I0702428

BOOKS BY MICHELLE MURPHY
Light's Awakening
Light's Lost

LIGHT'S LOST

MICHELLE MURPHY

BOOK 2: ALACORE'S APOTHECARY

1

Charlie had no business being in that alley alone at night. The waning winter air chilled her skin and left her throat feeling raw. Behind her, the walls of the building thumped from the heavy bass inside, echoes of the dance club.

The backdoor to Free House slammed shut, muffling its light and laughter. Blots of melting snow piled in the corners of the tight alley, around the corral of the trash dumpster and against the building where it turned toward the road. A dead rat stared up at her, its body spread halfway out from underneath the dumpster.

"You see? I was right, my dear," the man leading her cooed. His words pulled at her mind like plucked harp strings. They were rich and melodious; the sort of sound angels must make when they laugh. "Isn't it the most beautiful night for a stroll?"

Glassy eyes stared at her from beneath the dumpster. She blinked at the rat, in a daze, trying to make sense of something just beyond the perimeter of her understanding.

"A stroll?"

The man's slender fingers stroked her arm, turning her ever so slightly toward the lip of the alley. "Among the flowers, my sweet. That's where we'll frolic. Can't you see them, there at the end of the alley? How exquisite the arrangement. Row upon row of gardenias and poppies. And there, you see, a hedge of lilacs? Their perfume is intoxicating. Feel yourself fall into its heady embrace. They are all of them inviting us to visit."

Why was she doing this? She did not want to be out here alone with this beautiful man. The dead rat's eyes implored her to turn back. *You're not safe here. Go inside where it is warm.*

"I don't know," she mumbled, turning back toward Free House on wobbly legs.

The man laughed. He wasn't worried, for he possessed the mirror and with it control. It was a small hand mirror of hammered silver, quite unremarkable to the layperson. Its glossy surface rippled with his desire. The mirror was old magic, outlawed these days. He lifted it to her eyes, so she could see what he wished. The imagined fields of flowers opened before her.

"You see, my love," he murmured. "Off we will go on our adventure, over the hills and into the valley of spring. Surely you have never wanted to go anywhere so badly?"

He watched her eyes glaze over as the spell regained control over her, fogging her brain with his will. Her body language changed all at once. Suddenly, she stood straight and confident. Charlie coyly chuckled. She stroked his broad chest with her delicate fingers.

"I told you we should go," she insisted, as if it had been her own idea all along. "I don't know why you're acting so strange."

He tickled her chin and laughed. In an instant she bolted away from him, trapped in his illusion, straight down the alley toward the road.

"Come on, silly," she called back. "Last one to make it to the top of the hill is a peasant."

He relished watching her for a few minutes, enjoying the spectacle of the girl frolicking among imaginary flowers. She danced and twirled in a circle, letting the illusion of sunlight warm her face, her delicate lips smiling, her soft supine form folding with the wind. She was beautiful. And now she was his.

He pushed the mirror back into his shirt pocket and gingerly followed her, already wondering what Charlie's lips would taste like once he stole them from her pretty little face.

2

"Thank you, Lanie," a woman with a doe face said.

I do not mean to say she had demure features. Isa is a regular of mine, and she literally has the nose and ears of a deer, with a soft-tufted pelt covering her body. She's a talking deer person. How cool is that? I get to meet all sorts of interesting fae like her these days… because my life rocks now.

About three months ago, my world was drastically different. I used to spend my days working long hours at a florist, tucking myself as far back in the shop as I could manage. I scarcely interacted with anyone back then. Most nights I would work late in order to avoid declining a drink with my only friend, Deedee. Afterward, I would scuttle home to tend my rooftop garden, my absolute happiest place, then eat dinner alone and fall asleep either watching television or with a book hitting my face. That really was the bulk of what each day looked like. Lanie Alacore hiding from society. Alone.

Everything changed when my grandmother Rosalie died. Not only did Rosalie bequeath all her worldly possessions to me, but she also gave me the greatest gift of my life. She lifted a spell my mother had placed over my mind. That horrible spell kept me from seeing all the amazing things around me, places and people I should have been attuned to, since I too am a fae. Well, more aptly, a unicorn. That is, I have unicorn ancestry in my blood. This means I have deep mystical powers I must keep absolutely secret. Unicorn blood is supposedly one of the most powerful forces in the fae realm. I wouldn't know too much about it, since I can't access my own power thanks to my curse, but I had a taste of it for one evening. It was amazing. My grandmother's warning about our bloodline wasn't just lip service. The last person who found out about my lineage put my best friend in a coma. My friends and I almost died trying to stop his murderous rampage. So, we don't talk about unicorns around Alacore's Apothecary.

That's what I named my new business. It's so exciting and sometimes I have to pinch myself to make sure it's all real. I run my own apothecary! We sell poultices, herbs, crystals, unguents, and even the occasional elixir. Most of what I have to offer is behind the counter, on tiered shelves with jars and vials displayed for all. Each container has been carefully labeled, and all my ingredients are of the finest quality. It's been an incredible experience actually using my botany degree for something that gives me purpose.

Word of my shop is slowly spreading. It's always been a dream of mine to open an apothecary. I have a knack for growing, finding, and mixing the right ingredients to help those in need. It's ironic because Deedee used to tease me that I was going to end up joining one of those MLMs for essential oils. Now, I actually do prescribe them. Except, mine are infused with a bit of magic. I've noticed that no matter how much this curse blocks me from accessing my powers, a bit of it seems to seep out when I'm lost in thought over my workbench crafting remedies for my customers. It's not enough to make any major difference, just a trickle. But that trickle is something that gives me hope. Even better, I've discovered these amazing rose petals that help me harness a teensy bit more of my magic.

I found them when I was walking the hedge maze behind Greystone Chapel a few weeks ago around dusk. The rose petals glowed faintly with a ghostly blue light that drew me to them like a moth to a flame. They only retained their glow for a bit after I picked them, but I could still feel their magic as if it was calling to me. I've found grinding a couple petals into what I'm doing helps the magic locked deep inside me seep its way into my craft. It pains me to know what's lurking beneath the surface of my curse is far more powerful. I almost wish I never experienced its release during my brief time holding the relic, yet I'm glad I know what waits for me.

It would bother me more, but of one thing I'm certain – I am going to break that curse. One way or another, I will figure out how to free myself from its bondage. And in the meantime, I still get to help others and meet friendly doe-faced women like Isa.

"I hope you feel better soon, Isa," I said as she left the store.

My shop was practically destroyed a few months ago. I removed the debris of broken shelves and shattered antiques from the storefront. With

Lobo's help, we repaired what we could around the building. Luckily, we were able to replace the windows upstairs and fix the front door, but that pretty much dried up any savings I had left. The glass picture window on the left side of my shop is still boarded up, which doesn't look great. It's not exactly screaming *Fresh new apothecary that you simply must check out!* People like to shop somewhere they feel is successful; because if you're successful, there must be a reason for it. Customers want to discover what that reason is, with a subconscious hope that some of it will rub off onto them. I think we can make enough money in the next couple of months to replace the glass. I still have some of my grandmother's antiques on the remaining shelves in the shop. If Deedee was still around maybe I could sell them in the city. I felt sick to my stomach when I thought about what she must have gone through the night the changeling attacked.

Deedee's not going to be in a coma forever I told myself. *She's the strongest person I know.* I realized over the last few weeks that I'd relied on her to sort out my problems for too long. From now on I needed to take care of things on my own. I would find a way to remove the curse. Then once it's gone, I could use my unicorn magic to heal her and help her wake up.

I'm not going to be able to sell those antiques on my own, not even in Manhattan. They're an eyesore on the apothecary. If I had space in the basement, I'd store them down there for now. A cold shiver worked up my spine. Memories of crows and shifting shadows snuck up on me. I didn't like to think about the basement. Too many bad things had happened down there.

The shop door clinked closed on its springs as Isa left. I was able to replace the bell above the door with one I found in the basement. I like the way it sounds when people come and go. Less opportunity for someone to sneak up on me as well. That morning I felt lighter than air, so happy I thought I might be able to solve all the world's troubles with one of my salves. My life had certainly changed a lot in a short amount of time, and I loved it.

"Why are you smirking like you just swallowed a lizard?" Sacha asked from his stool where he read his newspaper.

Sacha is three and a half feet tall, with dark red skin. He's bald, loves wearing clothes that look like they're from an episode of Peaky

Blinders and has tiny leathery wings. He was smoking a cigar of his own creation, as usual. He claims he reads the news because he wants to catch up on world events. He was on year 1922. It was a good thing he was a fast reader. He always had his head buried in one of those dingy old newspapers while he 'worked' the counter.

"Who would smirk after they ate a lizard?" I snickered.

"A daemon," the little winged imp said.

"Touché." I snickered. "How can I explain it? For once in my life, everything is perfect."

"Whoa, there." Sacha's eyes flared a fiery red to match his skin. He dropped his paper on the checkout counter and scowled at me. "What are trying to do, jinx us? You don't just throw around the P word like a cursing sailor, damnit."

I could only laugh at his reaction. He'd seemed on edge ever since he came back from Hell. I tried to ask him about that trip a couple times, but he'd always blow it off like it was no big deal. I knew there was something else there, something he was hiding from me about the experience, but I wasn't about to force him to talk about it if he didn't want to. "Don't you think you're sounding a little paranoid?"

He scowled and opened his mouth to berate me, but I was saved by the bell of the shop door opening once more.

"Mr. Anders, it's lovely to see you today," I beamed, purposely cutting the imp off. Mr. Anders was a lovely old tephyr. A fae with three arms.

Mr. Anders tipped his cap to me. "And a good morning to you as well, Miss Alacore. It is certainly an exquisite morning to be out and about."

"I have the remedy to your troubles all set to go," I said, retrieving a parcel from underneath the counter. "Just lay it in your pantry and the ants will stay away." I handed him the wrapped sachets I'd prepared the evening before.

"Oh, wonderful." He smiled, folding the wrinkles around his eyes. He paused to inspect the packets through his thick spectacles. "It's rather early in the season for them to be out scavenging my larder, you know. But what kind of poison is this? It smells so lovely."

"No poison, just a little concoction I came up with. It's a bit of a few things: cayenne, mint, even some coffee grounds." *And a little of my magic of course, to seal the deal.*

"Well, whatever it is, if it works half as well as that honeysuckle tea you sold me last month, I should be pest free in due course." Mr. Anders took a polite bow before turning to leave.

I'm not sure how he managed to look so dapper in his out-of-date tweed jacket, but he always had an air of sophistication to him. His third hand stuffed the sachets into his breast pocket.

Sacha snickered as the old man opened the shop door to leave. "Coffee grounds to get rid of ants," he grumbled. Mr. Anders didn't seem to notice, as he was held up at the door chatting with another patron who had just arrived.

"What's your problem with my ant repellent?" I asked.

"We've got a busted window and no money." Sacha puffed a ring of smoke. "And you're over here peddling *coffee grounds*."

"What? They work," I said defensively. "It'll definitely keep the ants out of his pantry."

Sacha grumbled. "I don't doubt it, Lanie. Everything you make seems to punch the ticket alright. It's just… we need to drum up more business than *coffee grounds for ants* before we go destitute."

I sighed. He was right as much as he was wrong. "We're not exactly starving."

We were making enough money to stay fed and clothed at least, but that was about it. There was no overflow coming in to save up for a rainy day. Although, I discovered one of the truly amazing things about living in Willow's Edge was that there was no electric or water bills. Utilities were something fae handled in a more communal fashion. Everyone put a fair share into a communal pool based on their earnings. Appropriate amounts were doled out to the fae who ran the mill and so forth. I'm still clueless as to how the tree lanterns appear every night, but as far as basic utilities were concerned, Willow's Edge was covered. It was all very socialist and yet not at all. Living in a fae province was deeply confusing business.

"A happy afternoon to you, Miss Alacore."

Chulie was a tiny woman, just under three-feet tall. Other than her diminutive size and exceptionally large eyes and long fingers, she looked fantastically like any other human. However, she was not a human, she was a brownie who'd come into my shop several times in the last month and was quickly becoming a regular.

"Well, what a lovely day it is indeed, Mrs.… ma'am." I had no idea what her last name was. I almost winced, waiting to see if she noticed my slip. "Do you need a restock of your joint medication? It's awfully quick to have gone through that entire vial already. I can make it stronger if you need."

Sacha grumbled. He was clearly unimpressed with how quickly I veered away from his confrontation again. What the heck else was I supposed to do? We had a customer. Plus, I hate to argue, especially when the other person is right.

Chulie glanced sideways, as if she was trying to find a thought taped to the side of her head. "Not so much in the need of potions today, dearie."

I was going to point out that the unguent I had made her was not a potion, but her demeanor was odd, like an anxious dog waiting to be told it can lie down. Some of the fae had very strange ways about them and how they communicated. We stood there in silence for a few moments.

"Well? What is it you want for fucks sake?" Sacha snapped, cutting through the awkward tension.

Chulie's whole body twitched, and she spun about to flee the store. Sacha grumbled, and I held a hand up for him to settle down.

"Chulie, please don't leave," I called.

The diminutive brownie's retreat faltered to a standstill. I would be lying if I said her skittish nature didn't annoy me. But this was a business, and we needed all the customers we could get, as Sacha had pointed out only moments before.

"You came here today for a reason, right?" I said, slowly coaxing her back to the counter. "Sacha didn't mean to frighten you. He's just a world-class grouch."

Chulie shot him a nervous glance, then frowned at me. "He's a demon," she said, as if that explained everything.

"Yes, he is, a *daemon* to be exact, and he's also my business partner. Don't mind him though; his bark is worse than his bite," I said with a wink.

That was a lie. I had seen Sacha rake a serial killer's face open with his talons. Probably best skittish little Chulie didn't hear about that, though.

"Now, why don't you tell me what it is I can do for you today?"

"Well, since you asked," Chulie spoke slowly, unraveling her words like bundled yarn. "It's about the bazaar. I mean, I was wondering … that is, I was hoping …"

"Bazaar?" I didn't mean to cut her off. I do that sometimes, blurting out the first thing that springs to my mind. I had lived in Willow's Edge for four months and this was the first time anyone had mentioned anything about a bazaar.

"It's a huge marketplace in the fae realm," Sacha said, folding his paper and setting it on the counter in front of him. He was suddenly very interested in our conversation. His eyes practically lit up with attention. Sacha is, by nature, an aloof person. To see him expressing that much interest in anything made me all the more curious.

"Well, it was. You see, that is, your grandmother Rosalie, she would take things to the bazaar for me when she went every so often like," Chulie said. "And I was wondering if you could, if you would be a dear, deliver a package maybe, to my cousin, Bertie that is."

"Well, I've never been to the bazaar," I said.

Chulie's face dropped. She looked so distraught, I thought she might start weeping. "But Rosalie, she was the Warden. And now you're the Warden, I think. People are saying as much around town. At the end of the month the Warden goes to the bazaar. And you, being her granddaughter, and the new business, the shiny jars and vials, surely …"

"Yer ramblin' toots," Sacha cut her off. He was smiling despite himself.

The shop door popped open with a jingle. Lobo, my … well, what was Lobo? He was a detective for the province. Also, a werewolf. All werewolves are police for the fae provinces. Tae, my succubus friend and neighbor, told me it was for that purpose that the Court of Shadows created them in the first place. We never officially declared what *we* were, but I considered him my boyfriend for the most part. Even if he did try to rip me limb from limb while he was under the spell of a madman. Live and let live, right?

"Afternoon," he muttered.

As you can imagine, werewolves prefer to be out and about at night, although his mood isn't generally much different. He's a bit of a grump. Lobo always walked with a certain swagger that said he didn't give a shit about anything around him. The way he marched straight past Chulie to come around the counter and plant a kiss on my cheek was no more brazen than anything else he did in life.

I blushed as his lips and stubble grazed my tender flesh. Chulie's already large eyes grew so wide they looked ready to pop. I always liked the way Lobo smelled, like aftershave and cloves.

I giggled despite myself. "Hey, hun. I'm with a customer."

Lobo looked around the shop. When his eyes landed on Chulie, she wilted. He snickered. "I'm sorry, ma'am. I'm afraid sometimes I only have eyes for Lanie here. Please forgive my intrusion."

Now it was Chulie's turn to blush. I had to hand it to Lobo. Sometimes he could be just as charming as he was gruff. She averted her gaze from him, staring at the floor instead.

"Oh, young lovers. It is a splendid sight to behold. I'm sure you're both proper and decent in the way of our Queen's honor."

I did not know what any of that meant, but I nodded along with her. "Chulie, tell me more about this bazaar you mentioned."

Confusion clouded Chulie's oversized eyes. "Miss Alacore does not know? It is the Warden's place to attend these things, not a lowly brownie like Mrs. Etune."

Ah, so that was her last name. I repeated it three times in my head so I wouldn't forget. "What do you know about this?" I asked Lobo.

"Once a month folk come from all around the realm to hock their wares at a giant outdoor faire," he said. "It's called the *bazaar*."

"That sounds wonderful," I said, turning my attention back to Mrs. Etune. "But I still don't understand why you would come to me. This is an apothecary not a postal service. I wouldn't know the first thing about the bazaar. Besides, why don't you just deliver the package to your cousin yourself next time you go?"

Sacha snorted. "It's not exactly a place some folk can get to, Lanie."

I did not understand, and it was making me agitated.

Sacha rubbed his fingers and thumb together under the counter where Mrs. Etune could not see.

"Oh, money," I stupidly said aloud, instantly regretting it when I saw Mrs. Etune's cheeks turn scarlet. "Please don't feel embarrassed," I quickly added. "Things are tight here as well. Why, we haven't even made enough to fix our window yet. See? If the bazaar is expensive, I'm in the same boat as you."

Lobo cleared his throat. "Actually, as Rosalie's heir you would have a free pass whenever you want to visit. It's a perk of inheriting your grandmother's Wardenship."

There was that title again. Things had been so hectic since I arrived in Willow's Edge that I had yet to find time to learn what being a warden even entailed. I wasn't even sure I wanted to inherit that title. Running the apothecary was more than enough to keep me busy and happy.

Sacha snapped his fingers together, creating a little spark of flame that dissipated in a puff of smoke. "The mutt's a genius. Why didn't I think of it before?" He glowered at me briefly. "Probably on account of you starving me to death."

"You're hardly starving to death," I admonished. "I feed you the same as I eat every day."

"Leaves and berries." Sacha stuck his tongue out in disgust. "Not even scraps fit for a rabbit."

"It's called a salad," I groaned. "And I only served it to you once. How many times do you want me to apologize?"

"Doesn't matter," Sacha said. "The point is Rosalie used to go to the bazaar all the time. Quite the regular she was. Think the old bat even has a stall there for the shop."

"A stall?" I gaped. "Why is this the first time I'm hearing about a stall?"

Sacha's stomach emitted a loud growl, as if it was an empty echoing cavern. "Case in point," he said, flicking his rounded belly beneath his shirt and suspenders. "An imp needs to eat if he's going to be expected to think proper."

I rolled my eyes and ignored Lobo's chuckle behind me. We both knew full well Sacha made his stomach do that.

"If you go to the bazaar, you might be able to unload some of those goods in the corner," Lobo said. "Probably turn a pretty profit."

"Then we can get the window fixed," I said excitedly.

"And buy some steaks," Sacha agreed.

"Do you really think I can get in for free?" I asked Lobo.

"It shouldn't cost you anything to travel and enter the bazaar," Lobo confirmed. "All you need is Rosalie's Warden permit."

"I know right where it is," Sacha said. He hopped off the stool and scurried into the office. It was one of the few occasions I've seen the little daemon that excited.

The old antiques glared at me from the opposite end of the store. What looked like someone else's trash was actually a mixture of magical wares procured over time. I knew my grandmother peddled the enchanted artifacts, but I thought that business was done strictly through the shop. Except, in the months I had been there, no one had come by to inquire about them. I dared to hope the bazaar would be more promising. Could we have finally stumbled upon a solution for our financial woes?

"Well, then, Mrs. Etune," I said. "It would be my pleasure to deliver your package to your cousin."

She beamed and handed me a small plainly wrapped box. I took it with my mind already drifting off to dreams of all the money I might make selling the antiques at some big fancy bazaar. I felt that I owed Mrs. Etune a debt of gratitude for telling me about the bazaar and the delivery of one small insignificant looking box seemed like a poor trade.

If only it had dawned on me at the time to ask what exactly was in that package.

3

That weekend, I embarked on my adventure to the bazaar.

I left Sacha behind to run the apothecary, much to his chagrin, and brought along my new friend, Tae. Tae is a succubus who lives in the apartment across from mine. We've only known each other a short time, but we've been through some serious shit together and I think it's created a sort of bond between us. She's fun to be around, and she doesn't make me feel like a burden. Plus, she knows everything there is to know about all the different fae. Lobo and his partner, Doule, dropped us off at the train station. We only brought one stack of merchandise, but Sacha assured me it was valuable enough to make the trip worthwhile.

"You said the bazaar is in the fae realm, right?" I asked Lobo as two treants took my parcels from him at the loading platform.

Lobo grunted. He's a real conversationalist.

"Well, then, how is a train supposed to get us there?" I continued. "It's not like we're taking a daytrip to Pennsylvania."

One of the treants handed him the ticket for my belongings. Lobo leaned in close enough for me to smell his aftershave and slid the ticket into the front pocket of my blouse. "Relax and enjoy the ride, babe. You'll see everything soon enough." He tapped the pendant I wore round my neck. "And don't lose this. You'll need to present the sigil at the gates to be allowed free entry."

The pendant was the Warden's sigil that Sacha recovered from the office. It was a pink crystal obelisk with runes etched across its rough surface. I had tied leather twine around it in a weaving pattern to keep it in place, and I wore it along with the crystal horn my grandmother had left me.

Standing there in his arms, watching the tree people loading the luggage, steam billowing out from the tracks, I felt both anxious and excited, like a child who knows tomorrow is the first day of school. That wild expectation was muddied only slightly by the disappointment that Lobo couldn't join us.

He seemed to read my mind and nudged my chin with his rough fingers. "Don't be glum. I'll be out first thing tomorrow morning once my shift is over."

"It's not fair that you don't get any vacation time." I pouted.

Lobo chuckled. "Imagine that. A werewolf taking a vacation."

We both smiled, and he kissed me. Something about the way he did it so abruptly made me flinch and stagger back. It wasn't the first time something like that had happened between us. Ever since that horrible night with the changeling, I'd found myself jumping at shadows. I swiftly corrected my knee-jerk reaction and grabbed his arms to pull him back toward me. I didn't miss his pained expression, though he quickly tried to hide it.

Good job you big jerk, I thought. I knew in my heart it wasn't Lobo's fault that Brom had gotten ahold of his mind. Try telling that to my brain. It's only fair my body reacted to a memory of a murderous Lobo chasing me, all claws and teeth hungry for my blood.

The last thing I wanted to do was take off for the fae realm leaving him feeling shitty, so I rewarded him with a deep kiss. His stubbled jaw tantalized me where it grazed my skin. He pressed me to his chest with his powerful arms, and for a moment I was able to pretend everything was normal in the world. I lost myself in his embrace, each of us falling into the other.

I gently pulled away, breaking the spell before my body thought more was going on. No sense in blacking out on the train platform in broad daylight. I was still cursed, after all, and if I allowed myself to get too aroused, the curse would sense it and punish me. Lobo had no idea about my curse. I'm embarrassed to admit I couldn't bring myself to tell him about it. I told myself at the time that it was none of his business. The curse was my problem to deal with alone. What a crock of shit that was. The truth was I was afraid of how he would react. That little secret didn't make things easy between us.

"I wish you could join us tonight instead," I said, gazing up into his golden eyes.

"No trains to the fae realm run that late." Lobo smiled. "Anyhow, time passes differently over there sometimes, so pay it no mind and try to enjoy yourself. And stick with Tae. No wandering off on your own to explore."

It annoyed me when he started treating me like a helpless child. "Of course."

Tae signaled it was time to go. I finished saying goodbye to Lobo and waved a thanks to Doule. It was great to know the two of them had stayed so close, even after trying to kill each other that night. Doule, like myself, had completely forgiven Lobo for any transgressions.

"You're sure this isn't a waste of your weekend?" I asked Tae as we boarded the train.

"Are you kidding me?" Tae beamed. "I don't know a succubus alive who doesn't like a good shopping excursion."

Tae has an infectious smile. It could be because she exudes confidence and oozes sensual perfection in everything she does. The chick is smoking hot and has a mind that could knock the socks off even the best conversationalists. However, I prefer to believe she makes me smile because she is such a kind and light-hearted person. Even though Tae was shorter than me, she tended to be larger than life. I could scarcely blame other fae for being distracted when she walked down the aisle ahead of me, all curves and shimmery dark skin. Something about succubi made their skin look like it was mixed with a fine glitter that sparkled as they moved. Did I mention she's gorgeous? Next to Tae I feel like a prune left out in the sun too long.

We took our seats, and again I wondered how this ordinary train was going to bring us to the fae realm. Tae grabbed my hand and firmed up her grip "I can't believe this is the first time my girl Lanie travels to the fae realm. I'm so excited for you."

We both squealed. I felt light-headed as if I had just downed a glass of champagne. Soon enough the train announced our departure from the station. I braced myself for something amazing. The train vibrated as the locomotive powered up. Soon the whistle was blaring, and we were moving. Willow's Edge slowly rolled by at first, then the train lurched forward at a heady speed.

We left Willow's Edge and entered the countryside. We passed rolling hills, then forests and farmland. It was all quite ordinary. Soon enough, between the vibrations of the locomotive and the unremarkably mundane passing landscape I nodded off. This was just a train ride after all. I don't know what I was expecting to happen, but it wasn't this. Maybe something more like –

"What in the world?!"

I gasped as my stomach lurched like it was flipped inside out. Thick, impenetrable fog blanketed the outside of the train, blotting out my view of the countryside. I wasn't sure how long I'd been asleep. It seemed like only minutes, but my head felt groggy and disoriented.

"Here. Chew on some licorice root," Tae offered. "It'll help."

I greedily shoved a piece in my mouth, eager to fight the sudden nausea. My ears popped. I always relished that feeling, like when you're driving up and down a mountainous area and your ears delightfully pop. I know most people hate it, but I find it refreshing, like nature's way of resetting your eardrums.

The fog outside the window parted in little pockets giving me a tiny glimpse of the landscape. I spit the licorice root onto the window when I swore. Both my hands turned into a pantomime of frightened cat claws, one digging into Tae's thigh, the other my armrest. Through the holes in the fog, I could see the world in miniature detail, the way one would through the clouds on a plane. You might think that an odd analogy. I did too, until I realized with no uncertainty that we were indeed thousands of feet above the ground, barreling through the clouds in a train with no wings. Because trains don't have wings. Because trains should not fly!

Tae giggled and rubbed my forearm. I looked over at her and realized I was still digging my fingernails into her thigh. I let go, fumbling on an apology, but she laughed it off.

"I would have worn a different dress if I knew we were going to engage in a little S&M."

The way she winked at me was so comical, it suddenly took the air out of my fear. I looked around the rest of the train car. All the other passengers were entirely calm, some snoozing, others reading.

"Why is nobody freaking out that we're thousands of feet in the sky?"

I have never enjoyed flying. Any time I've been in a plane was filled with either pretending it was okay or drugging myself to sleep. The slightest turbulence makes me break out in a cold sweat. This was nothing like that. The train cut smoothly through the sky as the world below moved by in miniature detail.

Soon, a soft pastel pink bled into the clouds, followed by a pale yellow and then a baby blue. The colors were beautiful, swirling around and making the clouds resemble big tufts of cotton candy. Suddenly, brilliant bursts of color crackled inside the core of the clouds, like firecrackers with no sound. I watched them in awe as I pulled the licorice root off the window.

"The clouds are so pretty," I said. "Where are those lights coming from? Is someone lighting fireworks in the sky?"

Tae looked quite pleased with herself. "The border really is wonderful, isn't it? The best I have ever heard it explained is that we are entering the fae realms. What you see is the byproduct of us pressing through a sort of membrane that shelters the fae realm from its human counterpart."

I snickered. "Are you saying there's a giant force field around the fae realm?"

"More or less," Tae said in all seriousness.

As ridiculous and sci-fi as it sounded, it made sense. I had once used my magic to create a forcefield of sorts. It was a prismatic bubble that I used to deflect the changeling's killing blow from reaching Sacha. I reasoned that what I was seeing could be similar just on a far larger scale.

"But why doesn't anything like this happen when we enter Willow's Edge?" I frowned.

"You have to remember," Tae said patiently, "Willow's Edge is a province, a place that exists between both realms. By its nature it touches and belongs to both the human and fae realms. The provinces act as a conduit between them. Without the provinces, this trip wouldn't be possible."

That still didn't make sense to me, but I let it go. Soon the clouds cleared and with them the crackling colors. The sun was high, casting a brilliant light over the world below. I gasped as a swan as large as an elephant suddenly swooped down from above, opening wide its delicate wings so it drew up level with the train.

"There's a knight riding that swan," I said in disbelief.

Tae peered around me to get a good look. "Oh neat. That's a soldier from the Summer Court."

She waved excitedly at the man who was clad in shiny silver armor, with white wings on his heels and helm. A lance hung from the swan's saddle. It was easily one and half times the length of the gargantuan bird.

The soldier waved back at Tae and swooped his swan sideways, falling back toward the rear of our curving train.

"What was that all about?" I asked, unable to maintain what I can only describe as a shit-eating grin. If I had seen anything like that four months before, I would have promptly checked myself into psychiatric care. These days I only wanted to know more about this amazing world I had stepped inside of.

"All four of the great houses own a piece of the bazaar," Tae explained. "The Summer Court owns the rights to sky travel, so they are equally responsible to ensure those skies are safe. There's probably a few more soldiers out there with him, escorting the train since we entered the fae realm."

"Safe?" I glanced back out the window, scanning the horizon. What could be out there that would require a swan knight to keep it at bay? An involuntary shudder worked down my spine.

Tae patted a delicate hand on my lap. "There's nothing to fear. Now look at that. We're almost to the bazaar." She pointed out the window.

The first thing I noticed was that we were no longer alone in the sky. There were tracks below us in the open air and another train miles below them, aimed in the opposite direction. Beyond that were a myriad of flying objects. Some were giant pill-shaped zeppelins that cut through the air. There were giant hot air balloons dotting the area and even a galley fit for a pirate. I had never seen a galley at sea, let alone one flying across the sky. It was breathtaking, with billowing sails that drank the wind and a prow that looked like a wooden mermaid reaching for the sun.

And then I saw it. My first glimpse of the fae realm. Our destination was an enormous floating island.

I could see the port of entry, a harbor of sorts, where we aimed to land. What looked like elaborately constructed ivory scaffolding worked in crisscrossed patterns down the cliffside of the island. The cliffs stretched from the bustling harbor to the horizon beyond as far as my eyes could see, and then staggeringly curved back on itself upward into the air, like the lush green ring of a god. It was an impossible landscape that defied all known laws of physics. I had to stop tracing the horizon upward as I suddenly felt dizzy and insignificant in its wake.

Better to focus on the rapidly approaching harbor. All manner of vehicles came and went as we slid into port. The harbor was the best example of organized chaos I'd ever seen. There were no lights for traffic, nor signs to direct people, and yet everyone seemed to know their place in things. It was like watching an elaborate ballet performed by winged people, giant swans with riders on their backs, trains that moved across the sky as well as land, flying galleys, hot air balloons, zeppelins …

"Come on. We have to get off now." Tae tugged my sleeve.

I realized it wasn't the first time she had said that to me. "Sorry. I was so entranced by everything I guess I zoned out."

She giggled when she saw me blinking back to the present. "Oh Lanie, I'm so happy you brought me with you for your first time at the bazaar," she said with a broad smile.

I was glad too, but I did not want to look like one of those mooncalf tourists who visited New York City for the first time. So, I gathered my composure and hopped to my feet.

"I'm happy, too. Now, let's go make some money."

4

For a small fee, they offered us a cart at the harbor, and it was working wonders. It had no wheels and hovered in the air four inches from the ground. The weight of my parcels was completely absorbed by the cart's magical properties, much to my delight. I dragged it behind us as we passed through gates so tall I had to crane my neck to see the top of them. They towered over us like they must be the entrance to ancient Babylon, and connected to walls that encircled the outer rim of the market. I tried not to think about why such walls might be necessary. It was amazing how easily we were admitted entry. A simple flash of my grandmother's Warden sigil and black armored guards waved us through the gates.

What struck me most about the bazaar was the sheer magnitude of the place. It was as if every merchant in the world decided to go to the same farmers market.

But this was no weekend farmers market on the green.

Tents, stands, carts, and pavilions of all shapes and sizes littered the thoroughfare in a bazaar that could dwarf some cities. Farmers markets conjure to mind white tents and folding tables laden with goods. Not so with the bazaar, where all spectrums of color were represented. Most of the fabrics covering pavilions or the open-faced tents were not only vividly dyed, but also adorned with fantastic patterns. We passed by a large pavilion of stretched fabric that was dyed eggplant purple with violet and cream flowers printed in overlaying patterns across it. It was an expensive looking display. The pavilion practically screamed *Step inside and get a gander at our amazing wares! You will not be disappointed if you stop here to spend all your cash!*

Ironically, just beside it, was a ramshackle stand that was every bit as busy. They were serving something that sizzled. The aromas of garlic and roasted meat made my mouth water.

Patrons bustled up and down the dirt road that wound through the bazaar, passing one business after the other. Some of the storefronts were in wagons that blocked the thoroughfare at an angle, others were set in tidy rows. And some of the stores were no more than a carpet laid out on the ground, laden with goods. The one thing they all had in common was there was no room between them.

"I once visited an outdoor art festival that took up two city blocks," I said to Tae. "You could see people in every direction and only wonder how they all could be in the same place at the same time. I thought if that many people were there, then all the buildings around us must've been empty. It was a silly thought though, not even close to the truth, but that was when I first moved to New York." I waved a hand around us. "The bazaar is like that, times a hundred."

Tae grinned and asked me to stop the cart for a second. She went to a small wagon, a kiosk on the go. She gave the owner a quarter and came back with a handful of treats.

"Here. You have to try this," she said, handing me a small red and white speckled bean.

I popped it in my mouth to the immediate sensation of warmth, as if it came fresh from the oven. It tasted like a hot cross bun or sticky pudding or both. The bean dissolved on my tongue and left the flavors lingering in my mouth.

"That was wonderful," I exclaimed.

Tae giggled as she ate her own. "I know, scrummy right? A little happy discovery of mine from a few years ago. She grows them in her own orchard."

"I feel like I could walk for days and still discover new things," I beamed.

"There's something about the bazaar that always lifts my spirits." Tae agreed.

A wiry man wearing a shawl lifted a jug as she passed, offering a draught of his brew for a pence. Tae flashed him her sparkling smile as she declined. Not to be deterred, he swiftly moved on to the next passerby.

"I imagine if he can sell that to even five percent of the people going by, he'll be well off," I said. "Is it normal for sellers to take human currency, though?"

"Most will accept currency from just about anywhere in the world. Exchange rates are usually pretty fair at the bazaar. Oh, look up ahead," Tae said jubilantly.

A wooden building that looked like it fell out of the Wild West was coming up on our right. Fae gathered around its weathered deck, laughing and drinking. It was the first permanent structure I had seen inside the bazaar, with tents and pavilions on either side and across from it.

"That place looks old as dirt, like the bazaar grew around it. It reminds me of the way some roads wrap around hills. How long has it been there?" I asked.

"Not the saloon, silly," Tae said like an excited child. "In front of it."

As we approached the saloon, I noticed a small crowd had gathered out front on the thoroughfare. They had formed a semi-circle and were raptly fixated on a tall performer. He was a heavyset troll, stooped low. His large green hands tossed six ceramic bowling pins in the air, seamlessly juggling them as he told jokes. I instantly recognized his kind smile and wizened eyes.

"Droll!" I called over the gathering as we neared.

Droll was a regular at Free House. We had seen him perform his comic routine at least a dozen times. Tae and I always got a kick out of his performances. Seeing someone I recognized at the bazaar was thrilling for some reason, and I waved enthusiastically over the crowd.

Droll caught my eye and bowed his head in greeting with a wink. He usually wore a bent tin crown, proclaiming himself the *prince of fools*.' The crown shifted down to his forehead and threatened to spill off his head. I gasped, worried I'd just flummoxed his whole routine, but he seamlessly fixed the crown back in place and caught the next bowling pin. He juggled that pin without missing a beat.

I am ashamed to admit trolls scared me as a child. When I was a little girl, my mother told me a terrifying tale about one who lived under a bridge. The troll demanded a knight solve his riddle as toll for using the bridge. Affronted by this demand, the knight refused and tried to charge his horse across. The troll slaughtered both him and his horse, then strung up their bodies and ate their bone marrow. I don't know what my mother must have been thinking to tell that ghastly story to a child. She was ever a wicked person. I was delighted to find Droll was nothing like my childhood nightmares. He was a kind and humorous fellow, even if he did look bumpy and have oily hair.

We watched our prince of fools for a bit, laughing along with the crowd. "Let's not bother him while he's working," Tae finally said.

As we departed, Droll flicked a playing card in the air. It spiraled over the heads of the other onlookers and landed right in Tae's hand, then transformed into a daisy.

She giggled, and the audience cheered. Tae waved him goodbye as we cut farther into the bazaar. "I'll have to buy the old flirt a pint back at Free House."

"It's amazing that we can run into people we know all the way out here," I said. "Lobo and Chulie made it sound like coming to the bazaar is pretty uncommon.

Tae shrugged. "A brownie like Chulie hasn't much money to her name. A trip on the train alone would probably cost a month of her earnings. Besides that, brownies are notoriously lazy."

"Geez, that seems a bit racist, Tae," I said tentatively.

She seemed to consider it for a moment as we walked then shrugged. "Maybe it is. Though in Chulie's case, the stereotype fits the bill."

"How much farther is the stand?" I asked, wanting to change the subject. Fae could be very matter of fact with how they perceived different races, but I have always believed people are defined by their actions, not their bloodline.

Tae moved fast as whip, dashing sideways and slapping the hand of a child reaching for my cart. I hadn't even seen him approach us. He yelped and hopped back, holding his stinging hand. His hood fell back, revealing he was no child but a goblin with tusked teeth.

"Off with you before I call the guards," Tae snapped.

The little green man did not need to be told twice before promptly scurrying off into the crowd.

"How did you see that so fast?" I gasped.

"You have to keep your eyes open at the bazaar," Tae said. "There's a lot more than goods and entertainment here. There's a darker side to things and, unfortunately, thieves aplenty. Vile creatures like goblins – er, like *some* goblins, who pickpocket. Anyhow, doesn't matter the creature, just keep your eyes and ears open and you'll be fine enough. Let's keep moving. Your grandmother's place isn't much further."

Interesting. So even the realm of the fae produced criminals. I don't know why that revelation surprised me. In the short time I'd been around the fae, one practically roofied my drink and another tried to murder me. Naturally, there was a darker element to fae, as there was to any society.

"There it is, second one down on the left," Tae said as a seven-foot tall fae with four legs passed us in the opposite direction. "It's the orange tent."

I picked up my pace, spurned by an eagerness to see my grandmother's stall. An unoccupied tent stood to the left of it and an open produce stall stood on the right. The produce vendor's tables were laden with something exotic that could have been a hybrid of dragon fruit and bananas. The owner of the produce stall caught my eye. She waved heartily, beckoning me to come over.

As much as I ached to dash inside my grandmother's bazaar storefront, I forced myself to walk over and say hello to my new neighbor.

"I see you're excited at the prospect of eating some of my delicious fruit," the old woman said.

She was very ordinary looking for a fae, undistinguishable from any other old woman you might run across at a bingo hall. She had her white hair pulled into a bun and deep wrinkles around her sagging cheeks and hard eyes.

"Oh, no. I'm sorry; we aren't interested right now," I said.

"Come now, my dear, no need to haggle," the old woman said. "Magga will give you a fair price. No need for games. You could not hide such a look of exhilaration upon setting your eyes on my wares." Her wide smile didn't reach those hard eyes.

"It wasn't your stall," I explained. "Your neighbor's tent —"

Her smile snapped away as her hair lifted to reveal another, smaller face beneath. It looked very much like a turtle poking it's head out of a shell.

"That hag next door is out of business," Magga's smaller face snapped.

I took an involuntary step backward, so shocked by the sight of her scowling second face that I didn't have time to hide my revulsion. Both faces registered my reaction and scowled deeper.

"I'm sorry," I said. "I think you misunderstood. I know Rosalie passed away."

"Good riddance to the bitch, I say," the smaller face snapped.

"Excuse me?" Tae cut in.

Magga spat on the ground. "We're better off for not having that old witch around," she said. "Don't need someone always poking their nose in others affairs."

"So nosy she should have been a toucan," the smaller face agreed.

Magga digested this, then both faces broke into a howling fit of laughter.

"That's my grandmother you're talking about, you mean old … two-headed cow," I sputtered.

I could feel the heat rushing to my face. I don't know whether it was me or Tae who was more shocked by my outburst. Normally I did a fair job of taking it on the chin, thick skin and all.

Magga didn't even bat an eyelid before dropping a withering glare on me. "Cow, is it? Fine way to speak to your elders. 'Course you're her blood. Just another troublemaker. Go on, then. Off with you. Nothing better to do than waste an old lady's time."

We gladly complied, although I did feel perturbed it seemed to be on her terms of kicking us out of somewhere I did not want to be in the first place.

"Never mind that old crank," Tae said reassuringly.

"Great way to start my relationship with our neighbor," I said glumly.

Tae stepped in front of my path and stood to one side of the tent opening. "Just forget her babbling nonsense. In fact, I bet once you get a gander of your new pavilion you won't even care." She shot me a wide toothy grin and pulled the tent flap aside.

The fabric was a vibrant red-orange color, with a pastel orange pattern of braided lines printed all over it. I stepped inside with my jaw hung open in amazement.

"How is it so much larger inside?" It was like stepping into a pavilion three times the size of the small tent outside.

Tae shrugged. "Maybe a glamour on the fabric?"

A lush fur carpet blanketed every inch of the floor. The heavy wooden columns holding up the tent were ringed by display stands. These were wooden too, but they looked as if someone had grown rather than carved the wood into delicately curved forms with round platters atop each and set them in tiers. Cushioned ottomans and chairs were scattered around the pavilion, and soft music played from somewhere in the rafters. It was the melody of a forest stream in autumn, with birds and wildlife in the background.

The entire pavilion was lit by panes of light that trickled down from above, though I could not see where they originated from. There was a rounded counter to one side of the pavilion, beside which stood shelves brimming with teacups and saucers. Across the entire pavilion there was only one sign, a long wooden placard hanging below the checkout counter. It read *'Let Your Light Warm the World.'*

"Why are you crying?" Tae asked softly, placing a hand on my shoulder. "Did that mean lady get to you that bad?"

I shook my head and laughed. "I don't know what to say. I'm just so happy." I took in the serene pavilion once more. "This is all just ... I have never felt so connected to her. Not since that day under the willow tree."

I could feel my grandmother's love radiating across the place, like her aura was a piece of the pavilion. I realized in that moment that this was her true shop, the real place that she had poured her heart and soul into. Her storefront in Willow's Edge must have been her storage space, a backup for when the bazaar was closed. I hugged Tae sideways, and she hugged me back, sharing my moment of bliss.

"I thought I was going to have my hands full cleaning up some crummy tent to get it ready for customers," I said, breaking away to retrieve a French horn from the parcels on the floating cart. "But this place is ready for action."

I gauged the assorted display pedestals, then found one the right size and laid the French horn upright on it. It looked brilliant. I stepped back and could only laugh at how perfect the dingy horn looked in its new setting.

"In the shop at Willow's Edge, I would have sworn these things were total garbage. But here, in this lighting and setting, I don't know. That horn looks spectacular."

Tae appraised it with her arms crossed. "That's strange. It's like someone polished it when you put it there."

"I want to see how everything else looks setup." I grinned.

We both fell to work, quickly unloading the parcels from the cart and setting each item on its own display. Soon enough we had the pavilion ready to go, with a fair number of items for sale.

"I'm ready for customers," I said. "Sacha said I just need to pin the entrance open once things are setup, and folks will know we're open for business. Why don't you go shopping and have some fun?"

"If you're all set," Tae said, but she couldn't hide the eagerness from her eyes.

"Please go have some fun," I insisted.

Tae helped me pin the tent entrance open. She reminded me to kick out anyone who looked like they were up to no good and to shout for the guards if anyone gave me a hard time. It was cute that she thought she needed to look out for me. I lived in New York City for years. I know how to handle myself well enough, I think.

She practically skipped down the main thoroughfare in search of a new dress. I watched her go with butterflies in my stomach, ignoring the evil eye my neighbor's second face was shooting at me. It's not that I was scared. This felt more like a nervous sort of excitement, like the night before my first day at a new job.

In a lot of ways that was an apt comparison. I looked back at my pavilion and stroked the crystal pendant that hung from my neck, just beside the Warden's obelisk. It was an heirloom from my grandmother, a constant source of strength for me. It felt like, in some ways, my life was ready to truly begin in that moment, and everything that had come before was a dress rehearsal. I giggled at the notion and embraced the spirit of renewal. The pavilion looked excellent, chock full of shiny antiques.

"Now I just need to find some customers."

5

urns out, I didn't need to search for long. No sooner had I opened for business than customers started strolling in. It was only a few at a time, but between the notes Sacha gave me and the customer's needs, I was able to sell half my merchandise by the time Tae came back.

Sacha was right to make us bring the instruments along. It seemed fae really did have a penchant for human-made musical items. One gentleman told me it was because you couldn't find fae instruments that were as exquisitely off pitch as a human horn.

I proudly showed Tae my earnings when she returned from shopping. She didn't do too bad herself, making off with two armfuls of heavy bags.

"I'd better stay here for the rest of our trip before I blow any more money."

That meant it was my turn to go out.

"Did you want me to deliver that package to Mrs. Etune's cousin for you?" Tae offered.

"Thank you, but I made the commitment to deliver it. Pawning that off on someone else wouldn't feel right to me. Not after I gave my word."

Tae scribbled down simple directions for me to follow to meet with Chulie's cousin. I left her Sacha's notes and headed out, eager to see more of the bazaar on my way.

There are so many things to love about outdoor markets, like the feel of the warm sun on your skin and the fresh air comingled with aromas of roasting meats and specialty dishes all across the bazaar. There was an air of good humor everywhere I turned that charged my blood like electricity. I completely understood where Tae was coming from. Walking through such a spectacular place made it nearly impossible not to spend money. It was a good thing I left most of my cash back in the pavilion.

I passed an elfish woman who was selling hand crafted clay bowls, each with a moving landscape that washed across the surface like liquid once something hot was placed inside the bowl.

When I turned west, down a side lane, I spied a centaur selling clothes.

"One size fits all," he proudly and loudly proclaimed to a customer, meeting my eye with a wink.

A heavyset woman was trying on one of his tunics. It looked like the offspring of pressed flower petals and cotton. She slipped it on over her shirt. For a moment I thought the centaur would have egg on his face, as it was clearly three times too large for even a woman of her stature. He neighed a laugh as both the woman and I exclaimed with an "ahh" when the shirt suddenly shrank to the perfect-sized fit. It looked both flattering and comfortable, and I would have bought ten of them if I was rich enough.

Instead, I quickly moved along. A little farther down the lane I came across a frogman. He was my height, wearing a worn leather jerkin and breaches. His clothes looked like they were from a medieval fantasy. His skin glistened with an amphibious wetness, with a bright blue color that reminded me of the poisonous dart frogs I had seen at the zoo.

As if his appearance were not enough to intrigue me, he was selling marvelous sculptures. The frogman worked in front of his pavilion, chiseling through a squat wooden log as easily as if it were clay. Pieces flecked away like rain from his deftly moving hands, leaving behind an intricately carved curled dragon, scales and all.

"It looks like you're pulling that shape out of the wood more than carving it," I said without thinking.

He stopped and looked sideways at me with bulbous eyes, then blinked in the way frogs do. "My lady is quite astute in her observation," he said in a thick accent.

It sounded French, although it couldn't possibly be. Unless the fae realm had a Paris? Maybe they do. *Another question for Tae when I get back,* I thought.

"The wood, she speaks to me." The frogman ran his pod-tipped fingers over the curve of the wood as delicately as someone might stroke an infant's forehead. "The grains of the wood, I move with them, unraveling her secrets. For me, it is as eef the dragon is already there, and I am merely peeling back layers to free it so."

"You make it sound so poetic," I said.

There were larger sculptures inside the pavilion. One was shaped like a whale cresting waves, another an albatross, wings spread to take off in flight. However, it was a sculpture half my size that rested in the opening, securing the tent flap to one side, which caught my attention. I sprang toward it with unbridled jubilance. It was a perfectly carved unicorn, curled up as if resting but with its head and horn held high. Forgetting myself, I dropped down to my knees and hugged the statue. It was a stupid thing to do, a grown woman hugging a unicorn statue like it's a stuffed animal. Or her grandmother.

"Ah, my lady. She likes the unicorn, eh?" the frog sculptor asked.

"Um, I'm so sorry," I awkwardly apologized, looking up at him with my arms still around the wooden statue. I didn't know frogs could smirk until that moment.

"No, this is not right," he said with a dismissive wave of his webbed hand. "Enrique's art is for you to admire. I am one who is pleased to see your happiness. She is a legendary creature, but I see you already have a bit of unicorn with you, eh?"

His words jolted me like electricity. How could he possibly know? The secret that I had unicorn ancestry with powerful magic coursing through my veins was mine to keep. I followed his oversized frog eyes to my chest and giggled with relief.

"Oh, you mean my horn pendant." I hopped to my feet and closed the distance between us. "It's a family heirloom."

"She is as beautiful as my lady," the frog complimented, setting his chisel aside to face me.

Up close he was a bit intimidating with his large frog mouth. I could picture a grotesquely long tongue hiding inside and wondered what he ate. There was a documentary on TV one night where African bullfrogs ate rodents that came too close. The mouse wouldn't even know what was happening before it was buried to its tail in the frog's mouth; that was how fast they could strike. I wondered if I was foolish for getting so close to someone so dangerous. Could he swallow me before I could cry out for help?

"I have offended my lady," he said, slinking his shoulders.

I realized I was standing there in a growing silence. How horrible was I to be thinking such nasty things about this kind frogman?

"I'm sorry," I said. "I was lost in thought. Thank you for the compliment. You're too kind, and I do love your artwork so very much. It's wonderful."

He perked back up.

"You said your name was Enrique?" I offered an outstretched hand to him. "It's nice to meet you. I'm Lanie."

By the way he looked at my hand, you would have thought I was offering him a diamond necklace. He looked like he didn't know whether to take it or run away.

"It's a hand," I said. "For you to shake."

Enrique took my hand in his. His skin was cool and slick and a little clammy, but his grip was firm as only a sculptor's could be.

"My lady shows Enrique too grand a gesture," he marveled.

A woman gasped. I looked sideways to see her and her friends whispering among themselves, watching us as they passed. She looked mortified by what she saw.

Embarrassed, Enrique pulled his hand away with a bow. "It is my honor to meet one so fair, Lady Lanie."

I giggled. "You don't have to call me Lady. Just Lanie. Anyhow, I better get going, I have a package to deliver, and I need to be there by six or I'll be late. I'll have to stop by again sometime so you can show me and my friend Tae your other sculptures."

"That, too, would be my honor," Enrique beamed.

I told him it was a true pleasure to meet such a talented artist and went about my merry way. Everywhere I turned there were amazing shops along my path, but I couldn't shake the look of disapproval the fae woman had given me. *Was it a faux pas to touch another fae?* I wondered. *Or was it that they considered a frogman too low for such formalities?* Remembering Enrique's downcast face at their condemnation, I had a suspicion it was the latter.

I took a right at a curry vendor, just as Tae had marked on her notes. An open space twice as large as my pavilion was on the corner of the intersection. Tables were set up all around the space in neat rows that formed aisles for shoppers. Ancient looking bonsais were on display, with thicker trunks and boughs than I had seen before. These were not the typical windowsill bonsais of a New Yorker. They were carefully cultivated and crafted curving forms with finely manicured foliage.

I was admiring them with awe as I passed, when suddenly a sprite no larger than my palm fluttered down to a table and entered one. On closer inspection, I could see tiny glass windows and wooden doors had been carved into the bonsai she entered. I glanced back at the sign for the store. It read *'Bonsai Bungalows.'* How astounding must it be to be so tiny you could live inside a bonsai bungalow? I wondered what the inside of them must look like, trying to picture postmodern deco inside a hollowed-out trunk.

I can't wait to tell Deedee all about this trip to the bazaar.

It was a normal thought, one that would have occurred to me on any given day of the week. Because that's what me and Deedee did. She was my best friend. We shared all sorts of stories about the things we came across on an average day in New York City, which could range from how good my everything bagel was to seeing a naked man playing a trombone racing a taxi down eighty-eighth street. Except Deedee was gone.

My heart seized and a lump lodged in my throat. It hit me like that sometimes, out of nowhere, a choking despair that threatened to swallow me whole. Those panic attacks usually came when I was experiencing something enjoyable. They liked to catch me off guard. Because how could I be so happy while my best friend was lying in a bed, in the backroom of Free House, trapped in a coma? Shame weighed heavily over me.

Ever since I met her Deedee had been the only person I could rely on. We'd been together through thick and thin. For years she was my only friend. I wondered what she would think of Tae. I bet they would get along really well. There was so much I never got to share with Deedee. I wanted to tell her all about the fae; the province, Drys's willow tree, the fascinating creatures and culture, and most of all I wanted to tell her about my curse. It had been Deedee who was there for me when I first blacked out during foreplay. She had held my hand that evening, in my bed, and told me everything was going to be alright. When I had my heart broken by Ted, the jerk who tried to have sex with me even though I was blacked out, she was there to tell him off. Ted had been spreading rumors about what a slut I was and that he had to break up with me because I gave him an STD. It was the only way he could justify to himself how he had gone impotent for over a week after his perverted attempt to screw my unconscious body.

Deedee confronted him in the hall of the dorm in front of everyone. It was a Saturday night, so everyone on our floor was getting properly sloshed. Ted was bragging about how he'd dumped me for being a whore.

"Is it true though?" Deedee had asked.

Ted paused to turn a suspicious glance at her. He knew that Deedee and I were close roommates. "Is what true?"

"I heard your cock is huge," Deedee purred. The group laughed in that sort of salacious fervor typical of college students.

She said Ted blushed, but he popped his chest out like a proud little peacock. It stroked his ego to have his manhood chronicled before his friends. "Let's just say, I haven't heard any complaints."

Deedee sidled up to him and licked her lips. "Fascinating," she bit her lower lip. Ted was entranced. Deedee has that effect over men. If she was a fae I was certain she'd be a succubus. I've often wondered if that's why I get along so well with Tae. "Maybe you can show me?"

Ted gulped and chugged his beer. He couldn't believe his luck. "For sure. How about we … uh, maybe we can go back to my room?"

"Just show me now." Deedee wrenched Ted's sweatpants and underwear down to his ankles. He was completely exposed. All the kids in the dorm laughed at him. He covered himself up and ran down the hall then tripped over the sweatpants around his ankles. The hall erupted with more laughter.

"I guess your sex stories about Lanie aren't the only thing you lied about," Deedee called down the hall. "Huh, Tiny Ted?"

That name stuck with him all through his freshman year. At the end of that year he transferred schools. I haven't heard anything about him ever since, but I'll never forget how Deedee stuck up for me. She was a true friend. It shamed me to think there were times where I forgot she was trapped in a coma. It took the wind out of my sails to think of her, lying there in Free House alone in that bed. I wondered what she was dreaming about. I hoped they were good dreams. I hoped she was somewhere safe living her best life and that she didn't have to replay the horrible things the changeling did to her that dreadful night.

I was feeling fairly morose when I came to the circle where Tae had instructed I take the first left. At its center was a vendor selling drums of all sizes underneath a tall totem pole comprised of faces from different fae races. Hand drums, oblong drums as tall as me, short, round drums fit for slapping your palms against, even hollowed out wood that you could beat from the side with a stick were all on display. A group of percussionists demonstrated the wares, slapping and singing in beat with one another. Fae of all sorts danced around the circle, with the shop in the middle, like spokes of a wheel in a rotating line dance.

It reminded me of a maypole ritual, with dancers laughing gaily and holding long ribbons tied to the totem pole as they circled around it. My melancholy drifted off as I distracted myself with the musical celebration. The drummers beat harder, in rhythm, and the dancers sped up. The music made me feel alive. Everyone was so happy. It was contagious. I found myself tapping my foot to the beat and laughing along with them.

"Take my hand," a woman called, reaching out for me to join in as she circled closer, her other hand holding a green ribbon.

I fled, red-faced, mumbling my apologies. If you want me to dance, there usually needs to be a good amount of liquor involved. I moved hurriedly through the market until the drums were a distant thumping in the background before finally slowing to a normal pace. I wish I wasn't like that. I want to be the type of person who dances when they feel like it. I don't want to be so self-conscious all the time.

I think I'm improving, but for now it needs to be in baby steps, I told myself.

I was feeling a little deflated when I came to a small wooden stall with a library of books available. I had to stop and check them out. Not only do I love to read, but the idea of a fae authored novel was too tantalizing to pass up.

What kind of stories do they have in the fae realm? I wondered. Did they have the same fairytales as humans? I was intrigued, but one glance at the books told me they were far more expensive than anything I could hope to purchase. Each tome was leather-bound with opalescent embossed letters. Some were in an unfamiliar cuneiform language. All the books had a hand bound quality to them, with their uneven pages. A true treasure trove. A hunched wizard sat behind the counter reading a sloppy worn paperback of Stephen King's *Misery*. That is, I can only assume he was a wizard because of the pointy hat and long grey beard. He glanced at me, sighed, then went back to reading his book.

I snorted a laugh. *Even this old fart knows I can't afford anything.*

I moved on. There was a bridge just ahead with a stone watermill on the right and a path on the left. The path went down to the river waterfront. The watermill slowly turned, carrying its payload from the river gracefully in cupped paddles. From the sounds of merriment, there was a bar inside the building.

I stopped near the beginning of the bridge to admire the beauty of the wide channel. Small sailboats and yachts crowded the waterway in both directions. An enormous sturgeon halfway broke the surface, pulling chords behind it at a high speed. It was towing a small boat with a parasail. A fae held onto the parachute, expertly emerging from a swoop below the bridge. Her laughter carried across the sound and made me smile. There were picnic tables at the bottom of the hill, amidst trees, with families and friends milling about them. It was the only area I'd seen that wasn't clogged with storefronts. Everyone was having a lovely day.

Farther down the channel I saw a schooner descending from the sky at an alarming speed. It forced me to look up, and I suddenly felt dizzy seeing the curved landscape that went upward as if the world existed inside a bubble. I could see the other side of the bazaar in miniature detail upside down, directly above me. There were several hilltop castles where the landscape ended. I had to look down. Seeing a land that defied physics was more than my mind could handle. Suddenly, I was watching the schooner in horror, clutching the stone bridge with my free hand, as it crashed headlong toward the channel.

"Oh lord, no. It's out of control." I gasped. "It's going to crash!" I ducked down on my knees, with my head peering over the stone and bracing the package in my hands as if it could shield me from the imminent impact.

In the last moment, the ship pulled upward with alarming speed, its sails billowing backward. Within moments the schooner had gone from plummeting to delicately plopping down into the river. It was far down the channel, close to the edge of the floating island, and yet a rippling wave from the weight of it came roiling toward the bridge. The wave buoyed the various boats and swimmers, much to everyone's delight.

What a fantastical place this is, I thought for the umpteenth time as I stood back up. Red-faced, I checked around to see if anyone had noticed my overreaction. Thankfully, no one was paying any attention to me. I sighed gratefully and looked around to regain my bearings.

A stall on the opposite side of the street caught my eye; it was just before the path I was supposed to take that passed the wheelhouse building. Something people don't know about me is that I love to crochet. When I see yarn, it just makes me feel all warm and cozy inside. There's not a better way to pass the time waiting than with some crochet needles and a pattern. The stall showcased angled boxes overflowing with balls of yarn. I scurried over to feast my eyes on the fabric.

"'Ello there," the cherubic owner greeted me. He was a paunchy man with a green goatee and stubby horns. "Feel free to look and touch, but don't take them out of the box, if you please."

Each ball of yarn was soft and puffy as a cloud. The boxes were sorted by color. There were so many to choose from, but I had my eyes on the magenta stack. It was vibrant in the daylight, like a fluorescent marker. I just had to touch it. I reached my hand in and was not disappointed. It really did feel like stroking a fluffy wisp of air.

"I could make a wonderful pillow cover out of one of these," I said, leaning down to press my face into the fabric.

Then it moved.

The yarn ball I had stroked and those all around it began to wriggle. My face was only an inch from them when the 'yarn balls' flipped over and uncurled, revealing an undercarriage that looked exactly like those potato bugs you see under rocks in gardens. I screamed and jumped backward away from the box, much to the owner's amusement.

He bent over, slapping his thigh and pointing at me. "I knew you was going to do that, I did," he laughed.

I quickly turned away and ran.

And that was when I hit him.

I ran directly into a man who was behind me. I hadn't seen him a second before, but I bounced off his body all the same. I hit the ground on my back, and Mrs. Etune's package went skittering across the path.

The shop owner was howling with laughter. The man I ran into was as sturdy as a tree. Our collision knocked the air out of me.

He leaned over to glare down at me in disgust. His skin was pale but pleasant like polished alabaster, and his eyes were twin points of hammered silver that took my breath away. They matched his shoulder length hair and scowl. He studied me for a moment, as if inspecting an ant, and then his eyes shifted to clear recognition.

"You're that prince," I said stupidly. I'd seen him before, at Free House. Tae had explained he was a very important person, a Prince of one of the Great Houses.

His hands were on me, pulling me to my feet. He glanced back to where he had come from, a closing door on the side of the watermill.

"You should watch where you're walking," he snapped coldly, already leading me across the path as he moved with one hand on my elbow. We stopped, and he scooped up my package from the ground. He shook the dirt off it and sneered. "This smells like a wet toad."

"Oh, I, uh …" I managed. I know, I'm the Queen of Verbosity.

The door to the wheelhouse opened. Laughter and music spilled out from inside. The prince's head snapped around on a swivel, then he grabbed me again and ran for the path on the opposite side of the bridge that led down to the waterfront.

"You've ruined it," he snarled as he moved on fast feet.

I found myself following him with no objection, but instead of heading farther down the path. He cut to the right, and we slipped underneath the bridge. There wasn't much space for us to walk before the ground fell into the wide river. I had seen him at Free House several times, though we never spoke. He was always locked away behind his velvet VIP rope, in his own separate world, orbited by an entourage of fae that harbored a fashion sense that fell somewhere between goth hipster and leather punk. I finally recovered enough to recall his name.

"Lucien," I said loudly as it came to me. "That's your name, right?"

His eyes bulged at me as if I was deranged. "Keep your voice down," he hissed.

A rowdy group of drunken fae came out onto the bridge overhead. I didn't need to walk back up the hill to know they were Lucien's entourage. Someone called his name. There was lots of drunken laughter. Lucien looked desperate for them to go away, pressing himself tight against the side of the bridge. I leaned in closer to him, afraid they might see me and spoil his hiding spot. Cold air radiated from his body. It was like leaning into an open refrigerator. We waited like that, tense and silent, for a few minutes. Finally, the group moved on, across the bridge toward the other side of the channel. Once their voices were no longer within earshot, Lucien sighed.

"Thank you," he said, handing me Mrs. Etune's package.

"For running into you?" I smirked. One of the corners of the package was dented ever so slightly, but otherwise it was in decent condition.

"For not exposing me," Lucien said. "Most fae would have squawked away, hoping my cousin Finnely would throw them a little coin."

"Well, if I knew I was going to get paid, I would have screamed bloody murder. You should have told me earlier," I replied sarcastically.

He studied me as if he had never heard a joke in his life. "You're an odd one, aren't you?"

"That's what they tell me," I said, feeling squirmy under his inscrutable gaze. He was a beautiful man. Too beautiful. It kind of pained me to be around him, feeling all frumpy and blemished.

"They?"

"It's an expression," I said.

He stared blankly at me.

"A human saying. Maybe not so much in fae."

"Ah, yes. You grew up around those heathens did you not, Ms. Alacore?"

What the heck? How did this guy know my name? I felt like I bumped into Brad Pitt, and he knew all about me. I could only nod. My brain was taking a timeout.

He curled his lip. "I can only imagine how horrible an experience that must have been."

"Why are you running from your friends?" I blurted, desperately wanting the attention off Lanie-concerned matters.

He snapped his scrutinizing gaze away from me, glaring angrily out toward the water instead. "I do *not* run."

I laughed. "Okay. Walking quickly then."

"Someone like you wouldn't understand."

It was funny. He didn't say it to be an insult. The way he spoke, he genuinely believed I would not be able to see things from his point of view. Either way, it annoyed me. It's always great to get insulted by a specimen of masculine perfection.

"You're not that complex," I snapped. "Let me guess. You wanted to get a breather from that crowd of goons who hang on your every word and follow you around everywhere you go?"

He shot me a sideways glance. I could see the gears turning in his head. "I just wanted to look at the boats in peace."

My blood boiled, and I felt it seeping into my cheeks. I dug my nails into my palm to steady my nerves. The last thing I wanted was for this creep to see me blushing and take it the wrong way.

"Fine. Enjoy the water. You're the one who dragged me over here," I said accusingly, quickly turning around and heading up the hill. "And thank you for helping me up."

Lucien laughed. "I only meant from them, Ms. Alacore. Not you."

I stopped, confused. "Oh?"

"Yes. Please come back," he laughed again. "It's a lovely day and look, there's not even any trolls under this bridge."

Despite his disparaging joke about trolls, I found myself turning around. He was sitting in the grass of the sloping hillside beside the bridge, patting the ground next to him for me to take a seat. I felt like a foolish teen who just threw a tantrum and meekly took a seat beside him. He watched me with amusement.

"My name is Lanie," I corrected him. "Nobody calls me Ms. Alacore. Not since boarding school."

"Lanie, then."

He nudged me with his elbow. His smirk was hard to deny, and I found myself smiling back.

"Are they all loud like you?"

"Who?"

"The humans."

"I'm not loud," I said. I am by all accounts a fairly meek person. For the most part. People have described me as bookish, homely, and even a wallflower, but never loud.

He laughed. "I would have to disagree. Everywhere I see you go, your arms are waving about, and you are creating a scene. Don't be cross. I can see it on your face. Which only further proves my observation."

Wow. This guy was a piece of work. "How about you just shut your mouth and watch the boats?" I suggested.

Lucien snickered and nudged me again.

For some reason it was hard to stay mad at this insulting jerk. Everything seemed like a joke to him. I smiled back. "Yes, as a matter of fact a lot of New Yorkers, humans to you, are very loud people. But I am not one of them. Now watch the water."

He was content with that. We sat in silence for half an hour. Lucien leaned in toward me slightly, just enough to make me sweat, with his arm brushing up against mine. It sent a tingle across my skin. The wind ruffled his platinum hair, and the light reflecting off the water made his silver eyes seem to glow.

We watched the sailboats go by. There was a catamaran with sails painted like a curled octopus under the sea. When the wind billowed against it, the sails gave the illusion that the octopus was writhing its tentacles through the watery depths. Some children flew kites on the other side of the channel, where a boardwalk skirted the riverbank. One had a koi fish kite, the other a phoenix kite. They moved to make it look as though the kites were chasing each other back and forth.

I guess it was weird to sit there in silence with a complete stranger. But something about it felt freeing to me. I realized it had been a while since I was able to just exist without any sort of expectation. My stomach fluttered when his thigh rubbed against mine. What was I doing out there with some strange man?

"Lucien," someone called from the other side of the channel.

Lucien's entourage gathered quickly around the figure on the boardwalk, waving and pointing at us.

"Looks like your friends found you," I teased.

"Damn Finnely," Lucien muttered.

"Wait, that's Finnely?" I said. He was the broad-shouldered brute who always hung closest to Lucien at Free House. He was a rowdy drinker who looked like he was always itching to get into a fight. "With a name like Finnely, I expected a librarian or a butler, someone a little more ... *lanky*."

"Nothing to do but face them I suppose," he grumbled as if he hadn't heard me speak.

The entourage was already on the move, heading back toward the bridge. The idea of being surrounded by them, in their flashy outfits and drunken swagger spooked the hell out of me. My inner introvert screamed *head for the hills!* I hopped up and patted the dirt off my pants.

"Well, that's my cue," I said. "See you later, Lucien. It was nice watching boats with you."

Lucien looked surprised at my abrupt departure. "You can join us for a drink, if you'd like." He said it like he was giving me permission to do some great thing.

The idea of me grabbing a drink with his band of merry misfits was comical to say the least. It would be like a grandmother hanging out with Marilyn Manson and his gang.

I snickered. "Maybe another time. I have business to attend to."

He studied me in silence for a moment, then shrugged and walked past me up the hill. "Goodbye, Ms. Alacore."

It was such a strange reaction that I just stood there and watched him until he made it to the top of the hill before I started walking again. By the time I reached the bridge, Lucien was nowhere to be seen, lost among the throng of shoppers crowding the walkway. I could hear his friends getting closer and quickly slipped down the lane beside the watermill. The owner of the bug or yarn shop, I'm still confused as to what it actually was, saw me coming. I expected a barb to be thrown my way. Instead, he was solemn faced and bowed very deferentially toward me.

Is he doing that because he thinks I was with Lucien? The idea of that annoyed me far more than if he had laughed again.

I quickly moved past his stall and toward my rendezvous with Mrs. Etune's cousin. I checked my watch. I was running ten minutes late. I cursed myself for wasting so much time with Lucien. The sun was setting soon, spilling long shadows from the tents and pavilions across my path. It took a good twenty minutes of weaving through the bazaar before I arrived at my destination, a pavilion the size of a circus tent. Fae crowded the area, drinking and laughing. Inside the tent they were playing cards, throwing dice, and slapping money on tables with spinning wheels.

"It's a gambling tent," I said to myself. *This must be their version of a casino.*

I looked around for the sign. I found it on the far side of the front of the casino tent, a worn wooden circle on a pole. A faded symbol that looked like a mutation of an ankh was on its face. That was where I was supposed to meet Mrs. Etune's cousin. I ran over, searching the crowd for a brownie. There was no one around.

Oh no, I screwed it up, I thought.

"You're late," a cool voice startled me.

It was a man. No, a fox. A fox man, wearing white jacket and trousers, with a matching top hat. He held a cane, but judging by his swagger, I could tell he didn't need it.

"Percival?" I asked.

"The one and truly." He bowed eloquently and tipped his hat to me. "Come now, let's get down to business."

He strolled past me. I followed him until he made it to the space between the casino tent and a nearby pavilion half its size. It was a narrow alley, with crates piled at intervals against the tents. I stopped at the edge.

Percival sensed I was no longer following him. "Come on now, let's get this done."

"We can do it right here," I insisted.

He rolled his eyes and beckoned for me. "I haven't got it on me. It's just up ahead."

What the hell was he talking about? "Go get it then," I said flatly, improvising even though a voice inside me screamed for me to run the other way. There was something off here. I was pretty sure this fox was not cousins with a brownie. *But what if they are and you're just being an ignorant racist?* I thought worriedly. *Didn't I accuse Tae of something similar earlier?*

No. This was different. The alley felt primal to me, like a beast waiting for me to walk inside its jaws. There was no way I was going inside it. "Go," I repeated.

Percival lowered his beckoning hand. As he did, his mouth twitched and pointed fox teeth peeked out between his thin lips. His eyes were cold and dead. He turned his back to me and quickly marched deeper into the alley, past the shadows. A couple smaller, stooped figures emerged from behind one of the crates. I think they were goblins, but it was hard to make out their details. Percival spoke hurriedly with them, checking back over his shoulder for me. They handed him something. I moved farther away from the lip of the alley, looking around to be sure there were plenty of fae who could see me.

Percival returned, clearly annoyed by how far out into the open I had gone. "I don't usually do business like this," he growled. "Tell that brownie bitch next time it'll cost her double."

I handed him the package. He took it and gave the box a snuffle with his fox snout. Seemingly satisfied, he produced a sealed envelope from his jacket pocket. He held it out for me. I hesitated briefly. If this fox grabbed me and tried to pull me in that alley, would I be able to fight him off? His eyes met mine, and he grinned as if reading my thoughts. I was foolish to give him the package first. I snapped my hand forth and snatched the envelope from him before he could blink.

I know he was surprised by how fast I moved; people usually are. He was still gawking as I hurried away into the safety of the crowd. Even as I made my way past the wheelhouse I shuddered, picturing those huddled shadows in the alley.

What kind of devilry did Mrs. Etune get me wrapped up in? I brooded. *How close had I come to falling into something truly dangerous back there?*

I didn't know what that was all about, but I did know one thing for sure. Mrs. Etune was going to get some choice words from me when I got back to Willow's Edge.

6

could tell there was something off as soon as I approached my pavilion. The shopkeeper next door watched me like a vulture. Both of her faces wore smug grins that left a yawning pit of foreboding in my stomach. When I saw my tent flap was closed, that feeling intensified. My instincts told me to get out of there, but I stepped inside out of sheer stubbornness. There was no way I was leaving Tae behind.

"I don't care who you are," Tae snapped. "You've no right to do this."

It was disarming to see her surrounded by three armor clad knights. Their black steel seemed to steal the light from the pavilion. I quickly took in the scene, their grim looks of determination, Tae's exasperation, and the four-sided maces hanging from their belts. I remember thinking, *at least their weapons aren't drawn.*

That was as much as I was able to take in before a rough hand seized my arm from the side.

"Looks like we've got another one, sir," a knight said as he dug his gauntleted fingers into my flesh.

I didn't even have time to complain before he pulled me over to the group. *I'm getting awfully sick of men manhandling me today,* I thought.

"Who is this, then?" The man speaking held himself in high regard. He spoke beneath a thick matted black beard that looked dyed, oiled, and finely trimmed around the sides. With pointy ears protruding from his half helmet and his shimmery pale cream-colored skin, I marked him and his companions as shadow fae.

"Get your hands off of her before I make you grovel on your knees," Tae said with a steely danger I'd not yet heard from her.

"As you well know, using your magic against a lawman of the bazaar is punishable by death," the leader said dryly, looking unimpressed, but he waved a hand to his soldier. "No need to let things get out of hand. It's not like she's going to run off." He eyed me. "Are you, lass?"

"You are addressing the Warden of Willow's Edge, not your *lass*," Tae corrected.

He stared at me, waiting for a response.

"Of course not," I said. His man released me, and I rubbed my sore arm from where his fingers had been. "I don't even know what's going on here. Who are you? Why are you in my shop?"

"You don't ask Captain Finril questions," the soldier who grabbed me barked. "He asks the questions."

His words would have sounded so cheesy to me if these shadow fae didn't look like they meant serious business.

"This pavilion is gifted to the acting Warden of Willow's Edge by the Court of Shadows," Captain Finril said. "The *true* Warden of Willow's Edge passed away three months ago. So, who exactly are you that you trespass here and sell goods illegally?"

"I'm her granddaughter, Lanie Alacore," I explained.

"You claim. What proof do you possess of your identity?" Captain Finril asked.

"I mean, nothing on me," I said. "I don't make a habit of carrying around my grandmother's will." I patted my pockets subconsciously. "Oh wait, I have my ID." I fished out the contents of my pocket. A few dollars, Ms. Etune's envelope, and my New York State driver's license.

Captain Finril looked to one of his men. The soldier snatched the items from my hand. His face soured when he saw my license. "It's some sort of human placard," he said with disgust.

"It's called a license," I said softly and evenly, doing my best to remain patient. "My name and photo are right on there. See?"

"I've heard enough," Captain Finril said. He shoved Tae aside and snatched my cashbox from the counter. "You have trespassed and illegally peddled merchandise on this property. We are confiscating all these ill-begotten earnings and taking you to jail."

"But my license," I exclaimed.

"The only license that matters is an official permit bequeathed by the Court of Shadows. It is the great house which deems a shop has the right to operate in our portion of the bazaar. This human trash you peddle means nothing. You know very well we have no way of authenticating the validity of such a thing, nor would we care to sully ourselves in such an attempt."

"Wait," Tae demanded, shaking a soldier's hand off her. "Lanie has the Warden's sigil."

Captain Finril paused.

"That's right," I exclaimed, quickly fishing my necklaces out from beneath my blouse. The captain's eyes grew wide when he saw the sigil. I lifted the warden's obelisk from my neck and handed it to him.

"No, Lanie don't ..." Tae said.

"You see, my grandmother left this to me. I am really sorry, but this has all been a misunderstanding. If there was somewhere I was supposed to register or announce myself when I arrived at the bazaar, I didn't know. Please, it was an honest mistake."

I can't lie. The idea of being hauled off to jail was terrifying. I was about as shaken as I could be and fighting back budding tears. I balled my hands into fists, to try to stop shaking.

"She's lying, captain. This envelope stinks of fox." The soldier near me tore open Ms. Etune's letter.

"Hey, that's private," I yelled.

"Transporting illegal contraband, are we?" the captain said.

My heart sank. That seemed exactly like what the brownie had gotten me into with that sly fox and his allies in the shadows. I watched in horror as he shook out the envelope onto his hand. What if it was drugs? Sweat ran down the back of my blouse.

"What's this then?" the soldier asked. A tiny piece of paper fell into his palm. He tossed the envelope aside carelessly and unfolded the paper. "An address?"

"It's not important," Captain Finril said as he placed my grandmother's sigil into a pouch hanging from his belt. "I don't know how you came to have the Warden's sigil in your possession, but as of now I find no way of validating your identity. The Court of Shadows has not issued any title for a new Warden in Willow's Edge as of yet."

"No, that's not right," I said. Tae's deflated shoulders told me my battle was lost.

"Take this woman *and* her accomplice to jail," Captain Finril ordered.

I squealed embarrassingly as the knight seized my arm once more in his iron grip. "Please, we haven't done anything wrong."

"You bastards," Tae snapped as the other soldier roughly wrenched her wrists behind her back.

A snarl, feral and promising of blood soon to be spilt, cut through the pavilion like the crack of a whip. Everyone froze. All eyes went to the entrance. Lobo stood there, half in the shadows. His golden eyes reflected the shop light like two glowing orbs. His teeth were bared, his hulking muscular silhouette blocking the entrance.

"Get your fucking hands off of her," Lobo growled in a low voice saturated with menace. "Now."

The soldier holding Tae loosened his grip. The one holding me squeezed harder.

"Who are you to give orders to Knights of the Shadow?" Captain Finril asked.

Lobo stalked into the wider area, the light cascading off his feral face. The soldier between me and Tae licked his lips and looked at Lobo's hands. His talons were out; razor sharp claws protruded from his fingertips.

"Lobo Willow, inspector general to the province of Willow's Edge. And that's my girl you're pawing. So, if you don't let her go, I'm going to rip your fucking throat out before you can even think to grab that shitty little mace of yours." He spoke directly to the brute holding me.

Tae's soldier looked around at his companions uncertainly.

"You have no jurisdiction here," Captain Finril said, unphased. "The southern quarter of the bazaar is under the protection and governance of the Court of Shadows."

"Yeah. You're a long way from home, ya mutt," my captor said, shaking me as he spoke.

"That's true," Lobo said and growled. The sound of it sent shivers down my spine. "But I'm still going to rip your man's throat out."

Tae's captor released her and backed away. His hand quivered as it inched down to the mace at his belt. Lobo's gaze never wavered an inch away from the captain. His talons extended to their full length, an unspoken promise. I had seen Lobo attack before. He was brutally fast and extremely deadly.

"As an agent of the law, can you validate this woman's identity?" Captain Finril asked.

"What?" the soldier holding me barked incredulously. "You're going to let some werewolf push us around? We can take this mutt, captain. Just say the word."

"Shut your mouth, Rodger," Captain Finril said. "Well?"

"That's Lanie Alacore, heir of Rosalie Alacore," Lobo answered.

Captain Finril thought for a moment, then blinked and nodded his head. "Good enough. Release these women into Inspector Lobo's care."

"What? No way! We —"

Rodger's protest was cut off by Finril's gauntlet slapping the back of his head. He released me at once and shot a pathetic look to his leader. The way Captain Finril glared back told me Rodger was going to be in even more trouble later for questioning his orders.

I scurried behind Lobo. Tae stood to the side with her arms folded across her chest, looking properly chagrined.

"Give her back her money, too," Tae demanded.

"This money was earned through the illegal sale of goods on Court of Shadows property. Until such time as Ms. Alacore can confirm her appointment as Warden of Willow's Edge, this contraband will be seized and sent to the courthouse in Willow's Edge where it will be held."

Lobo gnashed his teeth.

With the speed of a cheetah… no, of a *shadow*, Captain Finril strode across the tent. He shoved his face a hairs breadth away from Lobo's. "Unless you would rather we spill blood and start a cross-house incident?"

Lobo snarled, baring his fangs in the knight's face. I placed a hand on his chest and squeezed my body between both men. "We don't want anything like that, captain. As I said, this has all been a terrible misunderstanding. I will correct this matter with the court in Willow's Edge."

Finril and Lobo both backed off at the same time. I watched helplessly as the knights seized the few unsold items I had remaining and carted them away, along with all the money we had made that day. The only thing they left behind was Ms. Etune's torn envelope and the folded sheet of paper that had been inside.

When the tent flap finally closed and we were alone, I let out my pent-up air. I rested my head on Lobo's chest.

"For once I'm happy to see you," Tae said to Lobo.

"What the hell was all that about?" Lobo's rumble petered into his normal voice as his talons shifted back into his calloused fingers.

"The old hag next door must have complained about me," I said.

"And they sent the captain of the guard out here to take care of it?" Lobo asked. "Not likely."

That did seem odd. "Well, one thing's for sure," I said. "I'm going to need to figure out how to prove I'm the Warden of Willow's Edge, or we're never going to get that money back and fix the store window."

"Why should she have to prove herself?" Tae asked Lobo.

He shrugged. "I have no idea. I assumed that mantle was passed down along with the rest of Rosalie's estate. Warden's, Guardians, captains, all of those titles are usually carried on by the bloodline, aren't they?"

"Geez, that's a good question," Tae said. "I'm not sure."

I eyed the address written on Ms. Etune's letter from the fox. That was a whole other thing to figure out. Why did she send me into such a dangerous situation for something as stupid as an address?

"Lanie?" Lobo pressed.

I looked up at him and shrugged. "I don't have a clue. But I think I know who can help us find out."

7

It's interesting how quickly your life habits can change. Not that long ago, when I lived in the city, I dreaded the idea of going out to a bar or nightclub. In fact, if it wasn't for Deedee, I might have never left my apartment at all.

Nowadays, it's not uncommon for me to go to Free House after working long hours at the apothecary, to spend time chatting with Tae or Lobo and unwind. Who doesn't like a good glass of wine or a tasty margarita at the end of a long day? However, I think the real reason I like going is to see all the different fae. Everyday new fae I've never seen before show up at the bar, and they all intrigue me to no end. It is hard to believe that these are my people. Then again, I never truly felt at home until I found Willow's Edge.

There was something about Free House that made me feel safe. I mean, let's get real, the *something* was a massive white willow in the center of the tavern, with cascading mystical light fluttering through its boughs. That tree was the heart of Willow's Edge, one and the same as the proprietor of Free House, Drys. Drys was a dryad, and the white willow was a part of her. She carried herself as stoically as a Viking commander. For all that she had a heart of gold. Besides being the heart of our province, Drys was a good friend to my late grandmother. I had come to see her as someone I could trust.

Free House was in rare form that evening, bustling with a crowd of fae. The dance floor in the other section of the tavern was alive and electric. We sat at the bar with throngs of patrons pressing in around us, eagerly waiting for the bartenders to come around. Drys had a full staff working, two dwarven barmaids, Luca and Lisa, as well as a succubus, Ellie, and a handful of barbacks that lugged cases of liquor up from the basement.

"I don't know how I'm going to get that money back," I said to Lobo as I traced a star in the condensation on my glass with my finger.

"We'll figure something out," Lobo said gruffly. "No sense in working yourself up until we know all your options."

"Says the guy who was going to tear out a knight's throat for me," I teased.

Lobo smirked. "You know you loved it."

He looked cute when he wasn't being all doom and gloom. He leaned in and kissed my neck, sending a tingle across my skin.

I leaned into it and kissed his lips, then smiled into his golden eyes. "My big strong wolf coming to save me? You bet your ass I loved that."

My attention wavered from his eyes, taking in the empty VIP area over his shoulder. Lucien and his entourage were absent from Free House that night. Why did I feel the need to check anyhow?

"Get a room you two," Drys said with a hearty chuckle.

I jumped. I never even noticed her make her way down the bar to us. She laughed even harder at my reaction; it was a rumbling sound like branches shaking in a storm.

"Luca said you needed to talk to me about something?" Drys said, tossing her bar rag over her shoulder and folding her powerful arms across her chest.

I quickly recounted the situation for her, leaving out the part about Ms. Etune's package. "Now I'm completely lost. They even took grandma's sigil from me."

"You shouldn't have handed them that sigil," Drys said.

"It's not like I told the jerk he could keep it," I replied a little too defensively.

Drys frowned. "There's still so much you don't know about our people. A relic like that sigil has power. Captain Finril would not have been able to take it from you."

"Unless you were dead," Lobo pointed out.

I scoffed at that. "You're saying he would have killed me to take a stone away?"

Drys shook her head. "You don't understand. He probably wouldn't have killed you. However, he could only remove the obelisk from you with your permission. Once he saw it, he had to have known you were who you claimed to be. Unfortunately, when you handed him the obelisk, you relinquished its protection."

I tried to digest what she was saying. "He knew I wasn't lying, yet he was still going to haul me off to jail? What a douchebag."

Drys fell silent, watching me with a serious intensity. "There's a few things that stink about all of this," she finally said.

"Oy, Missus Drys," called a wiry barback. He was a furry young satyr named Dando who always wore an ascot no matter what outfit he had on. I'd wondered in the past if he wore one with his pajamas too. I snickered as I thought of that again.

She excused herself and went over to him. There was some discussion about a group wanting to use the VIP area. Drys ordered Dando to bring up another set of tables and sent another barback to inform the incoming group. She was heading back to speak with us when a rowdy man dropped his glass over the bar, right into the ice bin. A group of patrons cheered for his mishap, but Drys was scowling.

"She's going to be busy for a bit," Lobo said.

"Yeah, looks like it."

The bartenders flocked to the ice bin, trying to clean up the mess and assess the damage. They were going to have to empty it and sanitize the whole area before it would be useful again.

"Warm ale is half off for the next hour!" Drys proclaimed with her arms held out wide.

The crowd went wild with excitement. She was firing off orders left and right, keeping her bartenders taking care of patrons. Barbacks hurriedly set up the VIP area for the new group that had walked in, all while she took on the duty of recovering the ice bin area herself. She looked over and caught me staring.

"Come back tomorrow morning," she called. "We can talk without any interruptions."

I shot her a thumbs up, feeling guilty for having dropped the burden on her in the first place. I'm sure she had enough to contend with on a busy night without also hearing about my problems. In fact, I wouldn't have bothered her the next day either, except I had no one else I could rely on who could advise on what to do next.

"Guess we're done for the night," I said glumly.

"I can think of something else we can do to keep the evening going," Lobo purred suggestively in my ear.

His lips grazed my cheek as he leaned in for a kiss. I could smell him, cloves and aftershave. Shivers rippled across my skin as he worked his way down my neck.

And I recoiled from him.

"Ha! Rejected, wolf boy," a man near us shouted. He was clearly over intoxicated.

Lobo snarled at him, flashing his fangs. The man sobered up quickly and made his way to the dance room next door.

"You didn't need to scare that guy," I said.

"You're right," Lobo growled. "He was only stating the truth."

"It's not like that," I said.

"Well, then, what is it like, Lanie?" Lobo snapped.

A few people looked over at us, and I felt my face blush. I knew why he was frustrated. We hadn't had sex since that first time. Whenever Lobo made a move, I panicked and made excuses. The thing is, only two people in the world knew about my curse. One of them was in a coma, and Tae only found out because of her succubus powers. It's not something I'm comfortable sharing. I don't want Lobo to know because it's none of his damn business.

Or at least that was how I justified keeping the secret from him, even though I knew in my core it was wrong. Relationships are supposed to be built on trust. I completely understood his frustration, but that didn't matter. It didn't give him an excuse to yell at me in the middle of a bar. His nasty response triggered my ability to be a stone-cold bitch.

"You should go home," I said coldly.

At least he had the decency to look slightly ashamed of himself. "Fine, it's been a long day anyhow. Come on, I'll walk you home." His voice was lower, but he was clearly still angry.

I turned away from him and waved Lisa over. "Nah, I think I'll stay here and have another drink."

Lobo growled through clenched teeth. Instead of scaring me, it made my blood boil.

"Fine."

"You already said that." I focused my attention on Lisa as she approached. "Can I get a glass of gnome-red, please?"

Lobo cursed under his breath and shouldered his way through the patrons crowding the bar. I didn't turn to watch him storm off until he was all the way to the front entrance. Guilt panged me as I saw his face, drawn down and sad, obviously wondering why I didn't want him. It was a scene that had played out too many times over the last month, and it sucked. I was sick of feeling like I owed him something, or that I wasn't enough for him. Still, I was mad at Lobo for behaving that way. *I'm not going to tolerate him yelling at me, even if he has the raging testosterone of a werewolf.* Thinking that didn't stop me from feeling like dirt about it, though.

I really like Lobo. He seems thick-headed and callous on the outside, the gruff detective who will smash a bad guy's head in, but there is so much more to him. I know he's hurting inside. I've seen it, when he's sleeping restlessly, and in the way people treat him for being a werewolf and the pained expression he sometimes hides behind false anger. He's been wounded by life as much as I have. To think I was adding to that pain tore me up inside.

The night we slept together lingered even more powerfully in my mind. The unbridled freedom of my sexuality, the well of magic waiting inside me… it was amazing. I cherished it and was determined to lift the curse, but I didn't even know where to start. What would he think of me if I let it go too far? I knew all too well where that led. I'd been there enough times to remember the look of disgust a man gives you when you pass out, when you make him impotent on top of it. They never came back after that, none of them. I was too afraid to lose Lobo that way.

I wondered why my drink looked blurry, then wiped the growing tears out of my eyes.

A sausage-fingered green hand with hardened bumps on it offered me a handkerchief. I was surprised to find Droll sitting beside me at the bar. For a troll, he had awfully kind eyes. Then again, he was the only troll I'd ever met thus far.

"Thank you," I said, choking back my anguish. I took the handkerchief and dabbed my eyes. When I went to hand it back to him, he gently pushed my forearm away.

"Keep it as long as you need, lass," he said softly. "No sense in rushing how we feel just because our pride says we shouldn't."

I cried more into the handkerchief, wishing my life wasn't such a hot mess. "Why can't I have a normal life, with a boyfriend and dates and no bloody magic?"

Droll rubbed his long, crooked nose nervously. His tin crown shifted slightly atop his head as he pondered my words. Then, he quickly switched gears, pressing one hand to his chest and lifting the other in the air. It was the vaudevillian stance of the melodramatic poet about to give a recitation.

"Love has nothing to do with what you are expecting to get – only with what you are expecting to give – which is everything," he declared in an imperious voice.

"That was wonderful," I giggled and wiped my eyes.

Droll bowed and sat back down. He took a deep draught of his beer.

"Shakespeare?" I asked.

He looked ready to spit the drink out, then feigned offence. "I shan't tell my royal court nor any other that you confused the late, great, Katherine Hepburn for that twiddling hack of a playwright."

That made me laugh harder. "I thought fae didn't have televisions."

"I cannot speak for the drooling masses of heathens," Droll said, making his voice high pitched and haughty. He would have been perfect in a Three Stooges flick, bent tin crown and all.

"I love those old movies," I said. "The black-and-white kind. Did you ever see the one with her and Cary Grant, with the dinosaur bones and the leopard?"

"A box office bomb." Droll nodded.

"Really? I love that movie. It's so zany," I said, realizing I forgot why I was crying in the first place.

Drys was still mobbed with thirsty patrons, and I was feeling tired. I slid the handkerchief back to Droll and hopped off my stool. "Thanks for cheering me up, Droll," I said. "You were spectacular at the bazaar this afternoon too."

Droll adjusted his crown and raised his drink in salute.

I waved goodbye and headed home. The problem of my grandmother's Wardenship still hovered over me, along with my anger over Mrs. Etune putting me in that shady situation with the fox. What I needed more than anything else was some rest.

Tonight I'll sleep, I thought. *Tomorrow I'll get some damn answers.*

8

The next morning came after a restless night of half-sleep. I felt shitty about the way I'd left things with Lobo, and the impending doom of losing my grandmother's Wardenship pressed down on me. I went down to the shop to organize things before we opened and found Sacha was also awake.

"Rough night?" he asked, puffing on his scentless cigar.

The little demon created an endless supply of them from the ashes of his previous cigars. I don't know what pleasure he got from smoking the odorless slugs but was grateful they did not stink up the shop.

I explained everything that had happened at the bazaar. First sparks and flames shot out of his nose, then he flew in a circle, raging and tearing his newspaper into confetti.

"If you keep doing that, we're not going to have any newspapers left for you to read," I said. I offered him the breakfast I had brought down. Part of our arrangement as partners was that I feed Sacha regularly.

Once upon a time he was trapped in servitude to my grandmother and then to me. He was a free imp these days, unshackled to do as he pleased, which was sit around the shop, complain, and read his newspapers. The food mollified him a little, as he fell to grumbling and cursing about the 'patriarchy' under his breath. By the time he was finished with his breakfast, the flames withered down to a puff of smoke.

I envy that moment in time, when my only problem was regaining my family's Wardenship. Looking back now I see how simple things were and how much I didn't understand about our realm.

"Do you know of any other way we can sell this stock?" I asked Sacha. We still had a bunch of antiques that could earn us a few bucks if we could only find the right buyers.

"Short of customers coming into our shop?" he asked. "Nope. Rosalie sold most of that stuff at the bazaar. Even when creatures came around to buy the stuff here, she was already expecting them. I can't

56

recall a single time back then when someone just wandered in and bought something."

"That would be amazing if they did, though," I mused.

The storefront door chimed as it opened. We both looked at each other in wonder. Had Sacha just manifested our destiny?

It was Lobo.

A pit opened in my stomach. The last thing I wanted to do that morning was get into another argument. Then, I noticed the bouquet of flowers in his hand. It was a bunch of irises and wildflowers, my favorites. Sacha eyed them with a frown.

"Hmm, left something out about yesterday, huh?" he said, putting the pieces together.

"Hey," Lobo said sheepishly as he came up to the counter. It wasn't a good look for him. Lobo was meant to be gruff and growling. It made me feel guilty to see him so reduced, but also resentful I should be made to feel that way in the first place.

"Hey," I replied softly.

Sacha groaned. "I have something I left in the office or some other excuse for me to get the hell out of here," he said, rolling his eyes as he hopped off the stool and fluttered to the back of the shop. We waited until he slammed the door behind him before looking at each other again.

"I owe you an apology," Lobo said.

"We were both stressed out." I shrugged.

"No. I overreacted," Lobo said. "And I never should have raised my voice at you like that."

He wasn't wrong there. "Are those for me?"

Lobo looked down at the flowers as if he forgot he was holding them. "The flowers? Yeah, I thought maybe they would –"

"Get me to open my legs? I'm kidding. They're beautiful," I said, taking them from him and smelling the bouquet. It felt a little lame, the whole 'he apologizes with flowers' routine was kinda cliché. The thing is, I just wanted the argument and awkwardness to be over as fast as possible, so I leaned into that cliché and gave him a kiss.

Lobo grinned from ear to ear with relief. He took me in his powerful arms and brought my body closer to him. His body was as hot as a radiator.

"Are you off today?" I asked. Lobo usually wore a button up and jacket when he was on duty.

"I'm yours for the whole day," he said. "Maybe we can go upstairs and run a bubble bath. Relax in style."

The front door chimed just in time to save me. I love that front door. I need to give it a raise. It was Ms. Etune. I glowered at her as she poked her head around the entrance. She had the look of someone who was trying to decide whether she should run for the hills or not. She took one look at my simmering rage and turned on her heels.

"Don't even think about taking off and making me run after you," Lobo growled.

The brownie gulped and walked over to us wringing her hands. "Is Ms. Lanie upset?"

"Guess you left out a few details about your cousin," I said, leaning over the counter. "Like that he's not actually related to you and some sort of shady smuggler who I'm pretty sure was trying to either rob or kill me."

Chulie sputtered out a tittering fit of giggles. I continued to scowl.

"Sorry," she said, straightening up. "A nervous reaction, I swear. Sometimes I laugh when I'm anxious."

"Well, it's not funny," Lobo said. "So don't."

When a werewolf tells you not to laugh, you sober up pretty quick. "There was no harm," Chulie insisted. "They assured me the information broker was reliable. No one said anything about *murdering* anyone."

"Information?" I asked. I pulled the folded paper out of my pocket and showed it to her. "Is that what this was all about?"

"Hey! That's mine," Ms. Etune complained reaching her tiny hands up over the counter to try and snatch the paper.

I moved it out of her reach. "You put me in danger to get this. Now tell me what it is, or I'll tear it up and you'll never get to see what was on it."

She blanched and held her fists over her chest trembling. "Just information. No danger, I swear."

"Then why did you lie to me?" I asked. "If you had told me the truth, I wouldn't have gone alone to meet with that Percival fellow. Why all the subterfuge?"

Chulie clammed up and put her nose in the air. "It is a family matter."

"Not good enough," I said, making a show of crumpling up the paper. I moved to throw it in the waste bin.

Ms. Etune threw her long fingers into a waving flurry. "No, no, please. It's my daughter."

I paused. "What about your daughter?"

"Please, I'll tell you the longness of the thing. My daughter, you remember her? She comes here with me."

She had come to the apothecary with Chulie one visit, a pokey teen girl who didn't talk much. She looked like she was going through the fae equivalent of a goth phase. I remembered her because she was almost my height, which is odd because most brownies are relatively small.

"Charlie, right?"

It was Ms. Etune's turn to scowl. "Yes, the silly girl. Charlie. She went missing a few weeks ago."

My heart dropped. Here I was giving this woman a hard time and she was just trying to find her missing child.

"Did you report this to the station?" Lobo asked.

"Pfft, lot of good that would do," Mrs. Etune said.

"Is that what this address is?" I asked, quickly passing the paper across the counter to her. "Why didn't you just say so? Here take it."

Mrs. Etune snatched the sheet from me and eagerly unraveled it, smoothing the crumpled surface as her eyes ran across the page. They landed on the tiny words scrawled there. I have seen hummingbirds move slower than the way her demeanor utterly altered before my eyes, from worry to outright rage.

"That two-timing fox," she shouted. "Of all the scams." She tossed the paper on the floor and kicked it away from her.

"I don't understand," I said.

"Worthless, nothing new, nothing found," Mrs. Etune exclaimed, her tiny brownie arms quaking.

"You're familiar with that address already?" Lobo deduced.

"Den of delinquents, Charlie goes to," Mrs. Etune nodded. "She is not there, hasn't been for weeks."

"But if the info broker sent that address there must be some lead there to find her, no?" I asked, hoping to ease her frustration. "If she's in trouble –"

"Charlie is always on the trouble," Mrs. Etune coldly retorted in her brownie way. "Damn mistake taking that babe in. Always trouble in my pains. I don't care where she is, just want broach back."

Lobo grumbled. "Is your daughter missing or not, Ms. Etune?"

She backed away from him but didn't drop her scowl. "Yes, missing, I say this already. Troublesome brat stole my broach and disappeared. Almost a month now she is gone. I ask those delinquents she wastes time with, and they tell me only lies. I hate that damn girl. To hell with her. I wash my hands." She spat in her hands and rubbed them together to emphasize her point.

I caught my breath. It felt as if I had been slapped. "Ms. Etune, surely you don't mean that. What if Charlie is out there somewhere in trouble? She needs her mother."

Chulie snorted derisively. "Then you find her. I am finish. Done. She can rot for all I care, little thief."

The air felt thicker in the store, and my breathing turned shallow. I felt like it was harder and harder to get air in my lungs. When I was a child, I used to have horrible panic attacks after I was first carted off to boarding school. This felt the same. I searched around the counter. My inhaler was still packed in some box somewhere upstairs. I needed a bag to breathe into. I clutched the counter to keep from falling over.

"Get. *The fuck*. Out," I wheezed.

"Huh?" Ms. Etune stood still, staring at me in silence, her eyes widening.

Lobo shifted uncomfortably beside me. He moved to put a hand on my back. I slapped his hand away before it reached me.

"I said get the fuck out of my shop!" I screamed.

The office door opened, and Sacha came fluttering out looking worried. Ms. Etune spun around and ran out of the store like a frightened mouse. I clenched my teeth so tight they ground together as I stood bracing myself upright against the counter and panting for air.

"Lanie, are you –?" Lobo asked.

"I'm fine," I managed to say through my chattering teeth.

Lobo ran into the office. I heard the water running.

"Sit down, lass," Sacha said softly.

I carefully leaned back onto my stool beside Sacha's, without taking my hands off the counter. Lobo rushed back into the storefront with a glass of water in his hand.

"Here, drink this slowly," he said.

I had to really concentrate to release my grip from the counter and take the glass. It shook in my hand, sloshing water on the floor and my shirt as I brought it to my lips.

"What is happening to her?" Sacha asked.

"I think it is what humans call ankhs-eye-ity," Lobo said quietly.

I laughed at his enunciation, spitting water back into the glass. "That bitch," I said between quivering lips.

Why does my body do this? I can be completely pissed off, ready to kill someone, and my body says, *"Hey, looks like it is time for a panic attack. Are you really truly angry? Then we should cry too, for good measure."*

I snickered at the idea of my body ordering me to cry. They stared at me the way men do sometimes, like all women must be crazy. "How could she just abandon her daughter like that?"

Sacha looked to Lobo for some explanation.

"Sounds like there's more to their family history than we know," Lobo said, ignoring the imp.

"How bad could it possibly be for a mother to turn her back on her child?" I realized I was crying, but I didn't care anymore.

"Just like your mother did," Sacha said softly, cutting to the heart of it.

"She just left me there, at that boarding school," I said. "Never even looked back. I've seen her, what, a handful of times since then?"

"Oh shit, Lanie," Lobo said. He pulled me sideways, almost spilling me off the stool into his embrace. "I didn't know."

He rubbed my arms and back to console me and kissed the top of my head. I let him. Soon my breathing was back to normal, leaving me only embarrassed and snotty. I found a tissue for my nose, then drank the rest of my water and straightened up.

"You have to find Charlie," I decided.

Lobo rubbed his stubbly jaw in contemplation. "The chief would never authorize me to run an official investigation. Ms. Etune would have to go down to the precinct and file an official missing person report. Even then it sounds more likely the girl's run off than is missing."

"Nobody knows where this girl is, and you're going to hide behind bureaucracy?" I raised my voice.

"I never said that," Lobo replied evenly. "Of course I'll help look for her. I can't do it officially, though. I'm still in hot water over that changeling incident. If Thosimir catches wind I'm investigating another unsanctioned case..."

"Then I'll do it," I said.

"Do what?" Sacha asked.

"Find the girl. I'll go out there and find her. Tiptoeing around it could make it impossible to find Charlie. I am not going to sit by while another mother turns her back on her child. What kind of mother is that bitch anyway?"

"Lanie, the fact is we don't know what has happened in their lives up until now," Lobo said. "For all we do know this Charlie is exactly what her mother says – a troublemaker and a thief."

I thought about Charlie. When she had come into my apothecary that day, she had been dressed like a rebellious teenager, but was polite and friendly. She wanted to know more about the herbs I was grinding and told me they smelled nice. She had inquisitive eyes. She was a kind and gentle person. I was certain of it.

"I don't believe that about her. Besides, no child deserves to be abandoned. She needs me, Lobo. I can feel it in my gut."

He didn't look convinced. He was going to turn me down. That was fine. I was determined to figure this out, even if I had to do it alone.

"Alright," Lobo shocked me. "Let me go down to the station and see what I can find out about all of this."

9

ree House is a different place when it's closed. Strip away the crowds of dancing and drinking fae, and you are left with a peaceful oasis. Drys's white willow tree is the heartbeat of the province. I could feel its lulling tranquility as its boughs swayed in a magical breeze. I've never felt as alive as I did when she let me sit under that tree, among its ancient roots, and speak to my grandmother's fading spirit. This morning, however, we sat at the bar beside each other as the dwarves set up for business.

"I gave a lot of thought to what you told me yesterday," Drys said. "And I found it led me to more questions."

"Such as?" I responded cautiously, unsure where this was going.

"Why do you even want to be the Warden of my province?"

It was a disarming question. "I was under the impression you were going to help me figure out what to do," I said. "This sounds more like a job interview."

Drys was a kind and caring woman whose age I would not deign to guess. She was an enigma to me, a dryad who was the heart of an entire province of fae. There were a handful of provinces on Earth, each of them unique in that they existed in both the human and fae realms simultaneously. I still couldn't pretend to fully comprehend what that meant, but around Willow's Edge Drys was something akin to a mayor. She had experience in both realms throughout her life, though she rarely talked about her past. She had the uncanny ability to go from doting grandmother figure to a hardened, stoic battalion leader in an instant. At that moment, she reminded me far more of the latter.

"Humor me."

"I don't know," I said. "I guess I hadn't really thought about the why of it."

"Come now, girl. There's no truth in that kind of talk. There must be some reason this is important to you."

Up until now I had taken it for granted that becoming the next Warden was something I was expected to do. Everyone around me acted as if stepping into the role was a forgone conclusion. My grandmother had served as the previous warden and now I would be. It was strange that I never really thought about what motivated me to fill those shoes.

Drys saw I was having trouble with her question. "Lanie, I am going to ask you something, and I want you to be completely honest with me. Can you do that?"

"I have always been honest with you," I replied evenly.

She ignored the petulance that crept into my voice. "Do you know what role a Warden plays in a province?"

"Of course. They help other fae."

"In what way?"

The way she asked me the question made me think I had answered incorrectly. "People come to my apothecary when they have all sorts of issues. I make salves and poultices, prescribe oils and herbs –"

"We have healers who do all of those things and more," Drys cut me off.

My mouth moved to speak, but no words came to mind. "What is this?" I asked, feeling cornered.

"Lanie, I loved Rosalie as if she were a sister," Drys explained, "and I have come to care for you deeply in the short time we have known each other. But you need to fully comprehend what it is you are throwing yourself into. This is my province; I am Willow's Edge, in spirit, in essence, and more. Do you understand what that means?"

My armpits were sweating, and my palms were clammy. I had never actually asked anyone what being the heart of the province meant, other than Drys was the de facto leader. Everyone respected her and showed reverence when her name was brought up, even some of the jerks I had met since coming to the fae.

"I think what it means is that you are Willow's Edge, that this land is protected by you and your tree. You are the magic that makes this province possible." I braced for her disappointment, certain what I believed was the fantasy of a daydreamer.

Drys beamed proudly. "You are such a bright woman, just like your grandmother."

"That was right?" I asked.

Drys laughed heartily. "Yes, my dear girl, that was correct. Each of us has a role to play in this world. Mine is to be the protector of this province. This land and I, we are one and the same."

"A protector?" I asked. "Isn't that what the werewolves do?"

"The werewolves protect the people of the province, as well as the interests of the Great Houses," she murmured the latter with open disdain. "I protect the province itself, the land and the bridge between realms. Without my protection, this land would be swallowed up by one realm or the other, barring one more way between."

"One more?"

Drys gave a melancholic sigh. "There was a time both realms were connected at every point. These days there are only five paths that exist to unite them. Four of them provinces."

"What happened to the rest of the provinces?"

"That is a story for another time," Drys said. "Let's discuss the Warden of Willow's Edge. A Warden is someone all people of this province can go to for help. Not just for their headaches or sore knees. Fae will come to you with their issues, big and small. I have never been able to fully understand why it works the way it does, but if a fae finds themselves on your doorstep, it is because they need you in some way."

"That's awfully vague," I said.

Drys peered at me with a smirk. "I think you know what I mean."

I did. I just didn't want to voice it. When I spoke the words aloud, it would make the situation real. I nodded and spoke softly. "Like the changeling."

"Exactly, like the changeling." Drys winked at me. "See, a very clever woman. The changeling was one of those unique problems that slips through the cracks of the established fae social structure. You saw what happened. The Great Houses were perfectly content to bury their heads in the sand and pretend Rosalie wasn't missing. They knew she was gone. We all did. We could feel it. Yet, look how eager they were to cover the whole fiasco up."

I shuddered, remembering Howard's sadistic glee when he had me cornered in my basement. How anybody could have tried to sweep that under the rug was infuriating.

"Ah, you see it now, the weight of the burden you are asking to carry." Drys wagged her finger at me. "To be the Warden is no small task. If you wear that mantle, the changeling would not be the last trouble you take on in this life."

I digested what she was telling me with care. "Howard terrified me. I still have nightmares about him chasing me through the basement," I admitted.

"An awful ordeal for you to go through," Drys said.

"But if I didn't, he would still be out there. Howard murdered my grandmother. According to Lobo, there were dozens of skeletons in the changeling's nest which means Howard murdered a lot of people. I'm not happy we killed him, but I am relieved we stopped him from hurting anyone else."

Drys smiled affectionately at me. "Spoken like a true agent of light."

I frowned. "Is that what a Warden is? An agent of light?"

She nodded. "And balance. If you take on that mantle you must be prepared for all you are committing to. There can be no halfway with becoming the Warden."

"Do or do not. There is no try," I said. I would need to fully commit myself if I was going to do this. That meant encountering more potentially dangerous situations in the future.

"That was perfectly said," Drys said, blanketing me with her approval.

"I stole it from a wise man in the human realm," I said, forcing myself not to crack a smile. "I do want to help people, Drys, but it's more than just that. There's something inside of me that screams this is the right path for me to take. Call it a deeper connection to my grandmother or the wishful thinking of a foolish girl, either way I know in my bones this is what I am meant to do."

Drys took my hands in hers and beamed. "This is what I hoped to hear. Now you will need to be just as convincing in two days' time. I have you all setup at the courthouse for an appearance before the council."

"Wait, what? You already set it up?"

Her eyes twinkled with mischief as she shook my hands and laughed heartily.

"Then why put me through the interrogation?"

She let go of me and slipped behind the bar. "It is not enough for me to believe you would make a perfect Warden, Lanie." She came around to the other side, across from me, and scooped some ice into a lowball glass. She set it on the counter and grabbed a bottle of scotch from the wall behind her. "It is *you* who must believe this with all of your heart. You were born to become our Warden of Light. Now that you fully grasp what that means, you can truly commit to the responsibility set before you."

A sinking pit opened in my stomach. "Can I still run the apothecary, though?" I asked.

"That is your way," Drys said, placing a napkin on the bar top. "Rosalie had her antiques. You have your poultices." She placed the drink on the napkin and slid it toward the seat next to me.

The door to Free House opened, flooding the dark tavern with afternoon sunlight as Lobo strolled in. I knew the news was bad as soon as I saw his expression.

"Afternoon, Drys," Lobo grumbled, taking a seat on the stool beside me.

"You look like someone dragged you through a pit," Drys said. "Have a drink, lad."

Lobo gratefully took the scotch. He downed it in one gulp.

"That good, huh?" I asked.

Lobo placed the glass upside down on the bar top. "Worse," he answered. "I spoke with Wilkins, from missing persons. Seems your friend Charlie isn't the only kid to go missing in Willow's Edge. In the last year he's had more juvenile runaway and missing cases than he had the whole decade before combined."

"How can that be?" I said. "Wouldn't people have heard about this by now?"

Drys set down another glass and poured herself a scotch. "Have you watched the news since you've been here?"

I wrinkled my nose at her. "'Course not. No one around here has a television. Oh, wait… right. There are no radios, either."

"Nor newspapers," Drys said. "Hence your little daemon's proclivity for the human papers he's always got his nose buried in. Demons and daemons love a good gossip column."

"So fae don't have news, huh? But people are bound to talk about that many missing kids, aren't they?" I asked.

"That's the thing," Lobo said. "Fae tend to stick with other fae of the same kind. We co-mingle here at Free House, but even then, you'll notice creatures tend to stick to their own. The neighborhoods are laid out that way, too."

"They're not laid out that way," Drys countered. "It has more to do with the way they settled here when they came to the province. A family of brownies comes to town, and they settle in where no one else has staked a claim. When other brownies come looking for a new home, they see brownies and naturally settle close by. And then their family or friends come and then theirs. Soon you end up with a small community of them, all living in this same area."

"Whatever the reason," Lobo said, shrugging noncommittally. He clearly held different beliefs as to the root of that issue but looked too harried to argue the point. "What's important is these missing kids are cross-species. A brownie, an ent, a pixie, a bogart, and so on. None of them are from the same neighborhood. If one person is targeting these kids, they're smart."

"Because one kid missing from your clan doesn't cause mass panic, especially if they're thought of as a troublemaker," I reasoned.

"And they were," Lobo agreed. "Almost every one of the cases we looked over was a kid thought of as a problem child."

"Which means they're being targeted," I said.

"Maybe," Lobo said noncommittedly.

"I think it's more than a maybe," I said.

Drys downed her second scotch and slammed the glass on the bar. "Explain to me why this is the first time I am hearing about this issue." There was an edge to her voice that made me uncomfortable for Lobo.

He looked like a cat backed into a corner. "Could be a dozen of different reasons. I can tell you the chief doesn't think this is worth my time."

"He said that to you?" Drys prodded. "In those exact words?"

"He said that most of the families never filed cases. More than eighty percent of the missing kids Wilkins logged were either brought in by another kid or through rumors he picked up. Without an official case being opened by an adult, we technically have no justification to allocate department resources in an investigation. This is the way it's always been. It's bureaucracy. To top that off, most of these kids have records. They're street rats, drug peddlers, petty thieves, vandals, the type of problem you don't bring home to meet your mom."

"So better off if they disappear. One less nuisance for the constabulary to have to police. Is that what you're saying, detective?" Drys said angrily.

"It's not how I feel," Lobo countered. "Though I don't generally deal with juvenile cases. I know a lot of these kids are repeat offenders, and they get let off the hook because of their age until one day they do something really stupid and then…"

"That's no justification to turn our backs on them," I retorted. "What if Charlie landed herself in some dangerous situation? She's just a kid who needs our help, Lobo."

"There is nothing I can do," Lobo said, "unless an adult of her family or *someone of upstanding respect in our community* directly opens a case." He pointed his words at Drys, then hung back quietly eyeing her.

Drys placed both palms on the bar top and leaned over it. An aura seemed to pass over her and for a moment the light bent awkwardly. I swore she suddenly looked three times larger.

"Lobo, as the heart of Willow's Edge, I am ordering you to investigate what happened to these missing children. You let your captain know that if he has a problem with that he knows exactly where to find me so he can share his unique *perspective*."

Lobo grinned wolfishly, clearly emboldened by the freedom her declaration gave him. "I will get out there at once," he said. "But Lanie, I think I'm going to need your help."

"My help? I'm not a detective."

"You were awfully passionate about finding Charlie earlier. There's another missing girl too, a dryad named Annabel. Sounds like she knew Charlie, and they both hung out at the same place." He was smiling like he couldn't wait to tell me where we were going.

"Let me guess. The address I got at the bazaar?"

"Yeah, we call it Punk House. A bunch of misfit kids hang out there," Lobo said. "Those kind of kids don't exactly get giddy to see a detective snooping around their stomping grounds."

"And you think they're more likely to talk to me?" I asked.
"Or at least you can help me soften the blow," Lobo said.
Drys agreed. "You've a kind way about you."
I shrugged. "It's worth a shot."

10

*P*unk House was pretty much what I expected from the outside. It was a ghastly green apartment building about three stories tall. The first floor was dominated by an old store front; the windows were covered from the inside with parchment paper and old newspapers. Like most of the buildings in that area, it looked abandoned. We were on the outskirts of the province, close to the warehouse district. Any closer and the landscape would be washed in grey lifelessness. There was a strange void around the outskirts of Willow's Edge, where it met with the human realm. Punk House wasn't as bad. It looked dreary, but that was due to age and lack of upkeep.

Some kids were gathered on the corner, animatedly talking and smoking while kicking around a hacky sack.

"They're dressed like they're auditioning for a Rancid video from the nineties," I snickered.

"What a shithole," Lobo complained as he pulled the car up to the curb across from them.

"At least *their* front windows aren't broken," I pointed out.

Lobo looked properly mollified. After all, he had been the one who broke my store window. "Not that building; that's not the right address. It's the old fire house over there."

Just down the side street, second building from the corner, was an old red firehouse. Sure enough, fae teens were milling about the front of the station, skateboarding up and down makeshift wooden ramps, trying to do tricks.

"I didn't know fae skateboard," I said.

"Is that what it's called in the human realm?" Lobo asked dryly. "Around here we just call it being a pain the ass."

We both climbed out of the car. "You sound like an old man," I chuckled. "Next thing you're going to be yelling at the kids to get off of your lawn."

"Lanie, you've been to my apartment," Lobo said as I came around the car to join him. "I don't have a lawn."

Ah, yes, Clint Eastwood references would fly over a fae's head. Which was ironic since Lobo and the actor had so much in common. "It's just an expression."

The kids on the corner spotted us. They fell into a hushed but fervent conversation.

"Are you sure you're up to this?" Lobo asked.

"Huh?"

"This is serious, Lanie," Lobo said. "We don't have time for jokes right now. If we go into that house, it could be dangerous."

"They're just a bunch of kids," I said.

The group on the corner quickly split off into two pairs, side-glancing us as they disappeared between buildings.

"Maybe in the human realm that's true," Lobo said. "These are fae, most of them with records. There's no telling what creatures we might encounter inside that firehouse or what powers they might possess. I need to know you're prepared."

"I mean, you make it sound like so much fun," I said. "How can I resist?"

"It's not a joke. I need to know you're prepared to use your magic if you get into a pinch. I know you don't like using magic, and that's your choice, but if things get hairy you might have to."

Ah, another lie I lived with. I squirmed uncomfortably under Lobo's scrutiny. He'd seen me use my magic to survive the changeling's attack. What he didn't know was that I was only able to use it that time because I had possession of the relic, which negated the effects of my curse. Unfortunately, I sacrificed that same relic to destroy the changeling's curse and end him. With the relic gone so too was access to my magic. How could I explain that my magic was sealed away without also letting on about the curse?

"If I have to use it, I will," I lied.

"Okay, good," Lobo said.

We crossed the street and turned the corner toward Punk House. The fire station looked like it was built in the late eighteen-hundreds, with red brick walls and two painted gates. Back then the firemen would need to open the gates by hand while another one cranked their siren horn. Paint was peeling off the gates, but they looked to be in decent shape. One of the gates was left propped open. The tall glass windows on the floor above were uncovered, unlike the buildings around it. I could see people moving around inside on both floors as we approached.

"Wolf," one of the kids called as a warning. A few of them rapidly dispersed from the area, skating away between buildings and down the street. It was like watching rats scurry away from the light.

Six remained. A teenage boy with falcon-like eyes. He wore an interesting red cap. By the way he positioned himself between us and the rest of the group, I took him to be their self-appointed leader. The cap he wore flopped over to one side, marking him as a powrie. Powries were goblin kin who lived on the fringes of fae society, many of them working as mercenaries for hire. Supposedly their caps were red from the soaked blood of their fallen enemies. His just looked like red yarn.

"What do you want with us, wolf?"

"Do you have a deed to be on these grounds?" Lobo asked.

"Claimed by the right of the dweller," the boy said, puffing up his chest.

"And you're old enough to claim that right?" Lobo asked. "Have to be a senior for that law to apply."

"All ages live here," one of the other skaters said sheepishly.

The powrie shot her a scowl, and she shuffled to the back of the group. He glared back defiantly at Lobo. I took a step forward, crossing the distance between us.

Lobo wasn't off to a good start. Already the teenagers were on the defense. "You don't see a lot of old school pig decks like that rocking chocolate wheels," I cut in. "How'd you manage to get one all the way out here in Willow's Edge?"

That got his attention. "What do you know about it?"

"Let me see that board and I'll show you," I said.

The powrie laughed knowingly to his friends, then handed it to me.

"You're going to let her mess with your deck, man?" another skater asked.

"The old lady's just going to wipeout, Gygax," the Powrie said, never taking his eyes off me. He wore a shit-eating grin I'd seen too many times before from cocky rich boys that liked to brag too much. "Little blood on the granite will look nice."

Butterflies fluttered in my stomach, but I refused to be cowed. I could feel everyone staring at me, including Lobo. I dropped the board and pushed off before I could psych myself out. Once I gained a little speed, I popped an ollie, tapping the board to fling it as I leapt in the air. I landed back on the board smoothly and circled around toward them.

The kids laughed, but out of surprise and delight, not to taunt me. I popped another ollie and they clapped, rooting me on. I hit the ramp at full speed, slid the deck across the rail at the top and then came back down to the powrie. It was all pretty basic stuff for a skater, but I hoped it would be enough to get me through. As much as it felt like a cheesy after school special, I needed to do something if I was going to get any of them to open up to me about Charlie.

"Not bad," the powrie said with genuine enthusiasm. "Where did you learn to skate?"

"I used to ride back in boarding school, behind the building when we were skipping classes." It was a lie. The truth was that I skated with a couple other kids, but I never owned my own board. And I was never maverick enough to do something like skipping class. We skated on our day off from classes, down at a local skate park.

"You grew up around humans?" one of the kids gasped.

They crowded in around me, excited to hear my response.

"Yup."

"Wow, what was that like?"

"It was like growing up, just without any magic," I teased.

It worked. They were laughing and loosening up.

"Have you ever tried marijuana?"

"Do you know any rappers?"

"What's a movie theater like?"

Questions were being rapid-fired at me. I was surprised how interested they were in human culture.

"Okay, okay, one question at a time," I laughed. "Yes. No, not in real life. There was a kid on my dorm floor in college who rapped when he got drunk, but I don't think that counts. Movie theaters in the city are dirty. The floors are sticky, and I'm sure there's roaches, but they're still amazing. Nothing compares to watching a film on the big screen."

"How big are the screens?" the powrie asked.

"The IMAX has a screen that's three stories high."

That earned a round of oohs and ahs.

Lobo cleared his throat for me to hurry it along. More questions were fired at me by the kids.

"Look, I'd love to answer all your questions, but I came here for a reason," I said with palms raised. "My name is Lanie. I'm going to be the new Warden of Willow's Edge, and I'm worried about a friend of mine. She's gone missing and I think you might know her."

The group of them fell quiet.

"Her name is Charlie," I said, gauging their reactions.

The powrie shrugged. "Never heard of her."

"Joss, she means Charlie Etune," Gygax said to him. "You know the…"

The words died in his mouth as he caught a withering glare from the powrie.

"C'mon, kid. This is important," Lobo growled.

"Joss, I just want to make sure she's okay," I added with all the sincerity I could muster.

Joss mulled it over for a moment, then waved for everyone to go away. In seconds they were all skating around the front of the firehouse again, as if we didn't exist.

"You'll want to talk to her girl, Sanji. They usually run together," he said, then walked toward the firehouse.

I glanced at Lobo, and he motioned for us to follow the boy. The bays that would have housed fire trucks and lockers in the building's heyday were now home to what effectively looked like a chop shop. A Corvette was on metal ramps with someone working underneath it. An orc girl with a dirty bandana tied around her head leaned halfway inside the hood of a minivan parked beside the 'Vette. I was surprised to hear the radio on their workbench playing Led Zeppelin. Radios were uncommon amongst the fae though human music not as much. The fae are lovers of artistic expression in all its forms. Also, it seemed every time a fae professed to like a human art they insisted the artist was actually fae. The girl must have felt me staring because she glanced over her shoulder, a cigarette hanging from her plum-colored lips. She almost swallowed it whole when she laid eyes on Lobo.

All the fae automobiles I'd encountered in Willow's Edge ran on a biofuel that was locally produced. These kids were clearly working on engines of a more human origin, as the odor of motor oil and gasoline attested. It was a crime to use such vehicles, as they'd harm not only the environment but also some of the more plantlike fae citizens.

"I'm not here for that," Lobo insisted as we followed Joss to a door in the back.

We entered a communal kitchen that looked like a long alley. A prep table dominated most of the space. On the other side of the table, set against the wall, was a six-burner stove with stacked ovens beside it. A large steaming pot filled the air with the aroma of simmering onions, celery, and thyme. Four fae were chatting while they chopped vegetables.

"Where's Sanji at?" Joss asked imperiously.

Everyone clammed up, wide eyes on Lobo.

Joss shrugged at them, then motioned for us to keep walking. "C'mon, she's probably playing Mario."

The fae watched us in stunned silence as we marched through their kitchen. "Smells yummy," I said, trying to be friendly. One of the girls gave me the finger. Fair enough.

We followed Joss up to the second floor, into an area that must have been used as the firemen's living room. There were four televisions setup, one for each wall, with a bunch of video game consoles split between them. Fae punks milled about the area on cluttered couches, blankets on the floor, and an office chair. The area was a hot mess, blaring with sounds of video games as they jammed away at controllers, oblivious to their visitors. Posters of human musicians and actors were spattered on the walls along with some graffiti. It was odd to see Billie Eilish and Denzel Washington displayed in a fae house, but I kind of dug it.

Lobo homed in on one wall, a mishmash of graffiti and old concert posters. His eyes tightened on an insignia that was painted in black.

"What is it?" I whispered.

Lobo shook his head, but I could tell the insignia meant something to him.

"You guys see Sanji?" Joss called over the racket.

One of the players pointed toward the ceiling without looking away from his game. I carefully sidestepped the clutter on the floor, trying to keep pace with Joss and Lobo as they made their way deeper into the building. There were rooms on either side of the hall. A girl was leaving one of them when she spotted us coming. She gave a small "meep" and hopped back inside, then slammed the door shut.

We passed a couple more closed doors, then I saw people inside a bedroom on the right. It was a young troll, a dwarf, and a doe, all wearing VR headsets. They moved their hands in the air to whatever virtual adventure they were on.

"What the heck was that about?" Lobo whispered.

"It's like a game," I explained, "but the screen is inside the headset. It makes you feel like you're really there."

"We're already really *here*. Isn't that enough?" he grumbled.

Wow, you're making that old man yelling at the kids to get off his lawn comparison easier and easier to imagine, I thought.

Then I paused. There was an open doorway on my left. A lone girl sat on the edge of a mattress inside the room with her back to us. Something about her caught my curiosity. She was slender and shimmering, clearly a fullblood fae, with iridescent faerie wings hanging from her exposed upper back. She wore an amazing dress that looked like she was cosplaying for a Final Fantasy game. It had an opalescent quality to it that altered as she moved. Her hair was platinum blonde with pink highlights that shifted color to a vivid magenta. She wore silver pointed nails on some of her fingertips, along with an army of rings. It wasn't just her fantastical attire that stopped me, but what she was doing. She tapped away at a keyboard in front of dual LCD computer monitors. Wires were attached to straps at her wrists, some lost inside her dress, and one plugged directly into a port on her arm.

"Come on," Joss said quietly. "K'lara doesn't like to be bothered."

"Is that a computer?" I asked. I wasn't using my inside voice. Oops.

The girl perked up and slid the headphones off her ears. Music spilled from them; steady bass mingled with an ethereal voice.

"But, how do you have internet?" I asked her.

She studied me with pale blue eyes, then looked over to Lobo. K'lara casually lifted a ringed finger and swiped it sideways. The door to the room slammed shut in our faces. When I turned away, Joss was already halfway down the hall. We hurried to catch up and found ourselves climbing another flight of stairs.

The third floor to the building was a wide-open space, other than a single enclosed room on the backside, by the stairs. Mattresses, sleeping bags, and even some tents filled the area. It was a communal living space, where most of the kids slept. It was deserted, apart from one girl reading a Zodiac Academy paperback on her cot and Sanji, who had her back to us on the far end of the room, by the windows. The girl reading flashed me a curious glance as we walked by, then fell back into her book.

"Hey-o, Sanji," Joss called to the other girl. "These folks want to know about Charlie."

"The fuck, Joss?" Sanji snapped. "You're bringing wolves after me? I said I'd get you your money."

Joss laughed at her in a way that told me his helping us was not the charitable act it had seemed. "Later," he called as he stalked back across the room to downstairs.

"We're not here because you owe Joss money," I explained.

Sanji scowled at me. She should have been pretty, had been once, with coppery skin that no longer shimmered and dark circles under sallow black eyes. I could picture her hair having a lustrous sheen at one point, but now it was a dull charcoal that was thinning around her forehead. She wore an oversized Tank Girl printed tank top, with a dirty bra beneath and oversized cargo shorts tied at the waist with a tattered belt. Sanji was in rough shape, and I could see why. Tracks marks dotted her arm, peeking out from a bandana she had tied around her bicep to hide them.

"Then piss off," she replied. "I don't want whatever it is you're here selling."

"We're not *selling* anything," I said. "We wanted to talk to you about Charlie."

"Never heard of him," Sanji said, folding her arms across her chest and turning her back to us. "And get your dirty shoes off my bed."

I looked down, alarmed to find my shoe overlapping her rough mattress and sheets. I quickly stepped back. It was hard to find a safe place to put my foot down between beds. *How could these kids be reduced to sleeping on the floor like this?* I wondered. It made me angry, but not at Sanji.

"Sanji, we know you and Charlie are friends."

"Leave me alone. I'm working," Sanji said, reaching down for a spray can.

Until then I hadn't noticed the plywood board leaning on the wall, between two windows. She added a curving outline to the graffiti she had been working on. It was her name tagged in abstract letters made up of purples and yellows with a neon green highlight. It was uncanny how much these kids wanted to mimic human culture. This was a side of the fae I hadn't seen before, and I found it intriguing.

"You know, humans don't generally tag using their real name," I said, hoping my insight into humans would give me another in.

Sanji was unimpressed. "That's because they're scared of people finding out who they really are."

"And you're not?" I asked. If I could keep her talking, she just might open up.

She dragged a chunky line of black paint underneath her 'J.' "What about me telling you to piss off doesn't compute? Maybe if you spent less time on your knees for your wolf and more time using your ears, you'd know I ain't telling you shit."

Lobo took two strides and snatched the spray paint out of her hand. My heart froze as he raised his hand for what I thought was a slap. Sanji cowered backward with upraised hands. Instead of hitting her, he flung the spray can across the room.

"Listen, you little strung out parasite," he snarled. "Stop playing games with us or I'll drag your drugged-out ass down to the station and throw you in a cell. How'd you like that? Want to detox in a cold iron cell for a few weeks?"

Sanji started crying, her body shaking in fear.

"Lobo!" I yelled.

He shot me an irritated glance.

"Get away from her," I demanded.

"I'm just trying to get her to talk," Lobo said.

"Can't you see she's shaking like a leaf?" I replied.

He ignored me and glowered at her. I felt myself grow cold.

"Lobo, I'll meet you outside."

He knew that tone. He looked back toward the door, then to me helplessly. I crossed my arms and glared back at him. How could he behave that way toward a scared child? Obviously, she *was* a junkie, and an extremely rude person to boot, but it looked like she was living a pretty hard life as it was. Once he could see I wasn't going to budge, he reluctantly stalked back through the room. I waited until I heard his footsteps on the stairs before looking back to the girl.

Sanji was wiping her eyes and nose with her forearm. I plucked some folded-up tissues from my jean jacket and handed them to her.

"What's this," she asked through sniffles, "your good cop, bad cop routine?"

"You kids have watched too many human movies," I said. "Wait, do fae even make movies? If they do, is there the fae equivalent of Hollywood out there somewhere? They should call it Trollywood." I snickered, picturing Droll performing his comedic routine in a black and white fae film.

Sanji frowned at me as if I was a three-headed duck. I was getting off topic again with my damn wandering mind.

"Look, I just want to find out what's going on with Charlie."

She took the tissues with trembling hands and mopped up her face, tossing the dirty tissues on the floor by her feet.

"I spoke with Charlie's mother. I know she's been missing for a few weeks now."

"Like that bitch cares," Sanji said.

"She doesn't seem to," I admitted. "But I do, and I'm out here looking for her."

Sanji narrowed her eyes at me. "Why would you care?"

I took a deep breath. This girl was a pain in my ass. "Let's just say we have a lot in common. My mother was a bit of a…"

"Bitch?"

"Yup. World class."

"I told those guys Charlie would never take off without her things," Sanji said, waving to the mattress beside hers. The two beds were pulled together to make one, with blankets overlapping both.

Sanji was more than just Charlie's friend, I realized. "Charlie's your girlfriend. These are her things?" I asked.

"Her clothes, her art." Sanji pointed to a stack of crumpled clothes at the foot of the bed and then to a wall on the left of the window where she worked. Three plywood boards leaned against the wall. The artwork on them was a mix of spray paint and brushwork, depicting the skyline of an emerald city. It was vivacious, brilliantly colored, and passionately painted with the name Soz in graffiti letters in the sky.

"Wow, this is really amazing," I said. "Can I look at the other two?"

"Charlie doesn't like people touching her pieces."

"Fair enough. Sanji, I just want to make sure Charlie is safe, that's all. Can you tell me what you think happened to her?"

"Who are you, though?"

"My name is Lanie. I own the apothecary on Main Street."

"Oh shit, yeah. Charlie told me about it. That's Rosalie's old place," Sanji said appreciatively. She sniffled then frowned. "I was sorry to hear about her. Rosalie was always a stand-up hoot, a real righteous babe always looking out for us."

"Yeah, it sucks," I said.

Sanji studied me for a moment. "Can you really help Charlie?" she asked.

"I want to try." It was as much as I could commit to in the moment. The last thing I wanted to do was give this fragile girl false promises.

She nodded. That truth seemed to satisfy her. "It's been almost a month now. We went to the lunar party in Proctor Park, back in the woods where everyone gets together. You know the spot? That was the last time I saw Charlie. After that, she never came back to The Brick."

"The Brick?"

"That's what we call this place," Sanji said. "Didn't you know? Anyhow, I waited up for hours, but she never came home. I probably fell asleep around four in the morning. At first I figured maybe she got smashed and crashed somewhere else. It wouldn't be the first time. But two days went by without a peep, so I went to her ma's house. She was even less interested in helping me than the jerks around here. Everyone says *oh she just ran off,* but that's bullshit. Charlie would never leave without me."

"Mrs. Etune is convinced her daughter ran off after she stole some family heirloom," I said.

"That old broach?" Sanji snorted. "That lying little brownie bitch. Charlie's grandmother croaked a couple weeks before she went missing. She left that ugly broach to Charlie, *not* to her mom. Charlie never goes anywhere without it on. Her ma's been trying to get it from her ever since the funeral, said Charlie doesn't deserve it because she's adopted and all."

That's what Mrs. Etune meant by taking her in when she was a babe, I thought. *It explains why Charlie's so much larger than her mother.*

"I see your gears spinning," Sanji said, sounding slightly panicked. "I'm telling you straight. I'm a fuck up sure enough, but Charlie, she's destined for greatness. She's no thief, I swear. Something bad has happened to her. I just know it. You have to help find her."

I grabbed her hands in mine to steady them. It was interesting how quickly she had shifted from not wanting anything to do with us to begging me for help. How long had this girl gone without hope? I imagined how horrible it would be to lose someone you loved and have no one around you interested in finding them.

"I believe you. I'm going to do everything I can to try and figure out where she is."

Lobo was waiting for me in front of the station. "How did it go? Did the kid give us any leads?"

"They're girlfriends," I said. "Looks like Charlie left all of her possessions up there though."

Lobo stroked his chin in contemplation. "Hmm, that's off. Kids like that, they cart around whatever they manage to scrape together. Even something like a blanket isn't easy to come by. It feels off that she'd leave one behind if she was planning to split. Let's head over to Free House and compare our notes."

As we walked back to the car, a girl came out of the door of the abandoned storefront I'd initially mistaken for 'Punk House.' "Excuse me, Ms. Lanie?"

"What's this about?" Lobo wondered.

I shrugged and walked over to her. It was the fae I had seen reading back on the third floor. She was wearing a faded Misfit's t-shirt and torn jeans. If not for her pointed ears, she could have been a human teenager from the nineties with her eyebrow ring and spacers. She still clutched her Zodiac Academy novel in one hand, her finger tucked in the book to hold her place. The area around her smelled like blow out matches.

"How'd you get over here so quickly?" I asked. The storefront was an entirely different building, and it didn't look attached to The Brick, not that I could see.

"She's a blink," Lobo explained as he eyed her. "They're teleporters."

The girl looked both ways down the street.

"Are you uncomfortable talking out here?" I asked.

She nodded and backstepped into the gloomy storefront. Lobo slid past her, appraising the room as I followed them inside. She looked between us, doe eyed.

"What's your name, dear?" I asked, keeping my voice low so no one passing on the street could hear us.

"Enjel," she murmured.

"You had something you wanted to tell me, Enjel?" I gently prodded.

"Sorry," she laughed nervously. "Wolves make me anxious."

"Was it about Charlie?" I asked.

"I overheard you talking with Sanji and Joss," Enjel said. Then her eyes went wide, and she quickly added, "Don't tell Joss I spoke to you. He'd be sore."

"I won't say anything to him," I vowed.

"Do you think Joss has something to do with where Charlie went?" Lobo asked.

"Oh no, nothing like that," Enjel insisted. "Joss is a good guy. He looks out for us. It's just, you know, *Brick business.* He doesn't really trust outsiders much. I bet he only brought you to Sanji because he was trying to rile her up. She owes him some money or something. But he'd never hurt none of us. Not Joss."

"Okay," I said. "Then what was it you wanted to tell me?"

"What Sanji said wasn't true," Enjel explained. "She acts like she and Charlie are this inseparable duo, but it's more one-sided than that. Charlie and her messed around a bunch, but she was way more into this boy Eli."

"Eli?" Lobo asked.

"He's a human. He used to hang around The Brick," Enjel said.

"Humans can come to Willow's Edge?" I asked Lobo in disbelief.

"Your friend Deedee did," he replied, wincing as he remembered how horribly wrong that had gone.

"I just assumed it was because she was with me," I said, trying to gather my thoughts. This was a profound revelation.

"That's one way to travel here," Lobo admitted. "Some humans though, they're born different. They can see fae or they dabble in magic. Enjel, what do you know about this Eli fella?"

"That's the thing," Enjel said. "Sanji acts like Charlie would never take off, but she's done it before, twice. Charlie has a taste for human cities. She loves going to visit them. Plus, her and Sanji had a pretty bad argument a few days before she took off."

"Do you know what their fight was about?" I asked.

"Oh yeah. I was there for the whole thing, trying to read my book," Enjel explained, sheepishly showing me her paperback. "Eli moved on a few months ago, back to his hometown for some job he got offered. Well, Charlie was fixing up to go on a road trip and surprise him."

"I bet Sanji didn't like that," Lobo guessed.

"No, she didn't. Not one bit. She was furious. Sanji called Charlie a human leech. After that, when Charlie didn't come back from the lunar party, well… everyone knows she took off to go hookup with Eli. Sanji's living in a delusion. She's been getting worse and worse lately. It's those human drugs she's been taking."

"So, you don't think Charlie is missing," I summarized as I wrapped my head around this new information. "You think she took off to go be with this Eli fellow?"

"I'm certain of it," Enjel said.

"Enjel, what about a girl named Annabel?" Lobo asked. "Have you ever met her?"

She looked sideways as she tried to remember. "There was an Annabel who used to run with the console junkies, but I haven't seen her in a while. We weren't really friends. I just like to read and mind my own business most of the time."

"Thank you for coming out here to tell us this," I said.

"Happy to help, just don't –"

"We won't say anything to any of the other kids at The Brick," I promised.

Enjel smiled and started circling the air with her free hand. A plume of pink smoke trailed behind it.

"Oh, before you teleport back to your room –" I said quickly.

Enjel paused.

"You wouldn't happen to have Eli's new address, would you?"

11

ree House was crowded for a Monday night. It was a good thing Tae saved us seats at the bar, probably something only a succubus could pull off. A few fae were surrounding her as usual, hanging on her every word. I thought of how alike her and Deedee were in that sense. Would they get along when Deedee finally came out of her coma? I should have visited her earlier that morning, before we set out for The Brick. Drys was far too busy to let me in the back, so I'd have to wait until the morning.

Tae shooed her admirers away and waved for Luca to bring us a round of drinks as we sat down. "How did it go today?" she asked.

"Well, it was interesting," I said.

Lobo hadn't spoken much on our drive over, and I was eager to hear his take on the information we uncovered.

"I guess I got a little carried away with our good cop, bad cop," he grumbled.

Was that why he was hemming and hawing the whole way here? I wondered. "Either way, it worked," I said, omitting that he did push it too far. When we discussed the strategy, it was just to get under their skin, not to reduce someone to tears. Besides, there was a moment there when I thought Lobo might actually hit Sanji. I didn't feel like getting into another argument though, so I played dumb.

"She opened up like a floodgate after you went outside, just like you planned," I said.

Lobo glanced sideways at me as Luca brought over two foaming mugs of mead.

"Thanks," Tae said. "Put it on my tab, eh?" She turned to us. "So, tell me all about it. Did you figure out where Charlie is?"

"Maybe," I said.

"One of the juveniles said she ran off with some human." Lobo took a sip of his mead.

"Really? Well, that's not great news but it's a heck of a lot better than missing," Tae said.

"A girl snuck out of The Brick to tell us," I said. "She seemed pretty reliable, but we won't know for sure until we check up on Charlie and the boy, Eli."

"What's The Brick?" Tae asked. "I thought you said you were going to the Punk House."

"That's what all the hip kids are calling it these days," I teased, secretly proud of the imaginary street cred I earned by using the proper moniker. "You better keep up, or you're going to be old before you know it."

Tae snorted. "I've lived through more fads and slang changes than you can fit into that cute head of yours."

I giggled, wondering again just how old Tae was.

Lobo slapped his mug down on the bar. "Look, I'm not good around kids. That's all."

Was he still griping about that? Feeling guilty much? Without thinking, my hand found its way to his back, rubbing him to console his worry. "Yeah, we didn't really think that one through. Let's move past it though, okay?"

He leaned into me and settled down. Sometimes I swear my Lobo was just like a puppy that gets all riled up and needs a little attention. Of course, he wasn't a pet, but an adult werewolf with complex thoughts and emotions. Still, petting him worked. I never liked to see him upset. Lobo tried his hardest day in and day out to keep everyone in the province safe. He sacrificed so much to that duty that average people took for granted. I respected him, even if he did act like a turd sometimes.

I gave him a kiss on the cheek. He smiled back at me and finally the tension unwound from his shoulders and flattened from his brooding brow.

"You think the kid really ran off with a human?" Tae asked.

"That girl seemed pretty convinced," Lobo said. "But what did Sanji say?"

"Just that she hasn't seen Charlie since the night they went to some party in Proctor Park," I explained. "The weird thing to me was that Charlie left all her things at The Brick, right next to her bed. It feels off, but if she got into an argument with Sanji about visiting this Eli… I mean, I couldn't blame her for not wanting to go back there to see Sanji before she left. Sometimes it's easier to just walk away."

Lobo frowned. "And Enjel said Charlie's done this before," he added, then leaned on his bar stool to talk to Tae. "Turns out the kids a city bug."

"Oh," Tae said. "Scandalous."

"Then we should go to that town, Old Forge, and check on Eli," I suggested.

"I need to check on something else," Lobo said. "There's a lead I want to explore on Annabel, that insignia I saw when we were in the house."

"But Charlie –"

"I think Enjel was telling the truth," Lobo cut me off. "And if Charlie is just off freewheeling with humans again, I need to focus my efforts on Annabel."

It made sense. I just wanted the door on Charlie to be closed by definitive proof. Not based on rumors and speculation. It was a shame fae don't use the human version of telephones or technology. At least that way I could have tried to track down a phone number for this Eli. It would have saved a long trip. *Maybe that interesting fae at The Brick could help me,* I thought. *She looks like she knows her way around a computer pretty well. She might have even been hooked up to one.*

"I see what you're thinking," Lobo said. "Just hang tight. Don't go back to Punk House… er, *The Brick*. What a dumb name. Anyhow, I agree with Enjel. That Joss kid only helped us to use it as leverage with Sanji. I don't want you anywhere near there without me."

"They're just kids," I said.

"Those *kids* are more dangerous than you can imagine," Lobo said. "And don't go off looking for this Eli until I get back. I know Enjel said he was a nice guy, but he's a human. They're even more dangerous."

"Yeah, you're probably right," I conceded half-heartedly.

A commotion across the tavern caught my attention. A rowdy group of fae piled inside. I recognized them as Lucien's entourage. I searched for a pale, moody face among them.

"I'm not fooling around, Lanie," Lobo said. "Don't go poking around the humans. Let me follow up on this lead, and if it's nothing, I'll drive out to the Adirondacks with Doule to check out Eli. I'm sure when we do, we'll find Charlie partying and strung out."

I sighed. "It would be a relief to find out she's just been on a bender this whole time."

"Great," Lobo said. He stood up and kissed my forehead. "I'll see you ladies later. I'm going to get some sleep so I can claw out an early start on Annabel's case tomorrow."

"You're not staying over?" I asked.

"I don't think either of us are really in the mood for that tonight," Lobo said. He smiled and stalked through the crowd toward the exit.

"Damn girl," Tae said. "I haven't seen anyone wound up that tight since… well, since I first met *you*."

"As he reminds me all the time," I grumbled.

"You still haven't told him about your curse?" Tae asked.

I ducked my head down and blushed. "Keep your voice down."

"Sorry, Lanie," Tae said, and I could tell she meant it. "But don't you think things would be easier if you opened up to Lobo and explained why you're not jumping his bones?"

"It's not that simple," I replied. I saw Lucien behind the roped off VIP area. He was surrounded by his friends. He looked miserable.

"Ah, I see," Tae tittered. She arched her brow and shot a suggestive glance in Lucien's direction. "Maybe the problem is that kitty wants a new treat?"

"What? It's not like that at all," I denied a bit too quickly.

"Any luck on your afternoon excursion?" Drys cut into our conversation from the other side of the counter. Bless her soul.

"Sounds like she ran off with some human," I said. Wow, had I so quickly adapted to the fae that I was calling Eli 'some human?' "Lobo thinks he might have a lead on the other girl, though. Sorry, we should have told you as soon as we got here."

"Never mind all that," Drys said. "I'm not your keeper."

"Well, you kind of are," Tae quipped.

Drys gave us a hearty laugh.

"Say, Drys, I was wondering," I said. "My little problem with getting the warden sigil back. Do you think someone like Lucien might be able to help with that? Isn't his family important or something?"

Drys's face went blank. "Hmm, it couldn't hurt." She eyed me shrewdly. "I didn't know the two of you are on a first name basis."

"Yeah, when the heck did that happen?" Tae leaned in hoping for some juicy gossip.

I giggled at her. "We ran into each other while I was at the bazaar."

"He could certainly be a great boon to your endeavors claiming the Warden mantle for Willow's Edge." Drys paused and chose her next words carefully. "Lanie, I'm not going to tell you who you should be friends with, but be careful around that one."

"Him?" I said, watching Lucien brood. "He's a pussycat."

Lucien might put on a good show of being aloof around his friends, but I knew better. No one could fake the kind of tranquility and joy he had exuded watching the waterfront with me. He and Lobo were two peas in a pod, with gruff exteriors hiding a warm gentle soul inside.

"I don't think so, but you have to trust in your own judgement," Drys said. "As long as you listen to your gut if things feel off." With that, she headed back to work.

"What was that about?" I asked Tae.

"Lucien's family."

"They're like important bigwigs, right?"

"Lanie, you really need to learn this stuff," Tae snickered. "It's important. There are four Great Houses in the fae realm. They aren't just *bigwigs*. Those families rule the fae realm. Your buddy Lucien is the Court of Shadows Prince."

"That sounds like a cheesy eighties band," I laughed.

Tae sobered up. "I like to kid around as much as the next girl, but not about the Great Houses. That guy's family are some seriously fucked up fae. The Court of Shadows are the fae who created werewolves, vampires, ghouls. They rule over the darker races of fae, and they do so with an iron fist. Your handsome prince over there is next in line to inherit it all."

I looked over my shoulder at her and smirked. "Hmm, so you're saying he's rich, too. Me likey."

She burst out laughing.

"I'm only teasing," I said. "It couldn't hurt to ask him if he can lend me some help though, right?"

"Depends on what you're willing to trade for that help." Tae smiled coyly.

I knew she was just teasing. After all, it's not like I could do anything remotely sexual thanks to my curse.

"I have a question though," I said. "If he's a pureblood fae or whatever, why doesn't he have faerie wings like some of the other fae in his entourage?"

"Lot of fae have wings," Tae explained. "No all of them are considered 'pureblood.' In fact, some of the pureblood purposefully hide their wings, as if it's an insult to have to show them to prove their lineage, like their above all that. Some like to flash them about. It's all a matter of personal taste. The real trick is who a fae will let touch their wings. That tends to be reserved for someone special."

"Why would I want to touch their wings?" I asked.

"Cause it's a huge erogenous zone," Tae laughed devilishly.

I eyed Lucien. He was sitting back on the sofa looking bored as usual. "Where does he hide his wings?"

"They retract," Tae said. "Do you really think the Prince would help you?"

"Won't hurt to try," I said, hopping off the barstool.

I cut through the crowd as fast as I could without running, heading for the roped off area before I could lose my nerve. If there was even the remotest chance Lucien could help me, I had to seize the opportunity.

I reached for the black rope, to slide underneath, when a hulking fae cut in front of me. I recognized him as one of Lucien's bodyguards.

"Private party," he said.

I had to look up to speak to him, that's how large this guy was. "I have to ask Lucien something really quick."

The knuckles in the brute's fist cracked. "That's Prince Lucien to you, half-breed."

My face reddened. I felt eyes on me and heard giggling. I hated the insinuation behind those laughs. To them, I was some fan girl trying to climb above my rank.

I looked around the behemoth and waved my hand. "Lucien!" I called.

He looked over, then turned away.

"Scram," the bodyguard ordered.

For a moment, I was stunned. Lucien had just blown me off without a second thought. The bodyguard opened his mouth to speak again, but I rushed away before he could. A table of fae watched me, whispering amongst themselves. One of the guys at the table laughed, elbowing his buddy. My blood felt like it was on fire.

Scram? Fuck those assholes. I was so sick of men telling me what I could or could not do.

I stormed out of Free House before anyone could see the budding tears in my eyes. *Lobo's not the only one who needs to get some rest for an early morning,* I thought. Because the next day I was going to do something stupid.

I was going on a road trip to pay our little friend Eli a visit.

12

I felt like a badass leaving Free House that night wielding my new determination. Unfortunately, a night of sleep tends to be a good equalizer for delusions of grandeur. A road trip sounded great in theory, except I was broke. A trip out to the Adirondacks was going to mean train fare and a rental car. I couldn't exactly hoof it from the train station to the town of Old Forge.

I had to ask myself something. *Is it really wise to be spending money I don't have to spare on what might be a wild goose chase?* The answer was clear.

Yes.

Charlie was out there somewhere, and I was the only one looking for her. If that meant spending what few dollars I had and scrounging to get by for the next couple of weeks, then so be it. Besides, if I could convince the court to correctly appoint me as Warden, I would have all the money from our trip to the bazaar.

I left my apartment early in the morning. It was still dark outside, but all the owls and hanging lanterns were gone. Drys had explained the owls to me. They were regular owls living their life, with one caveat, they worked for Drys. They acted as her eyes and ears throughout the province so she could keep her people safe. Transporting the lanterns was a part of their daily routine. I wondered how powerful she must be to maintain such an immense awareness through so many creatures as I walked to the train station. It was a brisk morning. The crisp air and smell of fresh dew filled me with a sense of adventure.

The train took me to the Adirondacks. From there, it was off to the car rental kiosk. I opted for the absolute cheapest model they had in stock and hit the road. Nothing beats listening to good music while driving around country backroads, so I tuned the car to 103.3 The Edge, but it broke in and out with radio static. Bummer. My cellphone no longer received service and I didn't think to save any music to it. I had cancelled my plan once I decided I was staying in Willow's Edge. I couldn't get any reception in the province with my human device, and even if I did, I couldn't afford the bill anymore.

At least the silent trip to Old Forge was scenic. Sprawling hills, smothered with trees, nestled at the foot of the mountains left me in a state of tranquility. It was very different than New York City. The air was still polluted, but nowhere near as bad as the city. I noticed the air had a more distinct smell and taste after spending time in a fae province. It was like charred rubber.

Why can't the fae share their biofuel with the humans? I wondered. *Maybe they run on some sort of magic mushroom biofuel they can't reproduce in the human realm. Seems like it would be better for everyone if it was possible though.* I made a mental note to ask Tae about that when I got back.

Spring was in full bloom. The trees were starting to bud, clusters of tulips decorated the front of rickety old porches, and birds chirped everywhere.

I drove with the window down. It was warmer here than in Willow's Edge. The sun kissed my skin, and the wind blew my curly hair about. *Deedee would have loved a road trip like this,* I thought somberly. *She would have had all our plans mapped out to the minute and filled the trip with the best things to do.* A lump lodged in my throat, and before I knew it tears streaked down my cheeks. I could not stop picturing my best friend lying in bed at Free House.

What if she never wakes up? I panicked. *Why did I have to be such a bitch to her that day? She came out to Willow's Edge to support me, and I acted like a spoiled brat, like she was in the way. That fucking asshole Doule was supposed to keep her safe. If he had stayed with her, she might still be –*

I shook my head in denial. *No, Lanie, don't blame Doule. You're the one who made the decision. You knew Brom was out there looking for you, and you left her there alone with a stranger. You're a piece of garbage, and now one of your only friends in the world is in a coma fighting for her life.*

Fucking hell. I hit the steering wheel. This is why you need music for a road trip. It helps keep your mind off how miserable you really are. Lana Del Ray's "Born to Die" broke through the static on the radio. I laughed at the irony.

Screw it. I embraced the feeling of despondency and cranked up the volume, then hit the gas.

Old Forge was a pleasant little town, nestled at the foot of the Adirondacks. Actually, it wasn't a town at all, as the welcome sign informed me. It's a *hamlet.* I'm not sure what the difference is but living in a hamlet sounded cozy. There weren't too many other cars on the road, which I suspected was because of the season. By summer, hordes of tourists would flock here to hike the mountain trails, camp, fish, and apparently go to the water park. Route twenty-eight cut right through the heart of the hamlet and led me all the way to my destination.

Fabled Forest looked like one of those amusement parks that sprang up in the fifties. They dotted the American landscape with juvenile promises of the American Dream that hailed from a simpler time, back when customers didn't know they needed three-dimensional rides that flip you upside down and twirl you through fantastical recreations of movie scenes. Surprisingly, the place looked like it had withstood the decay of time. If I had any money to my name, I would have been tempted to go inside for a spell and check it out.

Instead, I parked my car in front of the marquee theater down the road from the water park and waited until sunset. My only real option would be to try and catch Eli leaving work. As I waited, I watched groups of friends and families mill in and out of the water park. The ice cream parlor across from the theater was busy the entire afternoon. A little girl in a sundress held a cone stacked as large as her head. Her eyes were wide with wonder at the amazing treat in her hands. She took one excited lick, and the ice cream slumped over the side of the cone and hit the asphalt. The little girl cried as loud and surely as if she'd been slapped. Her mother quickly came to the rescue. She bent down and wrapped the child in a hug until she was done sobbing, then one of the workers, a teenager, came running out with a new cone.

And everything was right in the world again.

It should have been a heartwarming scene to behold. It wasn't for me. It left me feeling a tinge of irrational jealousy toward the girl, and I resented that. It wasn't that little girl's fault my mother would have handled things differently. First off, we never did anything remotely ordinary like getting ice cream. And if we had, you could bet your bottom dollar if I dropped that ice cream, she would have told me to suck it up. I could almost hear her imaginary reprimand: *That's what you get for holding onto it like a monkey. Next time, eat like a proper lady and you won't lose your food.* Then, she would probably take her time eating her own ice cream next to me while I cried. What a picture of maternal delight.

The little girl and her mother walked down the sidewalk holding hands. I envied her and tried to turn my attention away from them. They deserved their moment of bliss without my personal baggage sending negative energy their way. They walked past a massive pond that dominated the center of the town. The setting sun cascaded off of its surface in warm oranges and reds. The park would be closing soon.

I turned the ignition and drove closer. I couldn't risk pulling into the lot and finding out it cost money to park, so I found a spot on the side of the road across the street. At least the shade of the trees lining the road finally blotted out the setting sun so I could see without wincing. I regretted parking there once I made it halfway across the massive parking lot, since a large sign above Fabled Forest's fenced in property proclaimed, "Parking is Always Free for Customers."

A teenager was shutting down the small ticket stand at the entrance. He waved to me and shouted, "We're closing up for the night!"

No shit, Sherlock. "I know!" I called back, picking up my pace.

He waited for me impatiently. I hated every moment of it. If you've ever had to walk while someone stares at you, then you know how uncomfortable every step can be.

"I'm looking for a friend of mine that works here," I said. "His name is Eli."

The boy shifted his weight from one foot to the other, clearly mulling over what he was supposed to do in this situation. "We're not, like, supposed to give out information on co-workers. You know?"

"Can you just tell him a friend from Willow's Edge is here?" I tried.

"Um, I really have to finish my work." He walked over to the ticket booth to make sure the door was locked then grabbed a small broom and dust caddy. "I have to sweep the lot now."

And he was gone, off to clean the parking lot. At least he was dedicated.

More employees in bright teal polos and black visors came streaming out of the front entrance toward their cars.

"Eli?" I asked.

It was a group of teenagers. One shook her head, but mostly they just whispered amongst themselves and ignored me. With no better prospects, I leaned against the building and waited. Every couple of minutes more workers exited the park. I would call for Eli and they ignored me, shook their heads, or whispered among themselves. Soon there was a steady stream of them, but still no confirmations as I called out his name.

Then, they were gone. The boy was still sweeping the lot, looking for cigarette butts and soda cans. He periodically emptied his dustpan into large garbage receptacles that all the people who left the trash on the ground could have used.

Maybe I'm at the wrong Fabled Forest? I wondered. No, that was stupid. How many Fabled Forests could there be in upstate New York? *Could it be that Eli used to work here but lost his job?* It was within reason that someone who drifts from town to town might have issues holding down employment. In fact, it seemed highly likely. *This was so stupid of me. Why did I come out here looking for this kid? Lobo was right. I should have waited for him.* It grated my nerves to think of his cocky looking scowl when I would have to tell him I already went after Eli and turned up bupkis.

I heard voices and perked up. Two people came around the corner. I was about to ask if they were Eli, when I saw their faces. They were adults, both older than me, a man and a woman. The man frowned at me beneath his gray beard and sunglasses.

"Aw shit, we've got another one," he said out of the corner of his mouth.

The woman wrung her hands together. "Ma'am, were you looking for your child? The park's empty. We just did a final sweep."

"Oh no, nothing like that," I said.

She breathed a sigh of relief. "Thank God. You scared me for a second there."

"What are you up to then?" the man asked without masking his annoyance. "The park is closed, and this is private property."

"Oh, well, I'm just…"

Another cluster of college kids walked out of the park. One of them, a girl, quickly shoved something back into her pocket when she saw the bearded man.

"Well, out with it. What do you want?" the man asked sharply, his patience wearing thin.

"Willow's Edge?" I called to the group of kids. It was the first thing that popped into my head. One of the boys perked up and swiveled his head to look at me with sheer astonishment. "Eli?" I added.

The man grumbled. "Eli, do you know this woman?"

Eli was taller than the other kids and on the older side. He had dark short-cropped hair, an umber skin tone, and a flashy smile. He cut past the man, rapidly closing the distance on his long legs.

"Did you say Willow's Edge?" he asked me.

"Eli?" the man repeated, indignant that he had been ignored.

"What? Oh yeah, yep. She's here for me."

"You know friends and family are not supposed to be on the property after hours," the man retorted.

"I'm sorry," I said. "I didn't know." I turned to Eli. "I'm from Willow's Edge," I said in a lower voice. "Do you have a couple minutes? It's about Charlie."

"Yeah, c'mon. We can talk while we walk," Eli said. "'Nite Mr. Gothe, Mrs. Egle." He waved to them as we quickly walked away.

"I hope I didn't get you in any trouble," I said.

"Nah, he's just a bit grumpy by the end of the day," Eli replied. "He's a good guy, though. You should see all the crap we have to deal with. Some of the kids who come here can be real tyrants and honestly some of the parents are even worse."

He laughed. It was the sound of someone who hadn't a care in the world. It was contagious. I found myself smiling with Eli. He had a very likeable charisma to him.

"You mentioned Charlie. Is she okay?"

"Shit," I said. "She's not with you?"

Eli stopped to study my face. "Is she in trouble?"

I realized he could be trying to cover for her with misdirection. "Listen, my name is Lanie Alacore. I'm the Warden of Willow's Edge." *Or soon to be, liar.* "And a friend of Charlie's." *Another lie.* "Nobody has heard from her for about four weeks now, and we just want to make sure she's okay."

Eli furrowed his brow. "Damn." He reached into his pocket, then froze. "Wait, you said Warden. Is that like a faerie cop or something? You know you have to tell me if you're a cop. That's a rule out here in the human world."

"We're not in a different world," I said. "But no, I'm nothing like a cop."

"Oh good," he said, fishing a joint out of his shorts pocket.

He looked around to make sure we were alone on the edge of the parking lot. We were. Even the kid sweeping had gone home, and the sun was so far below the horizon the sky was rapidly turning dark grey. Eli lit his joint and took a few puffs then offered it to me. It smelled inviting, but I politely declined. I didn't even know this guy. No way were we smoking up together.

"Eli, Charlie isn't in any trouble if she's with you. And I'm not here to try and bring her back or anything," I said. "I just want to know she's safe. That's all, I swear."

Eli took a heavy drag. "Yeah, I can see you're good people," he said as he held the hit, before letting out a plume of smoke. "I haven't bumped into Charlie since I left Willow's Edge, though. Her mother is a straight whacko; I hope she didn't do anything to Charlie-beans."

"You think Chulie would hurt her?"

"Nah, more like lock her up in a rehab center. Charlie's a free spirit, and her mom's the most uptight bitch I ever met. You'd think fairies would be cooler. Guess there's plenty of uptight people on both sides of things."

"Her friend Enjel said Charlie was talking about coming to visit you," I said, gauging his reaction.

"Enjel?" Eli's face scrunched up in thought. "Was that the gamer dude with the funny hair? That silly fucker is obsessed with Fortnite." He thought about it some more, inspecting his joint as he smoked. "No, that was Benji."

"Eli, can you focus for me?" I asked sternly as a car whizzed past us. "Please tell me if Charlie is here. I just want to know she's safe."

"I'm sorry, my mind tends to wander. Seriously though, I haven't heard from Charlie in a bit. She called me just after I got here, talking about how she wanted to come visit. But I told her no. You can't have guests at the dorms."

"She called you?" I asked in disbelief. Those little shits at The Brick have a phone? That could have saved me a serious trip. Then again, I would have needed Eli's phone number. "Wait, there's a college around here?" I asked.

He snorted. "Nah, that's what they call the place where they shack up the seasonal help. The dorms. It's part of our pay, like a free summer vacation in the mountains, but one where you spend your days cleaning up kids puke and keeping them from hurting themselves doing stupid shit on the water slides."

Is he fucking with me? I wondered. *He seems legit, but what if he's throwing on this stoner act to get me out of here so he can run back to Charlie and warn her someone's looking for her?*

"You don't have much of a poker face," he said, blowing out the last of his joint. "I can see you don't believe me. I told her she couldn't come. She was pissed about it, too. This was like four weeks ago, sounded like she was at some big party, lots of loud music in the background." He flicked the roach of his joint out into the road. What a waste. "Look, I really do hope you find her. Charlie-bean's awesome. I hate to think anything bad has happened to her." He thought about it for a moment, then frowned. "Maybe I should have let her come stay with me."

"Shoot," I said. Either Eli was on his way to the Oscars, or he was being genuine. "I was really hoping this was all a misunderstanding, and she just ran off with you."

"Here, let me give you my number. I don't have a cell. Don't need the government tracking my every step. You know? But this will reach me at the dorms."

He pulled a tiny pencil, the kind you get at mini golf, from his pocket along with a strip of paper. He was suspiciously prepared for this. I wondered how many of those he gave out to girls at the park throughout the day. Eli was a little player.

"Can you hit me up when you find her? I want to know she's okay."

I took it. "I will."

Eli moved to walk away, then hesitated. "Charlie was always really good to me. It's not so easy for people like us over there, you know?"

"People like us?" I asked.

"You know, humans," Eli said. "A lot of those fae are kinda snobby, but not Charlie-beans. I really hope she's alright. 'Nite, Lanie."

"'Nite, Eli."

I watched him walk off diagonally across the parking lot. That was funny. Eli thought I was a human. It made sense. I don't have any outward characteristics that most of the different fae possess. I wondered if that was how the fae saw me, too? Did some of them think I was a human tourist like Eli? Did Lucien think I was a human? I remembered how coldly indifferent he had been at Free House and felt my blood boil. *Who gives a shit what that jerk thinks?*

A car was coming around the bend. I quickly moved across the street as I fished my keys out of my pocket. The car slowed as it approached. Suddenly a light came on, a blinding beam from the car to me. I threw a hand up to shield my eyes and dropped my keys on the asphalt.

"Is this your vehicle parked on the side of the road, ma'am?" a heavy voice asked me from the driver's side of the state trooper cruiser.

"Yes, sir, officer," I said.

"It's illegal to be parked on the highway like that," he said. He flicked on the flashing blue lights above the cruiser and got out to talk to me across the roof of the car. He was a tall man with a broom handle mustache. He looked like the poster boy for state troopers.

"Oh, I'm really sorry. I'm not from around here," I said. "I was just chatting with a friend, and we got to talking a little too long. I'll move it right now."

"Your *friend* should have stayed with you until you were in the car at least," he admonished. "It's not safe out here alone, you know."

That was an odd thing to say. "It seems like a nice enough town."

"Usually is, but a few weeks ago we had a girl murdered. Right up the road from here."

My spine stiffened.

"Are you okay?" he asked with concern.

I turned around slowly, as if in a daze, and placed my hand on the car to steady myself. "H-how old was the girl?"

"The Jane Doe? Just a teen. Horrible thing, too," he answered. "Somebody really went to town on the kid."

Fuck.

13

The constabulary for Willow's Edge was located at the heart of the province. Decades ago, the building was used as a human police station, but when the province moved to the area, it was taken over by the fae. Unfortunately, the constabulary was always busy. Even in a fae province there was no shortage of crime.

Lobo nodded curtly to the desk sergeant on duty, a hulking orc named Rodin, as he entered the building. Used to be the constabulary was the only place Lobo spent any amount of considerable time. However, lately he frequently found himself in Lanie's company. It was an unnatural way for a werewolf to spend their time, pining after a lover.

He made his way down the central hall, to the bullpen major crimes operated out of. A door to his left opened, and Cartwright, a break runner for the sixth district, came waltzing out dragging an inugami behind him.

The dog-faced prisoner caught Lobo's eye and whimpered pitifully. "Come on, brother. Don't let them do me like this. Throw me a bone, eh?"

Lobo grumbled. He did not have an affinity to the inugami, despite their shared canine bloodlines. "I don't help daemons," he growled, moving swiftly past them.

The hall ended at the bullpen; a wide-open space littered with desks that were overflowing with paperwork. There was only one computer in the basement of the constabulary. Technology like that wasn't something fae relished being around. Instead, every report, every note, and every addendum had to be typed or hand-written. That was the proper way of things.

Lanie found it annoying that the fae didn't have the internet pouring out of every orifice like humans do. She claimed they were missing out on all the wonders technology could provide. Lobo disagreed with her intrinsically. Computers were a by-product of science, a human plague that was destroying their half of the world. That and their incessant need for superiority over one another.

From what Lobo had seen, all the so-called conveniences humans had come up with had only led them to worse and worse habits. They turned their phones into mega-computers, where they could chronicle their every waking second, which in turn transformed them into slaves to those very devices. Instead of engaging with each other with this new connectivity, they shut out the world around them. Technology was inherently evil, and humans were lazy, greedy creatures. He did not envy them their ways.

Doule, Lobo's partner, sat at his desk working away on a report. He saw Lobo coming and shot him a slight wave with two fingers. It stung a little. It wasn't so long ago when Doule would flash a boisterous smile when he walked into the room.

Yeah, well that was before I fell into the changeling's trap, he thought.

The changeling's mind control had pitted him against his partner. The feeling of helplessness as he mindlessly gnashed and slashed at Doule haunted him. He had spent many a night in a sweat-laced fever dream, trapped and reliving that night. Except, instead of the changeling it was Lanie he was tearing apart. He had one of those nightmares the evening before and woke up in the middle of the night drenched in sweat. He had torn his sheets to shreds.

Doule still walked with a slight limp from the goring gash Lobo had scored across his left thigh. He claimed to have forgiven Lobo, but there was something utterly altered about their friendship that he worried they would never get back.

"What are you working on?" Lobo asked.

"A petty larceny case at the old mill. Open and shut," Doule said, typing away at his report without glancing up.

"I thought I would bump into you at Free House last night," Lobo said.

"Oh yeah? I didn't know you were hitting it up. Anyhow, I wasn't feeling up to it last night. Had a long day on my feet and my leg was starting to act up."

A reminder of his injury. Damn. Lobo felt a sinking despair. *I wish I knew what to do to make this all go away.*

The chief's office door swung open. Thosimir was a barrel-chested dwarven werewolf, perpetually red-faced from constant bouts of rage. His hands were like two hams, with hairy knuckles that were only surpassed by the mat of fur that perpetually peeked out of the top of his shirt. He was a vicious alpha and a force to be reckoned with.

And he's heading straight over here. Lobo almost groaned, wondering what he could have done to earn the chief's ire this time.

"Ho there, Lobo." Thosimir's voice rumbled when he spoke, more growling than speaking. It was enough to keep even a seasoned lawman like Lobo on edge. "Remind me what I've got you working on again."

It felt like a loaded question. "The missing girls, chief," Lobo said warily, wondering where this was going.

"Ah, yeah," Thosimir growled as he came up to their desk. "The great lady Drys's *niece*." That gnarled old trunk's got a niece like I've got free time on my hands." He barked a laugh at his own joke.

Lobo and Doule laughed along uncomfortably, neither of them at ease with disparaging the heart of the province. Still, it was difficult to know when the chief might blow a gasket, and neither of them were keen to set him off.

"But hey, her *ladyship* wants us to look into it?" Thosimir said. "Then that's what we'll do. Well, any leads on the lass?"

"There was something that stuck out to me." Lobo nodded. He pulled some folded paper out of his jacket pocket and handed it to the chief. "I went over to the punk house yesterday. Most of the little brats weren't too keen to talk, but I got some info out of them that possibly clears up one of the girls."

"What's this?" Thosimir asked, peering at the unfolded sheet. "You taking art classes in your spare time?"

"I saw this symbol in graffiti throughout the house," Lobo said. He had reproduced the insignia in pencil. It was a circle with a dagger piercing it at a forty-five-degree angle. Inside the circle the dagger's tip dug into a broken chalice. "There's something familiar about it that's been nagging me, but I can't place it for the life of me."

"A gang symbol?" Thosimir brooded.

Doule got up and circled around the chief to get a better look.

"That's what I was thinking," Lobo said. "Though I can't recall who sports this insignia."

Doule chuckled. "That's not a gang symbol. It's from a game."

"No shit?" Lobo asked.

"For real. It's a popular trading card game, Skrop. In Skrop, players form parties that delve into the lower levels of the underworld to destroy the high demons threatening to rise up and take over the fae realm."

Thosimir snorted. "Sounds like you know an awful lot about this game." He elbowed Lobo with a sly grin.

"I've just been to a few of the tourneys. Only to watch the spectacle unfold," Doule added defensively.

"Oh, come on now," Thosimir roared, shoving Doule. "Don't hold out on us. You've got your own deck of these cards, haven't ya?"

Doule's ebony skin reddened. "Maybe just a couple," he admitted sheepishly.

"Bah hah hah!" Thosimir howled, slapping his thigh and crushing Lobo's drawing in his palm. "This one's playing kiddie games, and you're chasing after the kids themselves."

Lobo felt embarrassed, but not entirely. "I don't know, chief. There's something off about it still, game or not. I've got this feeling about it, I'm telling you."

Thosimir's laugh petered off. He studied the two of them shrewdly. "Well, you know I always say follow your gut. If you've a hunch, then there might be something to it. Never underestimate werewolf intuition. You lads follow this down and report back to me on where it leads."

"Will do, chief," they said at the same time.

"Back to work for both of you. I'm off to break my fast." Thosimir handed Lobo back his crumpled paper and headed down the hall for the main lobby.

"Can you tell me more about this game?" Lobo asked.

"Oh man, I can tell you everything," Doule said, finally letting his excitement show now that the chief was gone. "But I don't think the game itself is your lead. Skrop is dominated by three major leagues. Players compete in leagues as a party, trying to climb the ranks. Two parties from each league move on to the finals, which are once every four years. It's a big deal to make it to finals."

"How the hell is that helpful?" Lobo asked, feeling frustrated. He had never had much of a penchant for the silly games fae occupied themselves with. Other than the glorious arena, of course. There was something to be said about proving yourself in hardened battle.

"Well, here's the odd thing. This insignia isn't from the Willow's Edge league."

Lobo furrowed his thick eyebrows together. "That is interesting."

"Right? The question is why would a league from outside our province be making time at the punk house?"

"How many people are in these leagues?" Lobo asked.

"A league represents thousands of players. It's their hometown team they're rooting for. The players themselves form into six person parties. That is who we want to target. Which party has been visiting the punk house?"

"How can we figure that out?" Lobo asked. "There's no way we can stake out that house. Those kids swarm around their turf like rats."

"Hmm, there might be one way. Parties have a different emblem they use in tandem with the league insignia. Each party uses a distinct emblem. Any chance you saw another marking beside these insignias?"

Lobo tried to picture it. The gamer room flashed into his mind. Human gaming consoles were set up all around the room, with fae juveniles cranking away in front of loud televisions. The racket was blaring. How did humans ever get anything done immersed in such noise? The northern wall was graffitied with a mural. That was where he saw the first insignia. Beside it was a painting of a fae gamer, hyper-realistic with massive breasts that stuck out from beneath her crop top. There was a spray can with a laughing face on it. A colorful tag of Soz. What else?

"Oh wait," he said excitedly. "There was something else there. It was sort of a glass rose shattered on one side."

"Are you sure it was near the insignia?" Doule asked.

"Yes, definitely. I didn't think they were part of the same thing because the rose was partially painted over by other graffiti."

"Would you recognize it if you saw it again?" Doule asked. His eyes flashed with a mischief that Lobo had seen too many times before.

"I would know it if I saw it again," he said slowly. "Why?"

"Looks like we're getting out of the office today," Doule said, happily plucking his jacket from the back of his chair.

"What? Wait, where are we headed?"

Doule grinned. "We're going to crash a Skrop tournament."

14

The murderer just left her body on the side of the road like trash. She was a Jane Doe, carrying no ID and unrecognizable by any of Old Forge's residents. Five-foot-two, brown eyes, black shoulder length hair, with a birth mark above her left eye. The state trooper said they marked her to be between eighteen and twenty years of age.

That was Charlie.

My mind spun with the grotesque possibilities. *Who could have wanted to hurt that poor girl? Could Sanji have followed her all the way out here and killed her in some fit of jealous rage?* The Trooper had said the girl they found was stabbed fifty-two times. I watched enough Law & Order to know whoever killed her had to be mired in emotional trauma. It seemed unlikely to me that Sanji could have looked me in the eye and lied after performing such a grotesque act on her girlfriend.

Then who? Eli? He was a true through and through stoner. *Guys like that don't hunt down girls on the side of the road. They spend their time listening to music and eating corn chips. Who then?* Was I supposed to believe that Charlie's murder was mere happenstance, a case of being in the wrong place at the wrong time?

Not likely.

I hoped to uncover some sort of clue once I saw her body. I followed Trooper Waits to the morgue like a mindless automaton, walking as if in a dream, numb to the world around me. I had lied to him of course, claiming I was Charlie's aunt and that she had gone missing. I'm not sure he would have let me identify the body otherwise, but it fit into my lexicon of police dramas.

The morgue wasn't what I expected. You picture a place like that being part of a police station, where the detectives leave their desk and stroll to the sub-basement for a debrief on their latest victim. More television propaganda polluting my mind. The morgue, or mortuary as it was listed on a small plaque beside the entrance, was on the bottom floor of the nearest hospital.

Apparently, that's a common place for them to exist. When you had to stop at a hospital to check in on a loved one, give birth, get blood drawn, every one of those times there was a mass of dead bodies just below your feet. It blew my mind, though I think that had far more to do with my frayed nerves than anything else.

My palms were clammy. I wiped them on my skirt and felt dizzy when I turned my head too quickly. "I've never seen a dead body in real life before," I said, meek as a mouse. *Liar liar*, I thought, recalling Brom's dead eyes gazing up at my basement ceiling, his face forever trapped in a rictus of terror. Some nights I could still hear Lobo's claws rending the changeling's flesh, kind of how you get a song stuck in your head, except that song was a nightmare that had been my reality.

I shook my head hard and blinked. The hall spun around me then reoriented when I caught my reflection in the glass window. I was pale as a ghost. The window was odd to me. It was eerie how similar this was to checking out the nursery after a friend had given birth. Those were always Deedee's friends though. I was just tagging along, feeling like I couldn't get more uncomfortable. Now I knew I could. Curtains were draped over the other side of the window. Trooper Waits' boot heels echoed down the hall as he rejoined me.

"They're rounding up the body now," he informed me. All business this one.

I nodded. If I spoke, I might lose my nerve. I could just picture myself blurting out, "I'm not really her aunt," as I ran out of the hospital with my tail tucked between my legs. I purposefully dug my fingernails into my palm. *Snap out of it you little baby. Charlie needs you to be strong for her right now.*

"It's normal to be nervous," Waits said consolingly.

Was I being that obvious? "I'll be alright," I lied.

He wasn't buying it. "Just remember to breathe. That's the thing to focus on. You'd be surprised how many people pass out when they have to do this."

"No, I wouldn't."

"Right," he said. We stood in awkward silence for a minute before he spoke again. "What we are here to do, this isn't your niece."

"It isn't?" I said, turning to him with a rising wave of panic. How did he know?

"What is on the other side of the curtain… it's just a body," Waits continued. "The girl that was inside, her soul has moved on to heaven. It's easier if you remind yourself of that."

Surprisingly, it was comforting to think of. I just needed to stay strong enough to ID Charlie's body. After that… Wait, what was going to happen after that? Would the police open an investigation? Where the heck would I tell them Charlie was from? My face felt flush, my temples on fire. This was crazy. They were going to see through my lie. Could I go to jail for something like this? My mind raced and the hall spun again.

A firm hand rested against the middle of my back. It felt warm through my sweater. Waits' eyes were kind, empathetic. He understood how I felt. *How many times has he been forced to stand in exactly this same spot and console a grieving family member?* I wondered. This man was not here to catch me in some aha moment. He only wanted to find out who murdered Charlie and bring them to justice. I read all of that in his expression and knew it to be true. *Could I tell him the real story, that we're fae and Charlie was not just some normal girl who got caught up in something horrible? I might have to, if only for his safety if another fae was involved.*

"Thank you," I said, feeling my panic attack receding. It left behind a cold sweat that made my sweater cling to my spine. "I'm ready."

Waits gauged my conviction then nodded and tapped on the glass. The curtains opened.

Did you know formaldehyde smells like pickles? I never knew that before. It's a strong odor too, hits you right in the jugular, even with a pane of glass between you and the horrifically desecrated body lying on a cold steel slab.

My mind reeled at the sight. The corners of my vision clouded. *Breathe.* I thought, closing my eyes tight. I let the air slide in slowly through my nose. *Pickles, gross. Why pickles?* I exhaled slowly out through my mouth. A few more of those and I was steady, my hands gripping the tiny metal window frame.

I opened my eyes.

Her arm stuck out from the smock. It had been gored, stitches crisscrossing almost everywhere there was skin. *She looks like Frankenstein's monster.* I felt guilty for thinking such a ridiculous thought. Her hands looked so real. Like they used to move and hold things and wiggle, like a real person. "Her fingernails look so neat," I heard my voice say from somewhere far away. It sounded as if I was in a trance.

Waits cleared his throat uncomfortably. "The coroner has to swab them for DNA, but they didn't trim them."

One of her fingernails was half gone. It must have snapped backward as she fought off her assailant. Her face was calm, nothing like the changeling's had been at the moment of his death. How much of that was the mortician's work and how much her final moments?

I tasted copper and pickle juice at the same time. My stomach lurched. I leaned over and puked. Somehow Trooper Waits already had a trash bin there waiting. Man, this guy was a pro. He handed me a handful of tissues. I wiped my mouth with one then my eyes with the other.

"It's not her," I finally said with a hoarse voice.

Trooper Waits frowned. "Many times, it can be hard for us to process the death of a loved one-."

"No, it's not that," I cut him off. "That's not Charlie. She's... the birthmark is different. Charlie's is sort of like the shape of an over easy egg, about the size of a quarter."

He still didn't believe me, or he did but didn't want to. Because that meant I was a dead end on finding this girl's killer. One look at her face and I knew that it wasn't Charlie. I felt ashamed of my relief. "Please, look again," Waits asked. "I'm sorry to ask, but sometimes our minds play tricks on us under emotional strain."

I forced myself to look at the girl. She was pretty, her face serene. Whoever tore her apart left her face unblemished. "I'm sorry," I said. "This isn't Charlie." I was certain.

Waits tapped the glass. The curtains closed.

"I'm so sorry to waste your time like this," I said. "I swear I'm not some weirdo who just likes to look at dead bodies."

"That's obvious enough," Waits chuckled. "Don't worry about it. Honestly, I'm glad. Not that I still don't have a lead for that poor girl though."

"I know what you meant," I said. The hospital corridor seemed so very ordinary suddenly. Now that I had been through the looking glass and back again everything else felt easier to accomplish. "I feel guilty for being happy right now."

"Don't be," Waits said, leading me away from the morgue. "There's enough sorrow to go around in the world without you heaping more on yourself over undue guilt. We'll find Jane Doe's murderer."

"That still leaves me with no leads to find Charlie," I glumly thought out loud.

"How long did you say your niece has been missing?" he asked as we climbed the steps to the main floor.

"About four weeks now."

Waits escorted me across the lobby then paused at the entrance. So, this was to be our parting point, eh? "Miss Alacore, I've been at this for almost twenty years now. When most of these kids go missing, they're off on a bender somewhere. Does that sound like something your niece might do?"

I thought about the people Charlie surrounded herself with and their angsty anti-establishment culture. Just because Charlie seemed like a normal angsty when I met her didn't mean she never did drugs. Her girlfriend Sanji was certainly an addict. "Could be," I admitted.

Waits looked sure of himself as he spoke. "Nine times out of ten they come back home after a month or so. Look, I'm happy that wasn't her back there. Here's my card. If you hear anything else or want to chat."

"Thanks," I said, stuffing it in my back pocket. I caught a glint in his eye. Now that business was over, Trooper Waits was definitely hoping for something a little more than just a chat. He was hot too for an older guy. But you know, boyfriends and sex curses and all. The fun never ends for me. "I really do appreciate the time you took with me."

I waved goodbye and walked swiftly across the moonlit parking lot back to my car. A chill wind blew down from the Adirondack mountains, sending goosebumps across my skin. Charlie was out there somewhere under that same moon. I could feel it in my bones. She wasn't off on some bender. She needed my help, but I had no idea where to turn next.

15

The waking world hit Charlie like a bullet to the brain. It was harsh and unyielding. She ached from her eyeballs all the way down to her toes as she stirred inside the dreadful cage that was her new home. It was hard to keep track of how long she had been trapped inside that dank basement. Slipping in and out of consciousness had caused all the days to blur together. There were no windows in the room, no glimpse of the outside world.

The best she could guess was that they were somewhere in the woods. Hordes of crickets chirped outside, and she heard the telltale hooting of an owl. There were owls in Willow's Edge, but they generally remained quiet and stuck to lantern duty at night. Those owls acted as eyes for the heart of the province, her way of safekeeping the streets, but they couldn't be everywhere at once. This owl sounded different to her.

The basement was cramped and musty, with a low ceiling blanketed by cobwebs. Cages identical to her own rested on either side of her, with three more lining the wall on the opposite side of the room. Her bed, if she could call it that, was straw. It was filthy and stank from the prince's previous prisoners. She tried to sit upright, but the room swam in a circle around her. Her head was throbbing.

What woke me up? she wondered. *There was a sound…*

"He's coming," one of the girls moaned pitifully from the cell across from her.

Icy dread froze Charlie's blood. There were sounds of movement on the other side of the rounded wooden door. *The prince is back*, she thought in a panic, quickly tossing herself into a sleeping position.

The door opened on rusty hinges that protested with a creaking that hurt her ears. Light flooded the dark basement. It was too much for her eyes to handle. She forced them shut to bare slits. The girl across from her whined. Charlie had never known what true fear sounded like until she was taken to that basement. Now she heard it all the time.

The prince's silhouette blotted out the light from where he stood framed in the open doorway. Charlie tried to get a look at the room beyond through her slitted eyes. There was a brick oven behind him, like the kind restaurants used to make pizza. Though she doubted very much that the prince was planning to be making pizza for them.

"Ah, a pleasant and fortuitous afternoon, my little dumplings," the prince elated as he crouched down and strode into the room.

"No, no, please," the girl across from Charlie begged. A second voice joined hers, moaning incoherently from one of the other cages. Charlie wanted to urge the girls to shut up. Didn't they know they were going to upset the prince? He did bad things when he was angry. She kept her lips clamped shut.

"What's this then?" The prince stopped in front of the protesting prisoner's cage. Charlie heard her shuffle backward across the dirt and straw. "Awake so soon? Ah, had I known I would have brought down your medicine hours ago." He removed a jingling keyring from his belt and found the proper one while whistling "The Farmer in the Dell."

That's how he thinks of us, Charlie thought. *We're his pets. Like animals he can do with as he pleases.*

Though she had not been touched in that way by the prince. Her first week there he had used the girl across from her to slake his depravity. The girl had fallen out of her trance midway through his rutting, screaming and sobbing for him to stop, which seemed to only rev up his twisted engines from the sounds of it.

"There, there. No need for troubles," he cooed. Charlie did not need to look to know he must have brought out that foul mirror of his. It was an evil thing. "Look. You see it there, don't you? This is a palace, your new home, a luxurious accommodation fit for Titania herself. Ah, yes, now you can relax over there."

"The bed," she whimpered in a daze. "It's so soft."

"Yes, and extravagant. Come now and rest. You must be tired from dancing all night at the ball, no? There you go, lean back. Sleep my treat, sleep."

Her breathing was soon heavy and steady. The mirror's magic was potent. To look past its glassy surface meant to fall under the prince's spell. There had been a time when Charlie had been intrigued by the idea of virtual reality that humans invented. Now she saw it as the stuff of nightmares, to be unable to distinguish reality from fiction.

"There's a good girl. Get some rest. I shall be back shortly to give you some medicine."

Ah, yes, *medicine*. The prince's idea of medicine was to stick human poison into their veins. The prince locked the sleeping prisoner's cell behind him as he exited. Charlie shoved her face under one arm, focusing on a steady breathing rhythm that mimicked sleep. Things were easier if he thought she was still out. Even if it only earned her a few hours before his next check in, to think with a clear head was a blessing. His key turned noisily in her cell door, startling her to twitch.

"Ah, but I've woken you as well," he chuckled delightedly.

Charlie tried to swallow the dry lump in her throat. Her breath felt trapped in her chest. The prince was carrying his pail. There was no faking her way through this one. His hands would be all over her soon. She forced herself to breathe. The prince preferred to keep his pets clean. *No diseases for my little treats,* he'd say. Despite herself, she let out a tiny squeak.

The prince paused halfway into the cell, soapy water from his pail sloshing over its sides and onto the cell floor. "Did I startle you?"

She had to think quickly. "My prince," she mumbled, slurring her words.

He knelt beside her bed, setting the pail to the side. A thick calloused thumb pulled her eyelid back, searing her eye with the light from the open doorway to the other room. She flinched but forced her eye to roll up until only the white showed.

"I don't want to go back down to the ball," she said, forcing false grogginess into her words.

"You *are* out of it still, aren't you?" he snickered, letting go of her eyelid. "Funny, I wasn't too sure about you at first. You seemed to have a strange resistance to my magic. But now…" His thick fingers pinched her inner thigh, stinging the naked flesh. "You're like playing with putty."

She suppressed a whimper as he slid his cold fingers up her leg. He squeezed, testing her flesh. "Not ready yet, though," he claimed, then slapped her thigh.

She clamped her mouth shut to keep from crying out. The prince's clothing rustled. He was searching his shirt pocket for something. Her heart grew cold. It was the cursed needle. Charlie had never understood Sanji's obsession with human drugs until now. One prick of that needle and she would fall through the veil into Shangri-La. She wanted to scream for him to stop. Once it was in her system, there was no telling when she would come out of it again, if ever.

The prince wrapped a tourniquet around her arm. "Make a fist. Gentle now. Yes, pump it." He cleaned her skin, just above the vein. "Here you are, my little treat. I've brought you your favorite medicine."

He guided her hand to the needle. She took it. She learned early on that it was better to go along. If she refused, he would use the mirror to put her to sleep and do it himself anyhow.

The girl across the room screamed at the top of her lungs. Charlie jerked and almost jolted upright. Thankfully, the prince's attention snapped to the other cell, otherwise he would have seen through her ruse. His face was inscrutable in the shadows as he grumbled.

Stab him in the leg with the opium, she thought in a frenzy. No. That was foolhardy. She had already thought through that scenario before. The prince was no fool. He administered the medicine to them on a need-to-basis, and she was quite sure that it was measured to her weight. He was much larger than her and would easily make it outside the cell before she could escape, that is if he didn't wrap those massive hands around her throat and choke her to death first.

"Let me out of here!" the other girl screamed, throwing herself against the chicken wire of her cage. The ceiling beams shuddered from the impact, raining dust down on them. "Momma, help me! I can't stay here anymore! Let me out of this cage! I want to go home! I want my mother." She was worked up into a frenzy.

The prince moved swiftly, out of Charlie's cell and across the room.

He left the door open! This was it, her chance at freedom. She just needed to make it past two doors, both of them left open, and she might see the sun again. His growl cut through the basement like a knife, stilling her thoughts.

"Ungrateful bitch," he snarled.

The girl in the cage across from her whimpered and backed away from him with upraised palms. Charlie flinched when she heard his fist slam into the girl's gut. She hit the ground on hands and knees, trying to suck in air between dry heaves. The prince kicked the girl hard, just below the ribs, sending her sprawling onto her straw mattress. Her breathing was a ragged bout of gasps for air. The girl in the cell beside hers stirred in her sleep, moaning quietly.

"You see what you've done? My little morsels are trying to rest, you ghastly little slut."

Charlie had to think quickly. Her opportunity to make a run for it had already passed. She looked down at the needle he had handed her. The drug pulled at her will. How much easier would all of this be if she just slipped it into her arm? That was her only real escape from this hell. One prick and everything would be right again.

She gritted her teeth and shook her head in denial. *I can't fall back into that abyss,* she thought. She jammed down the plunger and sprayed the needle out onto her straw mattress, then plunged the tip into her arm and went as limp as she could. The beaten girl was moaning apologies into the dirt where she lay, clutching her mid-section.

"Ugh," the prince sneered in disgust. "What a waste." He was already back inside Charlie's cell. He paused to appraise her. "What's this? Such a good girl, taking all your medicine like that. Alas, I cannot clean you up today, my treat."

He plucked the needle from her arm as she focused on the rise and fall of her chest. The prince shuffled out of her cage, taking the pail of water with him. He tossed it onto the floor just outside her cell and slammed the door shut. The light from the other room was blotted out for a moment as he passed through the open door. What sounded like a cabinet was opened and slammed shut. The prince stalked back into the basement.

"No," the other girl sobbed desperately as she still tried to gasp for air. "Please don't. I'll be good."

"There's nothing for it," the prince replied coldly. "You're broken. If I let you stay, you'll only continue to disturb my other treats. Such a shame, not even ripe yet, but better to harvest a little today than lose it all to rot."

Harvest? Charlie's body went numb with shock. She dared to peek across the room. Metal glinted in the prince's hand. He pressed what looked like a cross between a human blow dryer and a handgun to the protesting girl's forehead. A sharp sound, like a nail slamming through porcelain, resounded. The girl's body instantly fell limp to the floor. Charlie slapped a hand against her mouth to keep from screaming.

The prince put his weapon away, tucked it into his belt. He fussed with the girl's body, and then proceeded to drag her by her ankles out of the cell. Charlie knew the girl was dead even before she saw her blank staring eyes catch the light. A dark hole dripped blood from her forehead. The girl's arms flopped like limp noodles behind her as he dragged her out of the basement and into the adjoining room. The prince hoisted her dead body and slapped it down onto a wooden slab in the other room.

"At least I'll be eating well tonight," he remarked.

The prince casually walked back to close the door and resumed his whistling tune. Charlie flopped over and promptly vomited all over the straw. It had been bad enough living in fear of becoming a sex slave to her captor.

He's going to eat me. That fact hammered home.

A loud electric whir filled the air. It drowned out the prince's whistling, then grew louder. She realized with terror it was the sound of a table saw cutting through something thick. Thick and *meaty*. Charlie vomited again, emptying the food from her guts that the prince had spoon fed her earlier that day. She had thought it was his twisted way of caring for his prisoners, when in fact he just wanted to ensure his pets were plump and disease-free before he harvested them.

16

Sir Horrick's office was stuffier than I remembered from my first and only visit. Shelves laden with leather bound law books lined the wall behind his mahogany desk. He had been Rosalie's lawyer when she was still alive. Only a few months ago my wild journey into fae society began right there, across from the goat man.

"What's taking the goat so long?" Sacha grumbled under his breath.

"Don't call him that," I warned. Horrick had gotten very cross with me the first time we met, when I made the same comparison. "He's not a goat. He is a gwyllion."

Sacha snorted. "What's the difference?"

I honestly did not know. There were so many different types of fae that it was hard to keep up with who was what. Besides, I was finding it difficult to concentrate on no sleep. I thought to sneak a nap in on the train, but whenever I closed my eyes, I saw that poor dead girl lying on the slab in the mortuary. Sacha met me at the station, and we hopped right onto the next train. It was nice having Sacha along for the trip, anything to keep my mind off that dead girl's face. I rubbed my dry eyes and shifted uncomfortably in the leather armchair as Horrick reviewed the documents across from us.

"Please refrain from smoking in my office," Horrick said without looking up from his reading.

Sacha grumbled from the seat beside mine and shoved his cigar back into his breast pocket.

Sir Horrick made a show of putting the documents down in a neat pile before him, then folded his cloven hands together thoughtfully. He cleared his throat. It sounded exactly like a goat bleating.

Sacha snickered, but I nudged him quiet with my elbow.

"Yes, I see. Everything is in order," Horrick said. "It seems the heart of your province has gotten the chain of events rolling, cogs spinning as it were. Whatever analogy you prefer. You have a court date scheduled on –"

"I know when I'm supposed to appear," I interrupted. "But what am I supposed to be doing there is the question? Honestly, I still don't understand why any of this is necessary. Shouldn't the mantle pass to me as Rosalie's heir?"

"Traditionally that would be the case," Sir Horrick said, checking his wristwatch. "It is commonplace for a title or contract to pass along a bloodline. Although, it has always been at the discretion of the Great Houses to allow it. In your particular case, a house filed a petition of unworthiness."

"Why would they go and do that?" Sacha asked before I could.

Horrick cleared his throat and shifted in his seat. I got the impression he wasn't too comfortable having a daemon in his office. It was the way he made a point to look just past Sacha and turned his nose away from the imp's direction. He directed his answer to me.

"A petition of unworthiness is, as it sounds, quite directly a statement that you, as Rosalie Alacore's heir and next of kin, are incapable or too inexperienced to maintain the duties of a Warden. I believe the why of it is that they do not deem you up to the task."

"Just my luck." I took a deep breath. "They might not be wrong there. Still though, I don't understand why they would target me like this."

"Honestly, Miss Alacore, this all could have been avoided had you not disregarded the original court summons. It was likely a matter of routine, a chance for the local representatives to assess your character, as it were. To completely abandon protocol and not show up for that meeting was akin to biting your thumb at them. You could not have expected the Houses would have treated you kindly after such a stunt."

"What in the world is he talking about?" I asked Sacha.

"I don't know," he said. "Sounded like a bunch of bleats and bahs in between blaming you."

I agreed. Not with the bleats part, but the latter. "Sir Horrick, are you saying you knew this was happening before now?"

Horrick bristled. "Quite so. It was two months ago when we received their first correspondence. Please tell me you read the articles of indoctrination I couriered to you?"

"I never received any mail from you, sir," I said, feeling heat build behind my eyes.

"Alice," Horrick called toward the closed door to the reception area. His goat nostrils flared as we waited. "I say, Alice?"

Horrick's receptionist was a tiny woman who I believe is eternally grumpy. Her and Sacha would make great bed fellows. She burst into the room wearing her patented scowl. "I heard ya the first time."

"Miss Alacore claims she never received the articles of indoctrination."

"Sent 'em out seven and a half weeks ago," Alice snapped, shooting me a withering look for having the audacity to question her capability.

"Where did you send these papers to?" Sacha asked. "I ain't seen a thing come in the post for a while now."

"To her address in the big human city, ya bald dummy," Alice scowled. "I sent 'em guaranteed next day. Don't need you getting uppity with me about my business neither."

Smoke shot out of Sacha's nostrils. "Human city?" He looked at me in mock disbelief. "This is what you get for trusting a goat and a bug with your legal matters."

Alice clenched her fists, ready to holler at us. I raised my palm to stop her. "I don't live in New York anymore, Alice. I moved months ago, right after my grandmother died. I have been living above her shop ever since I met you guys."

"Oh dear," Sir Horrick bleated. For real this time. Alice looked like she just licked a hamster. "Oh dear, oh dear. Had we known…"

"That's okay," I replied glumly. "It's not your fault. I should have filed a change of address with the post office. Then again, it's not like they could have found Willow's Edge. It's rotten luck, but it explains a lot at least." I rubbed my eyes, leaving my vision blurry. I was going to need to get some sleep on the train ride back, dead girl's haunting my thoughts or not. "It might not have mattered anyhow. Who's to say that this council or whatever would have approved of me if we met a few months ago?"

"'Course they would have approved of ya, kid," Sacha said, fishing his cigar out of his breast pocket. "What's not to like?"

Sir Horrick shook his head at Sacha. The imp grumbled and pushed the cigar back down. The gwyllion checked his wristwatch. "Well, if that answers your questions, I have a rather pressing engagement."

"Wait, what?" I asked, perking up. "What about the case? Shouldn't we do some sort of prep work, so I know what to say when we're in court?"

Alice chuckled and shook her head.

"That will be all Alice," Sir Horrick said curtly.

She shrugged and waltzed back into the reception area but left the door wide open. Horrick turned his attention back to us. He looked like he was chewing on his tongue trying to find the right words.

"Miss Alacore…"

"Oh shit," I said as it hit me. "You're dropping me as a client, aren't you?"

"You must understand *you* were never really a client of this law office," Sir Horrick explained. "My duties to your grandmother's estate were what bound us together for our initial meeting."

"You're abandoning me?" I said, hating the whiny pitch of my voice. "My grandmother was your client for centuries."

I never knew what a flustered goat looked like until that moment. It was not pleasant.

"Rosalie Alacore was a paragon in this sad world. I adored her, I assure you. Which was the only reason I met with you today at no expense. But, Miss Alacore, we both know you cannot afford my further services at this time. You have no idea how overwhelmed I am with work. There is simply no way I can take you on as a pro bono client."

I lurched out of my seat and leaned across the desk to point an angry finger at him, feeling the indignation of a scorned lioness. "At least you have the common sense to wear your guilt for all to see. You know what you're doing is wrong. Rosalie would roll over in her grave if she knew you were abandoning her granddaughter like this." *If she had a grave,* I thought. It's not like we ever found out where the changeling stashed her body.

Horrick flinched with each jab of my finger, his hourglass eyes pockets of black. "Please, Miss Alacore, be reasonable. Would you expect a baker to serve you bread for free? Or a carpenter to build you shelves out of the kindness of their heart? Should we all go penniless until we lump ourselves into the same bread line, begging for scraps, so Lanie Alacore can get her way?"

I stormed out of his office, feeling the weight of the world on my back. Sacha followed me on fluttering wings, but not without throwing in the last word. "Never seen a fella with a gut like yours in no bread line."

We walked in silence to the train station. At first the anger buoyed me, fueling my muscles with fire, but soon that washed away leaving me with nothing but a sense of embittered defeat. We sat on a bench, waiting for the train to roll in.

All I do is let everyone down these days, I thought. Deedee was trapped in her coma. Lobo was never satisfied by our lack of intimacy. Charlie was missing with no leads. And my grandmother, dear Rosalie. What was I doing to her legacy?

"Hey, chin up kiddo," Sacha said, taking a deep puff of his newly lit cigar. "Who needs the stinkin' Warden title anyhow? We can run our apothecary fine without one."

"That's not the point," I said glumly. "That title should stay in Rosalie's family, as part of her legacy. I'm going to fight for this because it's worth it. I just don't know how I can win is all. Seems like whenever I think I've got things figured out, the world dumps more problems on me."

Sacha snorted. "Plenty have it worse, toots. Okay, no need to look like you wanna kill me. I'm just saying, there's more to life than helping other folks all the time. That Wardenship was constantly running Rosalie ragged, just like you are now. Look, it even got her killed in the end."

"That was different," I said, though he did have a valid point.

"I'm just saying there's nothing wrong with cutting loose to party once in a while, ya know."

Sacha's words splashed over me like a bucket of cold water. I perked up and grinned from ear to ear. "Sacha, you beautiful, brilliant bastard you," I elated.

"What?" Sacha giggled, confused as to why I was so excited.

He had no way of knowing that his words had brought back a memory of something Sanji had said. The last time she saw Charlie was at a lunar party in the woods, where a lot of local fae met up. Eli had also said the last time he spoke with Charlie over the phone it sounded like she was at a party. *Lobo said that lunar party is twice a month, following the phases of the moon. So, the next party should be tonight,* I thought, checking the time on the large clock above the train tracks. I leapt to my feet as the train rolled in.

"I think I know where we need to go next."

17

obo had never been one for playing games. His belief was that idle time was best spent doing something that fulfilled a purpose, like working out to strengthen your body or reading a book to feed your mind. He understood the drive people felt for competition, but it always seemed like a primal need, more akin to a baser human action than something any self-respecting fae should want to be involved in. Except, of course, for the glorious arena. Measuring one's worth in battle was a noble pursuit. So, when he walked into the gymnasium where the Skrop tournament was being held and found throngs of fae in attendance, he was taken aback.

"They're all here to play a card game?" he asked in disbelief.

Hanging banners decorated the walls of the gymnasium in intervals, each with different artwork depicting stylized heroes or villains of the game in what were supposed to be striking poses. One was bordered in cog work, the hero a leaping woman wearing a monocle with steampunk automatons flying around her. Another was a man clutching a glowing skull with an undead horde following him.

The center of the gym was dominated by round tables, each with twelve seats. There had to be fifty of those tables, each with floor length black tablecloths. A line was painted down the center of each tablecloth, dividing the teams into six on each side. If someone was not playing, they were hovering over the action, watching a match. The whole area had a palpable energy to it, akin to a beehive populated by fae nerds of all races. Except, instead of flowers and pollen, their trade was cards and laughter.

Doule nodded emphatically. "This is the province's calling," he explained with a glint in his eyes. "These events only happen twice a year. The top team today will go on to the pro tournament."

"Pro? As in for money?" Lobo asked, surveying the crowd. *These geeks actually get paid to play cards?* he thought. If he was being honest with himself, it looked an unlikely place for a criminal element to be up to nefarious deeds.

"You bet your hairy ass," Doule said. "Today, too. The top three teams will all walk away with some hard cash. My guess is it'll be around five thousand in human currency for first place."

"Damn." Lobo whistled. "I had no idea you geeks were making bank playing board games."

Doule sighed. "It's *not* a board game. Skrop is a battle of wits, where you put together your best hand of thirty-five cards that center around a paragon. This is a game of great skill and complex strategy, as you're playing off of your team's paragons to form a legion united."

Lobo grunted. "I really don't give a fuck. How about you stop masturbating over the pretty cards and help me find what we came here for?"

"Whatever, man," Doule chuckled. He handed Lobo a scrap of paper. "Here's a copy of the insignia. I'll take the left side of the event. Look at the center of each table. That's where the team insignias should be displayed."

Lobo took the drawing as they split off in opposite directions. He moved swiftly through the crowd, trying to blend in with a false smile and covert glances at the tabletops.

This'll go easier if I don't spook the players. Nothing like having a werewolf prowling in your midst to get the hackles up. The last thing I need is to scare off my prey. Not before I get some answers on these missing girls.

From what he gathered, the other missing girl, Annabel, was a bit of an outcast to the kids her age. This would be her graduating year. She was a juvenile delinquent in the same way Charlie was, getting into trouble for skipping classes, caught in possession of human drugs, petty theft, that sort of thing. That didn't mean she deserved to go missing. Her dad was a deadbeat drunk, and her mother had taken off years ago for the mainland, fed up with province life. Something about that stuck in his craw. *Living away from the fae realm wasn't for everyone, but how could she abandon her own daughter? Would she have turned out differently had her mother stuck around? I couldn't mention that information to Lanie. Not after how worked up she got about Charlie's mom disowning her.*

Three tables and none of the insignias matched the paper.

Maybe I should have asked Lanie to come with us. We could have covered a lot more ground faster that way. He chuckled ruefully at himself. What was he thinking? *Lanie isn't a detective. Stop trying to drag her around with you everywhere, you clingy bastard.*

That was the thing though, wasn't it? Ever since he had met Lanie, he found himself infatuated with the woman. Lobo used to throw himself into his work until he couldn't keep his eyes open any longer. These days all he thought about was getting off the clock so he could be around her.

Everything about Lanie enthralled him. The sweet way she smelled was intoxicating, leaving him heady sometimes. She smelled like no other fae he'd ever met, and she was fairly tight lipped about her lineage, but he guessed it had something to do with her race. Rosalie had a slightly similar odor. Lanie had a way of looking at the world with equal parts child-like wonder and cynicism that he found mesmerizing. It was the perfect balance to keep him on his toes. And she was sharp as a tack. Lanie absorbed information faster than most people he'd met. She was brilliant, gobbling up every scrap of knowledge she could find on the fae races, their cultures, their habits, all of it interested her. He hoped she was able to get the right to become Warden of Willow's Edge. *She'd make a great Warden. She's got one of the biggest hearts I've ever known. Just like her grandmother.*

Four more tables with the wrong insignias.

He frowned. *Would Rosalie have approved of me dating her granddaughter?*

It was a thought that had plagued him ever since the night she pulled him out onto the dance floor. It was one thing to show kindness to a werewolf and another entirely to allow him into your family. His heart felt like someone squeezed it. *Who am I fooling? Lanie doesn't even want to be around me much these days.*

The way she had looked at him the other night, at the bar, still stung like a fresh wound. Something profound had changed in their relationship. Things started off spectacularly, but ever since that horrible incident with the changeling, she had grown gradually colder toward him. It was all that bastard Brom's fault. Lobo spent so many sleepless nights recounting the events of the evening he went to the cemetery to track down the changeling. How could he have been so stupid as to walk into that trap? He should have smelled that wolfsbane as soon as he entered the tunnel. Some nights he could still feel that leech burrowing into his mind, dominating his will, forcing him to obey. He bristled, emitting a low growl as he shook off the filthy feeling of leeching tentacles probing his mind.

A nearby player watching a table looked at him fearfully.

Lobo flashed the boy a grin. That only made the color drain out of the fae's face. It wasn't often one found themselves face to face with a grinning werewolf. Lobo rolled his eyes and moved on. The next few tables had all the wrong insignias as well.

I need to stop fooling myself. It's not Brom's fault. It's mine for not being strong enough. How could I have let someone take control of me so easily? Even Doule hasn't looked at me the same since. If my own partner can't forgive me, what hope is there that a woman I've only known a few months is going to turn the corner? Does she think I can't see the way she flinches when I try to touch her?

The truth was Lanie could not stand the sight of him. *Let's face it. She's only still with you because she doesn't know how to break it off. If you were a real man, you'd make it easy on her and walk away. I think somewhere deep down she likes me so much that she's been trying to work through it, but how do you work through your boyfriend turning into a homicidal monster who tried to murder you? I'm fighting a losing battle, and I'm too pathetic to admit it and move on. Lanie deserves to be happy, not to be stuck with a jerk like me.*

A hand caught his shoulder.

Lobo wheeled around baring his fangs and ready to pounce. A few people around them staggered back.

"Whoa, big guy," Doule chuckled. "We're supposed to be low-key, remember?"

"Sorry." Lobo looked down at his feet. "I didn't get much sleep last night. Think it's fraying me at the edges."

"Yeah, no biggie." Doule shrugged. "C'mon, I found them. You're not going to believe this."

The two of them blended into the background again and cut through the crowded room as stealthy as two stalking wolves in a midnight forest. Not many eyes looked their way. There was nothing to see. Just two friends enjoying the event.

Lobo recognized his mark's face well before he saw the matching insignia. "Fuck me," he said under his breath.

"My sentiments exactly," Doule whispered.

They stayed back, hidden in the crowd. Close enough to confirm the insignia on the table matched the one he had seen on the walls at the punk house. Lobo didn't need that confirmation, though. As soon as his eyes landed on Sam, he knew this was their guy.

"This is the fuckface who tricked Lanie into drinking that prickly pink at Free House," Lobo grumbled.

"Oh, I remember," Doule said. "And the same little creep that you hauled into the station that time a couple years ago."

Sam had a checkered history of sexual abuse accusations. He was a blink, a less common fae, who could teleport short distances anywhere they could set eyes on. Blinks were very similar to pixies in that respect, though pixies tended to possess more powers than just teleportation. What he presented to the world was an average guy with freckles, curly red hair, and a dopey grin. It was the perfect bait, an innocuous nerd to ease his victims into letting their guard down.

"This scumbag's lured more nubiles into gangbangs than I can count," Lobo explained. "He used to have a pattern of hanging around watering holes, waiting for a fresh of age fae to come in for their first night on the town."

"Roofies?" Doule asked.

"Sam's too slick for that. He tricked those girls into hanging out with him and his friends. Made them feel special so they let their guard down. His drug of choice was to fool them into taking things only a succubus would imbibe. Nothing illegal to drink mind you, but strong enough to loosen their inhibitions. Then he'd share them with his friends and make them do things they'd never agree to if they weren't messed up. I took the fucker in twice for preying on them."

"Why isn't he locked up then?" Doule asked.

"Problem was the girls. They were always too shell-shocked from the ordeal to press charges. I think they would rather the world didn't know they had a train ran on them and who the hell knows what else by Sam and his buddies."

All of that stopped after Lobo had beaten Sam senseless behind Lucky's Pub two years before. *Until the night he tried that shit on Lanie,* he thought.

Sam laughed gleefully as he laid three cards down on the table. Whatever hand he had just played must have been good, based on the distraught reactions of the opposing team. Sam sat back with his hands behind his head as his friends patted his back. He wore a smug shit-eating grin that Lobo wanted to punch through to the back of his head.

"If he spots me, he's going to clam right up," Lobo said. "We should see what you can get out of him first, before we decide how to approach this."

"Alright, you hang back and cover me," Doule agreed.

He took off his suit jacket and dress shirt so all he was wearing was a tank top. Usually the captain made him keep his arms covered, hiding the tattoos up and down his arms, but in this setting, they blended right in. He mussed up his hair a bit and tossed his clothes to Lobo. One of the card players eyed them curiously.

Lobo flashed his fangs. "Mind your fucking business." The man quickly turned away.

Doule snickered. "Low key," he reminded.

Lobo moved further back until he was certain he was fully obscured by the crowd. He settled in against the wall of folded bleachers just as Doule made his way over to the table. The fact that werewolves have a heightened sense of smell is no secret. However, what most people don't know is that their hearing is just as astute. Lobo could hear as far as three miles away in the forest at night if he needed to. In a crowded room such as this, he could narrow that range of hearing to pinpoint accuracy if need be.

The players were talking back and forth about some of the plays from the completed match when Doule approached. He made his way around to their side, flashing a wide grin.

"Hey, that was a helluva hand you played there," he said to Sam.

Sam eyed him quickly, then flashed a disinterested smile. "Thanks, man."

"No really, using the prince's paragon ability to aggro that dude's wall defense and then sliding in a nice three card trample was killer.

Damn man, I've never seen nothing like it. What made you think to put that combo together?"

Sam looked at Doule with renewed interest. He knew his shit. Lobo might not like games, but Doule had been playing Skrop with a small group of fae for years.

"Just something me and the fellas were experimenting with. I'm glad it paid off."

"The prince's been mopping the floor with that strategy all morning," one of Sam's teammates proudly added. "You should see our tap in on the Hermit, too."

"*Tyler*," Sam emphasized his friend's name. "Maybe we don't wanna shout out our entire strategy to another player?"

Tyler looked like he just swallowed a crow. It was clear that Sam was the leader of his little group by the nervous glances some of the others threw his way.

"Oh, I'm not jamming out today," Doule added with a nervous chuckle, breaking the tension before it could get too awkward. "I'm more of a casual player than anything. Just like to watch the big dogs at work."

Tyler's shoulders relaxed. He was a pencil necked runt compared to the bear of a man sitting next to him. That would be Kezin, one of Sam's crew. Doule guessed he must have half-ogre blood judging by his size, but he couldn't pinpoint what other race the man might be.

"We're going to grab a drink before the next matchup," Tyler said.

"Hell of a win," Doule repeated, patting the monstrous Kezin on the back as he and Tyler left the table with a few of the other players.

"What deck do you usually run?" Sam asked.

"I'm a Queen of Pentacles guy through and through," Doule said.

He could see he surprised Sam with that answer by his arched brows. Not many players had the nerve to delve into the Queen of Pentacles. It meant sacrificing powerful cards to run abilities, a strategy that could easily blow up in a player's face. But if you timed it just right, the Queen could unleash a devastating power combo.

"Yeah, I love to push it to the edge, but you know that kind of deck wouldn't do too well in a tourney."

"I disagree," Sam said. "I've seen some decent maneuvers by QOP players. Where's your deck? I'd love to have a look at your build."

Shit. Doule cursed himself. He just had to push it, flashing around his deep knowledge of the game. He shrugged. "Got all the way here and realized I left it home," he said.

Sam's eyes narrowed. No respectable player would come to a tournament without their deck, playing professionally or not.

Doule hunched his shoulders and tried to feign embarrassment. "Actually, I only play with my mate's cards. Truth is I don't have enough scratch these days to hobble together much more than a commoner's deck." He hoped his gamble would work, flimsy as it was.

Sam laughed. "Hey man, we've all been there."

"Just living it day to day, you know, Sam?"

Sam paused. "Have we met before?"

Doule was laughing inside. The idiot had taken the bait again. "Oh man, that hurts," Doule said. "C'mon, really? We hung out at The Brick." He gestured to himself. "Dools."

Sam frowned.

"Damn, you really don't remember me?"

"Nah, man," Sam said. "I thought you looked familiar when you came up, but I just couldn't place it. Your Kike's friend, right?"

"No, not Kike. *Charlie*," Doule replied. He watched Sam's face for any flicker of recognition. A light flashed in Sam's eyes for only an instant.

"Don't remember a Charlie," Sam lied. "Is he one of the skate rats?"

"C'mon, brother," Doule said. "*She*, not he. You're thinking of Chaz. Charlie's the thick brownie, ass like a watermelon. You know her, man. Sanji's girl."

"Hmm, maybe. I don't know." Sam shrugged. It was forced. He got up quickly and murmured about catching up to his mates, then headed off.

Doule cursed under his breath. He cut through the crowd back to his partner. Lobo handed him his jacket.

"You spooked him," Lobo teased.

"Pushed it too far too fast," Doule agreed. "What do you think about what he said?"

"Sounded like a steaming pile of horseshit."

"Agreed. Fella got awful tense when I mentioned Charlie."

"He knew exactly who she was," Lobo said. "He's talking to his buddies now. Hang on."

"Where'd your little groupie go?" Tyler teased.

"Any of you recognize that guy?" Sam asked, cutting to the point.

"Maybe. He does look familiar," Kezin replied.

"Weirded me out," Sam said. "He started talking about that kid Charlie."

"From the lunar party?" Tyler asked. "That was a fun little piece of ass."

"Shut the fuck up man," Sam hissed. "You need to learn to stop broadcasting our shit all over the place."

"You worry too much," Tyler chuckled nervously. "Here, have a drink. We got plenty to go around before the next match."

"Interesting," Doule said.

Lobo nodded. "Looks like this wasn't a dead end after all, huh?"

"What's our next play?" Doule asked.

Lobo looked back over his shoulder, to the general area where Sam's team was drinking. "That party in the woods follows the phases of the moon, right?"

Doule nodded.

"Then it looks like we know where we're going next."

18

I was nervous about crashing the lunar party.

Tae reassured me we would be fine. "It's not a party the way you're thinking of. Anyone who wants to go is invited. All sorts of fae'll be there."

I have found Tae tends to know her shit. Nine times out of ten, if it pertains to the fae, she's dead on. I have learned to trust her expertise. That said, her words of encouragement didn't dispel the butterflies fluttering around my insides. Historically speaking, parties and I didn't see eye to eye. Even Deedee learned long ago to stop trying to drag me to them.

I am something of a magnet for disaster at parties. A few examples: one time I had a crush on the host. I went to talk to him, tripped, and accidentally pulled down his pants as I was trying to catch myself. He ended up falling backward into a folding table and the punch bowl flipped over his head. At another party, Cindy was telling Deedee a secret. I blurted it out in surprise just as I stepped on the chord to the speaker system, simultaneously unplugging the music and stating for the whole party to hear "You're sleeping with Kyle?" Spoiler alert – Kyle was her cousin. Gross. The party pretty much ended there when Cindy's boyfriend, Dan, started pummeling Kyle, and they both fell through the porch window.

That's but a glimpse of my track record at parties and I promise it doesn't even scratch the surface of my embarrassment. Suffice to say, a mountain of reassurance from Tae wasn't going to wipe out a lifetime of mishaps plaguing my memories. *Just cool it, Lanie,* I told myself. *You're doing this for Charlie.*

This was my best chance to try and figure out where Charlie had gone. My hope was that someone at the party would remember some clue I could use from the night she disappeared. It also gave me a chance to question Sanji again, to try and gauge if she was hiding anything. *And besides, I've done everything sensible I can to mitigate an accident this time,* I reassured myself, though I didn't believe it for a second.

I was determined to limit myself to one drink and even that would be nursed the whole time, just to give the illusion that I was drinking. I wore sensible boots I had dug out from the back of my grandmother's closet. *No slipping in the mud for Lanie tonight.* I hoped. Also, I wore tight-fitting jeans. I figured that way there would be no loose fabric that could get snagged on anything. Nothing is worse than having your skirt caught in a doorjamb and ripped off while you're walking down a hall tipsy. Trust me, I know. Plus, the jeans looked cute with the scoop neck crop top Tae let me borrow. The top wasn't tight around the chest, since she has way bigger boobs than me, but the way it slipped over one shoulder helped me channel my inner eighties child.

Proctor Park dominated the center of Willow's Edge. It was a sprawling seventy-two-acre park system made up of game fields, ornamental gardens, koi ponds, a wide river, and trails that wound through the crescent shaped forest that bordered it. A lot of work went into maintaining the grounds and it showed.

The full moon was high when we arrived. It lit up the forest, filtering down through the freshly budding branches. I smelled the bonfires as we turned the corner onto a path that dipped into a small gorge.

"Whoa," was all I could think to say. There were hundreds of fae in the clearing below. This was not some random teenage drunk fest. Fae of all ages and races were in attendance.

"Told ya," Tae proudly proclaimed as we entered the clearing.

I wore her and Sacha on either side of me, giving me the armor I needed to march into the party. Sacha fluttered in a circle, wearing a toothy grin as he took in the scope of the festivities. Loud dance music blasted from somewhere, though I saw no speakers. It echoed perfectly off the acoustics of the gorge, amplifying the sound as well as a dance hall. A deep throated man was rapping along to the music in a silky language I had never heard before.

"The music is amazing," I said.

Tae nodded. "That's Old Corinthian. He's dropped some new albums in the last couple years."

Three bonfires were spaced out across the clearing, long logs and straw piled into tall teepees, their flames licking the air. Fae danced around one of them, satyrs, faeries, pixies, boggarts, some of them fully naked, others barefoot and bare chested. They were covered head to toe with red paint, except for a man and woman who stood to one side, looking as if they were officiating the dance to ensure everything was proper. The woman wore an elaborate white dress with gold stitching around the hem and belt. A wide crown with three floating orbs, each a different phase of the moon, hovered over her plaited black hair. The man beside her was painted green, except his beard which was painted red. He wore a crown of red-feathered laurels that matched his beard.

I was mystified by their celebration. Surely this was exactly the depiction mid-century priests painted of Satan's children, engaging in lewd and devilish acts in the woods. "D-do we —"

Tae cut me off with a hearty laugh. "I couldn't wait to see your face when you saw the Brydnos," she said. "No, you don't need to go pants down tits out." She leaned in close and whispered in my ear. "Unless you want to."

I shook her off, and we both laughed.

"Looks like fun to me," Sacha giggled. His tiny leathery wings reminded me of a dog's wagging tail.

"The Brydnos celebrate the three sisters. This is their way." Tae pointed to the other bonfires. "There's plenty of tamer dancing going on over there to whet your appetite."

The fae dancing around the second bonfire were clothed normally, as fae can be, not a nipple or testicle to be seen. The third bonfire was even more casual. Clusters of fae gathered, either seated or in small standing groups, chatting and drinking around that bonfire.

"Let's grab a drink," Tae declared, leading us further into the festivities. Fae milled around the central area. Someone had brought wooden folding tables and set them up lengthwise to form one long tabletop laden with basins and bottles of ale.

"You alright, love?" Sacha asked frankly. "You look like your asshole is tight enough to crack a walnut."

I chuckled nervously. "Sure thing, just a little nervous. Probably just need a drink."

The night air was chilly as I tried to avert my gaze from my arch nemesis, the folding table. I swallowed down a flashback of poor Simon with the punch bowl on head. I forced myself over to the table, then froze in place.

"Wait, is that a punch bowl?"

The basin Tae had led us to was filled with a swirling liquid that gleamed in the moonlight. She grabbed two wooden mugs and ladled the concoction into them. "It's moon tea," Tae said, handing me a mug. "Try some. I think you'll like it. You want a mug, Sacha? Wait, do daemon's even drink?"

He must have been in a hell of a mood. Sacha's head was darting back and forth, taking in the festivities like an excited child. Normally a statement like Tae's would have left him scowling. Instead, he grinned impishly. "Would love one, sweetheart."

Tae took care of him, then lifted her mug in the air. "To housing mates and the troubles we find ourselves in."

We all toasted with a laugh. I took a small sip of the drink. It was an explosion of flavor, tantalizing my taste buds, transitioning between distinct flavors of tangerines and peppercorn, raspberry and almonds.

"This is tea?"

The flavors swirled over my palate with a tickling sensation. When I was a child, in boarding school, one of the girls snuck in candy one weekend. There was a powder called Pop Rocks that fizzled and popped on your tongue. That was the same exact sensation that the moon tea left in my mouth, long after I had swallowed the liquid down. The crackling and popping tickled my nose like chugging a fresh soda. Tae was right. I loved it.

"Aha, see," Tae said victoriously, pointing at me. "I knew you'd like it."

"Not bad at all," I agreed.

Sacha was still gulping down his serving. He emptied the entire thing down his throat, then tilted his head back for a massive belch. Sparks and fire flew from his lips in a long stream like a firecracker. Between the heady drink and impish antics, I found myself howling with laughter. Ever the showboat, Sacha did a head flip midair and wiggled his eyebrows at us wearing a toothy grin that cracked Tae up.

A squeal of delight demanded our attention. I turned to find three girls rapidly approaching us. They were from the nudist bonfire. I tried hard not to stare at their nipples. Underneath the red paint, I recognized one of them as the bookish girl, Enjel, from The Brick. By the glazed look in her eyes, I could see she was properly hammered and didn't recognize me.

"It really is a daemon," Enjel declared to her giddy friends.

"Look at his cute little wings," another said.

"Come dance with us little demon man," the other girl said.

Sacha openly grinned at the girl's painted breasts. He quickly remembered himself and glanced to me. I couldn't help laughing at the situation. "Go and have fun," I said.

The girls squealed. Enjel grabbed Sacha by the hand and tugged him toward the nudist bonfire. He winked at me over his shoulder, flapping his wings excitedly in tow.

"Little perv," Tae snickered.

"Wow, that's something coming from you," I said in jest.

"Oh, I mean that in the best possible way, Tae replied devilishly.

We decided to get to work. We would begin by circling the party to see if anything caught our eye, then head over to the milling fae and mingle to see what we could find out about the last time Charlie had been here.

Halfway across the clearing we bumped into a group of fae engaged in a game. "Oh, you've got to see this," Tae said, pulling me to the side. One of the fae, a tiny sprite, was sputtering on shimmery wings like a hummingbird, tying a brass ring to an upper branch of a nearby tree.

"What are they doing?" I asked.

"You see those rings?" Tae asked.

I noticed there were more of the brass rings hanging by string off different branches of the same tree and nodded.

"The four of them are competing, two versus two. They'll take turns trying to throw the sinch through those rings."

"Those bocce looking balls?" I asked. One of the fae, a broad-shouldered youth with dark eyes that glittered in the moonlight, was juggling three of the balls.

"Sure. But I never heard of a bocce. The balls are what we call sinch. For every one of them scored this way they get to take a drink."

"Oh, it's like reverse beer pong," I said.

Tae looked deflated. "No, Lanie. There's no beer involved."

I snickered. "Same difference."

She frowned at me. "Just watch."

The man who had been juggling sized up an aim with two of the balls... er, sinch... in his wide palm. He spun without warning and flung them at my face. I threw my arms up to ward the projectiles back as the sinch flew directly for me. They suddenly snapped backward as if caught on a rubber band and split off into separate directions, each heading for a different hoop. A blast of ice burst from the opposing player's hands. Three frozen circles, like tiny shields, sprang to life in midair. One of the sinch collided with a shield and fell straight down to the ground. The other spun in a spiral avoiding the shields and slipping through an exposed hoop.

The shooter shouted in triumph and snatched up his wooden mug from the grass. He lifted it in victory just in time for the sprite to clap her own diminutive chalice to it. They drank back two gulps of their beverage, then switched spots with the defenders.

"See, no beer." Tae smirked.

"That was spectacular," I said. "But you knew he was going to throw those our way, didn't you?"

Tae answered with a guilty giggle. We watched a couple more rounds of the fae's merry game before moving on. It was the first open showing of magic for sport I had seen in Willow's Edge. I couldn't help feeling slightly resentful of their joy. My own magic was bottled down deep inside underneath my curse. How wonderful would it be to experience that freedom? What could I accomplish if I could harness my power?

We found our way to the second bonfire. Tae stopped so we could ask a friend of hers about Charlie. Shiloh was a slaugh, a wispy faerie who floated in the air like smoke as she flickered side to side. She was at the last few parties but had no idea who Charlie was.

"You're sure?" Tae asked. "She hangs around with those kids from the Punk House. About yay high. The girl Chulie adopted."

Shiloh shrugged. "Sorry, Tae baby. There's always so much going on at these events, ya know? Everyone floats through here, singers, dancers, comedians, gamers, lovers; it's a plethora of diversity these days. Hard to keep track of everyone."

We politely said our thanks and took our leave. The heat from the bonfire warmed the side of my face as we passed. Its flickering light danced across the visages of nearby fae. I thought about what Shiloh said. These fae could be anyone, poets, lovers, spiritualists.

"Murderers," I finished my morbid thought aloud.

A cloud crossed Tae's face.

"Shiloh has a good point. Anyone could be here with us right now. Think about Brom and how easily he broke into our home."

Tae shuddered. "I'd rather not, thank you very much."

"That doesn't change the reality of things," I said, glancing around at the dancing fae. "How easy would it be to get lost in this crowd? Think about it. It's the perfect hunting ground."

"Let's not jump to any dark conclusions," Tae said. "We don't know anything yet. Hopefully the kid just ran off for some fun. We should keep talking to folk."

She was right. There was no sense in falling down a rabbit hole of depression just yet. Anything I told myself about Charlie at that point was just going to be a story until we had some sort of facts to lean into.

"Tae!" a satyr called from the dancing fae.

"Raphael!" Tae waved back excitedly.

He was a chestnut skinned fae, tall and heavy chested, just how Tae liked them. A curvaceous woman with deep set teardrop eyes was grinding against him. Her face lit up when she saw Tae. She flashed a come-hither wave with groping fingers.

"Another of your boy toys?" I asked.

Tae purred. "You have no idea. The man's a beast. And his girlfriend, Tasha, is sweet as honey. Honey you'd like to wrap around your ears and bury your face in, if you know what I mean." She nudged me.

I laughed. I had no idea what she meant, but I loved Tae's unabashed openness to sexuality. Even if it did make me feel self-conscious sometimes. The couple waved more urgently for Tae to join them. The music had shifted to a harder dance track. I still had no idea where it was coming from, though.

"Aw, sorry guys!" Tae shouted. "Maybe some other time." Her denial did not dissuade them. Tasha bent forward, pressing herself against the satyr and throwing Tae a look so sultry it needed its own movie rating.

"Oh, go on and have some fun," I said.

"No. I'm here to help you get info on this missing kid case."

I laughed. "You sound about as convincing as a politician. It's obvious those two are turning you on. A little dancing isn't going to blow our chances of finding some sort of connection here."

"Okay, just a quick dance." Tae flashed me a wide grin. "Maybe two."

She ran to her friends, and they cheered. I moved back away from the fire, still feeling its heat against my skin. I'm a bit of a voyeur. Always have been. I like to watch other people having fun. Back in New York I used to do the same thing with Deedee.

Raphael and Tasha parted so Tae could slip in between them. Tasha turned toward her, face to face, and kissed her on the lips. Tae pressed against her, biting her lip as she pulled her head away, then leaned back to kiss Raphael over her shoulder. I knew I lost her for the evening. It wasn't her fault. A succubus can only be pushed so far. Tae clearly had the hots for those two. Their bodies swayed in rhythm, like three intertwined serpents, their heartbeats pulsating to the music. I didn't fault her for it. I might have been a little jealous. Maybe wishing I could be so bold. Or capable.

I only ever wanted Tae to be happy, though. She had been a good friend to me since I arrived in Willow's Edge, taking me under her wing when she didn't have to. She reminded me a lot of Deedee. I wished the two of them had a chance to meet. *They would have liked each other.* I cursed myself for thinking of Deedee that way, in the past tense.

For Christ's sake, Lanie. She's in a coma, not dead. Guilt twined around my chest, squeezing my heart. I had not gone to see Deedee all week, ever since I agreed to deliver the package for Ms. Etune. What kind of friend was I to forget about her like that? *I should be ashamed of myself. Deedee would never leave me high and dry.*

"Enjoying the spectacle?"

I turned around to find Lucien's large friend staring down at me. The firelight worked shadows across the planes of his broad brow and jutting jaw. It gave him a real Frankenstein's monster vibe.

"Ah, Lucien's babysitter. You're Finnely, right?"

This was a man used to intimidating people through his mere presence. I enjoyed seeing the spectacle of shock that played across his face. He recovered quickly enough to his credit.

"*Prince* Lucien would like to invite you to the VIP lounge."

I looked around him, to the edge of the party where he thumbed over his shoulder. Sure enough, there was Lucien sitting on a couch. His black clad entourage swirled around him, as they usually did, sitting or leaning on another couch and plush chairs. It was a disarming sight. Not the furniture. People always left wild stuff in Central Park. This certainly wasn't the first time I saw a couch amongst trees, although they were usually pretty grimy looking and not padded with crushed red velvet cushions and accompanied by an intricately woven rug. What disarmed me was Lucien's eyes. They seemed to glow in the dark like twin LEDs, reflecting the light of the bonfire.

"He wants me to go over there?" I repeated, digesting the invite out loud.

I'm not one to walk into a hornet nest swinging. Lucien's entourage was intimidating. These were a tight knit group of people who only ever socialized with each other. *Yeah, but it would be a great opportunity to ask him for his help on the Wardenship,* I thought. Lucien might have the sway I needed to turn the court in my favor at that week's hearing.

I let Finnely lead the way. Some of the conversation died off as we stepped on the rug. A few of the entourage looked downright panicked, their wild eyes switching back and forth between Lucien and me. I couldn't tell if they were scared for my safety, having entered a forbidden place someone like me was clearly not allowed to be, or if they were terrified that I was approaching Lucien so boldly.

"Clear off," Finnely commanded, waving his massive hand sideways.

Fae scattered like disrupted flies, buzzing about to find new homes. However, one girl sat closer to the prince. She had a serious eighties goth vibe that was offset by her fiery red hair. I would have found her style endearing if her eyes weren't stabbing me with murderous intent. She ignored Finnely's glower and looked instead to Lucien. He turned deliberately away from her gaze, centering his attention on me.

"Good evening, Miss Alacore. Won't you have a seat?"

The girl scowled and begrudgingly moved over to give me space on the sofa. Finnely scooped up her arm with one hand and tugged her off, then nudged me to sit. "C'mon, Valia."

"Bone-headed brute," the girl hissed.

Finnely yelped and snatched his hand away from her as if he had been bitten by a snake. His eyes promised violence but instead they both laughed. The two of them hovered on the side of the couch as I plopped down beside Lucien. They were clearly not about to give me and the prince any sort of privacy.

"Hello, Lucien," I said. "I told you before, just call me Lanie."

Valia snapped her head around at me. "Who does this girl think she is?" she asked Finnely.

He shrugged. She clearly found my forwardness insulting. I ignored her.

"So, what are you doing here? I wouldn't think this sort of thing is your scene," I asked.

"What would *you* know about my scene?" Lucien said scornfully.

Something about the mixture of moonlight and nearby bonfire gave his skin a blueish hue. It was very appealing against his silver eyes and long white hair, a stark contrast to his venomous tone. A dry smile worked its way into the corner of his full lips.

"I have been known to enjoy watching the spectacle of the moon rituals."

"Is that what this party is?" I asked, feigning ignorance. I've found it's easier to get people to open up if they think they know more than you. "Of course. It's a full moon tonight. I had no idea that's why all these fae met in the woods."

"I suspect we could fit what you know about fae culture in a handbag and still have room."

I smiled awkwardly. Why was he being so rude? Or was this a casual observation of my past? I was new to the world of fae after all. I tried to be thick-skinned and let it slide.

"I'm curious. Why aren't you dancing with your succubus friend?" Lucien asked. "Perhaps the two of you had a falling out?"

Interesting that he knows I'm friends with Tae. Does this guy keep tabs on me or what? Stalker, I mused. "No, nothing like that," I replied. "I'm just not much of a dancer."

Lucien arched his white eyebrows in mock surprise. "I seem to recall a night not so long ago at Free House that would lead one to believe otherwise."

I felt the heat rush to my cheeks. "Oh, you saw that? I was… *under the influence* that night. Not my proudest moment."

Wow, he really is keeping tabs on me, I thought. A strange thrill of excitement ran through me. There was something insanely cool about knowing someone was interested enough in me to remember those details.

"Really? You seemed quite at home with that sort of thing," Lucien said. "Truth be told, I'm surprised you're not dancing with the Brydnos."

I frowned and followed his gaze to where the naked fae pranced around the first bonfire. Valia laughed cruelly at the scandalized look on my face. Finnely chuckled, too. Lucien's smirk grew a bit longer.

What is this? Did he call me over here to make fun of me in front of his fan club? I had been around the block enough to know exactly how to react to those sorts of situations. I laughed loudly, and playfully slapped Lucien's forearm. If you let a bully know they're getting to you, it eggs them on further. Best to flip the script.

"You're such a goof. I don't do that sort of thing. Truthfully, I have never been to a party like this."

Valia scowled again. I smiled at her. *Take that you fucking bitch.*

"Do they not throw parties in the human realm?" Lucien coolly asked.

"You've spent time around humans?" Valia blurted, suddenly deeply interested in me.

"It's where I grew up," I replied.

"Amazing," Valia gasped.

"No more so than Willow's Edge," I said.

"No, I mean it's amazing that you would openly admit such a thing," Valia laughed. "I couldn't imagine anything more disgustingly depraved than having to be stuck around those primitives."

Lucien snickered at her comment. Suddenly, the group of fae behind the sofa were all laughing, as if on cue. I felt smaller.

"They're not all that bad," I said in defense. "My best friend is human."

Valia pressed the side of her hand to her nose. "I was wondering what that awful stench around you was," she boldly declared. She turned to the nearby group, who were all listening in at this point. "That's the problem with half-breeds, they're more than happy to muck about in the mud with the filth. This one's even bragging about it."

"Why do you have a problem with humans?" I asked impatiently. I could feel the blood rushing to my head.

"Oh, you poor sad thing. If you have to ask, you'll never know," Valia laughed. "The only good human is a dead one."

A few of the fae nodded their heads in agreement, including Lucien.

It was too much for me. I don't know if it was the full moon or the weird tea fueling me, but I was suddenly too pissed to stop myself. "What did you just fucking say?" I demanded.

"Such foul language." Valia waved a hand as if warding off my stench. "This is why you have no business being over here. Go back to your own kind."

I leapt up before I could think, throwing myself face to face with her. "How about I slap that mascara off your pretty little face and make you eat my fucking boot?"

Valia shocked me. Instead of rising to the occasion, she cowered back with arms in the air to ward me off as she flinched. The entire group fell silent, leaving me red-faced and angry. I was shocked to find my fists balled up ready to hit her. Finnely looked at me as if I was deranged.

I looked down at Lucien. He sat on the sofa watching me as if I was a bug he didn't understand. How did I suddenly become the bad guy?

"You know what? Forget this," I said stupidly as I stomped away. *So much for getting Lucien's help,* I thought angrily. I cut swiftly through the trees, around groups of party goers. As soon as I was away from Lucien's group, my anger turned to unbidden tears and trembling hands.

"Fuck them," I muttered.

"Lanie, wait," Lucien called. The prince ran after me, his entourage left behind.

I glowered at him and spun back around, moving even quicker through the woods.

"Where are you going?" Lucien asked.

"Away from you," I said over my shoulder.

I was shocked to find he was directly behind me. I'm known for moving fast when I want to, yet Lucien was quickly catching up with me.

"Please, Lanie, stop for a moment. Let us at least speak."

I spun around to face him. "Your friend is a rude little bitch."

Lucien took a deep breath. "Valia can be a bit trying at times," he admitted. "Honestly though, you can't let every stuck up noble get under your skin so easily."

"She's a noble?" I asked, disarmed.

"Lady Valiara Medi'tu, her mother is a Duchess of the Court of Shadows." He nodded.

"Oh no," I blanched. "I just threatened a duchess's daughter?"

Lucien snickered. "I don't believe anyone has ever spoken to Valia that way."

"It's not funny," I said, pushing him playfully. "That's just my luck. I never get mad, and when I finally do, it's to threaten a duchess."

Lucien laughed even harder. "The look on her face was priceless."

"How come you're over here anyhow?" I asked. "Shouldn't you be back with your friends enjoying the party?"

"How could I enjoy the lunar ritual after your little scene?" he teased. "Honestly, you really do need to insulate yourself better from the harmless barbs of nobility."

"Easy for you to say. They're all tripping over each other to kiss your ass."

I said it in spite, to wipe that superior grin off his face. The effect my words had was harsher than I thought possible. Lucien looked positively wounded. He dropped his face in the shadows. His white hair reflected the moonlight in a ghostly aura.

"I'm sorry. I shouldn't have said that."

"No, you're right," Lucien said slowly. "They swarm me like leeches. It's intolerable. You cannot imagine what it's like to be constantly surrounded by people who hang on your every word and obsess over your every action. How can one know who is being genuine when every fae grovels over you as if your every word is gold spun from the ass of the gods. It's driving me mad."

"Well, I liked sitting with you by the river," I said.

He perked up like a deer catching a scent on the wind. "I enjoyed the time we spent together as well," he admitted.

"You have a funny way of showing it," I replied.

Lucien frowned.

"At Free House? When I tried to talk to you?" I reminded him.

Lucien's face was blank. "I have no idea what you're speaking of."

"Yeah right. Like you didn't hear me calling your name when your bouncer wouldn't let me into the VIP section? You weren't ignoring me or anything." I said sarcastically.

Lucien took a step forward, closing the distance between us so that his face was inches from mine. I caught my breath. His steady silver eyes gazed down into mine.

"I can assure you I would have jumped at the chance to speak with you again, Lanie Alacore," he said my name in a low voice that almost purred.

I felt foolish that my heart was suddenly aflutter. "And why is that?" I whispered, terrified to hear his answer.

Lucien struck without warning. He pressed his cold lips against mine. His kiss was firm and unyielding. I was bewildered by how icy his lips were, like he had just come in from a winter storm. Instinct propelled me. I shoved him away and slapped him square in the face. Lucien was wide-eyed with shock for an instant, then he laughed. His eyes sparkled in the moonlight, cutting through my pretense. We both knew I wanted him to kiss me. I grabbed him by his collar and pulled him in, pressing my lips against his. His tongue ran across my upper lip, then darted inside my mouth. He tasted like peppermint, matching the iciness of his shadow fae body as he pressed against me.

Lucien leaned into me until I was up against a tree. His mouth found my neck. Teeth nibbled on my earlobe and then his cool tongue ran across it. He explored my flesh, that icy magic of his seeping out into each kiss, and every nibble. It made my skin tingle. Waves of pleasure radiated wherever his lips moved.

What was I doing? One moment we were arguing, the next I was letting Lucien ravish me in the woods. I was making out with one of the rudest people I have ever met. This was all wrong, yet in that moment it was exactly what I wanted.

Lucien's hands wrapped around me, pulling me tighter against him. His mouth suckled my throat with a tiny bit of pressure that felt delicious. I could not remember the last time I had felt so wonderful.

His hands were ice cold beneath my crop top. At first the sensation made me jump, but I quickly longed for that touch. Everywhere he explored was ice and then radiating warmth as he moved on. His fingertips traced the curve of my spine as I thrust my tongue into his mouth. My core throbbed with excitement. As if reading my mind, his thigh suddenly pressed between my legs. I ground my pussy against it and let out a throaty moan.

"You like that, don't you?" Lucien whispered into my ear.

This was as close to dirty talk as I'd ever gotten. It was foreign to me. I should have been repulsed by his smug tone. Instead, it turned me on. I did like it. And I wanted more.

I made him kiss me again, more insistently this time, our lips and tongues hungrily exploring each other. Then it was my turn to run a tongue across his earlobe. Lucien groaned. I squealed in surprise when his icy fingers slipped underneath my bra. He seized my nipple between a finger and thumb and pinched it. It stung and yet felt delicious at the same time.

My pussy was soaked. I moaned louder.

Lucien laughed triumphantly.

What the fuck am I doing? I thought. My body felt electrified, tingling with pleasure. *This isn't me. But it feels so good.* I ground myself harder against his thigh, realizing we were moving to the beat of music in the near distance. It felt wonderful. The last time I had experienced anything remotely like it was the night I made love to Lobo.

Lobo?

My insides went numb. "What am I doing?" I murmured.

Lucien's lips were fervently working down my throat to my chest. I had to stop. If I let this go any further, I would do something I regretted. Also, reality hit home. I would blackout if I carried this on too long. Surely, I must have already done enough to trigger my curse. My mind spun. *How am I even still standing?* Panic racked my body. *What if the prince sees me like that, passed out on the ground in the dirt? What will he think? Who cares what he thinks? How can I be doing this to Lobo?* There were too many problems hitting me at once.

"I have to get out of here," I mumbled.

Lucien gripped me tighter. His lips suddenly back over my mouth. I felt suffocated. I flailed my arms in panic. *I can't be here. I don't want to blackout. Run, Lanie.* I shoved the prince away from me and sprinted into the woods.

"I forgot I have somewhere to be!" I shouted without looking back.

Lucien's laughter mocked me as I bolted deeper into the woods, putting distance between us as fast as my legs would carry me. How could I have screwed up that bad? Everything had gone horribly wrong.

Lobo shouldered his way past fae. He was a wolf on a mission. Words died on lips unsaid as party goers swiftly scrambled out of his path. His face was a mask of murderous rage set against the light of the bonfires.

Doule was trying to pry some info about the missing girls from a topless girl, one of the Brydnos celebrating the lunar cycle. Her eyes went wide as Lobo approached. She ducked away without another word.

Doule turned toward him. They had only just arrived at the party, barely enough time to get their bearings when Lobo had headed off on his own out of nowhere. "That was fast. Did you already find a lead?"

"No." Lobo's fists clenched and unclenched, talons digging into his bloody palms. "I need to go."

Doule smelled the blood. "Hey, man," he said slowly. "Is everything okay?"

"Just get me the fuck away from here," Lobo growled through gritted teeth.

Doule had known Lobo for a few decades, long enough to know when his friend was in pain. A werewolf in pain was a dangerous thing, especially on a full moon surrounded by relatively defenseless drunks. He didn't bother asking any other questions. There was no point. Lobo said he needed to leave, and that was enough for him.

They were exiting the party when Droll popped up in their path. The troll comedian had been entertaining the party goers with a debaucherous puppet show, with crude hand puppets of a rosy cheeked pixie and his love interest a satyr with a huge cock. "Why so glum chum?" Droll flapped the satyr in Lobo's face, making it's mouth move to the words.

"Get the fuck out of my way," Lobo snarled.

Droll blanched at the rough rebuff.

Doule frowned sympathetically at the kind-hearted comedian. "We're in a bit of a rush, Droll."

Having recovered enough of his composure, Droll affected a stately wave. "Then tarry these fields no longer, good knights." The troll stepped out of their path with a flourishing bow that almost spilled his tin crown onto the grass. "Allow the prince of fools and his royal court to convey you on your merry way."

"Go slink back under your bridge, troll," Lobo snarled as his shouldered past the comedian.

Doule nodded and led his friend away. He ignored the growling coming from Lobo's throat. It didn't stop until they made it to the top of the gorge, well away from the party.

The tears budding in Lobo's eyes were harder to ignore.

19

What in the world was I thinking? It wasn't like that was the first time a guy tried to kiss me at a party. I should have walked away after I slapped him. Instead, I rammed my tongue down his throat like a teen in heat. I thought of how I ground against his leg moaning, and my legs pumped harder, as if I could run away from my embarrassment.

How could you let it go that far? I thought. A lifetime of being careful blown in one single moment. The thing that really made my blood boil was I knew better. I wasn't some naïve college girl heady off one too many drinks ready to make bad decisions. This wasn't my first rodeo. Guys have been hitting on me since I first sprouted tits. *If I'd let that go any further, I would have been passed out in the dirt at a prince's feet. Then everyone would know my secret.* Shame and fear left me feeling queasy. The idea that any other fae might find out I was damaged goods, an incomplete woman who could never experience the intimacy and love normal to any other creature. It was almost too much to bear.

Then my other problem hit me.

What about Lobo? I stopped dead in my tracks. My clothes clung to sweaty skin. The chill air whistled past me as the revelation slammed home. I just cheated on Lobo. *Was it technically cheating? We never actually said we were exclusive.* That loophole was bullshit, and I knew it. Just because we had never explicitly defined ourselves did not make my actions alright. We were a couple. I cared about him, and I knew he felt the same way.

What do I do now? Panic pushed me to keep moving. Maybe if I didn't stop I could find a place where my problems didn't exist. I clutched my grandmother's crystal horn, hanging around my neck, and cut through the trees moving farther away from the party. I was still close enough to hear the music and the laughter. It felt like they were laughing at me and my plight. How could I have messed things up so horribly?

What was Lobo going to say when he found out?

How will he find out? I thought. *I don't ever need to tell him. I'll just bottle it down and pretend it never happened. That's what people do when they make mistakes, right?* It seemed sensible. Why hurt Lobo with something that meant nothing to me?

Didn't it, though?

Lucien's eyes invaded my thoughts. The fresh memory of his cold lips pressed against my throat left me unmoored. *Shit.* There was something there. I couldn't deny I was attracted to the prince. Was it fair to stay with Lobo if I had feelings for another man? *There's a difference between feelings and being horny,* I corrected. *Could that be all this was? After having tasted the sweet fruit of passion from my night with Lobo, freed for that instant from the curse, is my body simply craving more? Could I have lost control because I finally know exactly what I've been missing all these years? That has to be it. I'm no superhero. I'm only human. Wait, no... I'm fae. Whatever the fuck I am, I'm confused.*

Yes. That was my bullshit rationale. Because why take responsibility for my actions when I could redirect the blame? This was all the curse's fault. Lucien meant nothing to me. Why throw away what I was building with Lobo over a simple mistake?

Lobo never needs to know. Period.

A ghostly blue glow lit the forest to my right, drawing me to it like a mosquito to flame. It should have been a moth, but I felt too much like a parasite at that moment. I realized I must have run full circle, back toward the party. *I need to sit down.* My hands were shaking from the recent flood of adrenaline. I trudged toward the glow with slumped shoulders. It was time to head back to the party and find Tae. I knew I would have to tell Lobo. I could never live with that kind of secret, that betrayal. I could not bear the thought of his face when he found out.

It turned out the light wasn't coming from the party at all. Tiny clusters of glowing roses blanketed the forest floor.

"Hello there," I said aloud with delight.

I was happy to let my woes slip aside momentarily as I rushed over to the flowers. They were a fantastic discovery. These were the same roses I had been using to enhance my concoctions at the apothecary. I had discovered several different uses for their petals, grinding them up and mixing them with other herbs to help some of my natural magic seep past the curse. I first happened upon them when I was walking around the hedge maze behind Greystone chapel, after I had finished helping Father Willem weed the garden beds late one afternoon. In the daylight they looked like ordinary red roses with deeper crimson spots splotched on them like spattered paint. But in the dark, once the moon was out, they glowed a faint blue color. I had thus far only found a dozen or so of them. The forest around me was littered with hundreds. This was a rare find indeed.

I eagerly fell into a trancelike state, harvesting as many of the flowers as I could. I stuffed my jacket pockets full of them. Once they were full, I lifted my crop top halfway and created a makeshift basket.

"These are going to help so many people," I said to myself.

Within a few minutes my shirt was full. *I better mark where I am, so I can come back for more,* I thought, scanning the area for some sort of landmark. To my utter surprise, I found myself beside a bridge underpass.

What the heck is a bridge doing out here in the woods? I thought. It was a small bridge, a dark smudge of shadows that was greyer a short distance away. Trees ran up the hillside to either side of it, then abruptly ended. Is there a road up there? Curiosity got the better of me. I scrabbled up the grassy hill, clinging the roses close with one arm pressing my lifted shirt against my chest. I used my free hand to grab trees as I climbed the steep incline.

I found an old road at the top. The asphalt was cracked from frost heaves, and weeds grew out of potholes, but it was functional all the same. I dropped my shirt slightly to let the glow of the roses light up the surrounding landscape. *Yup. Definitely an old service road.* It stretched in either direction, slipping around a bend in the trees to my right. Dozens of tire tracks littered the weathered blacktop. I tried to picture the woods as they must have been before the fae arrived.

I bet this used to be a state park. But what state? I could picture families driving by, heading to camping areas for a weekend getaway. Naturally the fae still used the roads left behind. Not much of a mystery to see a road after all. I scrabbled back down the hill feeling silly for making such a big deal out of the discovery. Anyhow, there were more roses underneath the bridge. Clusters of them.

That was when it caught my eye.

The underpass was covered in graffiti. One particular mural stood out to me. I stumbled over to it in a daze. I recognized the flow of the lines, the style of colors mingled together. I knew without a doubt Charlie had painted that mural. It was a cat, with sunglasses on, and a spray can in hand. The art style was identical to what I had seen by Charlie and Sanji's bed.

That means she was here, I thought excitedly. *But how long ago?* She could have painted the mural at any time. Just because there was a mural in the underpass meant nothing. Charlie likely painted lots of graffiti around the province. It was only natural to assume she would find this place, coming to the lunar parties frequently.

I let the roses tumble out of my shirt onto the ground, then grabbed a handful and used them to sweep the area. Sure enough, the underpass was filled with different styles of graffiti. Plenty of fae had come here and tagged the bridge. It was a collage of styles and names. Metal glinted on the ground. Two cans of spray paint sat upright at the base of the wall directly beneath Charlie's mural.

A pit opened in my stomach. Cans of spray paint wouldn't normally be a big deal. *Except we're in Willow's Edge. A fae province. And fae don't make such things.* The paint fae used was made from homemade dyes, things like madder root and squid ink. They were the kind of medium you would need a brush for. Spray paint would have to have been transported from the human realm. That would make it pricey to procure for a fae living in Willow's Edge. No fae would so carelessly leave behind such a valuable commodity.

I snatched up one of the spray cans. The metal and plastic coating felt alien to me. It was part of a world I was losing touch with. I shook the can, and the pit in my stomach opened wider. It felt at least half full, if not more. *Charlie wouldn't have left this behind on purpose,* I thought. The chill night air sent goosebumps across my arms. I was suddenly painfully aware of how isolated I was from the party. I lifted the glowing rose heads like a torch, spilling a circle of pale blue light to throw back the shadows around me. Sounds from the party were distant, far enough away that no one would hear me if I screamed for help.

"Why the hell was she out here?" I said. Sometimes when I get nervous, I like to speak out loud, as if that will somehow make me safer. "Couldn't she see how dangerous it was to be alone? Why would she be so reckless as to come out here by herself?"

Maybe she ran from a boy she just kissed too, I thought, realizing I wasn't one to talk. Besides, who was to say she'd been alone when she was there? Another glint of metal caught the light, at the base of the cement slope of the underpass. It was another spray can. This one lay on its side. It might as well have been a dead body for the dread it filled me with. I started painting a mental picture of what happened here.

Charlie had been spray painting her mural when someone came along. There must have been a struggle, which knocked over one of her cans that rolled down the slope. I lit up her mural. It was really only two-thirds complete on closer inspection. The bottom portion was an outlined mess that would have been covered up by layers of paint if she had been allowed to finish the piece.

Another painting demanded my attention.

"Oh fuck," I whispered.

It was painted directly and deliberately over the breast of Charlie's graffiti cat, in yellow and black. It was the same insignia Lobo had been so concerned about back at The Brick. I finally knew something horrible had happened to Charlie.

There had always been a tiny piece of me that could lie to myself and say the girl was probably fine all this time. However, as soon as I set eyes on that insignia and the tipped over spray can, I knew without a doubt that something more disturbing than a sightseeing tour to human lands was at play.

There was no denying it any longer. Someone had taken Charlie.

20

It had been a few hours since the prince left Charlie's cell before she finally found the courage to move again. She deserved an award for the performance she put on when the prince found the mess she had made the previous night. He poked and prodded her, trying to determine why she had gotten sick. She dug down deep to find the strength to play catatonic. He needed to be convinced she was still high from the human drugs. Otherwise, he would've given her another dose.

It worked. He cleaned her and went about his business. The sound of electric saws cutting through bone plagued her mind. It was bad enough to be locked in a cage by this deranged lunatic. Now she knew his real purpose. The prince was harvesting them like cattle. She was there to be his food.

She didn't dare try to talk to the girl in the cage across the room. Other than when the prince was in the adjoining room, his workshop, she had no idea where he was. Sometimes she would hear the floorboards creaking above. A few times she thought he was talking to someone else, but the sound of their conversation was too muffled to make out properly. How many others might there be lurking in the house?

Would he be so bold as to have guests over with us locked in the basement? Was he so full of himself that he believed he could never be caught? she wondered. Judging by the condition of the cages, she guessed he had been at this for quite some time now. Who was to say others weren't in on it with him? Fae cannibalism had been outlawed centuries before. Could there be others, co-conspirators of his, who missed the taste of fae enough to kidnap girls from the province?

He was awfully upset that he had to kill that other girl so early. Kept talking about how she wasn't ready yet. If she wasn't enough meat for him then, how long could it be before he comes down here for another of us?

Charlie scrambled off the straw mattress and crawled to the edge of her cage. *This can't be real. It's a nightmare. I have to get out of here.*

She tugged at the chicken wire. It could have been cold iron for all the good her efforts produced. The cell, dingy as it looked, had been well built. It did not budge an inch. She flopped back on her bottom and pulled her knees to her chest.

A few good kicks should jog this chicken-wire loose, she reasoned. Her bare feet hovered in the air as she paused. *Think, stupid. Kicking that is going to make a hell of a racket. He hears that and he'll come running like a bat out of hell. He'll stick me with more drugs and make me look in that evil mirror again. The next time I wake up might be while I'm taking a bolt to the forehead like that poor girl.*

Charlie let her feet sag down to the dirty floor as she sobbed with her hands clamped over her mouth. It was hopeless. *Even if I can kick the chicken wire hard enough to get out of this I'll still be stuck in this room. Then what? The prince will find me and say, "aw shucks, you outsmarted me, I guess I have to let you go free."*

The situation was hopeless. She rolled over onto her side, in a fetal position, and watered the dirt floor with her tears. *I wish I never went to that stupid party.* Then she never would have been introduced to the prince. She would be with Eli, living it up in the human realm. Why did I waste so much time with Sanji when I could've been with him? That was the first time she admitted it to herself. She would have preferred to be with Eli over Sanji. Things had gone sour between her and Sanji months before she was taken. She couldn't stand her mother because of how controlling she always was, yet she had found herself in a relationship with Sanji, who turned out to be just as manipulative.

Charlie didn't want to be tied down. She wasn't someone's property to control. She was her own person, and she wanted to spread her wings and fly. Sanji had been getting more and more demanding: "Don't hang out with them, hang out with me. Why were you talking to her? You're going to leave me for that slut, aren't you?" There would be a big argument over some imaginary infraction Charlie had committed, and it would end with Sanji giving her a guilt trip about how her family abandoned her and she was just scared to lose Charlie. Blah blah blah.

All of it was true. Charlie felt horrible that Sanji had that done to her. But she recently realized something. That was Sanji's baggage, not hers. She wasn't happy with Sanji, and it was time to move on. That was the twisted irony of it all. She left Sanji that night to be free and here she was, trapped in a cage. Like a sheep waiting to be slaughtered.

She sobbed into her dry palms. *I hate the prince. I wish he was dead.*

It was a shocking thought for her. Charlie had never wished harm on any other living creature. She abhorred violence in all its forms. But now she really wanted him dead.

That's it. I'll have to kill him to get out of here. The reality of it unfolded before her as a cold brutal fact. There was no way around it. If she wanted to live, she was going to have to murder the prince.

She fell to all fours and scrambled back to the edge of her cage. On the other side of the chicken wire was a bucket of scraps, leftovers and refuse from when the prince brought in their meals. He spoon fed them every bite, and anything that was leftover went into the bucket. She curled her lip. *This is the sick bastard's version of a compost bucket, isn't it?* She had spotted the bone before, when she was lying down and staring blankly out of the cell. It was a big, jagged drumstick bone.

The chicken wire was woven into small, intertwined circles. They were far too tiny to slip through, but she just might be able to squeeze her hand through one. She studied the wire mesh, looking for an opening large enough. There was one spot that bent more to the left, slightly larger than the others around it. Charlie bunched her fingers together and thrust her hand as hard as she could through the opening. The metal caught on her knuckles, skinning them. She clenched her teeth together and shoved harder, biting back the pain as it shaved more skin away around her forearm. If the prince came, there would be no hiding what she was doing. She needed to act fast.

Adrenaline fed by fear pumped through her, numbing the pain. Her fingertips brushed the rim of the bucket. It was just out of reach. She forced her whole body against the chicken wire. The wall bulged out a fraction of an inch. Her fingertip caught on the edge of the bucket. *Just a little farther.* She grunted with the effort. Heavy footsteps padded across the room above her.

Fuck, he's coming down here.

The bucket slipped out of her grasp, wobbling suddenly away from her. *No, no, no. I can't be trapped here. I don't want to die like this!*

She pressed her weight harder against the fencing. The chicken wire wasn't budging any further. Her arm was raw with scrapes and cuts. Her fingertip scratched the side of the bucket, and Charlie's fingernail caught the wood. It was closer now. Her arm felt rubbed raw, slick with blood. Chains tinkled together in the workshop next door. The prince hammered something in loud thwacks. Her hand seized the bone, grasping it for dear life until it was firmly in her palm. She dropped back, letting her body weight pull her arm back through the tiny opening. Her head hit the hay mattress, but her foot slid across the dirt, rattling into the chicken wire fencing.

The hammering next door stopped.

She rolled around and threw herself onto the mattress with her body curled up in her best impression of sleeping and her forehead pressed against the cool brick wall. She heaved air in and out of her lungs. The door swung open, and Charlie caught her breath. She felt his gaze sweeping the room. His cool intellect, the mind of a predator, studied the shadows. The prince was a silent specter.

She focused on her breathing, slowly exhaling, softly inhaling, focusing on the rise and fall of her chest. He had to think she was sleeping, or it was all over. Her hands were tucked between her dirty thighs, the lacerations on her forearm burning against her soiled pants. It hurt like hell.

That doesn't matter. Either breathe through the pain or die. Those are your choices.

She could feel his eyes on her. Could he tell she was faking it? Boot steps padded across the dirt floor. She heard him breathing just outside her cage, in the middle of the room, watching them.

Just focus. Breath. Heavy and steady. Forget about him. He's not here. You're sleeping in your bed at home.

Time disappeared. All that existed in the world was her need to breathe.

The workshop door clanged shut.

Charlie snapped out of her stupor. The bone was between her legs. The prince resumed his hammering next door. She shuffled to the edge of the cage. It took her a few minutes to find the hole she had used. It was bent, warped out of shape. She wet her fingers with her mouth and used them to wipe away the drying blood, then reshaped the hole as best she could. She crawled back to her mattress and cradled the broken bone like a teddy bear.

This was her salvation. She fought a fog of exhaustion that descended on her. It was going to be a long night, and she dared not fall asleep. It would be feeding time in a few hours.

And this time I'm going to be ready for him when he comes.

Deedee looked horrible. For as long as I had known her, she was the light at the center of every room. No matter where we went, museums, pubs, shopping, it didn't matter, people flocked around her. I always admired how effortlessly she handled them too, with kindness and charity. Plenty of people would have grown pretentious under that level of constant attention. Not my Deedee, though. I still remember the first day I met her. She walked into my dorm room, flashing that bright smile. "I'm your new roommate!" she gushed. We talked for a little bit about our lives leading up to entering college, and at the end of it she insisted we were going to be great friends. And she was right. We had been best friends ever since.

Some best friend I was, letting her get tortured by that psychopath.

I watched the steady rise and fall of her chest as she lay in her coma. Her light was gone now. Only sorrow remained. The room was ripe with it.

"I'm sorry I haven't been here much this week," I said as I held her lifeless hand. Her skin was warm, and she smelled like aloe. Drys had been taking tender care of her. I set down the small pail of cold water by her bed and took a seat. Deedee seemed to like it when I massaged her forehead with cool water. I wrung out the towel and carefully moved her bangs aside.

"Guess what? I finally survived a party without making a complete ass out of myself," I said as I stroked her forehead with the towel. Deedee's eyes didn't flicker. She stayed sleeping, impassive to the world. "Well... maybe that's not entirely true. I did do a couple embarrassing things."

I half expected Deedee's mouth to quirk up into a knowing smirk like she did when I made a joke.

"I wonder what that stuck up snob Valia would say if she knew a human was lying in a coma in the backroom of Free House." I liked to talk to Deedee. Even if she couldn't respond. Drys said it might help to anchor her to my voice.

"She'd probably have a heart attack," I snickered. "I wish you'd been there, Dee. Can't believe I lost my cool like that. She wouldn't have phased you, though. You would've found exactly the right button to push to set that bitch on her heels. I don't know what got into me. I almost hit her. Can you believe that? I never lose my temper."

Never? Guilt pressed down on my chest. The last time I had spoken to Deedee was awful. Correction, *I was awful.* There she was, my best friend who had dropped everything to hop on a train and spend the weekend with me to help me sell my grandmother's estate, and I acted as if she was nothing more than a nuisance.

"If I had known that might be the last time –" The words stuck in my throat. "Stop saying that," I chided myself. *Deedee's not dead.* I squeezed her hand. "You're going to come out of this. I know you will. You've always been the stronger one, larger than life. If anyone can find their way out of a coma, it's you."

My resolution sounded weak and unconvincing. Deedee's chest rose and fell. My words had no effect on her. Was she even in there anymore? Not for the first time I worried that I had failed her twice. First when I left her at the shop with a mouthful of callous words. And a second time by not bringing her back to the human realm. What if human doctors were more advanced than fae healers? What if they could detect something in her physiology that Drys simply didn't understand? My brain screamed to stop thinking as the worst question lurked behind those thoughts.

What if Dee is already gone? What if she's a vegetable? I have watched enough television to know the harmful effects trauma can have on a person's psyche.

It doesn't get more traumatic than having a serial killer torture you for a couple hours and leave you for dead, I thought.

I wiped a tear from my cheek, angry with myself. I had decided early on not to cry around Deedee. She needed me to be strong for her.

"You *are* going to get out of this," I promised. I leaned over the bed and fixed her hair, brushing it out of her closed eyes, then gently kissed her on the forehead. "And if you can't, then I'm going to do it for you. I brought you something."

I rummaged around in my bag for the sachet. It was the size of my fist, packed with different herbs and infused with some rose petals I had picked the night before under the bridge. I had a lingering suspicion that if I could have harnessed my magic, trapped underneath that curse, I could have healed her. It was infuriating to be unable to use something so intrinsically a part of me.

There was raw power inside of me howling to be let out. It thrilled me to think about it. I needed to find a way to access that part of myself again. That magic was more than power. It was my chance to heal Deedee.

For now, I would have to rely on my newfound skills as an herbologist-slash-chemist-slash-alchemist. I did not know how to label it. I only knew the poultices and potions I was making at the apothecary were working. Deedee would be proud I was finally putting my botany degree to good use. I placed the sachet on Deedee's chest. It was a mixture I had put together that morning, typically meant to dispel nightmares. I have tried many different combinations on her over the last few months. Yet Dee was still in her coma.

"I'll never give up on you," I swore, even as shame reminded me I hadn't visited all week.

Someone cleared their throat from the open doorway, startling me out of my reverie. It was Lobo.

"Oh, I didn't hear you come in," I said, crossing the room to give him a kiss on the cheek.

He smelled nice, like aftershave even though sharp stubble covered his jaw. His body was rigid as I embraced him. It was awkward, like kissing a mannequin. I pulled back and searched his eyes, sensing something was off.

"We need to talk," Lobo said. He turned away and walked down the hallway.

I followed him, a gnawing pit growing in my stomach. I have heard those same words so many times before, from every boyfriend I ever had in college. From every guy Deedee set me up with and they always meant the same thing. Lobo cut a path straight across the quiet Free House. Drys was behind the bar, drying mugs as she readied to open. She shot me a questioning look. I could only frown and try not to cry. I knew what was coming.

"We're done," Lobo said outside, on the steps, in the noonday sun.

"Lobo, I –"

He raised his hand to stop me. "Lanie, it's not working out. We've both got to admit that to ourselves. It shouldn't be this hard. We've been arguing more and more lately. It's not healthy. And we need to be adults about this."

He was lying. Not about dumping me, that was definitely happening. Why was a different matter. The way he looked at me was mingled with distrust and despair. This was a man who was hurt and barely holding it together.

Oh my god, he knows, I realized. My face burned scarlet, and tears streaked down my cheeks. *How did he find out? Someone must have told him. I should have been the one to tell him. What is wrong with me? Just tell him what happened. Tell him now and you can fix this.*

"Lobo, last night –"

"Don't." He caught me off guard with a growl.

We both stood staring at each other, the unspoken confession hanging between us like a veil. Lobo closed his eyes and took a deep breath. He turned away from me.

"It hasn't been working out. End of story. I wish you nothing but happiness, Lanie. I really do."

He climbed down the steps and walked away from me. It was over. Just like that. I felt like the world was going to open up beneath my feet and swallow me whole. Actually, I wished it would. I never should have gone to that damned party. I never should have talked to the prince and his nasty friends. I never should have…

"Wait!" I yelled. "Lobo, please wait." I chased after him.

Lobo turned to me wearing a pained grimace. "Lanie, stop. This isn't going to happen."

"No. I know. I'm sorry," I said as I caught up. "It's not that, though. I found something that might help us figure out where Charlie is."

I quickly recounted what I had discovered under the bridge. I spoke rapidly before he could turn away from me again, though he clearly wanted to. It didn't take long for Lobo's detective side to kick in. He had me repeat the story as he carefully mulled over each word.

"It was the same insignia?" he asked. "You're certain about that?"

"Definitely," I said.

Lobo nodded. He ran his fingers across his jaw like he did when he was deep in thought.

"Do you think it's anything?"

"It confirms what Doule and I found," he replied.

Lobo filled me in on their trip to the Skrop tournament. I remembered Sam only too well. He was a slick one. I've been guarding myself against creeps all my life, especially in bars, but Sam fooled me good. He came off as shy, the kind of guy who finds it hard to talk to girls. While I'd been protecting myself from the cocky extroverts, I built a blind spot for the quiet nerd. If Lobo hadn't come along that night, I don't even want to think about what that creep and his friends would have done to me. Hopefully, my curse would have at least rendered them impotent for a week or so. Still, a guy like that, who would stoop to drugging girls, you never know what other nastiness they were capable of.

"What are you going to do now?" I asked.

"I'm going to go sit on him and see what he gets up to." Lobo grinned. "Hopefully, he'll lead us to the missing girls without knowing it."

"Like a stakeout?" I said. "Maybe I should come, too. Can't hurt to have another set of eyes, right?"

Lobo's eyes grew cold again. Our situation fell back between us like a wall. "I have to go, Lanie." He turned his back to me and crossed the street to his cruiser. "Good luck in court today."

"Court?" *Oh my lord, court!* What time was it? I was supposed to be in court at one-thirty.

21

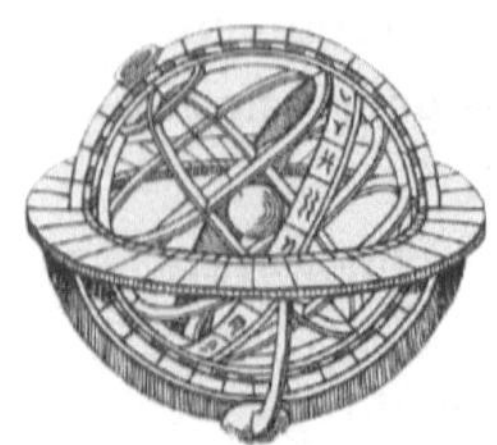

Court was a disaster. I didn't have a chance to change into something more formal. I was wearing the same jeans as the night before with a white tank top. I could only hope my jean jacket covered enough of my shirt to make it presentable for a court appointment. If Lobo hadn't mentioned court, I would have forgotten completely. As it was, I had to run all the way there straight from Free House. I was a sweating, disheveled mess by the time I arrived. I really need to buy a car. That is, if I ever get around to actually making extra money from the apothecary.

Though I had seen the courthouse, I had never been inside. It was a plain structure cut from heavy blocks of stone, the sort I'd expect to see in any human city. Kind of odd in a tiny town like Willow's Edge. Statues of griffons guarded either side of the entrance at the base of the steps. A relief of the blind lady of justice looked down at me from above the front doors, except her face was covered with a cloth and floated above her body.

I was still running when I burst through the front doors. A disinterested minotaur was reading a paperback I didn't recognize at the front desk. The odd cursive on the cover led me to believe it must be written in some fae language. It was intriguing, but I had to get to my hearing.

"Hello, I'm Lanie Alacore. I'm here for court," I said, trying to catch my breath.

"How grand for you," the minotaur said sarcastically.

"Can you tell me which courtroom I'm supposed to be in?"

His bovine nostrils flared with annoyance. He eyed me over his lowered book. "There's only one courtroom."

I took the minotaur's lifted book as a signal he was done with me. "Thanks for the directions. You're a real peach," I muttered.

The clock on the wall behind him read one-thirty. *Great, even after running all the way here I'm still going to be late.* I dashed away from the front desk, desperately looking for some sign of a courtroom. A pair of minotaurs stood watch on either side of a double set of sealed doors.

"Is this the court?" I asked one of them.

He snorted in response. These minotaurs were impossible. I burst through the double doors, accidentally flinging them aside so hard one bounced off the frame with a loud rattling. The sound of it echoed through a courtroom filled with fae.

I need to give you a good picture to understand how I felt in that moment. Half the large circular room was set up for those either awaiting their trial or spectating. There were four rows of wooden chairs on that side. It looked like every seat in the house was full.

A two-foot wooden barrier, very ornately carved to look like intertwining ivy and leaves, separated the spectator area from the rest of the court. Sunshine lit the room through a skylight in the center of the domed ceiling.

The judge's enclosed bench was on the other side of the court, looming higher than everyone in attendance. Five total judges presided over the assembly, with the center desk raised above the other four and two lower desks on either side. The setup represented the four great houses and the royal family. As Drys explained it to me, the idea is that the royal family's representative has the final vote in any tie-breaking situation. They otherwise act as an officiator of ceremonies but largely stayed out of the proceedings of day-to-day matters. I could tell which House each judge represented by the ornate emblems on the face of the woodwork just below their raised desks. I hoped I could remember their House names as Drys had taught me.

The royal judge, who sat in the center, was known only as Arbiter. This one was the only member to have a title. They were one of the most peculiar people I have ever set eyes on, the epitome of the specter that greeted me by the front entrance. Their head floated above their silver-robed body. The Arbiter's eyes glowed with an inner light. They wore a headpiece that reminded me of an Arabian scarf, except it was silver cloth that gleamed like polished metal but moved like delicate silk.

The fae woman to the Arbiter's left represented the House of Amber. Her bronze skin shimmered in the light. She wore a dress that looked like falling leaves in autumn, rippling around her in flowing waves. Her hair overlapped her shoulders in wild ringlets the colors of fire. The House of Amber's emblem was a clock embossed with colored leaves circling the face of a setting sun.

To her left was another pureblood fae, the representative of the Summer Court. He was a wizened old man with auburn hair and chocolate-colored eyes. He was the first fae I had seen besides my grandmother who had wrinkles. A roadmap of them lined his face around deep set twinkling eyes. Something about that gaze marked his age as ancient. He wore a duplicate of his emblem atop his head, a dazzling circlet of curving ivory with a gemstone in the center that sparkled like sunlight.

On the other side of the Arbiter sat two more judges. The first of which scowled at me with open malice. His skin was a pale blue while his eyes and pulled-back hair were white as ice. The black robes and fine ebony armor he wore were a stark contrast to the rest of the judges. He looked more like he was ready to march into battle than proceed over a courtroom. His armor reminded me of a woven basket, more wood-like than metal, but every bit as foreboding. The Court of Shadows emblem was a black circle with three phases of the moon cut in the center, a full moon and a crescent on either side.

The last judge, to the right of him, was from the House of Dawn. Her emblem was a burst of colorful peonies with birds and fish circling around the core. Her face was humanoid and floral at the same time, as if a giant chrysanthemum had sprouted a smooth graceful face. Glowing petals grew from around her wrists and circled where I would have expected her ear lobes to be. She was dressed in vivid blues and greens that wrapped around her ample bosom like flowing water. Her skin was a rich sepia that glistened as if she had just stepped out of a pool. She had pale blue eyes that cut through me with steely judgement.

Each judge would go by the moniker of the house they represented. Outside of that courtroom they were powerful and influential members of the realm. While there, they solely represented the interest of their House. They were not supposed to have identities. They were the embodiment of their Great Houses.

It was a lot to take in, and I only had a few seconds to process it all with every eye in the courtroom on me.

I have never been someone who enjoys attention. I know, big shock, right? The feeling of so many fae watching me made me want to crawl in a hole and disappear. The Court of Shadows judge, Shadow, was glowering at me like he wanted to skin me alive.

"Sorry," I meekly apologized. "Those doors are a lot lighter than they look."

No one spoke. I quickly spotted an empty seat in the fourth row, then apologized a million times as I shuffled past four fae to sit down.

"Right, then. Where were we before the commotion?" Dawn asked. She had an interesting lilt to her voice that sounded almost Japanese.

The clerk sat at a lower desk. He fixed his spectacles and examined a scroll. His arms were thin as broomsticks. He cleared his throat and scanned the docket with his forefinger. "Lanie Alacore, your lordship."

"Motion to move on," Shadow sneered.

"Wait! That's me." I jumped up and waved. "I'm Lanie Alacore." A few of the fae around me snickered, but the judges hardly looked like they shared their enthusiasm. I shuffled back down the row into the aisle, stepping on toes and almost tripping over someone's lap.

"Your hearing was scheduled to begin at one-thirty," Amber declared. She turned her attention to the other judges. "We have already called Miss Alacore, at which time she was not present. I second Shadow's motion to move on."

"Oh, but I'm here," I said unable to hide my mounting panic. "It's only one-thirty-two. Can't you please still see me?"

The Arbiter's head spun inside their shawl, revealing a different face. "It is this one's curiosity to allow Miss Alacore to speak."

Shadow grumbled to himself but waved for me to take the floor. I moved forward trying desperately to remember where Drys had told me I should stand. It had seemed like such a simple detail at the time, but now, with dozens of eyes fixed on me, I felt flustered. I quickly opted for the center of the floor, directly below the skylight. The sun's rays warmed my already overheated skin.

"Miss Alacore, though you arrive at this court late −" Amber declared imperiously.

"I am so sorry, your honor... err, your lordship," I fumbled the apology almost using the wrong title. I thought it wise not to share that I was running late because I was taking care of a human. Something told me the judges wouldn't be too keen to hear that little revelation.

"*And* you barge into these proceedings like a trouncing demon."

Shit, I didn't realize I cut her off. I needed to slow down and choose my words carefully. My lack of sleep and emotional turmoil over Lobo was going to get me in trouble.

"This on the back of snubbing our previous summons. Now you stand before this council with hat in hand believing we should show you a leniency your lack of decorum does not warrant?"

I waited for a moment to be sure she was done reaming me out before I spoke. I was all too aware of the crowd behind me. *Don't look at the audience, just look forward and keep breathing,* I told myself, fully aware that I might faint if I dared to turn around.

"Your lordship has every reason to be upset with me." I bowed. "I foolishly underestimated how long it would take to get here today and take full responsibility for that. I can see I have upset this esteemed council. Please accept my apologies and allow me to explain. You see, there was a mix up and I never received any summons to present myself until now."

"She speaks very much like her predecessor," Summer said with rosy cheeks.

Amber softened at his tone and sighed. The leaves of her gown rustled with the sigh. "Rest her soul."

"Is it your claim that this court did not send you a summons?" Shadow scowled.

"It is, your lordship. Well no, not exactly. It *was* sent, just not to me. You see, my family counsel led me to believe that all property and titles of my late grandmother were handed down to me, her successor. The first I knew anything otherwise was at the bazaar when my property was confiscated. Had I known earlier, I would have come here immediately to present my case."

There was a cruelty to the way Amber snickered. "Harcourt, did you not send the summons to Miss Alacore?"

The clerk bristled with a hem and haw at the scandalous accusation. "I most certainly did send the summons just as ordered."

"Oh no, I did not mean to imply…"

"I believe what this girl is insinuating is that she never received the post," Amber cut me off. She directed her next words down the line of judges with a wicked gleam in her eyes. "Could it be that the House of Dawn has grown lax in their duties to the realm?"

Dawn's face remained impassive, letting Amber's words slide off her like water. "The House of Dawn takes its duties with the utmost solemnity and honor. Not a single package, parcel, nor letter of import has failed to be delivered on our watch."

"I'm sorry, I think you may have misunderstood," I began.

"What? That you call a Great House inept or that you are simply a liar?" Shadow sneered contemptuously.

My face grew hot under his searing accusation. "Excuse me, sir, or lord, or whatever you call yourself," I heard the rising anger in my voice, but I was helpless to stop myself. I was suddenly standing a little taller, brazenly glaring back at him and Amber alternately. "I am no liar. I may have made some mistakes in my life, but I have always owned up to them. I will not stand here and let you twist my words, seeing as I never implied anyone in this council was at fault for my previous summons. Now, if you will allow me to explain myself, I would like to continue."

Summer's laugh was like tinkling glassware, yet warm and inviting. He shook his head with wonder. "Exactly like her grandmother," he said.

Amber looked more interested in me than she had been a few seconds before. I was no longer a speck of dust but now an enigma she was curious to watch.

"The previous summons was sent to my counsel's office," I explained. "The foolish man forwarded the letter to my previous address, and I never received it."

"Address?" Dawn asked. "I am unfamiliar with this term."

"Ah, it is a human term then," I surmised. "An address is a marking of location, so a human knows where to find their house."

"What a ridiculous assertion," Shadow said. "As if a person can live anywhere except inside themselves."

"Is this one stating she was recently living in a human city?" Arbiter asked. His glowing eyes were unnerving. Scandalous gasps ran through the seated fae behind me.

"For almost all of my life," I agreed. A few more gasps greeted me from the audience, and I had to stop myself from rolling my eyes. "Had I known about the summons earlier, I would have certainly been here. I swear, there was never any disrespect intended, just my ignorance of the meeting."

"Miss Alacore, oaths are not lightly given," Summer explained. "I accept yours on the temerity of your conviction and that of your grandmother's legacy."

"Thank you, your lordship," I said with a slight bow. "My grandmother's legacy is very important to me. I ask only that this council allows me to continue to walk in her footsteps. I promise that if chosen to be Warden I will do everything in my power to make her proud."

Surprisingly, it was Dawn who spoke first. The petals around her wrists pulsated with an inner glow of greens and yellows as she spoke. "The House of Dawn moves to allow Lanie Alacore to seek Wardenship through this Council's blessing."

"All those in favor?" Arbiter asked.

Summer lifted his hands, palms facing inward.

"All judges opposed," Arbiter asked.

Amber and Shadow lifted their hands, palms facing outward.

"Then the ruling of Houses is tied."

Arbiter's eyes dimmed, as if contemplating this. Shadow smiled cruelly at me as I felt my heart plummet. It had all happened so fast. In the blink of an eye my chance to follow in Rosalie's footsteps was snatched away.

The Arbiter's head spun suddenly, revealing a new face. It was statuesque, impassive, a copy of an original, that of a green skinned woman of immense beauty. Her eyes looked like glowing amethysts. "The Arbiter will cast their vote in favor of Lanie Alacore's bid," a deep woman's voice boomed the commandment across the court, as if spoken through a megaphone from far away.

The judges looked taken aback, and the room suddenly buzzed with whispers. The Arbiter's head spun back to its original form, a face of impassive glowing eyes. Something had transpired that I did not fully comprehend.

"The motion is so passed," the Arbiter stated.

I won? I thought, too shocked to take it in.

"Lanie Alacore," Dawn said over the crowd of whispers. The buzz in the courtroom died down. "This council will hear your bid for

Wardenship. Harcourt will give you the details before you leave, so there will be no further claims that you did not receive them."

"Wait, what? I thought that's what today was about?" I asked.

Summer chuckled. "This is a hearing to decide if you should be allowed to make a bid for Wardenship of Willow's Edge."

"She is awfully ignorant in our ways to be claiming such a title," Shadow pointed out.

Summer nodded in agreement but somehow there was nothing cruel about the way he did so. "And she will have little time to gather that expertise. Find yourself better prepared for our next meeting, Miss Alacore."

"I will," I said solemnly.

"And do not dare be late," Amber ordered. The leaves of her dress swirled as if caught in a wind. "We will not allow these proceedings to be disrespected by the carelessness of youth. This sort of thing might be okay in the human realm, but I assure you it is not here."

"Absolutely, your lordship," I bowed. "And thank you for the chance to prove myself. You won't regret it."

Big words. Now I just needed to figure out how I was going to back them up.

22

Left the courtroom feeling like I just got my ass kicked. It was demoralizing to think my Wardenship ordeal wasn't over. The bright side was I got an extension, more or less. Hopefully Drys would be able to prep me for the next court date. I wished I had money to pay for Sir Horrick's services. Well, maybe not him. He was a jerk for abandoning me, no matter how pragmatic his actions were. I wasn't that confident in his acumen as a lawyer anyhow. Regardless, I needed someone who could help me navigate the intricacies of fae law.

A slow clap caught my attention as I made my way down the courthouse corridor.

Lucien leaned against the wall, smirking at me and clapping his hands together. He was dressed differently than usual. He still wore a suit jacket, but this one was a double-breasted blazer with silver buttons and a stitched emblem of his House on the lapel. It felt more business-like than his usual tortured fashion-boi chic.

"Congratulations are in order for your *big* win."

The way he said it left me wondering if he was trying to be sincere or mean-spirited. His face was hard to read. His words were nice enough, but the quirk of his smile felt condescending.

I kept walking. "You saw all that?"

He pushed away from the wall to walk beside me. "The whole spectacle. You're lucky the judges were in such a good humor today."

"That was them being nice?"

Lucien snorted. "You have no idea. When you interrupted court barging in all sweaty and panting, I thought they'd haul you downstairs for sure." He inspected my hair with a frown. "You do look rather rough today."

I felt small under his scrutiny and painfully aware of how horrible I must have appeared. I mussed my hair back behind my ears. "I forgot about court today. Ran all the way here when I remembered."

Lucien's eyes went wide, and he laughed.

I wanted to punch him. The day was rough enough without a gorgeous prince telling me how crappy I looked. "Where's your entourage?" I asked, wanting to change the subject. "I thought they never let you have any time to yourself."

"I work alone," Lucien said, casually striding by my side.

"You work at the courthouse?"

"My duties take me throughout the province and both realms," he answered cryptically.

Why was he talking to me? I could still hear his mocking laughter chasing me as I ran off the night before. What did a pureblood fae prince want with someone like me? The more I thought of the previous evening, the more it felt like he had been toying with me. Quite successfully too, which was what really bothered me. The way he watched me as we walked reminded me of a hawk hovering over its prey. There was something else there as well, a feeling I couldn't place.

Was Lucien actually attracted to me? I was certainly attracted to him. Not just because of his looks either, although those piercing eyes and strong jaw are nothing to sneeze at. There was something broken about him that resonated with my unicorn blood. He was something that needed to be put back together. Unicorns are natural healers after all, and what could be more attractive than the possibility of fixing a prince?

A boy who only I can fix? I almost groaned at the thought. *Could I be anymore pathetic?*

I realized how ridiculous I was being. Lucien was the prince of one of the most powerful fae families in the realm. I was a fledgling apothecary owner. Our worlds could not be further apart. I was annoyed with myself for toying with the childish fantasies of a prepubescent girl. Besides, I had only broken up with Lobo that very morning. Deedee was in a coma. I lost my grandmother's Wardenship. And Charlie was still missing. The last thing I needed to do was bat my eyelashes at some unattainable miscreant. I grew angry with myself for being so absurd. Suddenly, I wanted to be anywhere except for there.

"I really should get going. I have a lot to do today around the shop," I said abruptly, speeding up and waving goodbye. "It was nice bumping into you, though."

"Whoa, hold on a minute."

Lucien's footsteps clapped faster after me up the hall. A surprising urgency was in his voice. It was unexpected enough to stop me in my tracks. He looked confused.

I bet Mr. Heartthrob isn't used to a woman who doesn't fawn over his every word, I thought.

"Your shop is a good distance from the courthouse. I was going to offer you a ride."

"You know where my apothecary is?"

Lucien looked slightly embarrassed but recovered quickly enough, resuming his formal stature and impassive mask. He nodded. "My driver is waiting for me. I'll give you a lift. Unless you would rather *run* all the way back home?"

"A ride would be great," I said. "Thank you."

Lucien took a right down a side hall.

"The entrance is this way," I said.

He smirked. "I prefer to avoid the crowds."

"Right, because you're a prince," I said, following him down the side hall. His dress pants were snug. *Hmm, nice ass there, Lucien.* I quickly looked away before he caught me. "I forget that sometimes. What's that like, being royalty?"

"Tedious."

I giggled. "Wait, if you work around the province why aren't you a judge then?"

"If I was the judge of Willow's Edge, then what would our representative do for a living? I'm not in the habit of depriving my people the ability to earn an honest living or miss out on a chance to do their civic duty."

I snorted. He probably didn't even know his representative's real name. "You just like to be free to party all day."

Lucien smiled amiably. He could take a joke. I liked that. In the movies you see royals stiffen up at the slightest offense, like a broom got shoved up their polished arse. Lucien was interesting; there was a cold and possibly cruel side to him that paralleled something softer he worked hard to hide.

"Actually, I work quite diligently through the day. I prefer to have my work completed early so I can spend the *evening* enjoying life."

"When the heck do you ever find time to sleep?"

"Not often," Lucien replied sadly. "Truthfully, I wish I could sleep more, but it just doesn't come as naturally to me as it does for other fae."

It was such a raw admission. Even Lucien seemed taken aback that he'd just shared such a personal detail with me. I felt immediate compassion for him.

"I'm so sorry, Lucien. That must be horrible."

Without thinking, I reached out a hand to rub his arm. He gazed down at it in surprise. My guess is princes are not used to people touching their 'royal person' unbidden.

He stopped walking, his eyes moving from my hand to my eyes. He was searching them for something. He must have been leaning toward me because I was suddenly very aware of the space between us, or lack thereof. Our faces were close enough that I could smell his skin, like a woodsy musk mingled with vanilla. His breath was cold on my face.

"So, I didn't imagine last night then?" he asked, penetrating me with those silver hammered eyes.

"No," I whispered.

"Did you run away because of the wolf?"

"Wolf?"

"Your boyfriend?"

It was a question with dual meaning. Was I with Lobo? If so, did it matter?

My heart skipped a beat as he gazed at me with an intense hunger. I felt like I could drown in those eyes. All the layers of bullshit I had thrown up were meaningless. It was obvious he wanted me, and he knew I wanted him.

"We're not dating anymore," I answered, trying to keep my breathing steady though it suddenly felt like my heart was racing.

Lucien smiled. That was what he was hoping to hear. "Then you don't find me appealing?" he teased.

"You're alright, I guess." I shrugged, trying to be coy. "It was just… I had somewhere to be last night. There are better things to do than make out with you, ya know."

He leaned closer with a wicked grin that made my knees feel like jelly. "Liar," he cooed playfully.

What was I supposed to say? *Sorry, I'm wildly attracted to you, but I have a curse that makes sure I can't have sex without blacking out. No biggie.*

"Maybe you're right," I said defiantly. "I'm not attracted to you."

Lucien placed his hands on my hips and wrenched me closer. I moaned despite myself. His grin grew more wicked.

"Right. I didn't think so. There's something else though, something that scares you," he deduced.

I felt heady staring back into that silver gaze. A cool wave of energy tingled from his fingertips, running across my hips and down my thighs like an invisible serpent. It felt amazing to be touched by his fae magic. He pursed his lips together. His lower lip looked delicious. I wanted to nibble on it. I remembered how good those lips had felt against my own, running down my neck, his icy tongue exploring my skin. We were so close I could feel the rhythm of his heartbeat. I nearly spilled my guts about my curse to him then and there.

"Are you going to play detective or are you going to kiss me?" I asked, then lunged forward and pressed my lips against his.

It was like jumping off a cliff blindfolded. But I couldn't help myself. It was exhilarating to dive into the deep end without letting logic fuzz up my brain. Nothing bad could happen from a little make out session, right? It wouldn't have mattered if I was thinking rationally in that moment anyhow. I was caught up in a wave of wanton abandon, and it thrilled me to my core.

Lucien hungrily met my lips with his own. They were cool and firm. He opened my mouth and ran his tongue across mine. I met him there. He pulled me closer against him. I could feel the bulging muscles of his biceps flexing beneath his blazer, pulsating with that cool energy and his need. The world spun as I embraced the madness. It was intoxicating. I wrapped my arms around his neck, my fingers sifting through his platinum locks. I let my fingertips lightly stroke his scalp, then gave a handful of his hair a firm tug. Lucien growled passionately, and suddenly I was thrust backward. He shoved us through an open door. It was a supply room for the custodial staff. He kicked the door shut behind him.

"Can't have loose lips wagging about the prince making out with a beautiful woman in the courthouse," he explained.

"You think I'm beautiful," I teased.

He laughed and pushed me farther into the room until my back was pressed against a shelf laden with cleaning supplies. His icy lips found their way to my throat, and ripples of pleasure cascaded down my body. I felt more alive in that moment than I had in months, lit up with the center of the universe. For an instant nothing else in the world existed except the two of us. I ached to be touched. The only time I had ever felt such unbridled lust was the night I possessed the relic.

That's when I realized something was drastically different. I dared to hope my theory about the curse was correct. My mind raced to remember. Had I ever gotten this far along before blacking out? Never. Lucien's cold fingertips circled my belly button, then ran down to my pelvis. I burned to have him reach farther.

My brain argued all the logical reasons why I should stop.

What about Lobo? I thought, ashamed of myself. He was the longest relationship I ever had and here I was, just a few hours after our breakup, making out with another man.

Why should I feel shame? I thought. *Lobo dumped me. He didn't even give me a chance to explain.* He could never know what it was like to live in my body, to be starved of something as primal as intimacy.

This isn't about intimacy, I thought. *You just want to feel Lucien inside of you.*

Yes. I do. And why shouldn't I? Don't I deserve happiness? Haven't I given up enough?

I bit Lucien's earlobe. It was his turn to moan. He slid the zipper of my jeans loose and tugged them down. My body froze.

Lucien paused. "Is this not what you wanted?" His icy fingertips hovered around my hips, waves of fae magic radiating from them. He searched my eyes.

It's not a question of want, I thought. I wanted it so bad I felt like I might burst from anticipation. My mind spun. *What if I'm wrong? What if the curse is still there?* The repercussions would be awful. Men had never reacted well to it. It's impossible to shake the look of someone you cared about, that you opened yourself up to, suddenly scornful and mistrusting. I'd been through this so many times before. What would Lucien do if I blacked out? But I wasn't blacking out. I was revved up, every inch of my body reacting to this arousal. Everything felt different. And I wanted him so bad.

"I do," I whispered.

Lucien's smile was devious. "You do what?"

"You know."

He fell on me. His kiss pressed my mouth open. Fingertips stroked my skin, tracing icy trails down to my panties. I was drenched. His thumb pressed just above my pussy in a way that opened up my world. This was it. This was where I should black out.

I moaned loudly even as I prepared to fall into the abyss. Except I didn't. It was working! Wave after wave of pleasure coursed through me as he worked my clit with his thick fingers. Why was it working?

His lips moved down my neck, kissing and sucking on my trembling flesh along the way. "Tell me."

"I want you," I moaned.

Two of his fingers entered me. They slipped in until they pressed against something that set me loose. Fire and ice danced deliciously across my skin, burning my insides with ecstasy as his magic kissed me from the inside out. "I can't hear you."

I moaned so loud I worried someone in the hall might hear. But I didn't care anymore. "Shut up and fuck me," I pleaded.

He laughed at that. His fingers worked me from the inside, ramming in and out of my pussy until I was soaking wet and bucking my hips to meet him. Suddenly, an orgasm wracked my body. Bursts of color radiated down my fae skin. It was coming from my open mouth. I rode that wave of pure pleasure, letting it bathe me with ecstasy. When it finally dissipated, I found Lucien grinning at me as he enjoyed the spectacle. I grabbed him by the shoulders and spun him around, slamming his back hard against the wooden shelves.

"My turn," I said with a mischievous grin.

I tore his shirt open. His body was completely hairless, like a marble statue. I was amazed to find he had a large tattoo spanning his chest of three phases of the moon, the crest of the Court of Shadows. His muscles were chiseled, each of them defined and cut to perfection. I held his shirt open, then ran my tongue down his icy chest and bit one of his pale nipples. Lucien flinched in surprise, but he laughed with delight. I gazed up at him as my mouth worked lower. I wanted to watch him watch me watching him, so I could see his lust play out as I toyed with his body. I moved my tongue slowly down the center of his rock-hard abdomen. He unzipped his pants as I dropped lower, a burning need in his eyes.

His cock was rigid. My mouth explored him, sucking the swollen tip. I loved how cold it was against my lips. I grazed it with my teeth in a playful nibble that sent a spasm up his body. I lived for the sounds he made. My tongue flicked across the bottom of his shaft, tracing a line back up to the tip so I could take him in my mouth. He wasn't as long as Lobo, but what he lacked in inches he made up for in sheer girth. I watched his expression as I let the rest of him slide into my mouth. His eyes closed tight. He tilted his head back as he lost himself in pleasure. His balls were cold in my palm, and I cupped them as I sucked up and down his cock, tasting every inch, feeling his body squirm.

Lucien suddenly snapped his gaze down to meet my own with the intensity of an avalanche. He wrenched me up to my feet as if I was weightless. He was a lot stronger than he looked! We twirled about, and suddenly my bare ass was pressed up against the shelves. The length of his cock rested against my opening.

"Do it," I urged.

He entered me slowly. My pussy stretched to meet his girth. I would have screamed with pleasure if his mouth didn't suddenly clamp over my own. His firm hands lifted my thighs, wrapping them around him as he eased himself inside me. He was so deep, thrusting and ramming himself against my world. I bucked my hips to meet him, ravenous to swallow every inch he had to offer. We worked as one, dancing back and forth, in and out. His icy magic entered me and probed every inch of my being. Pressure built inside my core. It felt like I might explode. This was it. This was what I wanted.

Lucien moaned and his body quivered. He let himself loose inside my aching core. It was more than I could handle. My own orgasm let loose, tearing me apart and putting me back together again. Rainbow light exploded out of my body, enveloping us in its radiance. When it touched Lucien his cock spasmed inside me and he screamed in ecstasy as a second orgasm hit him.

We slumped to the floor together, him holding me tight. As the light faded it left us in a pile of sweating panting bodies. I kissed his chest as he held me against him.

"And I thought court was going to be boring today," Lucien chuckled.

23

So that happened.

A few hours and a wardrobe change later, I made my way back to Free House, hoping to get advice from Drys on how to handle the nuances of my upcoming court date. While we spoke, my mind kept wandering back to my encounter with Lucien. I still felt tender from our excursion. I could almost trace the feeling of his hands on my hips. The taste of his kiss. I tried to imagine it was Lobo doing those things to me instead.

Was it right for me to be attracted to Lucien? He didn't have the best reputation and he was awfully nasty to me in front of his friends. I couldn't possibly be attracted to someone so heinous, could I? I told myself the only purpose he served was to dispel my belief that the curse was still on me. I'd successfully had sex. That proved the curse was gone. I don't know how it happened. The relic must have left a permanent aura over me when I used it against the changeling. I could have kicked myself. All those months of fighting against my urges, and spurning Lobo's affections and I could have been with him the whole time.

I could be with Lobo. The realization hit me, and I felt giddy. I smiled as I tried to focus on Drys's words. She was walking me through what the judges would likely do at our next appointment. It was important to remember. I needed to stay focused.

Of course it was the relic, I thought. *How could I have been so naïve? The relic's entire purpose was to break curses.* I had foolishly believed it needed to be worn forever to lift my malady.

"Are you sure you're up for this conversation right now?" Drys asked from the other side of the bar. "You seem a bit distracted."

"No, I'm listening," I lied. "You were saying to make sure I look Shadow in the eyes when speaking. Show no weakness. I must convey confidence."

183

Drys folded her muscular arms across her chest and eyed me suspiciously.

I sighed. "I was thinking about Lobo."

"Dear, I'm not one to get involved in the romantic relationships of others," Drys said.

"I know. I'm sorry to bring it up." I played with my glass of soda, watching the bubbles fizz as I twirled it on the bar in front of me. "It's just… my whole life I never had *those* kinds of relationships. I finally had my chance and I just wish I didn't mess things up so bad with him."

"Have you told him any of that?"

I snorted. "I was too much of a coward. Honestly, he'll probably never even talk to me again. If I had another chance to see him, I would confess everything. I think."

Drys nodded her head to something over my shoulder. "Well, here comes your chance."

My heart fluttered unevenly. I spun around in my seat, a million thoughts racing through my mind. A man was walking across the empty bar. It wasn't Lobo.

"Hey, ladies," Doule said, tipping his hat in greeting. "What's shaking?" He made his way around one of the dwarves who was pulling chairs down from tabletops in preparation to open in an hour.

"Luca, grab the detective's food from the back," Drys called.

"You knew he was on his way here?" I asked, though it was more of an accusation than a question.

Drys flashed me an unapologetic smile and made a face that said *here's your chance, girlie. Don't blow it.*

I grumbled. Don't ever let anyone tell you it's wrong to want to choke an older woman. They can be just as devious and cunning as the world's top con artists. Hell, they've had a lifetime to perfect their craft. I spun around on my stool as Doule reached us. He had bags under his eyes and his shirt and pants were wrinkled. Doule was typically a fairly buttoned up dresser.

"Long day?" I asked.

Doule sighed. "You don't know the half of it. We've been staking out that shit heel's building all day."

"Any luck?" Drys asked.

"Not a peep out of the guy. Some of his friends have come and gone, but we have yet to see the prince so much as pop his head up."

"I didn't know Sam was royalty," I said.

"It's his stupid gamer tag," Doule said. He must have seen the confusion on our faces because he chuckled and added, "It's like an alias. Gamers use them to identify themselves in competitions. Sounds a lot cooler to say Wildmagician24 wins the match than Bobby, you know?"

"So, are you guys done for the day?" I probed.

Doule rubbed his hands up and down his face. "I wish. We're going to be sitting on this until we catch a lead. Probably pull another all-nighter. Wouldn't be so bad if I wasn't already exhausted. I didn't get any sleep the last few days."

"Out late with the ladies?" I teased.

"Sometimes lately… let's just say I have trouble falling asleep," Doule said somberly. "My mind wanders at night."

His eyes had an inward look to them as if he was replaying a painful memory. It seemed I was not the only one haunted by the changeling's attack.

"How's Lobo holding up?" Drys asked, guiding me back to the point.

Doule frowned. "Honestly, I was going to ask *you* about that, Lanie. He's been acting really strange ever since we went to the lunar party."

My heart froze. "You went to the lunar party? What night did you go?"

"Saturday," Doule said. "I'm telling you something frazzled him bad. He dragged me out of there in a hurry. Did he mention anything to you about it?"

I swore under my breath. "I knew that's why he broke up with me."

"You guys broke up?" Doule asked in shock. "Shit. Course you did. It all makes sense now. Well, whatever happened between you two has got him shook up fierce. I've never seen the dude so tense, and this is Lobo we're talking about."

"I have to speak with him," I insisted.

"You're going to have to wait," Doule said. "My guess is we'll be tied up with this stakeout for a few days at least."

Luca, the dwarven barmaid, came out of the back and delivered a large canvas tote bag to Drys. "Two hot dinners fit for hungry wolves."

Drys handed the parcel over the bar to Doule who promptly opened it to give it a good sniff. If his tail was out, he would have been wagging it.

"Smells amazing," he said, practically drooling.

I put my hand on his forearm. "Doule, seriously, I need to talk to him tonight."

"I don't know," Doule replied. "Lobo wouldn't like it if I brought you there. He keeps things to himself, ya know?"

"Then you stay here," I said. "Better yet, take my keys and go catch a nap in my apartment. Let me deliver the food to him while you rest a little."

He looked ready to object.

"You have your radio, don't you?" Lobo and his partner used a pair of devices that looked similar to human walkie talkies except they were made of wood, and I am certain they did not use batteries. Most devices I have found around the province are either relics from when humans dwelled in this land or magically powered fae tech I couldn't wrap my head around.

Doule nodded.

"Then if Lobo sees anything he can give you a call. C'mon, you look like hell. A decent nap would do you good."

"I don't know," Doule said.

"Please, this is really important to me," I insisted. "Even if you give me an hour alone with him."

Doule finally caved. "Fine. Give me your keys. But only *two* hours, then I'm heading back. Thirty minutes of sleep will tune me right up anyhow. He's parked down at Lafayette and Blandina, just off the side street there. Make sure you approach him from the south end of Grant, though. We don't need these guys seeing you deliver food to a car. It's a stakeout, not a picnic."

Lobo's cruiser was hard to spot at first. There were no cars parked on the deserted street and only a few dusty automobiles in driveways. Boarded up doorways and overgrown weeds marked where humans had left behind the crumbling façade of a community neighborhood. The buildings reminded me a lot of where Sanji and her friends lived. This was an area of Willow's Edge that most fae had chosen to stay away from.

Lobo's cruiser peeked out from a driveway a third of the way down the street. I stayed close to the buildings, taking a circuitous route to his car that kept me out of view. As I walked, I played out a dozen different scenarios in my head that might unfold when I told him the truth about my curse. None of them ended well. I'm a pro at playing out the worst possibilities as if they are inevitable. I guess our brains do that to prepare us for what might come. It's like a defense mechanism.

Cause nothing says prepared like being scared shitless, I thought. Maybe I was wrong. Maybe my brain makes me live out the cruelest possibilities in the hope that I will chicken out and run away. Then again, that would still be a kind of defense mechanism.

I looked down at my outfit. Maybe I should have stopped home to put on something sexier. I was wearing a long grey skirt with white flower print and a t-shirt beneath my jean jacket. Between that and my Vans I felt rather homely looking. *Like Lobo cares what shoes you have on Lanie,* I chided myself, realizing I was psyching myself into running away again.

Most of the time that's exactly what I would have done too. It's easier to avoid than confront. I was sure Lobo saw me with Lucien. How could he forgive something like that? And why should he? It twisted me up inside, but I forced myself to breathe through it. I didn't want to run away from this one. I needed to make sure he understood the full extent of what was really going on behind the scenes.

I took a deep breath and shuffled up to the passenger door. The locks flipped up. I slid inside and closed the door softly, to avoid drawing attention to the car.

"Hey there," I said.

Lobo didn't look at me. No doubt he'd smelled me coming a mile away with his damn werewolf nose. "Where's Doule?"

"I told him to get a little rest at my place," I said.

Lobo mumbled something about a rat bastard that I was sure didn't bode well for Doule.

"Drys made you some dinner." I set the tote bag on the center console.

"Smelled it already." He didn't bother looking at the bag. "You're not supposed to be here."

"I know. I asked Doule to let me bring you dinner," I said.

"Why?"

"Because I need to talk to you. Why don't you eat something? You look tired."

Lobo snatched the bag and tossed it on the backseat. "I lost my appetite."

It felt like he just scooped my heart out of my chest and tossed it away. This wasn't going to be easy. *Why should it, Lanie? You messed around with another guy while you were dating. You're lucky he even let you get in the car.*

His attention remained transfixed on a three-story apartment building down the hill at the end of block. It was kiddy-corner at the intersection. The windows of the bottom floor were lit up from the inside but veiled with heavy curtains. There was a beat-up old sedan on cinder blocks in the driveway and another, in better condition, parked out front.

The tension between us felt thick as tar. I could feel the resentment wafting off Lobo. He knew what I'd done. I pictured him watching me hump Lucien's leg and felt queasy. Semantics weren't going to cut it in this conversation. I needed to start speaking, to cut through the awkwardness of it all and lay out the truth.

"Is that where the sick bastard lives?"

Lobo nodded. "Owns the whole block. Sam's folks were loaded, old money from import-export. I wouldn't have pegged him for merchant nobility. They worked for centuries to build themselves up from nothing. Hard workers, both. They died a few years back. Goblin pirates is the story, slit both their throats. Sam inherited it all. He's a fucking deadbeat though. Sold off everything and lives like a king off it. It's part of the reason I think some of those girls didn't talk. Hard to go up against a guy like that. Even in fae money can buy your way out of an awful lot. The perverted sack of shit knows it, too."

"Will it buy him out of this? If he took Charlie and Annabel somewhere against their will?"

"Not a chance," Lobo growled.

That shook me. The last time I heard him growl like that was the night the changeling sent him after me. On instinct, I eyed the car door handle.

Lobo must have sensed my trepidation. He scowled. "What are you doing here, Lanie?"

"I thought we should talk," I said, surprised with how meek I sounded.

"Just go away and leave me alone," he grumbled.

I thought about it for a moment. Maybe I should just leave him alone. The damage was already done. What was me confessing my secret to him going to change? It was just an excuse. Why go through the guaranteed rejection that awaited me? Far easier to run away and bury my feelings down deep where they could never see the light of day again.

Good lord Lanie, you went toe to toe with a murderer who spit killer crows at you. You can do this.

Lobo tensed up. The side door to the apartment building had opened. A man came out into the driveway. He was too far away for me to make out his features properly, but I knew Lobo could see him clear as day with his werewolf sight.

"Is that him?"

"Nah, just another of his goons," Lobo said, relaxing his shoulders. "He's got a whole group of the yokels in there. Been the same since we arrived; they come and go all day long, but we have yet to see the prince."

"The prince?" I exclaimed in surprise. Suddenly, my back broke out in a cold sweat.

Lobo growled again. "Don't worry. Not *your* prince. That's just what this joker calls himself. It's his club name or some shit."

"What do you mean my prince?" I asked tentatively.

His lip curled over razor sharp canines. The steering wheel groaned in protest beneath his curled grip. "Don't play games with me, Lanie."

The world dropped out from beneath me. *He just confirmed it. Lobo saw me kissing Lucien.* I was mortified. "It's not like you think."

He twisted his head sideways so hard I thought his neck might snap. His eyes glowed in the shadows of the car. "So you weren't all over the prince the other night, like a dog in heat? I imagined that. Right, Lanie?"

"It's not as simple as that."

Lobo's growl was guttural, vibrating up from his chest. The steering wheel whined as his hand clenched it tighter. When he spoke, his words were slow and precise. He was giving everything he had to control himself.

"You know what the sickest part of all this is? For months I've been torturing myself over us. Why doesn't Lanie want me to touch her? Obviously because she's repulsed by me. Obviously because I let that sick bastard into my mind to control me. Obviously because I screwed everything up." He laughed scornfully. "I'm such a dope. I never imagined it was because you were seeing someone else."

"That was the first time Lucien kissed me," I said. "I never did anything like that with him before that night. I swear."

Lobo's shoulders slumped, and he let go of the wheel. He reminded me of a deflated balloon.

"Then why, Lanie? I mean, we never had the talk. I know that. Somehow with you I didn't think we needed to spell it out. I haven't had many relationships. Sex, sure. There's always a horny fae or another lurking around the pubs wondering what it's like to get fucked by the big bad wolf. When I was younger, I used to think they were into me. Then I grew the fuck up and realized what it was all really about. Rebellion. Get one back on mommy and daddy for not paying enough attention or revenge on some idiot. *Oh yeah, you dumped me? Well, guess who I fucked?* Sex with a werewolf is taboo, you know."

"You didn't deserve to be treated like that." I said softly.

The car fell quiet. He looked so hurt. A guy like Lobo doesn't have it in him to be fragile. He was born to be a predator. He reminded me of a wounded dog that needed help, but if you moved wrong, he might bite you. Not that Lobo was going to hurt me. He was as uncomfortable displaying emotion as I would have been if I had a nail stuck in my foot.

"It was that night last winter," Lobo whispered with certainty. "The night I attacked you."

"That wasn't your fault, babe," I said.

"Yes, it was," he insisted. "I was the one who was supposed to keep you safe. Instead, I let that fiend get inside my head and use me as a weapon."

"That's on Brom," I insisted. "Not you. And he's never going to be able to hurt anyone else ever again thanks to us."

That palpable silence again. I needed to tell him. What was the expression? Like ripping off a Band-Aid. I hated that expression. Ripping off a Band-aid fucking hurts. But that was what I needed to do; just rip it off. Blurt it out. *I, Lanie Alacore, was cursed. But it is gone now, and we can be together.*

"It was supposed to be different with you," Lobo said sadly. "You're a good person."

I felt like someone punched me in the gut. "I'm really not."

"That's the shitty part. You are. You're a better person than most I've met in my life. Which was why I never expected you to hurt me like that."

"Lobo, I –"

"Were you even going to tell me?" Lobo cut me off.

"About the kiss?"

He growled.

"You dumped me before I could come clean about it," I said.

It was half-true. I liked to believe I would have told him the truth eventually. Once I'd built up enough courage. Seeing the pain on his face made me feel three inches tall. How could I have ever let myself lose control like that? Lucien was a horrible person. He was conceited and crass, just the type of uptight asshole I loathed to be around. Sitting across from me was a man who had only ever treated me with respect and dignity, someone I looked up to. Lobo spent his life protecting others. I could not stomach what I had done to him. If I didn't come clean then and there, I would lose my nerve.

"Lobo… I have to tell you something," I said.

He eyed me warily.

"The night we made love. You remember I was wearing the relic, right?"

"Lanie, what the fuck does that have to do with –"

"That night…" *Come on Lanie, spit it out. Just say it.* "It was the first time I was ever with someone. You see, I have this –"

"You were a virgin?" Lobo snapped.

"Yes, but that's not –"

"Lanie, you're a grown woman," Lobo said. "You're trying to tell me you'd never been with a guy before that?"

"It never worked out before," I said. "There were a couple times I almost did, even started to, but I was never able to go all the way with it."

"I don't know what to say. You waited all those years to finally have sex. Why waste that on me?"

I leaned over the center console and put my hand on his arm. His bicep was hard as a rock and steaming with heat. "I don't regret it. It was beautiful. You were... *amazing*. You said you haven't had many relationships? I've had even less. Honestly, between being with you and trying to navigate all the changes in my life, I don't know whether I'm coming or going most days."

Lobo put his hand over mine, pressing my fingers over his flexing muscle. He leaned in closer to me. I could feel the heat spilling off his body. I eyed his lips.

"Please don't give up on me," I whispered.

His lips pressed against mine, and sharp stubble grazed my delicate flesh. I leaned in closer, running my tongue across his. My hand found his chest. Lobo's muscles were like chiseled stone. My fingertips slipped into the space between the buttons on his shirt. His chest was hot. I could feel his heart pounding like a hammer underneath it. His hand found its way beneath my skirt to my exposed thigh. My body lit up like it was on fire. I wanted him to press himself inside me, to throw me on the backseat and ravage me right there. I parted my thighs, inviting him in as we frantically kissed.

The last thing I felt was his thumb slipping down past the waistline of my panties.

Then the world blurred. I tried to deny the curse its power over me, but it was too late. I was swallowed by the abyss.

24

Time passes in strange waves of eternity when you are trapped in a basement and locked inside a cage. Charlie tried tracking each second in a futile attempt to keep her brain alert. It had the opposite effect, soothing her nerves until she passed out from exhaustion.

She dreamed of her home. The garden on the side of the house was lush with violet bearded irises and tropical cannas. Hummingbirds flitted around the feeder that hung from her front porch. Her father sat in his rocking chair, a cobb pipe hanging from his lopsided grin as he waved for her to come up the steps.

She was home. No one could hurt her anymore. Something distracted her. A splinter from the wooden stair rail was stuck under her thumbnail. She stopped on the steps and wriggled it out from beneath her skin. A trickle of blood followed it. Her father was crying. She had only heard him cry once. It was the morning he died.

The sound of the metal door creaking open fractured the nightmare. She awoke in a panic, covered in a layer of sweat with her heart racing. Fear stole her breath as a flurry of panicked thoughts scattered across her mind like shards of broken glass. *No. No. No. I fell asleep. He can't be here yet. I'm not ready. I'm not ready!*

The prince stepped inside the prison room whistling the tune of "Maxwell's Silver Hammer." Hearing the Beatles was jarring. Human culture was shunned in fae circles. Charlie had spent her childhood fascinated with the taboo of it all, but her mother would scold her if she asked any questions about the human realm. It never made sense to her. Why should she not be allowed to ask questions about creatures who occupied more than half of their world?

When she met Sanji at school, they quickly fell together as friends. She was the first person to introduce Charlie to human music, mostly punk at first, stuff like the Sex Pistols and Dead Kennedys. Human music was unlike anything she'd heard before, so chaotic and frenzied with a raw emotion that starkly contrasted with the ballads or dance music fae were into. When she heard the Beatles it was revelatory, like finding enlightenment in simple notes and lyrics. She gobbled their music up and decided then and there that humans couldn't be all that evil if some of them had created songs like this.

To hear that same music spilling from the prince's cursed lips made her feel insane. It wasn't the shock of discovering the prince also enjoyed human culture. She had already known that. It was part of how he lured her away from the party, after all. It was the irony of "Maxwell's Silver Hammer," a song that sounded upbeat and whimsical on the surface but bore darker fruits beneath. That song was very much like the prince.

He shouldn't be whistling the Beatles, she thought, her blood turning to acid. That was her music. It did not belong in the mouth of a cannibal. Hearing it fed her just enough anger to hold her surging fear at bay.

The prince held a tray of food in one hand. He stopped in the middle of the room to study the cages. He liked to do that when he came in. She realized he was savoring the moment, like a man who peruses the cuts of meat at a butcher shop. She shuddered in revulsion.

Fortunately, he was looking at his other victim when Charlie moved. The prince's head snapped around as if on a swivel. She felt his eyes bore into her like red-hot pokers. He studied her in silence for what felt like eternity. He resumed whistling and set the tray on the dirt floor.

Charlie knew his routine well enough. He would gather up what he needed for the other girl's cage and go feed her. He liked to work around the room clockwise. *It's crazy that we're both prisoners here, yet I don't even know her name.* There was never any time to learn it. Charlie didn't dare so much as whisper across the room. It was always too great a risk. The third girl had tried one time, and he had immediately come down and beaten her senseless for 'disturbing their slumber.' When he finished hitting her, he made the girl look in his mirror and inject herself. Charlie knew better than to speak.

If I gaze into that mirror one more time, I'll never come back. She knew it was true. She felt much heavier than when she was taken prisoner, however long ago that had been. It seemed like years, eons even. It was something he put in their food. She always felt bloated after she ate. If he got her under his spell again, whether through the mirror or the human drugs, she would never find her way out of the stupor. It was too hard to fight against, and she didn't trust herself to find that willpower again. Not with knowing what waited for her on the other side of delirium.

She cursed herself for falling asleep. She had meant to be prepared for this encounter. It was going to be next to impossible, but she had to at least try. It was either that or lay down and wait to die. Her fingers probed the straw mattress. The broken bone was gone!

Her heart raced frantically. She scoured the straw around her side, careful not to move too much. *Don't move your head. If he sees you it's blown.* The only hope she had was the element of surprise.

She strained to see out of her peripheral vision. The bone was nowhere to be seen. Her breathing was coming in ragged bursts.

"Awake are we?" His voice was riddled with amusement.

Charlie murmured an unintelligible response. He had to think she was still in a trance, even if she was awake.

"Ah, no doubt you smell your dinner," the prince chuckled. Silverware tinkled onto the plate, and he rose from inside the other girl's cage.

Charlie's insides turned to jelly. *No! Don't come over here yet. I need more time, damn you.*

He turned back to his other captive. "Are you hungry too my sweet?" he cooed. "Have no fear, your prince is here to provide. That is what we do after all, as my royal court dictates. We are here to serve at our subject's whim."

This was her chance.

She had to find the bone. Without it she had nothing.

But if he sees me grabbing it, everything will be for naught. The prince was much stronger than her, and he had needles and evil mirrors to back that strength. Her fingers quietly searched the straw mattress. The bone had to be there somewhere. She had fallen asleep with it in her hand. It could not have fallen far.

The prince stood outside the other girl's cage with his back to her. She foolishly turned her head to watch him. His broad shoulders blotted out a shape in the darkness. Then his back stiffened. He lifted his head higher, like a dog who caught a scent.

"I can feel you looking at me." He said it playfully, like a child would use when playing hide-n-seek.

Her breath caught in her throat.

It was the wrong reaction.

The prince turned around to gaze across the basement at her cage.

She did not dare breathe. *Make it look like you're sleeping. Make him believe he's wrong. You're not awake, you just stirred a little. He has to go inside her cage first. I need to find the bone before he –*

"Hmm, you *are* awake aren't you," the prince said in a sobering voice, his levity replaced with calculating concern.

No, I'm not, she thought in a panic as if she could will it so. *Turn back around. Go into her cage first, not mine.*

The prince watched her in silence.

She focused on her breathing, slowly out, all the way in, concentrating on the steady rise and fall of her chest. Rhythmic. Steady and even.

He shook his head in disappointment. "You're faking it. This is my fault. I should have given you another dose of your medicine earlier." He moved swiftly across the basement to her cage.

A whimper betrayed her mouth in mutiny. The prince grunted as he rammed the key into her door. Charlie's head turned left and right as terror took hold. Where was the damn bone? Why did she fall asleep? Curse this world.

The cage door swung open. He stepped inside. He had to duck to squeeze into the cage.

"No, please," she begged.

"Hush now, my tasty little treat," he cooed, setting the plate on the floor by the open door. "This is just a bad dream. I have something right here to make it go away."

He pulled the mirror from his back pocket, twirling it like it was a toy.

Charlie shoved herself backward away from him, pressing her back against the chicken wire wall.

"Oh my," the prince chuckled. "You are a flighty one today. Come little sparrow, gaze into my mirror. All of your hurt will go away soon. There's no need to live in such fear."

He was right. There was no escape. Perhaps it had always been her fate to become part of the fae food chain. Her mother was right all these years. She should never have gone near the punks and their human nonsense. Better to have stayed home with the brownies and lived a life of menial purpose. Her father worked hard as a cobbler, her mother a maid. She had always resented that they worked for the purebloods hand and foot. How could she have ever looked down on that life? She would give anything to be polishing some noble's shoes at that moment.

He crouched over her. His hand roughly seized her chin and turned her face upward.

If you look into that mirror, you'll never come back.

And why shouldn't she? The mirror promised oblivion. No need to live through this horror when she could dream she was in paradise. Would she even know when she died? What if that dream was what waited for her on the other side? Was that not a better way to end things than watching as he cut her to pieces?

She peered past the mirror's rippling surface. Images danced inside. Her father was there. His rocking chair, the bearded irises, the hummingbirds. The flowers sang "Eleanor Rigby." She loved that song.

"There's a good lass," the prince chuckled. "Everything you need is here waiting for you, sweetie."

"I see them," she heard herself speaking distantly. Her father rose from his rocking chair and reached out for her. His arms were welcoming. Loving. His face was… The flower sang *died in the church and was buried along with her name.*

Her father's face was wrong.

Nobody came.

"Father's crying?"

The prince was a quick one. "Yes, of course, tears of joy to see his little girl."

He had done this enough times to know all the right buttons to press. Praying on the misfits always made sense. They were the least missed. Always had daddy or mommy issues. All they really wanted was to feel loved and accepted. It made them easy targets. A little push and they were putty in his hands. He felt Charlie's head sag. She was where he needed her to be.

She was more resilient to the magic than he had realized. He would not make that mistake again. As soon as she was in her trance, he would go upstairs and get some of the heroin. This time he would inject her himself.

"Is that true, Daddy?" she murmured. "Are you happy to see me?"

She was almost there. He knew better than to push too hard. The magic of the mirror would do the work for him.

Charlie's father wrapped his arms around her inside the glass dream. "I love you so much."

"I missed you, Daddy."

She closed her eyes and felt the warmth of his embrace. This was where she wanted to be. When did she get here? Where did the music go? It seemed like she had just arrived, but where was she before? She opened her eyes and glanced over his shoulder as he squeezed her in his arms.

A diminutive woman stood in the doorway. Her features were lost in the shadows of the house. Another version of her father stood behind that woman. He was crying too, but the woman wouldn't let him out.

"Daddy?"

Charlie tried pushed away from the man she was hugging. She was embracing the prince!

The prince laughed at her. "Yes, my love. You're safe now."

She knew it was true. It felt so right. She wanted it to be real. A glint caught her eye.

Her eyes focused closer to her face.

A glass mirror. In the reflection, beside her hand on the floor, there was something white.

The prince saw her gaze shift. Her features altered. Something was wrong.

"Now Charlie, stab him!" her father shouted.

She plucked the bone from the dirt floor and swung it as hard as she could.

She was too slow! The prince saw her slap coming and laughed. Something stung him. A tiny prick, like a mosquito bite.

The bone slammed into the side of his throat. She buried it halfway in.

He fell away from her, dropping the mirror on the straw mattress. Gouts of purple blood oozed from his wound. He looked around wildly as he tried to comprehend what had just happened.

She sprang to her feet.

A hand grasped at her. He was too slow. She darted around him and leapt through the door to freedom.

25

"anie, wake up!"

Lobo's frantic voice cut through the abyss. I opened my eyes. Where was I? Inside a car. It was dark out. A street I didn't recognize sprawled before me. Lobo was shaking me by the shoulder, repeating my name. I stared at him with the numbness of one whose body was more ready to wake up than their brain.

"Stop shaking me," I said weakly.

When my curse triggers, it hits hard. I felt like someone had cracked me across the side of the head with a hammer. Well, maybe not that bad, but it was at least a hangover-sized headache.

Lobo stared at me as aghast as if I had just pulled a third arm out of my mouth. "That's different," I mumbled.

"What is, Lanie?" Lobo asked. He spoke to me like I was a senile person he needed to coax back to reality. It was a pretty sound tactic.

"Your face. They never looked like that before," I answered sluggishly.

In all my horrible experiences with sex, I had received plenty of looks. There was disgust, shame, mistrust, and resentment. But never the look that was plastered on Lobo's face.

"You're not making any sense. What just happened?"

It took me a few moments to pinpoint his expression. "Were you afraid?"

Lobo's face turned red, and his cheeks puffed up.

"Are you going to blow my house down now?" I snickered drunkenly at my own joke.

"You just blacked out in the middle of kissing me!" Lobo yelled. "I thought you dropped dead for fuck's sake."

I cringed and shied away from him as if his words were blows raining down on me. The fog dissipated from my mind, blown back just as surely as if it were one of the little piggy's houses. I forced myself not to laugh at that comparison. Lobo wasn't in a laughing mood at the moment.

He had the decency to look embarrassed for losing his temper at least. Not that I would have blamed him for being mad. I suppose if I was in his shoes, I would have been pretty peeved as well. I sat up a little straighter and winced at the pounding in my head.

"I need to eat something." It was the only thing that helped with the weakness that came after the curse shut down my body.

Lobo reached into the backseat and snatched the takeout bag. The aroma of roasted meat made me salivate when he opened the box. Drys had arranged the food in a bento-style container made of finely carved wood. I snatched it from his hands. I don't even remember what I ate, just that it tasted like chicken and gravy and some fruit. I used my fingers to shovel it all in my mouth. I ate like a starved Neanderthal, gobbling up every scrap of food I could grab until my body finally stopped shaking. My forehead broke out in a cold sweat.

"Sorry," I said as I realized how I must look to him. "Doesn't always hit me so hard. Eating is the only thing that'll make the weakness go away."

Lobo handed me a cup of water from the center console. "Lanie, what's going on?" His voice was soft and kind. He was concerned for me. "I've never seen anything like that."

Two things stuck out to me in that moment. One, I was still cursed. Fuck me if that didn't suck ass to realize. I had no explanation for why I had been able to have sweaty, passionate sex with the prince earlier that day. It didn't matter. The curse that trapped me from a life of physical intimacy was still there.

Second, I had no choice but to come clean to Lobo. My greatest fear had come true. I blacked out in the middle of foreplay with him. In a way, it was liberating. The secret I had kept bottled up for a lifetime was revealed. The crippling fear of blacking out and waking up to find him loathing me had happened. Except he wasn't looking at me with disgust. I wondered if he would continue to look as concerned once he found out he wasn't going to be able to get any blood flow down there for a week or so. Better save that little tidbit for last.

I felt like I had just won the lottery. I could tell Lobo everything now. There was nothing left to hide. A small kernel of hope flared in my heart. Now we could stay together. Lobo would understand it wasn't his fault I had been so distant. Maybe he could even help me find a way to lift the curse!

I wiped my mouth with the back of my forearm. Yeah, I know. I'm disgusting. You try getting sucker punched by a blackout curse and see how pretty you look afterward. His eyes were hanging over me, longing for me to speak.

"Lobo, it's…"

Tires squealed on asphalt. Lobo's head jerked up. A van sped down the street, straight across our view. The driver turned the wheels hard, then braked right in front of Sam's apartment building.

I instinctively ducked down in my seat. "Did they see us?"

"Dunno," Lobo said, fixated on the spectacle unfolding before us. "I didn't catch a look at the driver. If they were looking our way, I would've seen their eyes."

The van switched gears and slid into the building's driveway in reverse. The driver side door swung open, and a heavy-set man with curly blonde hair hopped out.

"What are they doing?" I whispered, as if they might hear us half a block away.

"That's one of Sam's guys."

The side door to the apartment building swung open. At the same time, a blinding flood light switched on, throwing back the shadows up the street. Lobo dropped his seat back slick as a snake. I scrunched farther down toward the floor, not daring to peek over the dashboard. There was an insistent conversation. It sounded as if they might be arguing. There was a definite urgency to whatever they were saying.

"Can you hear them?" I whispered.

Lobo growled. I felt stupid. I have gotten to know him well enough to translate that growl as, *I could if you weren't yapping in my ear.*

Car doors were slammed. Telltale signs of the ignition firing up. The van peeled out, squealing rubber against the blacktop. Lobo's seat popped back up.

"Something's going down," he grunted. He started the car and spun out of the driveway. "You better hold on to something. We need to catch up to them."

"What do you mean?" I grabbed hold of the handle Deedee liked to call the "oh shit handle." You know the one, right above the side window. It's what you grab when the driver takes a turn too fast.

"They were talking about Sam. He hasn't even been here this whole time, damnit. He called one of them with an emergency. He needs them right away. Said something about losing their delivery. I'm not sure what any of it means. If I tried to guess, it's not good. Get Doule on the horn, quick. I have to catch up to them."

He tossed me the walkie while slamming around the turn in the road. My body was jerked right, against the passenger door. I fumbled for the walkie. It dropped between my legs onto the floor. We banked another hard turn, this one right. That pressed me right up against Lobo's shoulder.

"Lanie, come on. Stop messing around."

"I'm not," I huffed, scrambling to find the device between my legs. I snatched the walkie and turned the top knob. Feedback stung my ears for a moment. Lobo whimpered like a hurt dog. I can only imagine what something like that does to a werewolf, given their acute sense of hearing.

"Press the button on the side," Lobo said.

"I know how a walkie works," I snapped. I pressed the paging button and held on tight as Lobo took another turn. The cruiser suddenly decelerated. The van was up the road from us, only a few blocks away.

"Uhrm," Doule's half-awake voice cut over the walkie.

I looked from the van ahead to Lobo. He decelerated even more. "They'd have to know we're following to think to listen back here," he replied to my unspoken question. "I don't think they've got any fae with that ability anyhow. Not that I've seen at least. Go ahead."

I held down the talk button.

"Doule, they're on the move," Lobo said.

That woke Doule up as sure as a slap in the face. "Shit. I'm on my way. How far are you?"

"They're heading down Sunset Boulevard," Lobo said. "Maybe meet me.... oh crap. They're getting on the ramp to old 5S."

The van barreled up the ramp far ahead of us. That wasn't good. If they got on route 5, they could go as fast as they wanted. The old highway was fairly abandoned where it cut through Willow's Edge, since a lot of fae abhorred the idea of driving in automobiles.

"We're crossing the glen," Lobo said, easing onto the ramp just as they slipped onto the highway. "You're going to have to put on your running shoes, bud."

Static cut through the walkie. Doule was panting into the speaker. "Already on my way," he growled with the voice of a beast. "I can meet you just before the gorge."

"Right. Keep the walkie on in case we get rerouted."

The highway was pitch black. Empty-eyed human light posts watched over us. It felt like they were sentinels bowing their heads in reverence to the doom that lay before me. I suppressed a shudder and lowered the walkie to my lap.

"We still have them," Lobo snarled.

The van's lights were on, marking them clear as day. They were about half a mile ahead of us already. Lobo's lights remained off. He didn't need them anyway. His wild eyes could see in the dark as well or even better than in daylight.

I can't stand being a passenger in a car. Like it or not, I must admit to being somewhat of a control freak. If I am in a car, I prefer to be the driver. Especially since I'm a super tame defensive driver. Zero accidents under my belt. Sitting there with the world drenched in darkness whizzing past us at a dizzying speed was triggering my freak-the-fuck-out button.

Lobo must have sensed it. "We can't stop to let you out," he apologized.

"I understand. Just get Charlie and Annabel back from these creeps."

He nodded; his eyes transfixed to the highway ahead of us. "Roll down your back window."

My hands were shaking. I closed my eyes tight and lowered my seat. The car rumbled over a crack in the road. I yelped and gripped the seat for dear life, certain we were about to crash. I never should have taken my eyes off the road. At least then I could have slammed on the invisible passenger side brake that existed only in my head.

"Hurry up, we're almost there," Lobo ordered.

His firm resolve helped center me. I relinquished the headrest and stretched my arm back for the window lever. The car was an older model, with crank handles. The wind howled in, popping my eardrums, as I lowered the window all the way. The second I was finished, I spun around and popped my seat back up. The van was still a quarter of a mile ahead of us.

A dark shape suddenly shot up the hill to our right. I had just enough time to register its presence before a snarling werewolf leapt through the rear passenger window. Doule rolled around snarling and clawing at the seats for a few minutes before shifting back to his human form. Cracking bones and pulled sinew are sounds that stay with you long after hearing them. Doule panted, working to catch his breath.

Lobo hit the gas. The car shot forward like a bullet, pressing me back into my seat. Doule's human hand came around the seat and patted him on the shoulder.

"That was some fancy driving, brother," he managed between gasps of air.

"You just leapt through the window of a moving car," I said in awe.

"Yeah, well, we've had lots of practice," Doule said.

I peeked over my shoulder. Doule was buck naked, though thankfully most of him was hidden in the shadows of the unlit car. Doule retrieved a bag from under the back of the driver's seat. There was a change of clothes inside. They really had prepared for this.

"Did you catch anything else?" Doule asked. "Like where the hell these shady bastards are going?"

"Nothing useful," Lobo grunted.

I frowned at that. "Weird they're not talking while they drive."

"They could be," Lobo shrugged. He tried to make it look nonchalant, but I could see in his eyes it bothered him. "The shifty fucks are using deer whistles."

The first thing that came to mind was one of those duck calls hunters use. Then I remembered Old Forge. The rental company had slapped disposable plastic pieces to either side of the car. Deer whistles were exactly the opposite of a duck call. Air passed through them while you drove and alerted the deer to get the hell out of the way.

"But those are too high-pitched for human ears."

Doule chuckled.

I heard my words and felt stupid.

"Only fae who use those are criminals," Lobo said. "No other reason to keep a werewolf from listening in on ya."

"Well, we do have a right to privacy," I countered.

"Maybe in the human realm," Lobo grumbled. "But not here. Damn things are giving me headache."

"Like I'm being stung in the ears by hornets," Doule agreed.

"What the hell?" Lobo said in disbelief. The van lights cut off the side of the highway.

"Why are they getting off here?" Doule asked.

I looked around us. All I could see were the dark outlines of trees, trees, and more trees on either side of the road. "Is there anything around here?"

Lobo pressed hard on the gas, lurching the car forward. "Nothing but forests for miles."

"But what the hell are they doing in the forest?" Doule asked.

"I don't know. But we better not lose them, or we might never find those girls again. I may not be able to hear but my nose is working just fine."

Doule agreed. "I smell two things in that van. Women… and fear."

26

harlie's heart hammered so loud it blotted out the sounds of the forest around her. She had been blindly running through the moonlit forest for what seemed an eternity but was more likely only a few minutes. Escaping the house had been a blur, a mad scrambling nightmare to find her way out. Her brain screamed to block out what she had left behind. There was something back there, something she was forgetting. It was important.

Just keep running.

She pushed herself harder, pumping her legs until her calves felt they would burst. It was the wrong move. Her body was too weak from being pent up in a cage for a month. Pushing that hard made her careless. Her shoulder clipped a tree trunk, and she spilled into a sideways spin. Before she knew what was happening, she cartwheeled down a hill. Her arms flailed, desperate to grab hold of something. Her nails raked through mud. The world continued to spin, head over heels. Something hard cracked her on the temple.

It was another tree. The impact wracked her with a blinding pain so intense she could not think. She was reduced to an animal, like a wounded deer lying on its side, panting for air and trying to make sense out of what had just happened.

The moon peered down on the forest, mocking her from between wispy clouds.

"Stop staring at me ya big jerk," she mumbled. The moon was cozy up there in the sky. What right did it have to judge her? No one kidnapped the moon. He was safe. Not like the stupid girl below him who did dumb things and ended up in lousy situations.

"I'd be safe too if I had a cozy cloud quilt." She heard the scorn in her voice from a distance, followed by a sharp ache across her forehead.

Charlie tried to stand. She made it as far as kneeling.

I have to get up, she thought. *Need to keep moving.*

She tried again. This time she braced her weight against the tree, slowly pulling herself up the bark as if climbing. She was on her feet again, one hand holding the tree for balance. She was on a steep incline. *Or is it a decline?* She shook her head. It throbbed with pain. *I need to think straight. It's a damn hill. Which way do I go?*

The climb up looked treacherous. She had fallen a long way down. *Lucky I didn't break my neck.* There were roots she could grab ahold of. A large rock outcropping made her sick to her stomach. *If I'd hit that...* She swooned. *Maybe I should sit down for a few minutes, try to catch my breath before I do something else stupid.*

That dizzy feeling hit her again. Her stomach soured. There was something back at the house. She shook her head, refusing to listen to it. It left her dizzy, gripping the tree to keep upright. Unfortunately, the memory refused to go away. It pushed into the center of her mind.

There had been a sound. Just as she was running out the back door of the house. A sound from the basement. An angry scream.

"He's not dead," she mumbled. That was ridiculous. He had to be. She had planted the bone right into his throat. Nobody could survive something like that.

The angry scream echoed in her mind. It was unmistakable. It was the prince's shouting. He was alive. And he was coming for her.

Icy dread crawled up Charlie's spine like a hungry spider. She had to keep moving. She wiped the sweat out of her eyes so she could focus on the hillside. *I need to figure out a safe path out of here.*

She frowned in confusion. Her sweat felt like sticky sap. She looked down at her hand. Even in the dim moonlight the scarlet color of her blood was unmistakable.

"No, no, no. I need to get out of here," she mumbled, even as the corners of her vision pressed inward with the blackness of encroaching unconsciousness. She took a heavy step forward to deny the blackout, but it didn't care what her needs were.

Charlie fell in a heap against the tree, even as she heard the prince's familiar scream cut through the forest.

"Can't you smell who's in the van?" I asked.

We were a good half-mile behind Sam's goons. We left the highway and hit an old country road a few minutes earlier. We also hit a rainstorm as soon as we burst free from the province. We were in the human realm now. I could still make out the van's rear lights through the rain-streaked windshield. Lobo had switched the wipers on when the rain started. I guess even a werewolf needs a clear view.

"We're driving sixty miles an hour in the rain with an earful of deer horns, and they've got a decent lead. All I smell right now is engine grease and gasoline. Stop pestering us," Lobo grumbled. He had made no attempt to hide his annoyance that I was along for the ride.

"Guess even a wolf has his limits, huh?" I brooded. Yeah, that's right. I can brood too. Lobo's thick exterior might be romantically alluring for all the wrong reasons on a night out at Free House, but barreling blindly after a van full of could-be lunatics was getting my blood pressure up.

"I still can't figure what the heck they're doing this far from the province," Doule said from the backseat. He was a lot easier to look at now that he had donned his backup clothes. "This doesn't fit Sam's MO."

We left Willow's Edge about thirty minutes before. I felt the cold snap of reality, well human reality, as we crossed over the threshold. I wondered what was different about the train that I never felt it before. None of us recognized where we were, just that it was a rolling country road somewhere in Canada. Tae had explained to me that the provinces were not in a fixed place. They crossed over time and space in different places throughout the world. This was my first experience with that actually happening. Another way in which the train seemed to be different, as it always went to the same stations.

"I think I have an idea," I said.

I could feel Lobo's ire as I spoke, but Doule leaned in between the seats to listen.

"You said Sam has been caught before, drugging nubile fae and tricking them into like horrible gangbang situations, right?"

"Until I caught wind of it and almost tore his throat out," Lobo said.

"Well, what if he never did stop? We're always talking about this guy like he's dumb. I don't think he is, though. In fact, I think the bastard's pretty sharp. He was slick enough when he approached me. I felt like I was the one who engaged with him, not the other way around. He played the "I'm just a nerdy nice guy" routine to a tee. That doesn't feel like something a dumb guy can pull off."

"So, he's smart?" Doule asked. "What does that have to do with the human realm?"

Lobo growled. He understood without it having to be spelled out.

"What is one thing the human realm doesn't have that would appeal to Sam?" I asked Doule.

"Shit," he said. "Werewolves."

"The bastard's been taking these girls out to the human realm far from our prying eyes." Lobo punched the steering wheel.

I flinched at his outburst. I could understand it. Lobo blamed himself. If he had ended Sam when he caught him the first time, none of this might be happening. But what was he supposed to do? Lobo and Doule were bound by the same laws they administered. They were agents of the Great Houses, and if they were told to stand down, there was no choice in the matter. It seemed to me the fae realm had its fair share of classist hypocrisy. I thought it was funny how much fae looked down their noses at the human realm when our two races had so many similarities.

"They're turning." Doule pointed.

The van had its left blinker on. It disappeared down a hidden country road.

"Why would they signal?" I asked.

"If you were up to no good, the last thing you'd want is a human police officer to pull you over," Lobo grumbled, jamming down on the gas pedal. "They're lazy as shit when it comes to drugs, gangs, and rape, but heaven forbid you break a traffic law. Fuckers will be on you before you can fart."

We took the turn onto the country road hard enough to make me grab the oh shit handle and hope I didn't pee a little. The road was unfinished, dirt that was rapidly turning into mud under the steady rainfall. It was a narrow tree-lined country road, slim enough that you would have to pull over a little for oncoming traffic. The car fell into a rhythmic jig as it rode over the pocks and uneven terrain. I felt my teeth rattling with each bump. We snaked around a creek and then straightened out.

"There they are," I said, pointing to the right, outside my passenger window.

The van was driving away from us. On a different road.

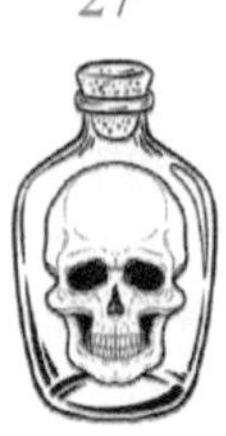

"**C**harlie!"

She woke with a pounding headache. Charlie found her feet and leaned against the tree for balance. She gingerly probed the tender skin around her forehead for the bump. When her fingertip pressed down on the swollen spot, she gasped. It stung like needling herself with electricity. No blood came away. That was good. The dizziness was still there but not as pronounced as it had been before.

Moonlight periodically lit up the forest when it peeked between gray clouds that drizzled rain. It felt like a miracle. It had been ages since she smelled clean air. The rain was light enough to be refreshing.

"Charlie!"

Charlie froze. Her guts flipped inside out. The prince was out there in the woods with her. He was searching for her, and he sounded close.

She spun around in a circle, looking for the way out. The hillside was steep, more of a ravine than a hill. If she went down any farther, she might trip on something. And there was no telling what waited for her down below the tree line. The wound on her forehead throbbed enough. Next time she might not be so lucky to walk away from a fall like that. Better to make her way back up the hill. It was not nearly as far as she had thought before.

Maybe it would be better to stay here and hide? No, that would be suicide. If I stay here, he'll eventually find me. She already knew he had the magic mirror. There was no telling what other evil tricks the prince had up his sleeve.

Her mind made up, she began the treacherous climb back up the steep hillside. She used whatever she could find to help pull her weight, digging her bare heels into the muddy ground. She grasped thick gnarled roots that were slimy against her skin. They were the sort of thing that would have repulsed her in the past. Now she clung to them as if they were her only friends in the world.

"Charlie!" the prince shouted.

Her foot slipped out from beneath her. She slid down the mud for a few heartbeats before snatching hold of a low branch from one of the trees. Charlie lay there, flat against the hillside, listening to the rainfall. It was hard to hear underneath the pounding of her heart. How well could the prince hear in this weather? She tried to recall if she had shouted out when she slipped. The night was silent, broken by the pitter patter of raindrops hitting leaves.

"I know you're out here, my little sweet," the prince called.

She flinched at the sound of his voice. A huddled shape above her seized her with dread. She watched it for a long moment, trying to hold her breath and be as still as possible. It took a bit for it to register in her brain that she was looking at a boulder.

"Stop playing games and get out here," he called.

She couldn't get a good read on where he was, but at least he didn't sound as close anymore. She scrambled on hands and knees back up the hillside, desperate to return to flat ground. Time moved in a blur. She clenched her teeth to keep quiet, focusing on keeping her breathing uniform and calm. She stopped at the boulder atop the steep hill to catch her breath. The hillside below her was a yawning plummet into shadows. She realized once more how lucky she had been not to break her neck in her earlier tumble.

No more of that. I need to think rationally. That's the only thing that's gonna keep me alive and give me some slim chance of escaping these fucking woods alive, she thought. *If I keep letting him run me scared, I'm gonna do stupid things. Like not watching where I'm running. Or like the house. Why did I go into these woods in the first place? The smart thing would have been to run to the front of that place, where the road is.*

Yes. The road. That was where she should have run. She could move faster on a road. And all roads led somewhere. *Like a town!* And there was a slim possibility someone might be out driving at night. Someone she could flag down for help.

"Charlie!"

His insistent voice froze her blood. She realized he wasn't calling her so much as taunting. The prince was a clever one. *He has his little act down slick. He lured me in with that nice smile and those gentle eyes.*

Now he's toying with me to get me to lose my nerve. I can't let him get to me. He's a master at manipulation. I need to stay focused. The road is the answer.

"Come out and play, my little dumpling," he implored with a laugh.

Charlie couldn't get a solid read on where exactly the prince was, but she knew one thing for sure. *He's not near me.* The prince's voice was coming from the south, the way she had been running before she got hurt. Away from the house.

A crazy idea formed inside her. The moon was muffled beneath the grey clouds, like a foggy nightlight. Charlie used that dim light to tread carefully back the way she had come.

That sonuva bitch will never expect me to head back toward the house, she reasoned. *Maybe I can save the other girl, too. I can run down to the basement and free her while he's out here grasping at straws. He'd never dream I'd do something that reckless.*

Her mind reeled at the idea. The things she had seen running out of that house. That was stupid Charlie talking again. That Charlie led her into nightmares. *Stop being a twit. The smart thing to do is find the road, get help, and have the wolves come back to take care of the rest.*

Charlie moved swiftly through the forest. She tread on feet as light as the rain drops coming down around her. She was the daughter of brownies. Her father had taught her how to walk as light as a grasshopper when she was still in diapers. She picked up his lessons like a natural, even if she wasn't a brownie by blood. Oh yes, she knew enough about the world to recognize she was adopted. At the age of eleven she was already taller than anyone in the brownie community. She saw the looks of pity they gave her when they thought she wasn't paying attention.

Nevertheless, her father had always treated her as if she were one of his own. She cherished the time they would spend in the woods, telling her old folktales while practicing brownie skills. No matter how many times she messed up, he was always there waiting to pick her back up again and tell her everything was going to be alright. How she ached to see him just one more time.

She liked to imagine their reunion. It was right in front of her, clear as daylight. He would hug her tight, and she would tell him all about how she had used the brownie steps to sneak out of the woods.

Wait.

The woods were wrong. This wasn't the way back to the house. She stopped to get her bearings. Something rustled behind her. She snapped her head around and crouched low. She held her breath as she scanned the forest. Nothing was there. Shadows of trees, gentle rainfall. Nothing else. She stood to go, and a branch snapped nearby.

Shit.

Charlie broke into a sprint. Something was out there with her. It had to be the prince. She heard his heavy footsteps barreling after her. Branches slapped her face and scraped her skin. Her brain screamed to stay calm, but she couldn't listen. She needed to run. Just keep moving as fast as she could.

A flash of lights ahead cut through the night. Was that a house?

"No, they're moving. It's the road! It's someone on the road," she cried with mad glee.

She stumbled down a short bank. The road was just up ahead. The headlights were moving fast. She would have to hurry to catch them. It was a white vehicle. A van. Her heart surged with hope. She almost fell, flipping sideways in the mud before regaining her balance. She made it to the road. The van was coming around a bend. She could see it through the trees. She waved her arms frantically for them to see.

"Help me!" she cried.

The prince's body hit her in a tackle. They rolled across the dirt right down into the ditch that lined the road on the other side. Charlie flailed about trying to break free from him. If she could scream, the people could still help her. He squeezed her tight as a python, jettisoning all the air out of her lungs. Her forehead hit the dirt, spinning her thoughts in a dizzying wave of pain that radiated from the lump already there.

The van roared past. It was so close. She could have reached right out and touched it. Why didn't they see her? They had to come back to save her.

The prince pressed his cold lips to her ear. "You've been a bad little girl, Charlie."

28

e followed the van in uneasy silence. The forest was broken up by pockets of farmland. It was hard to see the landscape with the light of the moon trapped behind the retreating rainclouds. At least the rain was moving on, petering out to a light drizzle. Fields of corn hungrily swallowed the rain and any dim light from the moon was lost in their stalks. Even in the happiest of times, I have always felt a certain unease around corn fields. Anything could be hiding inside of them, waiting to snatch you when no one was looking. And that was before I knew anything about faeries and werewolves and murdering changelings. I tried to ignore the fields as we trailed the van.

"They're slowing down," Doule warned.

Lobo grunted his agreement. He slowed the car to a crawl, then pulled off to the left. We parked between some trees off the side of the road. Lobo took a minute to turn the car around so the headlights were angled facing the road.

"In case we need to make a quick getaway," he explained.

We were out of the car in seconds. There was no argument about me staying behind. I didn't know whether I should be relieved or insulted that Lobo wasn't worried about my safety.

We moved through the woods like the wind. Well, the pair of them did. I scurried behind and tried my best not to slip in the wet grass. Lobo moved with a grace that was inhuman. There are times I can forget he's a werewolf, but nothing about his agile loping gait through the rain drenched detritus screamed ordinary. The woods fell away to a rolling hill that we quickly climbed. There was an open field beyond that, with hills on all sides.

Doule sniffed the air and broke into a sprint across the field. Lobo raced after him, quickly closing the distance. They were laying on their bellies at the top of the next hill, on the far side of the field, by the time I caught up. Lobo held a hand up to warn me to be quiet.

I stalked up the hill and laid between them. The wet ground soaked into my t-shirt. Their body heat was palpable, like being next to an open fire. That was what it felt like just before Lobo would shift, as if all the cells in his body were boiling with anticipation.

An old two-story farmhouse rested at the bottom of the hill with the side of the house facing us. There was a barn farther to our left and a wide-ringed coral of wooden fencing behind the farmhouse. It looked like an old horse ranch that had fallen victim to the recession. Several of the windows on both floors of the farmhouse were lit. The backdoor was wide open, spilling angled light through the shape of the doorframe onto the grass. The white van was parked in front of the house along with a few other vehicles and a pair of Harleys.

"They're inside already," Doule whispered so quietly I could barely make out his words.

Lobo sniffed the air. "Someone's still in the van." He sniffed again. "A few people, actually. Shit."

Doule growled. Even though I knew Doule would never hurt me, the hairs on the back of my neck stood up. It scared me in the same way a dog growling with its face inches from the side of your head would make you flinch.

"Why are you pissed?" I whispered.

"There are girls down there," Lobo explained.

My heart surged with hope. We had found Charlie and Annabel! "But that's a good thing, isn't it? Just go down there and get them out of the van."

Doule growled again.

Lobo explained, "He's not saying just inside the van. There're girls in the house, too."

My mind reeled at the implications. How many girls were these perverts trapping?

"There are a lot of different scents in that house," Doule said. "Different fae, there's men and women, and *humans*." He spoke the last word as if it were the filthiest thing he could imagine.

"Humans?" I was at a loss. "Why would humans…"

"We fucked up, Lanie," Lobo sneered. "I don't know how I didn't see it before. This whole time we've been treating this as a couple wayward girls that these perverts are drugging to have sex, but it's obviously way bigger than that."

The reality of it hit me like a punch in the gut. "They're trafficking them?" I asked it in disbelief. That was something that only happened in Hollywood movies about angry fathers seeking retribution, right? Except it wasn't.

A documentary I watched one night, a year earlier, alone in my apartment, came back to me. Every year *millions* of unsuspecting people are trafficked. In the US alone tens of thousands of women are sold like they're products. The MO was to grab them when they were fresh off the bus or snatch them at crowded events. The kidnappers would immediately get the women drugged up so they couldn't fight back. Opium is an evil beast. Once the women were addicted, they were easier to catalog and sell.

Naturally, Lobo felt angry. All the signs were right there in our face the whole time.

"He was going to take me that night I met him at Free House." I shuddered with the realization.

Lobo put a hand on my shoulder, his golden eyes a tinge softer. "I never would've let that happen."

"We can't let them sell these girls as sex slaves," I said.

"Humans are involved," Doule said. "It might not be just about sex."

Lobo shot him a cross look. I felt a little warm inside. He was trying to shelter me from something ugly. What could be uglier than selling women as sex slaves? Normally, I would find that annoying, but it was something I could latch onto. Lobo still cared about me, even after I'd blacked out.

"What do you mean? Humans traffic women, too. Don't sugar coat it for me, damnit. What's going on here?"

"Humans do buy fae for sex as well," Lobo said. "Rich cretins looking for an exotic pet, some of them practicing arcane arts. This sort of thing hasn't happened in decades. Werewolves in the Ruby Thickets province shut down a major operation. Not all humans are blind to fae. And even some that are still like to buy themselves a muse, or a woman they think has magical powers. But humans are more likely to be involved when they're buying the fae for meat, Lanie."

"What the fuck?" I swore. Both of them shot angry glances at me. I lowered my voice again. "I'm sorry. But meat? What sort of sick fuck would eat another person?"

Lobo snorted. "You'd be shocked to hear some of the stuff rich humans can get up to."

I thought about it for a few seconds. "Actually, I wouldn't."

"Head's down," Doule said.

The front porch door opened. One man held it as another, the blonde we had seen earlier, went around to the back of the van and unlocked it. He said something I couldn't make out from so far away. It sounded like a short command. Lobo's body tensed up next to me. My heart seized in my throat.

Two girls stumbled out of the van. They had their hands tied and canvas sacks over their heads. The blonde led them to the porch. One of the girls tripped in the dirt and landed on her side. His partner kicked her and barked an order for her to get up. Lobo's heat dialed up to the point of spewing lava. Seconds later they were inside the house, and the screen door bounced on its hinges. Deep bass came from the house. Someone had turned rap music on, and it was wicked loud.

"Fucking pieces of shit," Lobo snarled.

"We need to get in there," Doule said, already slipping his boots off.

"I'm going to rip their fucking throats out," Lobo agreed. His talons were out, tearing the grassy hillside to shreds of upturned dirt. He turned his feral gaze to me. "You're waiting here. It's too dangerous down there for you. We'll try and send the girls out through the back. Wave them up the hill and lead them to the car. When you get them in the car, leave."

I recoiled from him. "I'm not leaving you here."

"Lanie, we don't know how many people are in there," he explained as he kicked off his boots into the grass as well. "These girls, their best chance to survive this is going to be if you get them out of here as fast as possible."

"But –"

"We don't really have time for this," Doule said, already heading down the hill in a crouched lope.

Lobo took both my shoulders in his firm hands and softened his words. "I understand your fear. But this is what werewolves are made for. The only thing that matters is that you get those girls out of here. Promise me."

I nodded, trying to hold back the tears forming in my eyes. "I'll get them to the car."

Dark spatters stained the surface of the butcher block table in some pantomime of a Pollock painting. Charlie had marveled over images of Pollock's work after she had discovered an art book Eli brought from the human realm. The asymmetry of chaotic colors brought to life by a truly passionate hand had thrilled her. It was a distinctly human artistic expression. Ironic how those images would go on to inspire her to pursue her own art, which would inevitably lead her to that tabletop.

Fuck Pollock.

The prince was busy tying her ankles down as he had done her wrists, so she was spread eagle across half the butcher block.

"Why don't you clean your table, you pig?" Her voice was hoarse from having his hands wrapped around her throat.

Her words surprised her as much as the prince. He paused to peer over the tabletop at her and cocked an eyebrow. "The table is clean. Never fear little treat, you shall not fall ill. There are no crusted over fluids or diseased tissues lingering, I assure you. All that remains for you are the memories of pleasant moments."

A piece of her broke inside, unhinged by his lunacy. "I'm not worried about catching a cold, you demented fuck. Why don't you take one of those knives over there and shove it up your ass?"

He pulled the knot tight enough to sting her ankle. He pantomimed a wounded look, but the lie was broken by a creeping smirk he tried to hold down.

"You are a feisty one, I'll give you that. I had a feeling when I first saw you at the last lunar party, watching you squabble with that riff raff of dysfunctional misfits. I said to myself then and there I must taste her sweet, delectable thighs. I prefer dark meat usually, but a dearie such as yourself, a lost little half-blood, there's something to say for splurging on junk food now and again. It can be fun." He caressed her thigh, then gave it a firm pinch. "You certainly haven't disappointed me in that regard."

A freezing tingle worked over her body, but instead of filling her with dread, it fueled her anger and disbelief. How could anyone be so cruel? What kind of a monster could gloat over another creature as they were about to slaughter it?

"I hate you. You're completely insane."

The prince placed a hand to his heart. "Charlie, you wound me."

"Don't you say my name. Don't ever say my name. I'm not a person to you. I'm just your livestock. Go on then, you demented piece of shit. Just do it. Get out your gun and put me out of my misery so I don't have to listen to your bullshit anymore."

The prince scowled. He quickly turned his back to her and moved over to his workbench. Cleavers, meat knives, tongs, and zip ties hung from a metal grate that was chained to the wall behind it. He mumbled to himself as he opened and promptly slammed drawers in the workbench, searching for something.

He's not used to girls talking back to him, she realized. *He usually has them drugged and glamoured by the time they're on his table.* A spark of hope lit inside her. Perhaps there was one last chance for survival in all of this. If she could just bait him into making a mistake. *With your arms and ankles tied to a butcher table, Charlie? Fat chance.* She laughed at the hopelessness of it all as madness descended on her.

The prince's shoulders bristled on the other side of the room, and he growled. He thinks I'm laughing at him. There could be a chance. It was slim, but she had to take it.

"You're a fucking coward," she snarled venomously.

"Oh yeah?" He whirled around to face her.

His face was a mask of rage. She realized how grossly she had miscalculated when she saw the cleaver in his hand. It looked sharp enough to slice a blade of grass.

"You think yourself a clever girl, yes? Let's see what your clever mouth makes of this. Yes, scream all you want. Nobody is coming for you. Do you know why? Because you're worthless. A good for nothing, no better than a rodent or a louse on the back of decent society."

He paused to flick the switch on a radio receiver nearby. Blaring music filled the room to drown out her screams.

Her body trembled with terror. The prince's smile returned as he took his first step toward the table.

The pungent odor of fear made Lobo curl his lips back in disgust. It was a foul scent, like piss and sweat had fucked and given birth to a grotesque child. A normal person knows danger when they encounter it. They might not realize what it is, a feeling of unease, a pit in their stomach, but they know something is off.

A werewolf's heightened sense of smell is powerful enough to track prey up to a mile away. Doule's hackles raised. He caught the scent, too. It was coming from the window above them on the first floor. They pressed tighter against the peeling white edifice of the farmhouse.

Lobo cocked his ear like a dog and listened. Music thumped inside the building. It was so loud he could feel the bass vibrating against the grains of wood. Underneath it was the sounds of many voices.

"This place is packed," Doule whispered.

Lobo tried to focus his hearing, to narrow it down to just the room above them. It took a moment to filter out the background noise. He had it. There were women in there. They were crying. Not all of them. Two maybe three men, breathing heavy and laughing.

"Those sons of bitches," he snarled.

Doule met his gaze. His fangs were out, razor sharp canines nature designed for tearing flesh. Except, it wasn't nature that had created werewolves. He owed his existence to the brilliantly demented minds behind the Court of Shadows. The shadow fae decided they needed a powerful lawman. A creature capable of holding its own against the worst criminals the fae and human realm had to offer. He often wondered what kind of experimentation it took to come up with something as cruel as a shapeshifting wolf man.

He leaned back enough to get a good look at the window without being seen. Leaded glass. The old school kind. Nowadays humans mostly used tempered or plexiglass for windows. Humans were fragile creatures which was ironic given their capacity for destruction. They liked tempered glass. One rupture of the glass would cause a chain reaction across the rest of the pane, shattering it into smaller chunks instead of shards. Less injuries that way. Old leaded glass like the one above was different. When that glass broke it would be into jagged shards that would be begging to dig into exposed flesh.

The gouges did not worry him so much. It was the other side of the window that made him grumble. Four metal bars were fixed to the inside of the window frame. Cold iron, of course. Most fae wouldn't be able to so much as touch that metal without being wracked by pain or weakening. Another benefit of his shifter heritage was the ability to handle cold iron with impunity. It was something the shadow fae worked into them when they created the werewolves, so that they could handle prisoners and build dungeons made of the crude metal. *This is an old house. How sturdy could that window frame be? If I hit the window with enough force, I might just be able to knock the bars loose.*

Doule shook his head, sensing his partner's thoughts. "Can't risk it. If those bars don't give with the first jump, they'll know we're here."

"We need to get inside," Lobo insisted.

"I agree. But there's at least a dozen people inside, maybe more," Doule reasoned. "Our best bet is to surprise them."

Doule's logic buzzed in Lobo's ears like angry flies. His dander was up. The wolf inside of him did not want to hear logic. It wanted to rage, to rend flesh, to punish the bastards responsible and drink their hot blood. He was lucky he had such a good friend in Doule, someone to keep him from devolving into a raging beast. Doule was right. If they rushed in there like wild animals, there was no telling what those cretins would do to their prisoners.

"Right. We'll need to stay stealthy as long as possible, see how many we can take out before the whole group discovers we're here. Our first priority is to get those girls out of there. If we hit them from both sides, we'll have a better chance of blocking both exits, too," Lobo said.

Doule agreed.

They split up. Doule headed to the front porch while Lobo loped around the side of the house to the backdoor. The rain clouds were replaced by wispy grey tendrils fleeing from the angry moon. Lobo felt its light strengthen him, hardening his muscles, and honing his resolve. Sam and his gang needed to be punished for what they were doing. What could be worse than turning another person into a product to be bought and traded like some commodity?

The stark odor of fear was replaced by an acrid smell that stung his nose. *Human cigarettes.* They were an unmistakable odor of aged leaves sprinkled with chemicals and fiberglass. How anyone could inhale that smoke willingly was a mystery. The worst part was how appealing they smelled to Lobo. The cigarette smoke called to him like a siren's call. *Come lose yourself in the depths of my ocean, drown yourself in my cloying delight as I fill your head with a dizzying delirium.* He bared his fangs at it in response.

Lobo pressed himself tight against the building. He peered around the corner, to the back of the house. An old tractor rested between the house and a dilapidated barn. The tractor looked like it had run out of gas one day, and the owner just left it where it stalled out and never came back. Rust, weeds, and two flat tires decorated the tractor. Light cut through the night, spilled across the weedy yard like a wedge of yellow painted earth. The backdoor was wide open. The music was louder there. Men laughed inside the house. Lobo's talons tensed. He wanted to rend them through their laughing flesh.

One of them was in the yard. He was the source of the cigarette. The bastard looked pleased as punch with himself, completely satiated after whatever despicable things he had done inside. He was taking a deep drag of his cigarette, staring up at the moon in silent reverie.

That fire scorched Lobo's brain again. *I'm going to tear him apart and eat his flesh. I'll gorge on his liver and kidneys.* Lobo crouched, ready to charge the man and disembowel him. He paused. *If I pounce just right, I can hit him hard enough to knock that cigarette free. Nothing like a smoke after a nice meal.*

Lobo shook his head, curling his upper lip. What was he thinking? This damnable brain fog was like a curse. It had grown increasingly worse ever since his run in with the changeling. Having someone fiddle around inside his head had left him damaged. Guilt was at the root of it. He had enjoyed the feeling of letting go, falling fully into the raging lunacy that coursed through his blood. For that single hour he was no longer a man-wolf, but fully wolf. A primal being that needed no acceptance or affection. His only need, his sole reason for being, was to devour those around him. It was the most liberating experience of his life.

What the fuck's wrong with me? he thought. *No wonder I scared Lanie away.*

Lanie.

He cocked his head to the side. Lanie was up on that hill watching them, waiting for him to free the girls. She was depending on him. Lobo re-centered himself. *Doule's right,* he reminded himself. *We have to be as quiet as possible if we're going to get these kids out of here. But I already knew that. I shouldn't have to keep reminding myself. Brom's dead. It's just me now. I have to forget that other nonsense. It was a perversion of my mind, not who I really am. I'm here and now. Keep moving like you always do. Just keep moving.*

Lobo pounced.

He hit the man hard, tackling him to the ground. They rolled in a bundle, his hand already clamped over the man's mouth. When they stopped rolling, Lobo had his legs wrapped around the man, one hand still over his mouth and the other twisting his arm back.

"Move or scream and I'm going to break your arm, understand?" he growled in the man's ear.

The guy mumbled incoherently, his hot breath against Lobo's palm.

Lobo clamped his legs tighter and twisted the man's hand so his arm was bent farther than it should go. "Nod you understand."

The man nodded fervently.

Lobo sighed and relaxed his grip a little. "Good, now listen carefully…"

Tension spilled out of the man. He understood. There was no way out of this. He would do as Lobo said or he would die.

Lobo jerked his arm hard, snapping the man's neck in one fluid move.

"Fucking moron," he spat.

He rolled the guy off him and stood, quickly surveying the open backdoor for sounds. Deafening music blared out. With luck it was enough to drown out the sound of their accomplice's tumble in the grass. Lobo grabbed the dead guy's wrist and dragged his body to the tractor, never taking his eye off the farmhouse. He left the man there, tucked behind the tractor's shadows where no one would immediately see.

His fingers stank like nicotine from the man's lips. He pointlessly wiped them across his duster in disgust. It would take days to remove enough of the oily taint from his skin before his canine senses would stop picking it up. Lobo loped inside the house with a grumble, moving like a stalking predator.

The first room was a narrow kitchen that shot off shortly to the left. An exposed lightbulb hung over the sink. The countertops around it were covered with dirty dishes. The rotting food remains swirled with flies. Three fat sticks of incense were burning in a holder on top of a rusty refrigerator. The pungent odor was masking something else he couldn't put his finger on. Thankfully there was no one occupying the kitchen. Anyone standing at the sink wouldn't have seen anything outside anyhow, not with the bright light from the bulb directly in front of the only window in the room.

There was an open basement door on the opposite wall. He paused at the doorway to listen. The music was cranked up high, with a subwoofer that made the old floorboards thump. There was somebody downstairs in the basement. A lot of somebodies actually, but it was tricky to make out exactly how many through the deafening music. He didn't recognize the song. Some human rapper bragging about their wealth and fame while also proclaiming to have a hard life. Humans were weird. The other scent he had detected was down there. Something cloying. He sniffed the open door. A thick miasma of wolfsbane hung in the air.

Bastards aren't as stupid as they look, he thought. In fact, this whole operation was far more sophisticated than anything he would have dreamed Sam could put together. The man was sly as a fox. He'd always known Sam's bumbling buffoon routine was an act, but he'd never suspected the depths of depravity the bastard was getting himself in. Pretty good cover for a trafficking ringleader to hide under. If things ever went tits up, Lobo would never have had him on his top ten list of suspects.

He continued straight ahead, past the basement door on his left and down the central hallway. The living room was at the other end of the hall, with two rooms off to the right on the way. At the end of the hall was the front door and a staircase on the left-hand side going up to the second floor. The hallway doors were closed. Lobo listened at the first door. The basement music thumped across the wood. If he opened the door, he was going to have to do so like everyone else in the world. Blind. He turned the knob as gently as he could. It moved counterclockwise all the way around. Lobo let the door slide open a crack, listening and smelling as best he could. Nothing moved.

He let the door open farther. The room was dark. A bed, some ruffled clothes on the floor, the smell of dust and wolfsbane. There were cold iron bars across the windows. He could smell the foul metal. It was a different room than they had seen from outside, though.

He quickly moved down the hall to the second room. Someone had opened the door since he had entered the room next door. It was Doule. He was crouched over an empty bed, sniffing the air and waving for Lobo.

"Where the hell did they go?" Lobo growled.

Doule shook his head. "Fuckers have the place laced with wolfsbane."

"I know. I smelled it as soon as I came inside. It's coming from the basement."

"I heard someone going up the stairs when I was coming up the front porch," Doule whispered, pointing a taloned finger to the ceiling.

Lobo tilted his head to one side. He strained to focus his hearing on the floor above. The blaring music blanketed everything. Finally, he heard the floorboards creak.

"There's definitely someone up there," he agreed. "Bunch of them in the basement, too."

"Shit," Doule said.

"Yeah."

This was a predicament. With people on both floors, there was no way to determine which level the girls were on. If they picked the wrong floor and anything went sideways, there was a chance the other floor would be alerted. The girls' lives would be in jeopardy. Either the traffickers would make a run for it, taking their captives as hostages, or they might execute the girls to get rid of witnesses. Neither of those scenarios were good. They were going to need to split up.

Doule nodded, knowing what was necessary with the words unspoken. He looked just as chagrined as his partner to part ways. Together they could watch each other's back. There were a lot of unknowns in this house. This was certainly a far more sophisticated operation than they thought walking in. If the traffickers knew enough to drown out the ability to hear and laced the house with wolfsbane, then Sam was sure to have other tricks up his sleeve.

"I'll take upstairs," Doule said, already moving for the door.

Lobo grabbed hold of his arm. "These guys aren't going down without a fight."

"I'll be careful, brother," Doule promised.

Lobo followed him out into the hallway. He felt the wrongness of it as they split in different directions and paused at the kitchen doorway to glance over his shoulder. At the end of the hall, by the front door, Doule rounded the stairs and disappeared.

Fuck, if this isn't one of the world's worst ideas.

He shook his head in frustration and pressed on. Because what other choice was there? These girls were in danger, and their only hope of getting out of this mess alive was two down-on-their-luck detectives.

Without a second thought, Lobo crept into the belly of the beast.

29

I watched Lobo from the hilltop with sick fascination. The first time I ever saw someone die was the night the changeling tried to murder me and my friends. Lobo moved with such brutality, pouncing on the man smoking a cigarette, that it stilled my heart. They tussled in the shadows, and moments later he dragged the man's limp body across the grass. I knew the man was dead. The way Lobo moved was so casual, as if he was taking some recycling to the curb. That bothered me more than the violent swiftness of dispatching another person's life.

Don't get me wrong. I am not shedding any tears over some creep who makes his money trading women like they're livestock. It was just the aloofness of the whole act, like it was a foregone conclusion, which I guess it was. I mean what did I expect was going to happen when two werewolves confronted fae traffickers? But there was no hesitation. No moment where Lobo stopped to think about the life he had just taken. One moment he was crouched, ready to pounce, the next he was moving on to the targets inside the house.

I should never admit this out loud. I feel guilty even thinking it. But I liked it. I was happy those bastards were getting their due. They traded people, destroyed their lives, and broke families apart forever. The psychological ramifications of family members never knowing what happened to their loved ones was something that might never be healed, either. What were those girls inside the farmhouse feeling? How much disgusting depraved shit had happened to them in the last few months? If I was a spitting person, I would have slopped one out right there like an angry cowboy from one of those old westerns.

Fuck these assholes.

I imagined their faces when a werewolf busted into the room, all rippling muscles and bared fangs. I bet they would soil themselves. I played it out in my mind: Lobo busts in as the villain is slapping a girl around. The bad guy turns with wide eyes, mouth hung in awe. Lobo grabs him by the throat. The man begs for his life. Lobo looks to the girl, and she shakes her head no. Commence the blood and gore.

My heart was racing. Vengeance consumed me for a moment, and it was tantalizing. Then, reality set in. Those were people down there. Some of them were fucked up complete pieces of garbage that the world would be better without. But did that justify cold-blooded murder? What about the justice system? How did any of that even work in fae culture? Surely detectives didn't always play judge, jury, and executioner? Was what we were doing right?

I was mired in the moral dilemma of it.

I heard the motors before I saw the vehicles. They came from the road beyond the tree line. I knew something bad was coming before I ever saw their headlights through the woods that skirted the house. This was not some lone car traveling through the countryside at night. This was a convoy. The lights slowed as they neared the bend in the road. I ducked down flat on the grass just as they pulled into the driveway down the hill.

Two motorcycles led the motorcade followed by a slick black SUV. They pulled into place, kickstands thrown and drivers hopping off. They were human! One of them opened the backdoor to the SUV. A tall Korean man got out; his jet-black hair pulled back into a ponytail. Fuck me if he did not look like a stereotypical cliché of a gangster from a Korean crime flick. Except this wasn't some buddy cop comedy. This was real life, as the semi-automatic hanging from a harness across his side informed me in spades. There were six of them, but they moved as one, like a shark cutting around the SUV to retrieve something from the trunk.

Fuck.

Things were going sideways faster than I could think. These guys were the real thing and deadly as cancer. Lobo and Doule were going to get caught completely off guard. This wasn't the movies. Bullets kill. Fae, werewolf, human, it didn't matter. Sure, some things hurt certain fae more than others. But you know what hurts everyone universally? Metal slugs to the chest. You spray a werewolf's organs with enough bullets and they're not getting back up anytime soon.

I was already on the move before I had time to register how absolutely insanely stupid my reaction was. I dashed in a crouch to the left until I had the corner of the house between me and the parked vehicles. Then I sprinted with everything I had for that back door. Dangerous or not, I had to warn Lobo before it was too late.

Lobo crept down the basement stairs, oblivious to the new threats above. The bass thumped in his chest. The music was deafening to his canine ears; he already felt lightheaded. There was a large cache of wolfsbane somewhere down there, and the closer he crept to it, the weaker he would become. It was a precarious position to be in, especially split from his partner. In a normal situation, there would be no way he would move forward without backup close behind.

Just keep your eyes on the ball, he thought. *As long as you don't go waltzing into a room full of that shit again, you'll be fine. Hell, me and Doule have been through worse scrapes than whatever these assholes can muster.*

That lie withered to dust in his brain. This whole situation was as dangerous as a demon's tits. It was all he could do to lean into the lie and let it bolster his confidence enough to keep moving. The stairwell reeked of wolfsbane as he neared the bottom of the stairs. It left his mouth as dry as sandpaper. He quickly looked over his shoulder, half-expecting to see the changeling swinging his club across the back of his skull. These flashbacks needed to go piss off. There were only empty stairs and the walls of a finished stairwell. He almost growled. How long would that night haunt him?

The basement floor was carpeted. Even better to creep across, barefoot or not. There were two directions he could go. The right led to a dark room with a furnace and an old water heater with rusty water pooling around its base. His wolf sight easily cut through the dark. Clumps of wolfsbane dangled from the ceiling above the water heater. His lips curled back to bare razor-sharp canines.

That must be the way to go. Why else would they leave so much wolfsbane in one room? He flexed his fingers, extending talons that were eager to rend the flesh of whoever had hung those wretched herbs. Lobo crept cautiously inside, quickly scanning left then right. There were old paint cans and a boxy ventilated human contraption plugged into the wall. No lights were lit on the equipment, though. It looked like it hadn't been used in many years. The walls were cracked and damp. He felt around them, and even behind the water heater. There were no secret doors, no passages, no hiding holes. The room was a dead end.

Then why put the wolfsbane in here? he wondered. Dust drifted down onto his hair from the ceiling. He stopped to cock his ear. The music made it impossible to hear anything without a ton of effort. He placed a hand to the ceiling. *There's someone up there, though. I can feel them walking around.*

Lobo mulled over the layout of the house that he knew of so far. The bottom of the basement stairs would align, more or less, with the front door. *The room I'm in would be just below the living room. Hmm. Great place to stack with wolfsbane in case a nosey detective comes calling. That's why those fucks have all that incense burning. By the time the poor bastard knew what was happening, they would be springing an attack and he would be as weak as I feel right now. Knowing it's here is one thing, but catching yourself off guard, with no time to pump yourself up... that could be the difference between life or death.*

It was a well-laid trap. Lobo shuffled out of the room, his feet dragging across the carpet. His hands were shaking by the time he reached the stairs again. He risked pausing there for a few minutes, to regain his strength and shake the miasma of wolfsbane from his addled brain. He had to recover quickly. Time was of the essence. He could feel it in his bones. There was something bad going down that he didn't fully understand yet. He hated not knowing what was happening. It made him grouchy... well, grouchier than usual.

He shook the blood back into his arms and flexed his chest. It felt overly macho. *Doesn't matter how I look. I need to get adrenaline pumping to overpower this shit.* He would set the foul stuff on fire if he thought he could get to the girls before the whole house became alerted to the smoke. *Problem is there's no telling what else is down here.*

With a deep steadying breath, he turned the corner of the stairwell and marched down the hall that shot to the left. It abruptly ended in another turn. Lobo pressed himself against the corner and peeked around the wall.

Fucking humans.

Whoever had lived there in the past had remodeled the largest basement room into a dance studio. Humans were sentimental like that. The owner probably had a child into ballet or ballroom dance or some shit that involved jazz hands. They would rearrange their entire world to suit a loved one's dreams. It was one of their more redeeming values.

The far wall was lined with floor to ceiling mirrors. A long rail ran the length of that wall. Sam's gang had appropriated the space with their predictable brand of sleaziness. Black lights hung from the ceiling with a chintzy disco ball in the center. Crushed velvet couches were set up around the perimeter of the room with cardboard boxes stacked behind and on the sides of them. Chopsticks stuck out of some takeout Lo Mein containers that sat atop large floor speakers, the source of the ear-splitting music.

Lobo took it all in with one quick glance around the corner. There were four humans, three men and a woman, dancing under the disco ball. They were dressed like they'd just come from a business meeting. The black light made their teeth glow in a demented parody of happiness. Their eyes were glazed over, glassy and distant with a look he knew too well. They were drugged. Even worse, there were two fae dancing with them in the center of the room. They were young women, half naked with only thin strips of translucent lingerie between their bodies and the gyrating dancers. The fae were completely out of it as well. One of Sam's men, a satyr, was blowing smoke from a hookah into a floor fan that was aimed at the dancers.

The stench of the drug assaulted Lobo's senses.

Shimmer? he thought. *Of course these bastards have shimmer. They're kidnapping and selling their own kind. The next logical step in such depravity would be to peddle shimmer.*

It was a potent drug hailing from darker times. Human wizards were the first to fathom such a monstrous creation. Shimmer was made by grinding the wings or bones of a living fae. The more pain they experienced during the process, the better quality the drug was. Apparently fear released a hormone that latched itself to their blood, which the ground bones would be soaked in. The result? For a human it meant opening a new sight, to see the world of the fae and all of its mysteries. Couple that with a powerful libido and sense of euphoria, and you have a fantastic recipe for addiction. If a fae used shimmer, it heightened their natural powers, sometimes unlocking hidden potential as well. Pureblood families started using it, subjugating the "lesser races" to its creation and using it to bolster their strength in conflicts with other Houses. King Oberon and Queen Titania had long ago banned its use. To be caught producing or imbibing shimmer was a death sentence, even for the long lived fae purebloods.

Lobo glanced back the way he had come. Maybe it would be a better idea to go upstairs and join Doule. Besides the satyr, there was no telling if any of Sam's gang were using the shimmer. That would give them an undue advantage, particularly without them being hampered by the wolfsbane he and Doule were affected by.

One of the businessmen suddenly backhanded the dancing girl. She fell flat on the floor, her eyes still unfocused and glassy. The man laughed hysterically. The girl spit blood onto the hardwood floor, a dark splotch in the black light, then giggled as if in a fever dream. The man helped her back to her feet and pressed her body tight between himself and the female human.

Lobo's veins throbbed with coursing blood. He wanted to kill the humans so bad. *I have to get these kids out of here, damnit.* Everything inside of him urged action. *Dash into the room and take out the satyr first. His throat would feel perfect between my jaws. The spurt of hot blood as his life ebbs out of him would be delicious. The weak humans would probably be too shocked by the brutality of it to act quickly enough.*

He tensed up for the second time that evening, readying to leap around the corner after the satyr.

Wait! Think rationally you fool. Sam has at least four other guys in his little entourage. So far I only know where one of them is. Dead behind a tractor. With the satyr in view, that left Sam and three others still unaccounted for. *It would be madness to go in with claws tearing. If even one of them alerts Sam or his goons, this whole thing gets a hell of a lot harder. And it's already difficult enough. These guys are good. The deck is stacked in their favor. I have to play this cool. Think smarter, Lobo.*

One of the humans danced in front of the stereo receiver responsible for the loud music. All he had to do was hit the power button, or even fall over onto the system in fear, and that would be enough to alert Sam something was happening.

I need to figure out where the rest of his guys are before I attack.

There was a doorway on the right side of the dance studio with one of those accordion style doors from the seventies. The door was folded to one side. Lobo crouched down low to the floor. He focused hard on the smells coming from the hallway beyond that doorframe. The wolfsbane muffled his senses. Now that he knew the source of the wolfsbane though, he could center himself. *That scent is behind me, in the mechanical room. What's down that hallway?* He stubbornly sniffed the air in that direction. *Shimmer, acrid and wrong. Sweat from the dancers. The smell of sex. The satyr's fur matted with sweat. Rust.*

He probed further, demanding his sense of smell push aside each new scent as he encountered it. *Come on, Lobo. You can do this. What is down that hallway?* He strained to cut through the cloying wolfsbane.

There it was. Blood. And fear.

He popped upright, his muscles straining against his shirt. *They've got one of the girls down there for sure.* Lobo dashed into the dance room on all fours, low to the floor. He moved swift as a shadow, darting behind one of the sofas on the closest side of the room. He peered over it. No one noticed him. They were too involved in their drug addled depravity. The satyr laughed and blew more shimmer into the fan. Lobo dashed behind the next sofa and then slipped into the hallway beyond. There was a small lip from the doorframe that he pressed himself upright behind.

Most of the group had their backs to him, but it was still too risky to openly walk down the hall. He used a talon to slowly slide the accordion door shut. Once it was in place, he relaxed a little and surveyed the new area. The hall ended in a large metal door.

No way that was here when the original owners had this place. That door's cold iron was meant to keep out unwanted fae. How the hell do they get that thing open? he wondered. Two other doors lined the hall leading to it, one on either side.

Lobo loped to the first one on the right. He smelled around the wooden frame. Dust. Old clothing. Rotting food. Refuse. No fae. He slowly and firmly turned the doorknob all the way until it disengaged. He pressed the door open a few inches. It was a small room. Old, with a dirt ceiling that roots poked through. This room was outside the border of the house above. Soiled mattresses were huddled together on the filthy floor. This was one of the chambers they kept the girls in. But there were no locks on the door. *They wouldn't need it. Who knows what other drugs they're pumping into these kids to keep them docile.*

He crossed the hall to the second door. This time he could smell the room's inhabitants. *There's at least two people. Fear. Blood. Pain.*

Adrenaline pumped through his veins. For a moment his eyes were blinded with anger. Lobo burst into the room, all caution thrown to the winds of a rage he could no longer keep pent up. In the back of his mind he knew he was making a mistake, but his body refused to listen.

He took in the scene before him in a flash. A naked dryad was chained by the throat and hands to the wall across from the door. Her skin was raw beneath the cold iron bindings. She watched him enter with wide eyes. A panel was fixed to the wall beside her, housing all manner of whips, clamps, and blades. Another kid was chained to the room's left wall. He couldn't have been more than twenty years old. His right eye was swollen shut, a meaty purple welt beneath it. He was crying in pain as one of Sam's guys punched him in the stomach. Lobo recognized the man. He was the behemoth, Horace.

"Is that how you get your rocks off?" Lobo growled. "Torturing kids?"

Horace spun around with lips pulled in a snarling rictus and frothing white at the corners.

He's high on shimmer, Lobo thought, followed quickly by, *Aaand he's a werebear!*

Unlike werewolves, which were bred by the Court of Shadows, other shifters were borne from curses or genetic afflictions. In truth, they were the basis for the arcane magic that the Court of Shadows manipulated to create the fae realms lawmen. Horace's snout was black and furry, his body too wide and taller than the last time Lobo had seen him. His hands were black paws as large as a man's head that ended in deadly claws.

Lobo attacked while he still had the advantage. He sprang from the open doorway onto Horace, swiping his talons for the man's throat.

Fueled with the strength of a bear, Horace backhanded him in midair. It felt like being hit by a Mack truck. Lobo's skull struck the opposite wall. The pain blinded him. He swiped a warding hand out in front of him, certain a follow-up attack was coming. Sure enough, his talons caught Horace's reaching paw, tearing the flesh of his padded palm. Horace pulled back, gaping at his torn paw.

Have to stay on the offensive, Lobo thought, forcing himself to his feet. He crouched and spread his arms wide.

Horace eyed him a little more warily this time, some semblance of realization seeping through the effects of his shimmer addled brain.

"You're that detective from Willow's Edge that's always sniffing around Sam's ass." He chuckled. It was a rumbling guttural sound. "Guess you picked the wrong place to stick your nose this time."

"Come on, you sorry sack of shit," Lobo snarled.

When you live your life as a werewolf, you get used to being the strongest, fastest, and deadliest predator in the room. Lobo realized how deceptive that confidence could be when Horace made his move. Bears aren't just brutally strong, they are also bloody quick. A black bear can run as fast as thirty miles an hour and has jaws strong enough to fracture a bowling ball. Both of these things came to mind as Lobo was suddenly tackled flat to the floor and found Horace's snapping maw lunging for his face. Once those jaws clamped down, it would be game over. There was only one thing Lobo could do. He bit back.

Lobo's extended wolf snout was filled with razor sharp canines capable of doing their own bevy of devastation to a foe. He snapped his neck forward and chomped down on Horace's incoming mouth. This was no lover's kiss. He caught the bear's lower lip with his teeth and tore it in a strip of flesh as his head snapped backward. Horace emitted an inarticulate gurgle and quickly pulled his face away, but that only made his wound worse. It was a wonder the brute kept his paws firmly locked on Lobo's wrists.

"Fucking mangy mutt," Horace rumbled. Dark blood dribbled down his chin and onto Lobo's chest.

Lobo violently thrashed sideways. He bucked his body up and down like a madman. He gnashed his teeth snarling.

Horace rumbled out a laugh. "You're a tough little fucker, I'll give you that. Let's see how the big bad wolf does when he can't breathe."

One of his bear paws released Lobo's right arm and clamped down over his throat instead. Lobo could hardly believe the strength in that one paw. His throat squeezed shut, cutting off his oxygen flow in an instant. He flexed his corded neck, struggling to keep the bear's insanely powerful grip from crushing his windpipe entirely. It was all he could do to maintain his werewolf form. Horace let out a gloating growl in response. He could see what a struggle it was for Lobo to barely keep him at bay.

Lobo raked his talons over the man's muscular arm over and over again, coming away with clumps of fur matted with blood. If the damage of those wounds hurt Horace's shimmer charged mind, he wasn't showing it. His grip didn't loosen at all. If anything, it got stronger, and his torn smile spread wider. He was a sadist to the core. Lobo needed oxygen. The corners of his vision were already darkening. What could he do to break free? He was being choked by a man who delighted in torturing others. Lobo was nothing more than another distraction for him to get off over. The corners of his vision seeped further. Soon he wouldn't be able to see anything.

Lobo's scrambling swipes were getting slower, weaker. Between the wolfsbane hanging in the air and the surprise of grappling with a werebear, he was completely outmatched. *I never should have split with Doule.*

It was at that moment Lobo realized he was about to die.

30

oule stalked silently up the stairs, glad for the dampening effects of the carpet. Even with the blaring music rising up from the bowels of the farmhouse, it was good to have an extra layer of protection from detection. There was no telling how many of Sam's gang might be on the second floor. The upstairs was unlit. A short hallway with two rooms on opposite sides ended in an open window. Curtains billowed with the night breeze.

Doule smelled the fresh air, dewy with rain. The breeze slightly cleansed the wolfsbane miasma from his system. He lingered outside the first door. Sounds of a struggle came from the other side. He worked the doorknob carefully, before letting the door drift open a few inches.

Sam's wiry goon Tyler was wrestling a girl on the bed. Doule recognized her as one of the captives they had corralled out of the van. Tyler's belt jingled as he straddled her on the bed. She was putting up quite the fight.

"Fucking tease," Tyler complained. "Just let that shit settle in, and this'll be so much more fun."

There was a needle on the side of the mattress, and a tourniquet still hung from her left arm. Doule gauged there was no one else in the room. He threw the door open wide and lunged for the bed. He grabbed Tyler's skinny neck from behind, clamping his taloned fingers tight and squeezing.

"Get off her, you sick fuck."

Doule pivoted his weight, thrusting sideways so Tyler was flung across the room into the wall. His head caved in a section of the drywall. He looked to Doule wide-eyed for a second, then slumped to the floor with his eyes rolling in the back of his head.

The girl on the bed scrambled backward until she was pressed against the headboard. She pulled her knees up to her face and cradled them. She was mumbling to herself. "Asshole. Stupid, coward prick."

Doule let his wolf form slip away. The girl was spooked enough without having a werewolf hovering over her on the bed.

"You're okay now," he promised. "We're here. I won't let him hurt you."

"How did you find us?" she asked. "They took us in the van. Put something in my arm." She showed him. Two red needle marks.

Doule sniffed it. "Human drugs," he snarled.

"I feel sick. I don't think it did what they expected."

"Probably not. They wanted you out of it. You're a boggart, right? Human crap isn't going to work on you. You'd think these halfwits would know that much at least."

"He said we were going to a party." She spit toward Tyler's unconscious body on the floor. "Fuck their party."

"I'm Detective Doule from Willow's Edge. What's your name, kid?" Doule asked.

She looked to him like names were a foreign concept. He saw her searching her mind for the answer. "S-Sandy? No. That's my mom. What's wrong with me? Stupid jerks. Gretcha. I'm Gretch – what the fuck?!"

Her eyes popped open, the irises pinpricks staring at something over Doule's shoulder.

He had just enough time to turn his head and register the werebear charging through the open door. Doule tried to move, but the bear was already on him. Its gaping maw clamped onto his shoulder. The room flipped as he was thrown across it. The wall should have broken his fall, but the last thing he saw was his body crashing through it. That and all the blood.

"I'm gonna die," Lobo realized.

The thought felt detached from his situation. It was as if Lobo was floating above himself, watching the grisly scene of his murder unfold like one of Droll's vaudeville plays. He was outmatched and outclassed. That was reality. His body was weaker because of the wolfsbane. Horace was already a behemoth with his werebear abilities. Layer on top of that

Horace's increased strength from the shimmer, and Lobo realized he didn't have a chance in hell of getting through this alive. The muscles in his neck were weakening. It would only be a few more seconds before he could flex them no longer, and Horace's bear paw would crush his windpipe. If he even made it that long. His vision was a smear of blacks and grays. How long had it been since he breathed?

It's going to be weird to be dead, he thought. *I wonder where I'll go. Wish I got to save those kids. I'd feel better about it if they were safe at least. What will Lanie think of me now? Oh shit, Lanie. These fuckers are sure to check out the perimeter once I'm dead. What if they find her? Of course they're going to find her, you ass. Damn it. Why did she get in my car tonight?*

"Who's Lanie?" Horace asked. Lobo must have mumbled her name. "Who else did you come here with? Got a bunch of mutts sniffing around our operation?" Horace gloated. "Don't worry, we'll make good use of you stinking cops. There's a pretty penny to be had for wolf pelts at the knight market."

The world dwindled around Lobo. His time was up. His body was numb. His free hand no longer slashed at Horace's powerful arm. It rested on Lobo's stomach. Lobo focused on that hand. He tried to stretch his talons. He grasped feebly at open air until he found his mark. His talons tore into Horace's groin.

The bear brayed and bent away from Lobo's clutching talons. Air flooded Lobo's stinging throat as he heaved in and out. Horace clutched his bleeding groin, but the weight of him still pinned Lobo to the floor. Suddenly, a pair of legs wrapped around the werebear's throat.

It was the dryad chained to the wall. She flexed her outstretched legs as hard as she could to wrench the werebear back farther.

"Hurry," she urged.

Lobo thrust both of his taloned hands into Horace's mid-section, goring the bear. He worked hard, goring the werebear's entrails in a stinking mass of blood and guts. Horace tried to howl as he was disemboweled, but the dryad's bark-like legs squeezed even harder over his throat. Horace flailed side to side and broke free of her. He staggered off of Lobo and crawled to the side of the room, holding his torn guts and mewling.

Lobo leapt on him from behind. His teeth tore into the sadist's neck. Horace tried to fight him, but too much blood was pouring out. Even with the shimmer he was too weak to fight the mad snap of Lobo's jaws as he tore the werebear's throat and spine to shreds. Lobo lost himself in the kill for a bit, tearing and chewing, lapping hot blood, rending sinewy flesh from Horace's shifted body. He caught a flash of the dryad's eyes. They were filled with terror. It was enough to snap him out of his blood craze. He was there to protect her, to save her.

"I'm not going to hurt you," he lamely promised, stubbornly pulling one more strip of Horace's flesh away with his teeth. Lobo slid to the opposite corner of the small room and slowly shifted back to normal. He laid there gasping for air for a few minutes as he worked his way out of the blood craze.

"I've been searching for you, kid," he finally said. "We came to get you and your friends out of here."

She looked uncertain, her eyes lingering on his chin.

Lobo realized what he must look like to her. *Oberon only knows what the girl has been through.* He wiped Horace's blood from his face with the back of his forearm.

"Let me get those chains off you," he said, finding his feet.

He seized the cold iron chain that connected a manacle to her left wrist with both of his hands and pulled in opposite directions. Lobo's muscles flexed, corded veins rippling under the exertion. In a normal circumstance, he would have no problem breaking such a chain. Werewolves were practically built to cut through such defenses. However, with the large amount of wolfsbane in the area and having just fought for his life against Horace's bear form, he simply did not have the strength.

"All of their gang have keys on them," the dryad said. Her voice was hoarse and tired, more like that of a woman who had seen battle than the teenager she looked to be.

"Right," he said. "Of course, keys."

Lobo went over to Horace's shredded remains. He had to study them for a few moments to decipher which end was what. All that remained of his clothes were strips of blood-soaked cotton. *Wow, I really went to town on him once he was down. No wonder the girl's spooked. How long was I eating this rat bastard?*

It took him a bit, but he eventually found Horace's pockets one by one, sifting through unspeakable remains in his search. He found the key. It was attached to a flimsy plastic keychain with their Skrop team insignia on it.

He dashed back to the dryad and released her neck manacle. She gasped for air with it gone. The skin around her throat was raw from the despicable metal. A little light entered her eyes as she took deeper breaths. Cold iron can feel like it's suffocating a fae. Lobo quickly freed her wrists in turn. The girl slumped forward against him.

"Steady now. It's going to take a while before you feel normal again. Cold iron's nasty stuff."

"I'm so dizzy."

"That's the dampening effect of the cold iron being removed. Your essence is realigning with the universe. I've got you."

She pushed away from him, staggering backward with the key in her hand. Lobo hadn't even felt her take it. *Damn kid's a pickpocket.* He would have laughed in admiration at how slick she lifted it if not for the gravity of the situation.

"I have to free Dacha."

"Okay, of course we will," he said gently. "But you can't touch that cold iron. Give me back the key so I can unshackle Dacha."

She looked at the key in her hand as if it was an alien artifact. The girl didn't even realize she had lifted it from him. She sheepishly handed it back to Lobo. "The drugs," she said sluggishly. "They're always poking us… needles. It's horrible. Hard to think most time."

Lobo took the key and fell to work releasing the beaten boy from his shackles. "Well, you're a tough lass. Fought through that shit well enough to leg wrestle that bastard. I owe you my life."

Dacha fell limply to the floor before Lobo caught him. He was light as a branch. He shifted the kid so he was sitting upright with his back pressed against the wall. He was a spectre, a fae who could move through lights and create dazzling rainbows. Spectres were known for having a sunny disposition that was uncanny. To see one so badly beaten was heart breaking.

"You're safe now, baby girl," the dryad crooned, cradling Dacha's forehead against her chest. "The detective is going to get us out of here."

Dacha looked dreamily up at her. "Krysta?"

A tear strolled down Krysta's cheek. "Yes, dear. It's me."

"Wait. Your name is Krysta?" Lobo asked. "Not Annabel?"

She nodded, pressing Dacha's head against her bosom and stroking their hair. "Krysta Arabel. I'm from…" She struggled to think.

"You're not Annabel? Annabel Silf, from Willow's Edge?"

Krysta's eyes shot open. "Oh goddess! Annabel!"

Lobo leaned next to her and readied to catch the girl. She swooned as if she were about to faint.

"What is it, girl? Do you know Annabel? Is she here too?"

"The cold room. The prince, he took her to the cold room."

"You mean that big metal door at the end of the hall?"

Dacha whimpered and Krysta whimpered at the mention of the door. Krysta peered at Lobo with terror-stained eyes. "Today was her day. Sam promised. They're making her into shimmer."

"Shit."

Lobo eyed the open door to the hall. He needed to get into that room before Sam cut the girl to pieces. He might already be too late. Maybe those humans were here for more than a little light dancing. They were known to buy fae organs.

But how am I going to free her? I can't leave these kids here alone and defenseless. He knew he needed to figure something out and fast. Time was of the essence.

That's when the gunshots began.

31

I don't know what rare brand of stupidity compelled me to rush headlong into that house.

Running that fast in a long skirt was a pain in the ass. I knew I could get to the house before the new arrivals. Put me side by side with any professional runner, and chances are I can match them step for step. It's this weird ability I've always had. Now I understand it's due to my unicorn bloodline. In boarding school, the athletics teachers were always trying to talk me into running on their track teams. The problem with that was I have absolutely no desire to run. It's exhausting. I get out of breath, my muscles feel like they're on fire, and I get all sweaty. I hate being sweaty.

I cut across the field in record time, well before our newly arrived and fully armed surprise guests entered through the front door. I was panting by the time I crossed the threshold of the back door. I paused in the kitchen to catch my breath and get my bearings. It was a tiny affair with barely enough room to prep food, let alone cook. The sink was overflowing with a gross pile of dirty dishes. Loud music came from an open basement door. I could sense the armed men climbing the front porch.

What was I going to do? *What was my brilliant plan?* I thought. *Run into a house of depraved traffickers with no weapons and no way of knowing where my friends are?* It seemed a no brainer a few moments ago. Warn Lobo before these guys got the jump on him. But how? Where the heck was he? Judging by the staircase at the end of the hall by the front door, there were three levels to the farmhouse. So which was he on?

Do I call out his name? What if that blows his cover? What if he's sneaking up on someone and I screw it up? Shit. Shit. Shiiit. Why did I do this? I need to hide.

Panic fell over me as the reality of my foolhardy plan set in, but it was too late. The front door opened down the hall. I glanced around me. There was a chef's knife sticking out of the dirty dishes. I snatched it up. Remnants of food clung to it that I wiped off on the edge of the counter before I realized how moronic that was. *Better make sure the blades clean before I stick it in someone.* My stomach flipped at the idea of having to follow through on that. I could hear the men shuffling into the front room.

I can't use this. Isn't there a saying? Don't bring a knife to a gun fight?

My entire plan buckled before my eyes. I needed to get out of there. This whole thing was a huge mistake. I quickly dashed for the open back door. I've never been known for my good timing; just as I reached the door, the music in the basement went silent.

"Hey!" someone shouted. His voice was immediately followed by the telltale click of a readied gun.

I froze in place, my back to them.

"Where are you going, little faerie girl?"

Oh crap. The knife was still in my hand. I quickly slid it into my right pocket, tearing the fabric and poking myself in the leg.

"You hear me talking to you? You speak English?" the man at the end of the hallway asked.

By the sound of it, he wasn't being cheeky. It made sense. Did all fae speak English? It was a legitimate question.

"Looks like one of their strays is running away," another man said.

His voice was as cold and indifferent as a dead body. The sound of it made my skin crawl.

"Just shoot her in the leg, and we'll sort it out with Sam."

My hand shot up in surrender out of reflex.

"Ah, so she does speak English."

I winced. There was no way I was getting out of this, and I was pretty sure bullets moved faster than me, awesome runner or not.

"Come over here," the cold voice commanded. "Now."

The music kicked back on from the basement. It was a new album with loud bass thumping the floorboards. I slowly turned around to face the hall, my hands still raised high. A short Korean man had the muzzle of a mean looking handgun trained on me. I immediately knew who the other speaker was. He stood beside the gun wielder. He was the man I'd seen from the hill. He had long jet-black hair, dead eyes, and a semi-automatic weapon hanging from his side.

"I was just going out back for some fresh air," I said, slowly walking down the hall toward them.

Dead eyes laughed. You've never heard such a harsh sound, like sandpaper scraping across glass eggshells. There was no mirth to it, only scorn.

"You mean running away."

These guys weren't part of Sam's crew. They were professionals. The five of them moved as a unit as I entered the stuffy living room, like a swarm of hornets circling their food.

"Put your hands down, silly girl," the gunman ordered.

Dead eyes grabbed me by the arm and yanked me closer. He wanted to inspect me. He penetrated me with his hawkish gaze in a way that left me feeling unclean. It was difficult to meet his eyes, like if I stared too long I might see all the horrible things he'd done in the past. And he wanted me to see them. He had a cold gaze, indifferent to the world around him other than how that world could be manipulated to serve his whims. The guy fucking terrified me. He knew that. And he enjoyed it.

He brushed my hair out of my eyes. His fingers were soft. They shouldn't be, not with what they've done. They should be hard and calloused and blood-stained, but they were smooth and smelled like lemons. He smirked at me.

"She's a pretty one. Not the usual trash Sam peddles." He forced me to turn in a circle. "What are you?"

I flinched and fought tears from welling up in my eyes. His fingers brushed my spine. I could feel the heat of them seep through my clinging top.

"No wings." His palm slid slowly down my back until he reached my waist. "No tail, either."

His face was suddenly near my neck. I flinched, certain he was about to bite me. He smelled my skin.

"Interesting. You're no fae I've ever seen. I'm intrigued. What *are* you?"

"Yong-Gi?" a heavy voice called.

We all turned to see a beast of a man overlooking the living room from the stairs to the second floor. He was a behemoth with shoulders wide enough to fit a man and half between them. Remnants of a shirt hung from his shoulders. A massive tear down the center of his shirt revealed a torso matted with black fur.

Yong-Gi's men bristled at the sight of the monstrous arrival. Evidently they too were shocked by his appearance. Their leader casually put me behind him and raised a hand to calm his men.

"Kezin, we almost didn't recognize you in your other form. What a pleasure for us to view. Having a spot of trouble, are we?"

Kezin grunted exactly like a bear. He trudged down the stairs with heavy footsteps that made the floorboards rattle beneath the carpet. Something thumped after him. Something he was dragging.

"We weren't expecting you so early," Kezin said, clearly trying to recover from his surprise. "There's no trouble. Nothing we can't handle."

There was nowhere I could run. They had backed me into the corner of the living room. My only escape was to hide behind a sofa with a quilted blanket thrown over it or an armchair with dark blotchy stains on the seat cushion. Yong-Gi's men were all focused on the behemoth trudging toward them. There was a tension among them. I noticed several of them kept their hands close to their weapons. I had already been forgotten as if I was nothing but a minor amusement that had lost their interest.

Kezin rounded the stairs, but I couldn't get a good look at him around Yong-Gi and I didn't dare try. I was trying to make myself as small as possible. I needed to buy time to make a run for it.

"What do you have there, then?" Yong-Gi asked coolly. "One of your girls get out of line? We're not paying for her if she's broken."

"Don't sweat it," Kezin rumbled. "He's not for sale anyway. Not yet. He was a... *distraction*. Hang tight; I'll go downstairs and get Sam for you."

One of Yong-Gi's men said something to him in Korean, and his body tightened up. He replied in Korean, and suddenly the entire room shifted. All of his men trained their guns on Kezin.

Kezin stopped. A deep growl rumbled inside of his chest. "What is this bullshit?"

"You tell me," Yong-Gi said. "Werewolves are lawmen in your land, are they not?"

Holy shit. The thing Kezin had been dragging was a werewolf. I couldn't get a good look at him, but the room suddenly felt like it was closing in around me. This monstrous person had taken out one of my dear friends.

Kezin chuckled. "Is that all? Yeah, he's a cop. So what? Does he look like he's going to be causing any trouble for us?"

My heart raced, and I groaned.

Kezin frowned. "Who's your little friend back there?"

I felt the weight of the room shifting toward me. Once the attention was on me, it was all over. Not only were my friends in grave danger, but I was about to join them. The only fate waiting for me was a needle in the arm and unspeakable horrors. I moved with blinding speed. The knife slid out of my pocket as if it had a life of its own. I pressed it to Yong-Gi's throat. His men started shouting in Korean. Some pointed their guns at me, others at Kezin.

Yong-Gi slowly lifted his hands for his men not to shoot. I pressed the blade so tight against his throat it drew a line of blood. There was no halfway to a decision like that. I had no doubt someone of Yong-Gi's size and apparent criminal capacity could flip me over if he wanted to. I intended to make sure he would receive a permanent neck grin if he tried.

"What the fuck?" Kezin gaped.

"Call off your girl or we kill everyone in this house," the short man who initially trapped me ordered, waving his pistol in Kezin's face.

Kezin dropped the weight of the body he'd been dragging. Doule groaned on the floor, blood oozing from a gash across his forehead. Kezin's eyes centered on me in shocked recognition.

"You're that girl from Free House. But what are you doing here?"

I pressed the knife tighter against Yong-Gi's throat, forcing him to move with me as I shuffled backward toward the fireplace. "You can drop the act, boss. I got him like you wanted. You were right." It was my turn to press my lips close to Yong-Gi's ear this time. "He's a sucker just like you said. Let a little girl like me get close enough to kill him."

The Koreans lost their shit. They started shouting and waving all their weapons at Kezin. Doule crawled across the floor behind Kezin, making his way for the porch.

"What are you playing at?" Kezin rumbled at me. His body rapidly expanded, muscles rippling and growing, fur thickening. A toothy snout erupted from his enraged face.

"Oh shit," I gasped, my trembling hands loosening on Yong-Gi. It was all the space he needed.

In the blink of an eye, I was flying head over heels. I hit the couch upside down. Somewhere in that tumble I lost the kitchen knife.

Kezin's growl grew louder.

"Kill this motherfucker," Yong-Gi ordered.

Yong-Gi's men sprayed the room in a hail of bullets.

32

"What was that?" the prince rumbled.

Charlie froze, her ears open wide. Something loud had cut through the music. It sounded like firecrackers. It came from the hall beyond the massive metal door.

The prince growled and stretched talons from the tips of his fingers. He flicked off the loud music and listened at the closed door. Something crashed just outside the room.

Charlie's heart soared with hope. Someone was there to save her! She shook her hand, trying to free the rope binding her wrists.

The prince slid the large metal door open. His body was bent over, ready to pounce on whoever had come into his house.

"Watch out!" Charlie screamed. "He's coming for you!"

The rattling cacophony of gunshots coming from upstairs set the hairs on Lobo's arms on end. A gunshot is a peculiar sound, like a sharp biting firecracker dropped in a steel kettle. The first few shots were followed by a staccato of insanity, bullets fired, bear roars, heavy thuds, and screaming. Whatever was happening upstairs took a deadly downward spiral in seconds.

"Doule," he growled, turning back to the dryad. "Krysta, I have to go help my partner."

She was shaking and clutched Dacha to her chest. "What about us?"

Another volley of gunshots rang out. The music in the dance studio was cut off. There was a commotion in that room. Lobo would not have much time before the humans and the satyr were added to whatever madness was unfolding above.

"I need to get to my partner. It sounds like he's in serious trouble," he called over his shoulder, already springing for the door. "You stay here with Dacha, help them back on their feet and wait for me to come back."

He hit the hallway running. His body slammed into someone else who had the same idea, a man who had been coming from the far end of the hall. Lobo's weight slammed into the man, tackling him sideways into the wall. Lobo's legs got jumbled underneath him. They rolled across the floor together. He quickly shoved away from the man and sprang into a snarling crouch with talons splayed wide.

It was Sam.

The cold iron door at the end of the hall was wide open. Lobo could see a girl's feet dangling from a table inside. She wasn't moving. His heart sank.

Sam sat up, clutching the back of his head. "Damn man, watch where you're running." His eyes popped open when he saw who he was talking to. "Detective Lobo?"

"Surprised to see me, you piece of shit?"

Sam quickly recovered and chuckled. "Nah. Figured it was a matter of time before you stuck your snout in our business. Man, it's going to be a bummer having to kill you. I always enjoyed our little games around town."

Footsteps hit stairs on the other side of the basement. The humans were fleeing. Lobo growled. "I'd love to stand around and shoot the shit, but it sounds like my buddy might be tearing your friends apart up there."

Lobo lunged across the space between them. His talons tore into Sam's shoulders as he bowled him into the wall. Sam's body rapidly changed. At first it was pudgy and malleable, but by the time they bounced off the wall, he was already solid muscle, his face protruding into the yawning jaws of a bear.

Sam clacked his teeth trying to eat Lobo's face. Lobo slammed him into the wall again, smacking the back of Sam's head on the concrete. Sam's eyes glazed with pain.

"What the fuck?" Lobo said. "Didn't I already kill one of you werebear freaks? What did you and pal get bored one night and decide to go get cursed together? What's next, matching tattoos?"

Sam's muzzle shifted back into his normal face. He was wearing that shit-eating grin of his.

"What the hell do you think is so funny?" Lobo snarled, shaking him with each word.

"You think there's only two of us?"

"What?"

A menacing rumble came from down the hall behind Lobo's back. It was the satyr who had been overseeing the dancing humans. Krysta and Dacha were still in the room across from him, clutching each other in terror.

"We've all been blessed by the spirit bear, detective," the satyr said.

Something loud broke upstairs followed by a scream. Another volley of gunshots. Sam's body slipped out of his grasp, sifting into a cloudy form as he used his fae magic to blink. Lobo had just enough time to register his shock before the satyr, turned werebear, tackled him sideways into the wall.

I had no idea about the impossible odds Lobo was facing downstairs. It was all I could do to simply keep moving. I haven't been around many gun fights. By many, I mean zero. I have been around exactly zero gun fights, like most average Americans, despite our reputation. When a gun goes off it's not just loud, it's jarring. A ringing covered everything I heard, and I felt each bullet in my chest as if my body was bracing for the impact. The best thing I can compare it to is being underwater. More bullets are shot, and people are screaming while a murderous werebear goes on a drug-induced rampage, but I heard it all muffled beneath an incessant ringing.

Kezin made short work of the first two thugs. One of them had his face stuck in the drywall; his body hung like a limp doll. The other was thrown through the front door.

Somewhere in the chaos I managed to crawl behind the beaten-up armchair. It didn't afford much cover from the bullets being sprayed around the room. Kezin slammed one of Yong-Gi's men over his knee. His spine sounded like splintered wood. The screaming man's gun slid across the carpet. I thought about grabbing it, but so far their weapons hardly seemed to matter against the werebear.

If they can't take him down, what the hell chance do I have? I thought. I couldn't even tell you where the safety is on a gun. *I think it's a little red button. Or is that just something I made up from watching too many cop shows? Yeah, nope. Not worth risking my life over.* My only option was to try and get out of there while they were all distracted fighting each other.

One of Yong-Gi's men straddled Kezin's shoulder from behind as the monstrous beast tossed his broken companion aside.

"Go for his throat!" Yong-Gi ordered, ducking a paw swipe from Kezin.

I saw something move out of the corner of my eye. Doule had found his way behind the nearby sofa. I quickly scrambled over to him on hands and knees.

"Oh no, Doule. What did he do to you?" His face was a pulpy mishmash of bruises and cuts. A chunk of his ear was missing. "Did he eat your ear?"

His lips moved, but I couldn't make out the words between the ringing and the vicious battle. His body was shaking. I pulled his head up on my knee and hugged him.

A radiating wave of energy wafted off Doule. It was a strange sensation. I got similar feelings from time to time when I was helping someone in the apothecary. That energy usually guided me to what they needed, what herb or concoction would be just right to alleviate their pain. It has something to do with my unicorn blood, something I don't yet fully understand. This time the energy was telling me Doule was dying.

No, that can't be right, I thought. *Werewolves can't die like this, not unless silver is used against them.* I pressed my hands flat against Doule's temples and reached out with the trickle of magic that had been seeping out of me since holding the relic. He wasn't hurt by silver. *It's...*

shit... what is that? There's something blocking your werewolf ability to heal, but what?

Doule's lips moved.

"Wolfs...?" I voiced his word, trying to decipher it. What about wolves? "This infernal ringing is making it hard to think." *Damn this curse. At least in my shop I could use the church roses to bolster my ability. Wait. The church roses!*

I was wearing the same jacket I had on the night of the party in the woods. I reached into my pocket and found one of the rosebuds I'd gathered from underneath the bridge. I crumpled its petals in my hand and stuffed them in my mouth. I swallowed them down in a dry gulp. My stomach warmed as the magic did its wonder. Bolstered by the rose's power I was able to see Doule's aura clearly. He was suffering greatly and on the verge of death. His body was floundering to access his healing magic, but something was in the way. It was a miasma of sickly smoke that was coming from just beneath our feet.

It finally hit me. *Wolfsbane! Of course, that's one of the only things that could weaken Doule or Lobo's abilities. If I could only access my magic, I could heal Doule's wounds.* The power of my unicorn blood made me particularly adept at healing. However, with the curse smothering my abilities, I was practically powerless. My friend's body spasmed. Blood came from his lips. Dread seized me as I realized I was going to watch as Doule died in my arms.

Was this what my life had been reduced to? A series of events where I would be forced to watch helplessly as the people I cared for were taken away one by one? First it was Sacha at the church, then finding my best friend Deedee tortured and comatose. Was I to now lose Doule as well?

Kezin roared as Yong-Gi soared backward into the armchair. The chair flipped over on its side. His semi-automatic came up almost immediately spraying bullets. One of them went through the couch, skimming my shoulder and burying into the wall by my head.

I screamed in pain.

Kezin finally got a good hold of the man on his back. He flipped him over, hurling him into the window above me. Glass rained down over us as the man crashed through it. His body hit the outside porch with a solid thud. Suddenly, the couch was tossed aside. Kezin towered over me. He crouched down and roared in my face, his bear lips peeled back away from giant fangs. I covered my ears and closed my eyes tight. It was too much. This was not how the world should be. All of it was wrong and dirty and depraved. My stomach felt like it was on fire. I screamed my denial, knowing Kezin's teeth would be buried in my flesh any second. Something inside me broke loose.

I felt like a broken bauble. My insides unhinged and let loose a ball of fire. That ball grew rapidly outward, spinning like a tornado. It was my will. I wanted to cleanse the world of all that pain. An orb of light burst from my body, rapidly expanding like a soap bubble across water. It was a rainbow membrane, translucent and brilliantly glowing. My light washed everything dirty away from the world. It was blinding and pure. It was me. I didn't know how I created it or what I should do with that power. All I knew was I did not want Doule to die. I wanted to heal him, to cleanse everyone. I didn't want to be surrounded by all that pain and hatred anymore.

My light swept even the monstrous Kezin off his feet.

It expanded like a shockwave until it reached the walls of the house and popped. When the light cleared, I was left as weak as a mewling kitten. I fell over onto my side and could only watch the world around me. There was no ability to move. I could only lie there and breathe. All my energy had been dispersed like a firehose, in one giant gout.

Kezin mumbled something and sat up. He was still a werebear, but that glassy insanity was gone from his eyes. Whatever drug he had been on was dispersed from his system. Yong-Gi crawled from behind the armchair, blinking and looking around the room in confusion.

Something rumbled against my leg like a sleeping cat. Doule rose to his feet. His cuts were rapidly healing before my eyes. My magic was healing him and had washed all the toxins out of the house. The wolfsbane no longer had a grip over him.

"But how did you –?" Kezin asked, dumbfounded.

Doule, in full werewolf form, leapt on him. They rolled across the living room. Without the drugs and no longer hampered by the wolfsbane, Doule was quickly beating Kezin senseless. I had just enough time to register that I had helped before I blacked out.

Of course, I had no way of knowing what special level of hell my magic had unleashed downstairs.

257

33

shockwave of magic had hit the basement like a tsunami. Everyone was tossed against different walls as the bubble of expanding light hit them.

Lobo came to his senses to find Sam lying on top of him, half transformed and mumbling incoherently. He felt like he had just gotten the world's best nap. The wolfsbane no longer dulled his senses. Any weakness he had felt in his muscles from his near-death battle with Horace was gone as well. It was a miracle.

He had seen exactly this type of magic once before, on a far smaller scale. "Lanie." He grinned.

He let her power course through him, muscles expanding, fur thickening, and mouth turning to muzzle as he transformed. He tossed Sam away and got to his feet.

"What in the nine circles of hell was that?" the satyr behind him groaned.

Similar sentiments came from over his shoulder. The kids in the dance studio at the other end of the hall were getting to their feet.

Before Lobo could respond, Krysta leapt from the torture room screaming like a banshee. She swung an engorged wooden fist at the satyr. The dryad's fist and forearm were three times larger, covered in overlapping layers of freshly grown bark. Her fist slammed into the satyr's gut before he could so much as blink. Dryads are known to be gentle souls, only growing malevolent if their mother tree is threatened. Befriend them and they were sure to nurture you with unsurpassed kindness and connection to nature. Piss one off and you would be facing a world of hurt.

The blow was powerful enough to toss the satyr on his back. He slid into the dance studio cussing up a storm. His hand slapped down with a transformed bear paw to stop the momentum. At the same time, two massive, black-furred arms wrapped around Lobo from behind. Sam bear-hugged him, lifting him off his feet with a rumble.

"Don't know what the heck kinda spell your partner pulled upstairs, but it didn't work," Sam goaded.

Lobo was forced to watch as the satyr rubbed his stomach and growled from a rumbling bear snout. "That actually stung, you little bitch."

"Not so easy when we fight back, is it pig?" Krysta shouted.

"You may have gotten a lucky shot in, girlie," the satyr said. He spit some blood to the side. "But did ya really think a wee thing like you could take me on all on yer own?"

"Who says she's alone?" Lobo snarled.

Sam chuckled up at him. "That's rich. You really think you're in a position to help her, wolf?"

"Wasn't talking about me," Lobo growled.

The satyr had just enough time to glance over his shoulder in surprise as the two fae dancers, unshackled from their drugged stupor by Lanie's magic, fell on their captor. Krysta rushed in to help them. Her arms stretched like the roots of a great tree. She snared the satyr's ankles with those tendrils and pulled hard, knocking him onto his back once more. One of the smaller fae, a pixie with shimmery wings, leapt on his chest screaming. She jammed a chopstick from the takeout Lo Mein right into his eye.

Sam loosened his grip as he gasped at his friend's plight. Lobo wrenched his right arm free of the werebear's hold. He slapped his hand over his shoulder and raked his talons wildly about. Sam roared as he let Lobo go, leaning away from the danger. Lobo hit the ground on his toes and spun around swiping his other hand toward the werebear.

But Sam was gone. A hazy cloud of purple smoke marked where he had been. It was the power of a blink, a fae who teleported at will. They called it blinking. Sam would be able to blink anywhere he wanted as long as he could see it. Fortunately, that meant he couldn't have gone too far.

Lobo darted his head back and forth waiting for Sam to reappear farther down the hall. A soft popping sound came from behind him. He tried to spin around in time. Sam was faster. He swung both his paws down at once. The attack would have hit Lobo in the top of the head if he hadn't desperately dodged. Instead, the devastating blow crushed his collar bone.

Lobo went down hard, but he was too stubborn to let the flaring pain in his shoulder stop him. He slashed his talons at Sam's furry leg. Tendons were torn. Sam roared. Lobo rolled away from him as the werebear's paws crashed down a second time. The floorboards splintered under Sam's impressive assault. Lobo was forced down on all fours. That was fine with him; he preferred to move that way, anyhow. His collarbone was rapidly healing under the magic of his werewolf blood. He swiped another taloned claw out for Sam. It raked across his bear paw. Lobo felt his claws tear through one of Sam's fingers. The bear howled as the severed appendage dropped to the floor. He cradled his hand in agony.

Lobo tensed his muscles to pounce. The satyr in the dance studio was screaming in agony. Lobo snapped like a rubber band, flinging at his prey all claws and teeth. The air he hit was purple. The smoke of Sam's blink tasted like sulfur. Lobo hit the hall in a roll, skidding and already spinning back around.

Sam was stepping out of another portal, his jaws open wide as he fell straight down from the ceiling above Lobo.

"Shit," Lobo snarled.

A werebear can weigh as much as its more common forest dwelling cousins, upwards of six-hundred pounds of muscle. That was enough weight to crush Lobo and break every bone in his body. He desperately scrambled across the floor even as Sam fell over him. Sam pinned his leg. Lobo heard his femur snap seconds before he felt the blinding pain. It was a strange, muted popping sound for so much pain.

"Oops, that sounded like it hurt," Sam goaded. His bear paw dug into Lobo's shoulder, just where his collarbone was mending. The pain was excruciating. "You know, I really should be thanking you. After all, it was you who gave me the idea to become a werebear. After you beat me senseless in that alley, I vowed to never be that weak again. Cost a pretty penny too. So, you see, I've been looking forward to this. When I'm done with you, I think we'll make a nice wolf pie out of that smug face of yours. I'm going to serve it to those brats in the other room after I punish them for hurting my friend."

"You talk too much," Lobo growled.

Lobo snapped his teeth down on Sam's forearm. He bit as hard as he could, forcing his canines through muscle and sinew. Sam roared, trying to shake him loose. His blood tasted wonderful, then it tasted like a mouthful of sulfur. Lobo choked on the leftover smog from Sam's blink.

Sam growled like a cornered bear. His back was to the dance studio. Lobo flipped back onto all fours but spilled sideways. His leg was broken. It was going to take a while to mend, even under his considerable healing magic. Sam licked his torn forearm like an animal in pain, but his angry eyes remained alert on Lobo. The three captives were locked in a fierce battle behind him. None of them would be coming to Lobo's aid anytime soon.

Sam's braying laugh shook him. "Face it, mutt," he said. "You're outclassed and overpowered."

"How's your forearm feel?" Lobo snarled.

"Already healing," Sam said sourly. "That's the beauty of the werebear curse. Just like you, I'll heal. Except soon my wolfsbane will be seeping back in here. Did you know wolfsbane doesn't impact werebears? It's not called were-bane, right?" Sam chuckled at his joke. "When that hits, you'll be weak as a baby again while I'll still be strong as a…" He left it open for Lobo to answer.

"Limp dick?" Lobo said.

The lips of Sam's bear snout pulled back to reveal his fangs. "Go ahead, take your shot. There's nowhere you can go where I won't blink."

Lobo sprang forth. The pain in his leg was blinding. He fell flat a few feet away from Sam's blinking cloud. The werebear appeared on his side, already stepping from another portal. He swiped a paw down to pin Lobo's chest.

Except Lobo was already rolling toward him. He had expected the maneuver when he faked his fall. Sam had just enough time to register his mistake before Lobo sprang from the floor and hit him in the chest. Sam's back hit the wall as Lobo wrapped his legs around his torso. The werewolf raked his talons across Sam's face.

"Going to be hard to blink with no fucking eyes," Lobo snarled.

Sam howled in agony as his vision was torn away. He desperately tried to blink. Smoke sifted from his pores. He went nowhere. He needed to see to blink. He was trapped.

Lobo's teeth tore at his throat. The werebear roared and tried to pry him loose. Lobo was tenacious, tearing and gnawing at his flesh. Sam slid sideways down the wall, blindly swiping his bear paws in front of him. Lobo ducked under a swiping paw and came up like a piston, slamming his forehead into the base of Sam's snout. Sam's eyes rolled back in his head. He was knocked out before he even hit the floor.

It would be such a simple thing to finish the job. Lobo could tear Sam's throat out with one swipe. He growled as he fought the urge. Sam needed to be brought to justice for what he'd done. There were too many questions that needed answering about this whole thing, the shimmer, the fae trafficking, the human involvement.

The satyr's screams of a well-deserved death had died out in a gurgle only moments before. Lobo crouched over Sam's unconscious body and slammed his fist into the man's face twice more for good measure. Or maybe just because he wanted to. The girls in the other room were sobbing and holding each other. It was over. Blood dripped down Lobo's chin to his chest. They did it. They saved Annabel and Charlie.

Wait, Annabel! he thought, remembering where she was. The cold iron door at the end of the hall was still open. A girl's feet dangled from the table. Krysta had said Annabel was in there.

Am I too late? Did he already carve the poor kid up? Lobo hobbled as fast as he could toward the room.

Charlie held her breath as she watched the prince open the metal door.

The prince leapt into the hall roaring like a lion. There was a clatter of metal, some struggling, and then silence. After a few moments, the prince spoke again.

"Oh Mr. Mittens, what have you done?"

Charlie's body grew numb. She gazed out the opened doorway. The prince's pet cat had knocked over an entire stack of metal sheet pans. He was pinned underneath a shelving unit, whining as the prince entered the hall. The prince carefully lifted the unit so he could pull the cat free.

He cradled Mr. Mittens in his arms. "Looks like someone got a booboo," the prince said.

The cat meowed in response.

"There, there. It's going to be okay. Daddy's going to get you to the vet, little buddy."

Charlie's felt like puking. Tears streamed down her face as she choked on her sobs. The prince sauntered back into the room, holding his wounded pet close to his chest as it mewled.

"That was a naughty thing to do, Charlie. Didn't think you still had any fight left in you. That's all the better. Your meat's tastier this way."

He kept the cat cradled in one arm as he punched her in the temple with the other. The room spun in a sharp circle as she blacked out.

"You actually thought someone was here to rescue you? I told you no one cares about street trash." He shoved a soiled cloth in her mouth. "Now you stay here and try to keep out of trouble for once. I have to get Mr. Mittens to the doctor, but I promise when I get back this will all be over. No more pain, no more misery. Cross my heart."

He punched her in the side of the head once more. The prince was right. Nobody was coming to save someone like her.

"What do you mean Charlie wasn't in there?" Lanie asked, back at the constabulary.

Lobo could still picture Sam's room in his mind. Cauldrons bubbling with unspeakable ingredients, alembics dripping his foul drugs, and rows of knives. Annabel laid on the table, strapped down with cords. She was crying hysterically. Sam had been just about to sever her wings when Lobo arrived. He had gotten to her just in time. He hugged the girl tight, promising the nightmare was over. It took twenty minutes before she spoke anything even remotely coherent.

He shook his head, walking around his desk to stand before her. "The other girls don't know anything about her, but Annabel confirmed Sam had her."

"What did she say exactly?" Lanie asked.

"I asked her about Charlie. She said Charlie went with the prince."

"That's it? Maybe I could ask her more."

Lobo shook his head. "The girl's been through hell. She's in and out of consciousness. What she needs right now is sleep and to feel safe. It's going to be awhile before she's normal again... if that's even possible."

"But what does that even mean, though?" Lanie asked. "Who is the prince?"

"I told you, that's Sam's nickname. His pals call him the prince, remember? Because he's the heir to merchant royalty. It's also his gaming alias. He claims they never had her, but I'm sure he's lying. He won't even admit he was trafficking the women we found there. Claims they were all just partying too hard. Like anyone's going to buy that bullshit. I'll get him to talk, though."

"Do you think..." Lanie had to gather herself. The idea of what happened to Charlie was unspeakable.

"She's gone, Lanie," Lobo said morosely, trying to shake the memory of the boiling cauldron from his mind.

"So, after all that, we didn't even manage to save her." Lanie folded her arms over her chest and shivered. She was cold, had been ever since she woke up in the backseat of Lobo's cruiser. He thought it had something to do with the spell she'd cast. "Why did I stick my nose in this in the first place?"

Lobo shuffled his feet. "Look, Lanie, I know you really wanted to save that girl. Oberon knows I wish we had gotten to her in time. But all those other kids are alive today because of you. If you never got involved, they'd all still be back there in that farmhouse."

She nodded, biting back a trembling lower lip. "No, I know. It's good. I'm really happy for them. I can't even imagine what horrors they went through." *But I failed Charlie,* I thought.

"What about that human you saw?" Lobo asked. "Do you remember anything else about him?"

"Just when he escaped. Yong-Gi stared at me in disbelief as he staggered to his feet. I was too weak though. All I could do was watch helplessly as he dashed out the front door. He shouted something in Korean. Which I don't speak..."

"But?"

"*But* it sounded like a threat if I've ever heard one."

Lobo frowned. "How can you be sure?"

"It's the way he said it. Anger tends to transcend cultural boundaries," Lanie said, hugging herself tighter.

Her shoulders were trembling. It hurt his heart to see her in pain. There was no thought involved in his response. He wrapped her in his arms. She pressed her face against his chest and hugged him back. It felt right. It was like coming home. He wished it never had to end. He wanted her to stay in his arms forever.

Lanie gently pushed away so she could gaze up into his eyes. She looked so soft and innocent. It was almost easier to believe she had never betrayed him. Never strung him along for months on end when she wanted none of this.

"Lobo… what happened… I never meant to –"

But she had hurt him. He could still see her all over Prince Lucien. Hear her moaning. Her lips hungrily kissing the prince. His hands exploring her body. His smirk as he saw Lobo staring at them. Maybe Lanie was innocent. Maybe it was just the prince up to his usual dirty tricks.

"It doesn't matter," Lobo said. "Either way it happened."

A glimmer of hope entered Lanie's doe eyes. "Then, we can start over?"

Her hair smelled like coconut oil. It would stick to his skin for hours. He used to love it when that intoxicating aroma would cling to his clothes. It would remind him of her beautiful smile, and he would play out an interesting conversation they'd had the night before. Then, he would daydream about Lanie when he was supposed to be working. He had never felt like that about any other person.

She took his silence as acquiescence. Lanie closed her eyes and rose on tiptoes with her eyes closed and lips pressed together. Lobo wanted to kiss her like the sun wanted to heat the earth. He needed her in his arms. With Lanie, the world changed from a duty to be done to a life worth living.

But if that was the case, why did we spend so many months unable to connect? Maybe I just want to dwell on those good moments, but there were plenty of bad ones in between. It would be a mistake to forget how gutted he had felt. Lanie did not want to connect with him in the same way he needed. There was a piece of herself she kept closed off. And it was a major piece of who she was.

Because she thinks I'll hurt her. I can never take back what the changeling stole from us. She'll never see me as anything other than a monster. Just like the rest of the world.

Lobo pulled away from her. "I can't…" he whispered.

Lanie stared at him in shock.

"When you're done making out with your girlfriend, we have actual work to do, detective," Chief Thosimir barked from his office door. A few of the constables in the room chuckled at the jape.

"She's not my girlfriend." Lobo's voice was low, sad, and definite. He kept his eyes locked on Lanie's as he spoke. "Not anymore."

I left the police station in a daze. It felt like someone had hollowed my insides out with a dull spoon. There was no going back after all. Why did Lobo have to be so cruel? Why hug me like that then coldly dismiss me in front of all his colleagues? It was so unlike him. I knew I'd lost him for good, just like I'd lost Charlie. If I had only been faster, smarter… *better*, more like my grandmother, then I could have gotten to Charlie before Sam…

I couldn't stomach the idea of what that creep had done to her.

The early morning air felt like heaven against my skin as I stepped out of the station. Was it already daytime? We had worked the night through to bring the girls back to the province. I had woken up in Lobo's cruiser and gathered my composure. The girls had been through enough. They needed to see their rescuers as strong and confident. I put on a brave face and drove Sam's van. Some of the girls felt gross being back inside of it. I kept them talking as much as I could until we got to the station. I couldn't even remember the words now. Everything that happened seemed like a distant dream.

Damn, I'm tired. I checked my watch. *I've got six hours before my court appointment. If I run back to my apartment, I should have enough time to sneak a quick nap in and get freshened up.*

I groaned at the idea of having to run anywhere. It seemed that's all I'd been doing lately, running from one fire to the next.

"Heard you had a big night."

I blinked twice at the dark limousine that was parked in front of the constabulary. Somehow, I'd been too tired to even notice it. *Or too preoccupied feeling sorry for myself,* I thought. Not that those were mutually exclusive states of being. The backseat window was open. Lucien sat inside, wearing a lopsided grin as he stared at me.

"What are you doing here?" I asked, quickly mussing my hair and wondering what I must look like.

"We were heading home from the club. I heard there was a big bust, and my new friend Lanie was involved."

"So you came all the way down here? You miss me that much already, Lucien?" I teased.

"Knowing you, I figured you could use a ride home." Lucien grinned with a mischievous gleam in his eye.

My aching feet hollered at me. A ride home would be a godsend. "Okay," I said. "But just a ride. I have a long day ahead of me, and I need some rest. Don't be getting any dirty ideas."

Lucien popped the door open. "I wouldn't dream of it."

34

ucien held the door for me as I climbed inside his limo. Nice of him to leave me only a little room to squeeze inside, forcing me to brush up against his chest as I shimmied over his lap. Cold air radiated from his body. It felt good on my sore muscles. He placed a hand on my side to steady my weight as I climbed over him.

"Already getting handsy, I see," I teased.

I had never seen the inside of a limo outside of a television show. It was bigger than I expected. The backseat curved. It was a bench that ran on the opposite side of the car and connected to another bench that faced the back. I took a seat across from him, with my back to the driver. The pungent aroma of sandalwood hung in the air. Someone had recently burned incense.

"It's awfully dark in here," I said as I sat in the seat across from Lucien.

"Helps me unwind after a long day," he replied as he closed the door.

He leaned back in his seat and eyed me with a look I couldn't read. His blazer was neatly folded on the seat beside him. He wore a leather vest over his black dress shirt. The shirt had fine lines of white stitching around the mandarin collar and wrists. It was unbuttoned down to his midsection revealing his porcelain skin. The black lines of his tattoo teased the edge of my view beneath his shirt. It was a more relaxed side of Lucien than I'd seen before. He was the sort of guy who made a bonfire party in the woods look like it should be a formal event.

Maybe this is how he unwinds, I thought. *Am I'm getting a peek behind the curtain?* That didn't feel right, though. There was still an air around Lucien of being perfectly manicured and tended to. He was a man who thought each step out carefully. None of what I was seeing was by accident. His presentation of aloofness was a show put on for my benefit. But why?

"Gregor." Lucien rapped two knuckles on the roof of the limo.

"Very good, sir," his driver said. He was a square-jawed fae, dressed exactly as I had always seen chauffeurs in movies, even down to the belted flat cap, though his had tiny wings above where it rested over his ears. He slid a wooden partition closed, and we were on our way.

"You look rough," Lucien said.

"I think you need some lessons in flirting." I already knew I looked like dirt. I didn't need this perfectly tailored mannequin of a man pointing it out even more.

"Don't be so sensitive," Lucien chuckled. "I was only going to suggest you have a drink." He lifted a hand to stop me before I could protest. "It's not spirits. There's some balmy limonum in the console."

There was a minibar on my left side, built where the second passenger door should have been. Tiered shelves of cherry wood with smoothly polished holes held glass goblets and bottles. Some of the bottles were dark, only hinting at the secret treasures harbored within.

"It's the clear one with the yellow liquid," Lucien said.

"I've never heard of *balmy* limonum. What does it do?"

"We grow it on the hills behind my villa. It's good for your muscles; it'll loosen you up a bit."

"Ah, so that's your game." I felt a lascivious grin form on my face under his scrutiny. "You trying to loosen me up, Lucien?"

Lucien frowned. I felt the air fizzle out of my sails.

"Such an odd girl," he said to himself.

Suddenly, he crossed the gulf between seats and slid beside me. Glass clinked as he leaned over and pulled two goblets free. His throat was so close to my lips. I fought an urge to nibble on it. He held the goblets in one hand as he pulled the bottle free with the other.

"Do you really mean to imply I would need to resort to such base trickery in order to bed a beautiful woman?" he teased, leaning back into his seat. He held the tip of the bottle toward me and looked pointedly at the stopper.

I pulled the glass top free. It produced a popping sound like a champagne cork which was followed by the pleasant aroma of fresh lemon zest. Lucien filled each goblet a quarter of the way, then offered me the tip again. I pressed the glass stopper down. The bottle seemed to suck it firmly back into place of its own volition. Lucien replaced the bottle and offered me one of the glasses.

"To good health." He raised his glass to me, then took a sip.

"To good health," I repeated.

The balmy limonum lived up to its name. It reminded me of the warm sensation you get sucking on a cinnamon candy. It felt wonderful running down my throat. The liquid magic hit my stomach and sent hot rippling sensations through my insides. I sighed as it crawled across my muscles like groping tendrils, easing and soothing my aching body.

"This is very good. Sorry for being so crabby. I guess after everything we went through last night, I'm still a little on edge."

"Who could blame you?" Lucien said. "How bad was it?"

I remembered being a curled-up ball of fear on the side of the couch as bullets sprayed the wall. I could still hear the sickening sound of the werebear tearing the Korean gangster's body apart. The memory made me feel queasy.

"Worse than you could imagine. They were going to turn those poor girls into shimmer."

Lucien's body stiffened beside me. I felt the muscles in his leg flex where it rubbed up against my thigh.

"Nonsense. No one has seen shimmer in decades."

I took another sip of the balmy goodness and let it ease my nerves. "Well, that's what the creep was doing; that and selling fae to humans."

"To what end?" Lucien finished his drink and casually set his goblet back into the console.

"We don't know. But nothing happens in a vacuum. Their operation looked like it'd been running for a while."

"It's a shame the wolves dealt with this, then. If we had sent in some soldiers from my house, we would've been able to question those brigands," Lucien said. He waved a dismissive hand. "Wolves are only good for killing. Can't blame them, I suppose. It's their nature after all."

"Oh, they didn't kill all of them. Their leader, Sam Usou, is still alive. Don't worry; if there's anything to learn, Lobo will pry it out of that creep."

Lucien raised an eyebrow at me. "Interesting."

"What?" I said it too defensively.

"Thought you and the wolf weren't a thing?"

I shrugged. "We're not."

Because he dumped me, I thought. I had tried to take it like a big girl, but I was pissed about the way Lobo had so callously dismissed our relationship in front of his colleagues. *I ran into a fucking building packed with psychos to save him. How could he treat me like that?*

It was a dumb question to ask myself. I already knew the answer. It was, as the Talking Heads had so profusely serenaded so many times, *'same as it ever was.'* As much as my life had changed, things were still the same old bullshit. Lobo saw me black out. My fears had come to fruition. Now he was permanently done with me. *That's how it always goes. How could I think anything different was going to happen?*

Lucien chuckled. He stared at me with those silver eyes. "Wow, you really got it bad for the wolf."

I slammed back the rest of my drink and handed him the goblet. "Go screw yourself."

Lucien took the goblet with a cocky grin. He enjoyed pushing my buttons. I grinned back despite myself. Maybe a little levity was what I needed at that moment, and Lucien knew it. What was I doing pining after Lobo anyhow? I had a bonafide prince who I was wildly attracted to sitting right next to me.

"No thanks," Lucien grinned. "There's someone else I'd prefer screwing instead."

He leaned in closer and kissed me on the lips. His kiss was soft, probing, his lips tingling with that cold energy. It hit me like a static shock, tickling my skin in the most delicious way as I kissed him back.

"I said not to get any dirty thoughts," I murmured.

Lucien pulled back to look me in the eyes. "There's nothing dirty about kissing a goddess."

It was a cheesy pickup line but laughed. My hand was on his chest. I loved the way his skin felt, so cold and yet so inviting. I traced the curve of his rippling muscles, then slid my hand underneath the shirt to his nipple. I circled it with my fingertips. Lucien smirked smugly at me. I gave his nipple a sharp pinch. He sucked in his breath in pleasure.

"Oh, we're going to do a lot more than kiss," I promised.

It didn't take long before we ended up pulled over and naked. Gregor found us a secluded spot in the park and went outside somewhere. He was barely out of the limo before our clothes were ripped off, our mouths exploring each other's bodies. Lucien leaned back in his seat.

"Hop on," he teased with that playboy smile of his.

I wanted to fuck away all the darkness from the night before. It made it less real, stripped its power over me. I'd never felt as alive as when I was lost in the throes of passion. I needed that escape. I finally understood why all of those romance stories were so popular. Except this wasn't love. It was my need to fill my reality with something better, even if for only a few minutes. I couldn't do that with Lobo. The curse was still there. But for some reason the curse didn't work when I was with Lucien, and I meant to take full advantage of that opportunity.

I hovered over him, grazing the head of his erection. Lucien licked his pale lips. His eyes burned with need as they traced a line from the curve of my breasts up to my eyes. He lifted himself to enter me, and I let myself part only slightly, then lifted my ass just out of reach of his probing.

Lucien made a sound of exasperation, but I filled his mouth with my breast before he could protest. He hungrily nibbled on my flesh. His icy lips sent ripples of pleasure through me. He caught my nipple between his teeth and held it firmly. It was a sharp sensation of pain followed by a burning delight that made me squirm in the best way possible.

I lowered myself once more, letting his cock graze me. His thumb was there, delicately stroking my clit. Each brush of his thumb increased my arousal more and more, and I was soon lost in the feeling of it. I slid a little lower, letting him enter me. I still wasn't used to his sheer girth, and I stretched to take his thick cock. His skin tingled with his icy magic, filling me and making way for the heat of our passion. I finally succumbed to him, sliding all the way down to the base of his cock as I ground my throbbing clit against his body. Light cascaded over my skin in dim waves. I enjoyed every inch he offered me.

Lucien grinned triumphantly as I straddled him. I wasn't a lover to him. I was a conquest. A plaything he could use to get his rocks off. And I loved it. It made me angry at myself, but two could play this game. I dragged my nails down his chest. He gasped, startled. His shaft grew harder, pulsating with his desire. It was my turn to grin wickedly. He was my toy just as much as I was his, and that was enough for me in this moment. He laughed and bounced me up and down on his cock, filling me with waves of ecstasy as his icy magic penetrated my body.

Moans spilled from my open lips. A rainbow light cascaded out of my mouth, pouring down my naked throat and across my breasts, down to my belly and between my thighs. By the time it reached my swollen pussy, every sensation was heightened tenfold. Lucien's throbbing cock felt delicious as I grinded against him with an animal urgency. I slammed him all the way in harder and harder, unable to focus on anything but the waves of pure pleasure washing over me. How could anything feel so amazing? The light felt so powerful, my magic given a momentary reprieve from the addling curse that locked a piece of me away. Lucien's ice magic swirled together with my light, the two of us working in and out of each other. Our magic gathered in a pent-up storm until I felt I might burst.

Lucien slid two of his fingers into my mouth. They were cold as popsicles. I sucked on them, sliding my tongue between them and enjoying the way it turned him on. He lifted his pelvis, ramming himself into my core. The more I sucked on his fingers, the harder he fucked me, meeting my rhythm, slamming deeper and deeper inside me. I was beyond moaning. He pulled his fingers away from my sucking lips, and he grabbed me by the back of my neck, forcing me to lower my face to his. Our lips locked together, our tongues fervently tasting each other as if we could never get enough. His icy fingertips, still wet from my mouth, traced a path down my back. He pressed one finger to my ass, stroking the flesh there, circling my hole.

I was going to tell him to stop, but I was surprised by how much I liked this new feeling. He slowly eased his fingertip into me, increasing the pleasure of this new sensation. That pent up pressure exploded. Blinding ecstasy rocked my body as an orgasm overtook me. Wave after wave of it washed across my skin. The light inside the limo was blinding. Lucien let himself loose inside of me, pulsating and thrusting as he erupted with a long moan much to my screaming pleasure.

We collapsed in a panting heap. My head rested against his chest as he ran his fingers through my hair. His heart was beating like a hammer. We were both slick with sweat. I looked up at him, and he chuckled.

"That was fun."

"Loads of fun." I snickered and slid off him, retrieving my crumpled clothes from the floor of the limo. I watched him while I dressed, enjoying the view as he buttoned his shirt back up. "But I really should get going. Court and all."

Lucien shot me a devious smirk.

Gregor, his driver, was across the park, feeding pigeons hunks of bread from a brown bag. I wondered how often he did that. Did he carry stale bread around, like some sort of emergency ammo, just in case the moment presented itself?

Lucien unrolled the window and stuck his head out. "We're ready to go, Gregor. My *business meeting* with Ms. Alacore is complete."

I rolled my eyes as I tossed my jacket back on. He was so lame. But something about the situation was a major turn on. I felt naughty, like I just got away with something. I am not so naive as to think Gregor had no idea what we were doing in the limo while he was sent away, but somehow that was part of the fun. It made me feel more adventurous than I am.

"You've dropped something." Lucien gestured to the floor by my feet.

It was a few rose petals from my special flowers. "Oh, thank you. They must have fallen out of my jacket. I almost forgot I had these."

I felt guilty for blanking out on them. If not for the rose petals I had swallowed back at the farmhouse, my magic never would have worked. I shuddered to think how things might have turned out then. I felt like I owed the remaining rose petals I owned a debt of gratitude. I would put them in my special jar when I returned to the apothecary, before heading to court.

Gregor got in and opened the partition.

"To Alacore's Apothecary," Lucien ordered.

"Very good, sir."

The limo pulled out onto the park road and headed toward my shop as I retrieved the last of the rose petals. The sunlight hit them in a lovely way that made their dappled red spots reflect like fluorescent paint.

Lucien knitted his brows together, scrutinizing my prize. "Why are you carrying around grave lumeria?"

"Is that what they're called? I found a bunch of them the other day," I said brightly. "I like to use them when I'm making poultices and salves."

Lucien studied my face. I wished I could peel back the layers to tell what was going on in that beautiful head of his. He watched me like I was an alien being he just came across in the wild.

Suddenly, he flashed a grin of his too-white, perfect teeth. It made me uncomfortable. When Lucien grinned like that, it looked more like a predator about to enjoy a snack and reminded me of the foreign nature of fae compared to humans.

"You're such an odd person, Lanie. I can never figure you out."

"Yeah? Don't tell the world, I might get caught."

He smirked at that. "Either way, I wouldn't be so braggadocious about using grave lumeria to too many people. Most fae aren't as discerning as Prince Lucien."

I laughed hard. "Did you just refer to yourself in the third person?"

Lucien wiggled his eyebrows up and down in jest. The move was so out of character, I almost choked. "Wait. Why would anyone be mad at me for using these flowers? They're not poisonous, are they?"

Lucien pulled a speck of lint from his cuff with disdain. "Grave lumeria are considered sacrosanct in most fae cultures. Since they only grow once and only from the remains of a fae, they're particularly rare. It's taboo to pick them, said to bring misfortune to the culprit. An old superstition naturally, but the common folk do love to wallow about in their traditions."

My smile withered. "That can't be right. Are you sure that's what these are?"

Lucien flashed a look of mild annoyance at me. He wasn't a fan of anyone questioning his competence. He looked pointedly at the petal I held in the light.

"Of course. They're rather distinct. Red roses spotted with crimson, glow at night like a ghostly lantern. You're holding grave lumeria."

I spun around and banged on the wooden partition. It slid aside almost immediately.

"Is everything alright, sir?"

"Gregor, turn the car around," I demanded. "Go back to the park, to the inner road."

Gregor shot a questioning look to Lucien through the rear-view mirror.

"What about court?" Lucien asked.

"This won't wait," I insisted. "There's something I have to see."

Lucien shrugged to Gregor. "Go ahead. Humor her."

"And drive fast," I ordered.

The limo pulled an abrupt U-turn that hurled me backward into Lucien's arms. He grinned salaciously at me from the side as I gathered my composure. I unrolled the window and watched intently as the landscape rolled by. If what Lucien said was correct it changed everything. I couldn't think about the implications. To do so would make it real. But if I was right...

"Please don't let me be right," I whispered.

Lucien frowned at me.

We circled into the park. I had Gregor take the road that skirted the gorge. A knotted tree was coming up on the right.

"That's it! Stop up there on the bridge," I shouted.

My feet were already out the door when the limo rolled to a stop. I dashed down the length of the bridge and around the side. The hillside was steeper than I was prepared for, and I recklessly careened down it, barely managing to stay on my feet.

The bridge looked so different in the daylight. The graffiti was washed out in the sun, a fading spectacle of teenage rebellion. Somehow beneath the bridge still felt ominous even in the clear light of day. I searched the landscape for what I was afraid to see. The flowers couldn't be here. I must have made a mistake the other night, embellished it in my memory.

My heart sank.

There it was. The clump of grave lumeria, right where I had found them just underneath the bridge. And beside them was another mound. And another farther on. And two more beyond that, deeper beneath the bridge. The flower beds were everywhere. Except, according to what Lucien said, these weren't just flower beds.

"They're the buried bodies of dozens of fae," I whispered.

Lucien's cold hand on my shoulder made me jump out of my skin. "Why couldn't you just leave this alone, Lanie?"

35

Standing alone with Prince Lucien, immersed in the shadows of the bridge, with no one else around for miles, I realized something. I hardly knew this man. I studied his eyes, so silver they almost glowed in the shadows of the bridge. It was uncanny some of the things he and Lobo had in common. Except, where I knew with no uncertainty that Lobo would never willingly harm an innocent, Lucien had an aura about him that always felt dangerous. In the human realm, the rich and powerful very rarely stayed that way without performing some dark deeds.

It was folklore to tell your children anyone can become rich through hard work and determination. That was true, to an extent. Roll up your sleeves and get that hard work done. You can go far. You might even carve out a nice life for yourself. That's not who I'm talking about, though. No, I mean the truly rich and powerful. Politicians and presidents, media moguls and sheiks. Men like Lucien. People like that didn't stay in power without getting their hands dirty from time to time.

Who knew what skeletons lurked in Lucien's closet. I decided at that moment it was awfully foolish of me to wander out into the middle of nowhere with someone I knew so little about. Something else struck me, too.

What was it Annabel told Lobo about Charlie? She never said Sam took Charlie. Her exact words were that "She went with the prince."

Lucien studied me with his cold eyes.

I backed away from him, trying to wrap my head around what was happening. Lobo said the prince was Sam. But that was a nickname he used with his friends. Who was to say he made the girls he kidnapped call him that too? Standing in front of me was a man everyone knew as a prince.

He was there at the lunar party the night Charlie went missing. He already told me as much the night he first kissed me. He said he never missed one.

My body felt heavier. All this time I'd tried to understand why a guy like Lucien would be interested in a girl like me. He was one of the most powerful men in the fae realm. Why would he waste his time with a nobody from one of the provinces? Unless…

My mind went back to that night at Free House. I had tried to talk to Lucien. He claimed he never saw me, but I clearly remembered him looking directly at me, then nodding slightly for Gregor to turn me away. He lied. He knew I was there. So why the sudden interest the night of the party?

To distract me from asking questions about Charlie, I realized with dread. It made sense.

There was something different about his eyes as he gazed at me. Was it anger? Was he mad that I figured out his little game? No, that wasn't it.

"You feel guilty," I said. It was barely a whisper, but Lucien flinched as if stung. I was right. He felt guilty about something.

Lucien shook his head in wonder. "I don't get you. I have to imagine it's because you grew up around humans. You're reckless and impulsive, like a child who finds a gun and decides to look down the barrel."

"What makes you think I don't have a gun in my jacket right now?" I asked. I was bluffing of course. How much had he been paying attention when he took my jacket off, before we had sex? And where was Gregor? I tried to get a look out of the corner of my eye, but I didn't dare take my eyes off Lucien. *That behemoth could be coming at me from behind.*

"Why would you say something like that?" Lucien scowled.

"Just in case you were wondering," I said, trying to put on a brave face. "I'm not some helpless girl, you know."

"Then stop acting like one. Court is in four hours. You should be home getting rest and prepping for your appearance. Instead, you came running out here chasing… what?"

"Wait… what?" Those weren't the words of a man about to murder me. *What the heck is going on?*

Lucien eyed me seriously. "Do you even want to be a Warden?"

"How can you ask me that?"

"Your grandmother left behind a powerful legacy," Lucien said. "Believe me, I know all about living in the shadow of your predecessors. There's no shame in saying you're doing this for her. What would be a shame, however, is to turn your back on your own dreams in pursuit of that goal."

This was all too confusing for me. His words stung and made no sense at the same time. If Lucien wasn't the *prince* who took Charlie, then what was he doing out here with me?

"I don't have to explain myself to you," I insisted.

Lucien bowed his head in acquiescence. "You're right, Lanie. You *don't* have to answer me. But stop deluding yourself. If you really wanted to be warden, you wouldn't be out here in the park right now. You'd be back at your apartment preparing to make your appearance with the council."

"You're one to talk. You're the biggest liar of them all. I watch as you pretend to be what people expect of you everywhere you go. Meanwhile, you keep your big secret from them all. But I know it. I know who Prince Lucien really is."

I could not believe how much impact my words had on him. Lucien's cold indifference melted. He shocked me by looking wounded and afraid.

"And who is that?" Lucien carefully asked.

"Someone kind," I said softly. "Someone who enjoys sitting by the river and smiles as they watch children playing. Someone who would drive all the way across town to offer a girl a ride home."

"It was on my way home," he whispered.

"No. It wasn't."

Lucien looked confused. I leaned in close to him and took his hand in mine. He frowned down at our fingers locked together. When he looked up into my eyes, I saw his uncertainty. I kissed him softly.

"You're right," I said. "I shouldn't have come out here."

"Then why are we out here?" Lucien asked. "Let me get you home so you can get ready for court."

That brought me back. "Look around you." I pointed to the mounds of grave lumeria, one after the other, as I spoke. "If what you said is true, then someone has buried an awful lot of fae under this bridge."

Lucien took in the scene around us, seemingly for the first time. His expression was hard to read, but he did offer the slightest of frowns. "That *is* odd."

"Was this area ever used as a graveyard that you know of?"

Lucien shook his head. His eyes shifted from one flowerbed to the next. "These woods are protected land. The humans who defiled this area did enough damage. The idea is for this forest to recover and take back the land. This would be the last place fae would leave their dead."

"Then who the hell is buried beneath our feet right now?"

"That's a good question."

I tried to see the bigger picture. Someone had buried an awful lot of bodies under that bridge. There was something else staring me in the face, something obvious I was missing. The warm sunlight kissing the back of my neck was a stark contrast to the chilly shadows under that bridge.

"They're not just under the bridge though," I mumbled to myself.

The area past the underpass was dappled in shadows from the tightly clustered trees. I walked in that direction, moving from one flowerbed to the next until I left the cover of the bridge. The undergrowth was thick, but there was a path there. Someone had tread through the detritus on a routine walk.

"They like to come and look at their flowers," I realized.

"What?"

"I watched a documentary. Well, a few actually, on serial killers. Many of them like to take some sort of souvenir," I explained, continuing to follow the trodden path. It was hard to track, but it was there if anyone stopped to look close enough. "It's like they just can't help themselves. There's some sort of perverse rush they get from what they do. It's like an addiction for them, a compulsion. The souvenirs are a way for them to bring the memory back up and relive that rush all over again."

"You think whoever buried those bodies back there is coming by for a nature stroll to get their jollies?"

"That's one way of putting it," I said. *Also, who the heck says jollies?*

The path abruptly ended. A concrete wall rose out of the forest like the ruins of some lost civilization. It was so out of place, I could only stand there and stare at it in confusion.

"It's an old bridge," Lucien said dryly. "There used to be a road cutting through this area. I told you, the forest is reclaiming the land around it."

"Another bridge? Damn it."

Once the killer hit the road above, there was no way of finding them. *It's not like I'm some sort of tire track expert. I should have taken forensics in college instead of botany. At least that would have been useful right now.* I found myself walking the length of the bridge despite the hopelessness of the situation.

"What the heck is that sound?" I said, looking around us.

Lucien shrugged. "I don't hear anything."

"Shhh, listen. It's there." I focused on the forest around us. There were echoes of water dripping and splashing into something deeper. The trickling sound was coming from somewhere nearby. "It's water."

"Okay, it's water. So what?" Lucien grumbled. "There's streams and creeks all around these woods."

I held a finger up for him to stop talking. "That's not a stream. It's something else... There's a weird echo."

I rushed toward the source of the sound. A dark splotch marked an opening on the side of the bridge. It was a culvert, a large yawning hole that allowed flood water to channel beneath the bridge. The trickling water echoed from inside its dark depths.

"It's coming from in there," I said, my voice echoing down the tunnel.

"Surely you're not suggesting we go inside this filthy hole in the ground like a pair of dwarves?" Lucien turned his nose up in the air.

Admittedly, there was a foul stench of sitting water coming from inside. I knew he was right. There was no rational reason for me to want to enter that dark hole. Except there was this thing inside urging me to keep moving. I needed to go down that tunnel and see what I found. I felt it in my bones.

"You're serious?" Lucien said.

"I have to."

Lucien made a show of checking his watch. "Well, I have a busy day ahead of me, and I'm pressed for time as it is. There's no way I'm trolloping around some sewer. You're a fun fuck, Lanie, but not that fun."

I rolled my eyes at him. "Geez, thanks."

"I'm going. I suggest you do the same. Let us drive you home so you can prepare for court," he insisted.

But I was already walking down the tunnel. There was nothing I could do about it. I knew it was stupid even as my feet started moving. I also knew the answers to my questions lay ahead of me.

I could feel Lucien shaking his head at the bizarre girl walking into a filthy tunnel. It didn't matter. I had to find out who buried those bodies.

36

The tunnel was not what I expected. A culvert is a simple conduit built underneath a bridge to prevent flooding. The tunnel I was in was much larger.

At first, I had to crouch low to walk down it, but soon it widened out as I hit an intersection. I had entered a connection to an old sewer system. It smelled even fouler.

I'm way out of my depth, I thought. *Lucien was right. What am I doing down here?*

I grumbled as I trudged forward. *I should be getting ready for court, not mucking about in sewers.* I was ready to turn back when I spotted a flash of red. I turned my head to train my eyes on it and lost the color. It was too dark in there for me. I was no werewolf. *Lobo's night vision sure would come in handy right about now.*

I shook my head. I had to forget about Lobo. We were done. *I need to solve my problems on my own from now on. Nothing knew there. I've been doing that my entire life, give or take.*

There was that red again. It was a shirt on the ground. I stared at it for a bit to try and make sense of what I was seeing. It was a girl's shirt, small and torn on the sleeve. I reached down to pick it up. There was a loud snap.

I tried to will my feet to move, but the cord was already looped around my ankles. I had just enough time to let out a yelp before the trap flipped me head over heels and dangled me from the ceiling. A small alarm clock chimed.

Because why just set a trap when you can also alert yourself that someone has stepped inside it?

The next thing I knew, I was walking down a dank tunnel with Lobo. I don't know when he arrived. His hand was in mine, firm and calloused. He looked down at me with a serene smile as we took our stroll.

"Everything's going to be okay," he assured me.

Deep down, I knew this man wasn't actually Lobo. My guts were churning, and a voice in the back of my mind howled to get away from this stranger as fast as possible. Which was silly. *He's here to keep me safe.*

Rats scurried out of our path.

"Why are we going deeper into the sewers?" I asked. "We're going to get lost."

"Nonsense, my little dumpling," Lobo crooned. "I know my way around these tunnels like the back of my hand."

I knew he was lying, yet I believed him. Being put under a controlling spell is very confusing. It was like watching from the outside as someone else steered my body. *Get the hell away from him,* I thought. But his words comforted me. I squeezed his hand affectionately. This was all I really wanted, to be with Lobo and share our lives together.

"Now that we're back together, I want to tell you my secret."

Lobo watched me like a cat toying with a mouse. The hungry glimmer in his dull yellow eyes terrified me. *Lobo doesn't have yellow eyes, Lanie!*

"A secret, you say? That sounds positively delicious."

Run, you stupid girl! Get away from this man!

The rats around us danced in a circle singing *tra-la-la-la-laaa*. They were happy for me that I'd found Lobo again. So happy, they promised not to eat my face at all. Pinky swear.

We came up out of the tunnels through a manhole. We were back in the woods. *Why do they call them manholes?* I thought. *Is it short for maintenance hole? I should get a cookie-cutter shaped like a man. Then I could have little man cookies to bite the heads off. Wait… that's just a gingerbread cookie, right?*

I snickered. "Gingerbread-hole."

"What's that?"

I shrugged. "I think I'm a little drunk, babe."

"And what a wonderful morning it is to be inebriated," he crooned, leading me by the hand through the dense forest.

The morning air was crisp, and a magpie chirped from a heavy bough overhead. "You know they sound more like monkeys than birds to my unsophisticated ear," I said. "I could see the appeal to go bird watching, though. In an old forest like this there's bound to be some interesting-looking species. I wonder if there are fae birds?"

Lobo pulled me along through the forest. His palm was slimy against my skin.

"Where are we going?" I asked as we climbed over a root thick enough to be a tree trunk.

Lobo steadied my weight with his slimy but firm grip as I climbed over the root. "To my cabin, little sweetness. Remember, we're spending a quiet weekend alone." He splayed his other hand in the air dramatically. "A romantic retreat."

"Mm hmm, romantic," I mumbled. I had seen him do that hand gesture before. Several times. Not Lobo. The person wearing his face. He liked drama, in a vaudevillian sense.

We arrived at a log cabin. Smoke billowed from a stone chimney. The porch had a cozy swing. I moved to test it out, but Lobo held my hand firm.

"Plenty of time for swinging on chains later," he promised. "But first, I have something exquisite to show you downstairs."

My mind screamed to escape. There was a road behind us, at the end of a long driveway. I could call for help if I reached the road. That was a wiser choice. The last thing I should do was enter this man's house.

I obediently followed him inside, cursing my traitorous body for disobeying me. The living room was quaint. Everything was wooden. It was a genuine log cabin. There were built-in shelves lined with old hardcover books. I didn't realize Lobo liked Clive Barker so much. His armchair recliner had a faded Afghan blanket draped over it. I felt the electric hum of a television. It was an odd sensation.

"It's been a while since such an ordinary thing was in my orbit," I said sleepily.

How long did I live around electronics without realizing the palpable energy they radiated? It looked like the man who wore Lobo's face had been watching a movie when he came to my rescue. It was an old black and white flick. Cary Grant was on top of a reconstructed dinosaur fossil of a brontosaurus. Katherine Hepburn was talking to him from a nearby ladder with a bone in her hand.

"Well, when I go back down, I'll go down quietly, David," she said.

"I love that clear punchy way that Americans used to speak back then," I said.

Not-Lobo grinned admiringly at the television. "Yes, the world was a simpler place then. Every creature knew where they belonged and did as they ought to."

I watched their banter with a grin. "Oh, this is the movie you were telling me about, isn't it, Droll?"

Lobo turned to me wearing a severe frown.

"Droll?" I repeated. "Droll the troll…"

Lobo's features melted away from him like smears running down a steamed mirror. Along with his mask came the feeling of tranquility torn away from me, splashed from my being like a bucket of icy water to the face. That false sense of peace was replaced by horror. The man before me was taller than Lobo, even though he stood with a slightly stooped hunch. His skin was the slimy green of seaweed and swamps. He had a long hooked nose and feral yellow eyes. And he wore his familiar bent tin crown.

"You're a troll," I stated the obvious again.

"Yes, and you're a very clever girl," Droll deadpanned, reaching down to turn the knob on the television with an audible click.

"But… you're such a sweet old man," I said, still trying to wrap my head around what was happening. It was obvious. Droll had kidnapped me. I walked into his shitty trap, and he came along to scoop up his prize. Which meant Droll had been the one kidnapping girls and burying their bodies under the bridge. The harmless comedian that put on bawdy puppet shows, and juggled gourds was the man responsible for all the graves underneath the bridge.

"Shit, bridges," I said. "That was where I should have pieced it together. Stories about trolls under bridges are as old as time. And that shitty crown you wear, always talking about your royal court and calling yourself the prince of fools."

None of it felt real, though. Droll wasn't a devious kidnapper. He was a comedian, a foppish vaudeville flavored act. Nothing to take seriously.

"You were so kind to me the night Lobo and I got into that argument. But you're not kind, are you? You're nothing but a creep who preys on defenseless girls."

Droll planted a hammy fist into my gut. He wasn't interested in talking. I bowled over trying to suck air into my lungs. I'm not a werewolf. I don't know what secrets my unicorn blood holds beneath this curse, but it's not heightened strength, that's for sure. A troll punch to the stomach is agonizing. I struggled to breathe as nauseating waves wracked my body. Somewhere inside that agony I realized Droll was carrying me over his slimy green shoulder down into the basement.

"Put me down you brute," I gagged out.

Droll chuckled. "Is that the best insult you can come up with?"

He sounded jovial, crooning like he was playing with a child. Any advantage I had gained disarming him by cutting through his mesmerizing spell was lost. He flipped me off of him. My back thudded hard against a wooden slab. I fought for air once more, curled on my side like an infant.

I was looking right into the eyes of another person!

"Charlie?"

Charlie struggled against her bonds beside me on the table. Her screams were muffled by a soiled rag that was shoved into her mouth.

Droll worked the large metal door to the room closed, carefully sliding bolt locks up and down the edge of it. I took in his workshop with a terror I had only ever read about. It's like fear, but it grips you from the groin, seizing your body in this cold numbness that feels like your heart is going to explode and you might be driven insane. Metal hooks dangled from chains fixed to the ceiling above. They were stained with dark brown splotches. Across from me was a workbench with various boning knives and cleavers hooked to the wall. A roaring coal stove stood beside it. The oven door was open so I could see the red-hot coals and polished skull inside.

"You're murdering these kids?" I gasped.

Droll surprised me with the flash of shame that crossed his face. He looked down to the floor, shoulders drooped.

I decided to seize on that guilt as it might be my only possible lifeline. "But everyone adores you. How could you do this to them?"

"They *adore* me?" Droll snorted.

I realized instantly that I'd touched on the wrong nerve.

"Do you have any idea how tough it is being a big ugly troll?"

"You're feeling sorry for yourself?" I said, unable to contain my disgust. "Aw, poor Droll, and his self-pity."

"What would you know about it?" Droll growled.

I flinched when he slammed his palm down beside my head. His face was massive, hovering over me all bloodshot eyes and jagged tusks. He dragged his yellow nails across the wooden slab.

"You could never know what it feels like for everyone around you to be repulsed by your appearance. You're pretty and delicate. Can you even guess how long it took other fae to speak to me? Can you imagine a childhood looking like this?" He snorted. "People are shit. They laugh at you right in your face. They say mean things, then brag about what good people they are to their friends. Our society would rather see me drop dead than be around them. And the only way I could hope to manage that was by turning myself into a joke. *Oh look, there's Droll. He's not like other trolls, he's good. See what a joke he is? He must be harmless. He's a buffoon.*" Droll scowled. "You don't get to judge me. I'm a troll and I need to eat, simple as that."

"You're not a troll," I whispered, fighting my fear to keep my lips moving. If I stopped talking, the alternative was to curl up and wait to die. "You're nothing but a monster."

"You think I don't know that?" Droll growled. "All my life it's been rubbed in my face by pretty girls just like you." He pounded his chest with a fist as large as my head. "I didn't ask for this. I didn't make myself a troll. Do you know how much easier my life would have been if I'd been born a pixie or a brownie, like little Charlie here?" He shook his head in disgust. "These kids… they have it made. They'll never know what it's like to live as a *freak*. They're born into this world with everything at their fingertips. And what do they do with that opportunity? They squander it with petty righteous indignation, inventing new reasons to be angry. *Down with the patriarchy. Momma doesn't give me enough attention.* Blah blah blah."

Droll shoved his face inches from Charlie's. "Do you know what troll matrons do to their young, Charlie? The bitches spill thirty or so of us from their womb. Problem is trolls only have six nipples. So, what happens to the rest of the litter? What do you think? Can you figure it out?"

Charlie shook her head violently, tears streaming down her cheeks.

"We're forced to fight for the nipple. We have to kill our brothers and sisters to get to it or die ourselves. But that's not all. When mommy sees who the runts are, she takes her time eating them. Yeah, that's right. She ate my siblings in front of me. When your mommy got mad she probably yelled at you too loud, and it hurt your delicate little feelings. So, you popped some rings in your face and pouted about how rough your life is. Talking to me about monsters... Save your bullshit for someone who gives a damn."

"What happened to you was horrible," I said, unable to express in words how horrified I was of that revelation. "But that was done to you when you were young and defenseless. No one is forcing you to kill other fae now. This is a choice. What you're doing is wrong and you know it. You don't have to be evil."

Droll snorted. He grabbed some rope off the workbench and snorted again. His hand clamped down on my ankle like a vise.

"Is a lion evil?" Droll asked as he tied the rope to my ankle and then to the leg of the table I was on. "Lions kill 'innocent' helpless creatures, don't they? We don't stop them. Do you see fae wiping out the big bad evil lions? No. You know why? Because it's the lion's nature to hunt."

"Lions aren't cruel," I said.

"Oh please, predators are predators. It's the way Mother Earth created us. Take Komodo dragons, for example. They're brutal hunters. They poison their prey with a bite and wait for the paralysis to kick in. Do they then simply snap their prey's neck? Nope. They eat their catch alive, taking their time to feast as it lays there knowing what's happening. There is no love in that transaction. It's the brutal act of a predator. At least I take care of these silly runaways. They're not free-range," he chuckled. "But look at humans. Look at their meat. I follow similar principles here. Cage the bitches, stuff them with drugs and fatten them with food, then a bolt to the head. It's over in an instant. I only draw out the slaughter on special occasions. When you deserve it. And admittedly the meat tastes so much better when you're scared."

"You disgust me," I said. "You're taking advantage of innocent kids."

"Oh yes, they're all *so* innocent," Droll said sarcastically. "If they're such innocents, how do you think I get them to come with me?"

That was a weird thing to say. Droll's gloating smile hammered something home. It was a suspicion I'd had for a while but had been unable to believe possible.

"One of them is helping you take the others," I said in disbelief.

I looked at Charlie and saw anguish written in her eyes. It *was* true. One of her friends had delivered her to Droll.

"But why?" I asked the universe.

Charlie replied by crying. I was wrong. Anguish wasn't the only thing she felt. Charlie was betrayed so badly that her heart ached. That level of betrayal confirmed my worst suspicions.

I looked back to Droll. He was very pleased with himself. "Sanji brings you the other kids," I said. Charlie's junkie girlfriend had sold her out to the troll after all. "In exchange for the heroin you provide her."

Droll shook his head and wagged a finger at me. "You're far too clever for a fae. Sanji's been serving me well for years now. You can imagine my delight when she brought Charlie to me that night at Free House."

Charlie's sobs were muffled by the gag in her mouth. Droll leaned over her taunting. "She caught wind you were leaving her, you know. Oh, how that tore her up. When she told me she was bringing you, I almost couldn't believe it. You just can never tell about people these days, eh Charlie-pie?"

"You're a sick twisted fuck," I snarled.

Droll chuckled again. It was as if my vehemence and moral outrage made him feel better about himself. *How can anyone take so much pleasure from hurting another person?* That's when I realized we weren't going through the same thing. What was happening was, for Droll, a matter of routine. I wasn't a person to him, more of a passing interest. Our whole conversation was more like talking to himself while he prepped his dinner than anything else.

"Well, me oh my. You're a vegetarian, right? That must be why all this talk upsets you." He eyed me coyly, knowing full well I was not. "Then you have no right to stand there… oh, silly me. I mean *lie there* and lecture me."

"Oh, go fuck a knife," I said.

"Enough talking."

A dirty rag was suddenly stuffed into my open mouth. I tried to spit it out, but his slimy fingers shoved it deeper, until I was gagging. "Darn, this is my last piece of rope," he grumbled as he tied it around my face to keep the gag secure.

"I have a lot of work to do, and I don't need you distracting me. Charlie there's been a naughty girl, so I have to cut her up tonight."

Charlie squirmed trying to protest underneath her own soiled rag.

"No, no, none of that. You know you were a bad girl."

He flipped the table saw on across from us. It whirred to life on his workbench as he grabbed a cleaver from the wall. The conversation was over. Droll was preparing his knives.

That was the last straw. I was trapped like a rabbit in a snare. Tears rolled out of my eyes. Droll turned to me, sharpening his cleaver with a whetting stone.

"I don't know how you cut through my mirror's spell like that though. Usually takes a few weeks before one of my dumpling's minds can ignore its call. It's a shame, seeing how skinny you are and all. Normally, I'd have stuck you in a cage and fattened you up a bit more before the slaughter, get some more meat to work with. Can't do that now, though. You're too dangerous." Droll shrugged. "Well, you'll make a good stew at least."

My body was shaking uncontrollably. That can happen when a person is terrified. It's all that adrenaline coursing through their body with nowhere to go. Usually that sort of reaction results in a fight or flight. I could do neither. My ankle was bound tight to the table leg. My wrists were still free, but any punches I might land on Droll would be useless. He was a troll and they're built like a brick wall.

Droll set down the whetstone and shuffled over to the coal stove, humming a happy tune. "Eh, we're going to need a little more flame to keep us warm."

He grabbed a section of wood from the floor and eyed Charlie and me. He wanted us to see what he was up to. He slapped the wood down over the spinning table saw with a chopping motion. Metal squealed in protest as it tore through the wood, efficiently severing it into two pieces.

I winced.

Droll chuckled. "Sounds beautiful, doesn't it? Believe it or not, your bones will sound even more exquisite. Did you know certain cultures eat dogs? Talk about barbaric. Poor little pups. But there is some good to come out of that. You see, they figured out the more scared a dog is, the better the meat tastes. It's a clever little trick; works just as well with fae. Not humans so much, though." He slapped another branch into the saw, locking his gaze on me.

Don't give him the satisfaction of squirming, I thought. Despite myself, I slapped my hands over my eyes. I wanted to be strong, to defy the cretin, but there was only so much my mind could take. Droll laughed. *He knows I don't need to see the blade to feel terrified.* I worked at the rag in my mouth, trying to free it so I could tell him how revolting he was.

Droll grumbled. "You're a royal pain the ass, you know that?"

Charlie made a noise, and I lowered my hands. She was leaning her face toward me, flailing around and screaming something. Her words were muffled beneath the soiled rag in her mouth, her wrists and ankles bound tight to the table.

Her muffle is different than mine, I realized. Droll had simply shoved a piece of dirty fabric into her mouth too far for her to push out with only her tongue available. Since her hands were bound, it would be pointless to use more rope, which he apparently had in short supply. *If I could free her gag, maybe she can call for help.*

I snatched Charlie's rag and tugged it out of her mouth. Charlie choked on the air. Her throat was raw from the gag, her lips cracked and dry. Droll got a kick out of watching his food squirm. He looked like a honey badger playfully toying with its prey moments before it ripped out their throat.

"Help!" Charlie screamed. "Help us! Someone!"

Droll laughed so hard he dropped his cleaver. It must have grazed his bare foot because a second later he yelped and hopped backward. "Sonuva whore," he snarled.

I laughed at him beneath my muffle. It would serve him right to lose a toe.

Droll's glare turned to me. "You know what? I think you better go first. You're a little troublemaker. Charlie can call for help at the top of her lungs while she watches me slice you up into bacon and steaks."

He reached for me. I slapped at his hands and clawed at his slimy forearm. It did nothing. Droll picked me up like a ragdoll and hurled me over his shoulder. The rope at my ankle pulled against the table.

Something glinted in the light from the oven fire. It was the hand mirror sticking out of Droll's back pocket. I hit the workbench hard, all the while Charlie screamed for help.

"Keep wasting your breath, dimwit," Droll said. "Nobody is around for miles, and this basement is soundproof."

He grabbed my forearm and dragged me across the workbench. I tried to kick him, but my leg was pulled taught, my ankle still tethered to the table across from us.

Droll lowered my arm to the saw as easily as turning a lever. I fought him with all my strength. It was futile. He stopped just above the spinning blade. I could feel the air from the whining metal whipping inches away from my flesh. Droll held my hand there, deliberately turning to face Charlie. He wanted her to see him grin. He was all in on the scare your dinner thing.

Charlie stifled her scream. "Wait, Droll! Please... just wait," she whimpered. Then she screamed. "Lanie, take his mirror!"

The mirror! I thought. *That's how he controls the girls he kidnaps.* I snatched the handle of it with my free hand and tugged.

Droll tried to block his back pocket, but I was faster. "Damnit, you little rat. Be careful with that. You're going to break it!"

I held the mirror firm, thrusting it up to his face.

Droll laughed. "You have to be able to speak, you nitwit."

Charlie choked on something. "Look into Lanie's mirror!" she shouted.

Droll snarled, ready to tell her to fuck off, but his eyes suddenly drooped. He stared blankly at the looking glass. His shoulder twitched as he tried to turn his body away.

"You can't use it against –" he mumbled.

"Shut up and look into the mirror," Charlie commanded again.

Droll's mouth went slack as his eyes glazed over. It was working. I did not dare move an inch, holding the mirror close to his face.

"See how happy you are to be with us?" Charlie quickly stammered. "So happy. This is the best place you've ever been." She stopped to cough hard. "We're your best friends in the whole wide world."

"I love you girls." Droll smiled sheepishly. "Momma always warned me what whores you are. I wasn't allowed to talk to pretty girls. But look at us now. We have so much fun together."

He let go of my other forearm. It was so abrupt, and my arm was so numb from the pressure, that it almost fell right onto the whirring blade. I screamed and snatched it back in a flurry that made the mirror waver. Droll groaned and shuffled backward shaking his head.

I clambered sideways, trying to get away from the table saw. The taut rope attached to the opposite table pulled my weight wrong, and I spilled off the workbench. My elbow cracked into the concrete floor, and I lost my grip on the mirror.

The mirror went flying in the air and smashed onto the floor in a burst of shards.

Droll bent over rubbing his eyes. "No! What did you do?"

The troll's dropped butcher knife sliced my shoulder when I tried to roll over.

Droll roared. "You fucking bitch, you broke my mirror!"

He slammed an angry fist on the workbench, then charged after me. He bent down low, his jaws opened wide. He was in a state of blind fury.

I swung my hand as hard as I could as he came in close. They say people can perform feats of unimaginable strength when they fear for their lives. It's all the adrenaline. In my case, it gave me just enough strength to bury Droll's dropped clever six inches into his forehead.

He stopped short, eyes wide with disbelief, hands opening and closing.

"What? But I?" He slowly backed away from me, blood already spraying down his face.

I pulled my leg back so the rope tied to my ankle was taut again. Droll's heel caught on it, and he lost his balance, spilling in a jumble of flailing arms and legs. His spine hit the spinning saw. Four-hundred pounds of troll was too much to maneuver to escape his fate. The table saw stuttered and tore through muscle and bone while Droll screamed in agony. It was a sound I prayed I would never hear again as long as I lived.

But fuck him, I thought.

He deserved every second of his death.

I don't know how long we laid there crying. Somewhere in that span I freed my ankle and untied Charlie. Droll was about as dead as anyone could be. The saw motor still ran, but the blade had shattered into pieces inside his mutilated body. Charlie sobbed uncontrollably in my arms, and I joined her.

I heard myself reassuring her. "It's okay. You're safe now. I've got you."

"Thank you," Charlie murmured. Her body finally stopped quaking. "There's another girl in the other room, Warden."

"Oh, I'm not Warden yet," I started to explain. "Not until…" I glanced down at my watch. "Oh, shit. Court."

37

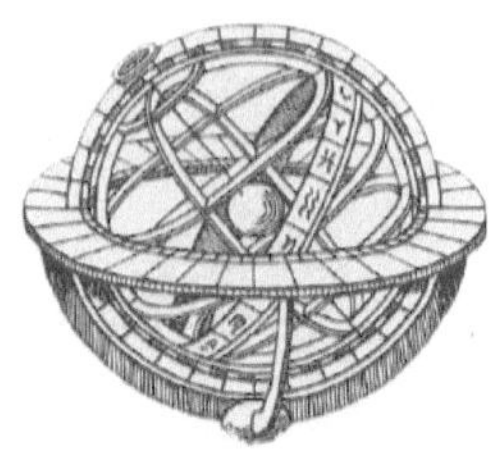

Droll owned a cell phone. I guess I shouldn't have been that surprised to find it, the troll had human devices all over his cabin. I imagine he never fathomed one of his captives would escape. I had ninety minutes to get to the courthouse. Lobo and Doule were able to get to the cabin in forty. It wasn't hard for Lobo to lookup the troll's address at the station. We were off for the courthouse half an hour after that. We pulled up at five past ten as Charlie cradled her shell-shocked friend in the backseat of Lobo's cruiser. I felt miserable to think about what they had gone through.

"You sure you don't want me to come inside with you and explain everything?" Lobo asked as my bare feet hit the curb.

I leaned into the window. Charlie was rocking the whimpering girl in the backseat. We still didn't know her name.

"She probably won't be able to talk for a few days," Doule said from the passenger seat, following my gaze. "Not until we can wean her off that human poison Droll was pumping into her veins."

"No, you guys go on ahead. These girls need to see a healer," I said. Besides, facing the firing range was going to be bad enough without the humiliation of having Lobo watch me grovel in front of the judges for being late.

I raced into the courthouse. A few wary glances were thrown my way by the minotaurs as I ran down the hall. The pair guarding the courtroom doors rolled their eyes as I raced past them. At least the one on the left held the door open for me.

"… is already late, so this council will not waste our time on such flagrant –" Shadow broke off as I rushed into the courtroom.

"Please wait!" I shouted far too loudly. "I'm here."

Shadow openly sneered at me. "Ah, Miss Alacore. We see you're arriving in your customary ideal of punctuality and looking like a disgraced mess to boot."

"As you well remember, this council warned you of the repercussions should you arrive late for this meeting," Dawn added.

"I do remember, your honor," I panted, trying to catch my breath. "But if you'll just hear me out —"

"Then *if* you remember, you know full well that this matter is adjourned." Shadow raised his black gavel.

A mumbling curiosity arose from Summer. It was an interesting thing, both soft as a whisper and yet powerful enough to garner everyone in the courtroom's attention. And there were an awful lot of fae in attendance that morning.

Summer shuffled in his seat, his white robes rustling like a fresh morning breeze. "Hold on a moment. It would be in our good nature to at least allow Miss Alacore to explain why she comes before us looking as bedraggled as an alley cat who just went ten rounds with a gorilla." He chuckled, his chocolate eyes twinkling.

Shadow opened his mouth to protest, but he was cut off by Amber.

"I agree with our cousin," she tittered. Her dress of copper and crimson leaves whirled around her shoulders as she sat back to study me with scalding eyes. "Tell us, Miss Alacore. Why do believe it appropriate to come before this court in such a disrespectful manner?"

My mouth was fuzzy. The last time I had any water was the afternoon before, at Free house. Have you ever tried speaking in front of a room full of people with a dry mouth? It's fucked. My lips felt like they were sticking together, and my teeth wanted to glue themselves to my tongue. I felt like everyone was staring at my sticky mouth instead of listening to me. I glanced nervously around at the crowd of fae sitting in the courtroom, then back to the expectant council. Everyone *was* staring at me.

"Last evening, we uncovered a trafficking ring," I said.

"We are aware of Detective Lobo and Detective Doule's exploits in this matter," Dawn cut me off. "Having your boyfriend come home late is no excuse for your tardiness."

Shit. That disarmed me. Last time I stood before the council, I felt Dawn was an ally. From the look of annoyance clearly painted on her face, that may have changed. It was, after all, she who had warned me not to be late. How could I sum this all up and explain it before they hauled me out of there?

A growl came from the doorway. "Miss Alacore was not sitting up late pining for me to come home."

There was a stir among the crowd as Lobo entered the courtroom.

"How dare you intrude on these proceedings, detective," Shadow hissed, slapping his gavel down for order.

The minotaurs at the door were right on Lobo's heels. One of them clamped a meaty hand down on his shoulder. Lobo snapped his head around and bared his fangs with a snarl. A murmur of excitement and disapproval worked through the crowd of fae. There were remarks of the wolf "not knowing his place" and even calls to "take him out back and flog him." As usual for me, things were quickly spiraling out of control.

The Arbiter's empty eye sockets spilled golden light, its cold, indifferent metallic face watching Lobo. Charlie slipped between the minotaur and Lobo. She wrapped her hands around his arm for support. She was still wrapped in the blanket he brought when he came to pick us up.

"Your grace, if you can forgive my boldness," Lobo said, shaking the minotaur off. "I would request the right to be heard in these proceedings."

"Your request is denied," Amber said firmly.

"Are we not the least bit curious to hear what the werewolf has to say?" Summer asked.

"We are here to discuss the worthiness of Miss Alacore's petition," Shadow answered. "The exploits of the mongrel she is rutting have nothing to do –"

"Hey!" I snapped.

Shadow flicked his gaze to me, scandalized that I would have the audacity to raise my voice at him.

"I don't care what your title is. You're way out of line talking about me like that. I would expect a representative of one of the Great Houses to behave with more dignity and respect for the people they serve."

The court was quiet enough to hear a needle drop. Shadow's face reminded me of a tea kettle about to explode. Even the minotaurs in the courtroom looked baffled. I realized I had completely overstepped my bounds and wondered how bad it was going to hurt to be flogged behind the courthouse.

It was Dawn who broke the silence. Her laugh started as a titter and grew to the sound of crashing waves in a bay at high tide. "The girl has moxie, I'll give her that," she said.

"Detective, if you have something worthy of these proceedings to share, then speak it," Summer said.

"Miss Alacore wasn't home *pining* for me, because she was there with us during the raid. Lanie played a pivotal role in the apprehension and destruction of Sam Usou's fae trafficking ring. She was the one who pushed us to investigate the missing girls in the first place. It was Lanie that rushed into the house with us, and it was she who used her magic to free the girls of their imprisonment."

"That may very well be true," Shadow said, each word like the slow cracking of an icicle. "However, this council knows full well that the entire matter you speak of was brought to rest early this morning. Miss Alacore has had ample time to prepare herself for this council."

"I am in agreement with the Court of Shadows," Dawn said.

My heart sank into my stomach as Amber too nodded along with the statement. "Miss Alacore, you present us as a tragic heroine fresh from battle. Coming here in this manner reeks of the spectacle the humans you were raised around love to bandy. I can tell you such tactics will not work on this council."

"How can you say that?" Lobo snarled.

"We've heard enough from you, Detective Lobo." The crowd broke into a hectic murmur once more, like a gaggle of geese drowning out the words of the judges.

The Arbiter's voice carried over them all in a booming command. "There will be silence."

It worked. Everyone stopped speaking at once.

"Miss Alacore, you have turned these proceedings into a mockery with your wild interruptions and paltry theatrics," Amber said. "We will offer our ruling on your impeachment now."

"Please, no." Charlie broke free from Lobo.

"That is enough," Shadow shouted, his pale blue skin was turning a shade of purple. "There will be no more of this disrespect in our courtroom. Take this girl away."

The minotaur behind Lobo grabbed his shoulder again and wrenched him toward the exit. The bailiffs moved away from either side of the council bench toward Charlie. She clutched her blanket tight and mewled in a sound of pure fear. I threw myself in front of her with outstretched arms.

"Don't you dare touch her. I'll leave, but don't lay a hand on her."

"Let the girl speak," a rich velvety voice boomed over the court chambers. It was the Arbiter, except his head had spun to the marble aspect of Queen Titania.

Everyone stopped to gawk at her. I could hear Lobo suck in his breath at the sight.

"I would hear her words."

Charlie stammered as she clung to me. "Q-queen Titania? I, uh –"

"Have no fear child. No member of this court will harm you," Titania said softly. "Speak your words freely."

Charlie looked to me. I shrugged. I had no idea what the right thing to do was in that moment.

Charlie took a deep breath and began. "I-I haven't always been the best citizen of our province. There're dozens of kids like me. Outcasts really, to the rest of our society. See, we were born in the provinces, stuck between the two realms with only our curiosity to keep us going. I've done some things I'm ashamed to admit. I haven't always been the best... as I said. But what happens to kids like us? When someone like me goes missing, it's not exactly the top priority for the detectives." She stopped to nod at Lobo. "I'm not saying you, Detective Lobo, but –"

"I understand what you meant," Lobo said. Then to the judges. "We never would have went looking for these girls if Lanie Alacore hadn't gotten Drys involved."

"Right. But she did," Charlie said. She stood a little taller, with her chin raised so she could look each council member in the eye in turn. "It was Lanie who kept fighting. She kept searching for me when everyone told her I wasn't worth it." The bravery of this teenager, who had just spent weeks as a prisoner in a cannibal's dungeon, sticking up for me, humbled to no end and touched me deep in my core.

"We are humbled to hear the words of a survivor," Summer said kindly. "Though Dawn's judgement still holds true. Miss Alacore had ample time to prepare herself for these proceedings and failed to do so."

"And she had no right to be interfering with province investigations in the first place," Shadow added.

"But she –" Charlie said before Dawn cut her off.

"Child, we feel in our heart of hearts for the ill you've suffered. But objectively, it does not speak to the candor and professionalism of one who would represent the province. I must agree with Shadow once more. Lanie Alacore does not seem fit for the role as Warden."

Someone began laughing from the crowd. I had never heard such a contemptuous sound before. Their laugh was loud enough to interrupt anything the judges might say. The crowd rippled from the center, buzzing like a swarm of angry bees.

Shadow slammed his gavel down repeatedly until everyone except the laughing person fell silent.

"Who is that? Who dares?" Shadow shouted. He rose to his feet and reached for the dagger at his belt. "Who are you to laugh at this court's ruling?"

"Careful, old chap. A martial threat is not a thing to be taken lightly. If you pull that dagger, I will be forced to brandish my own weapon."

The crowd parted, quickly distancing themselves from whatever punishment was about to befall the culprit. There was a gasp as Prince Lucien rose from his seat, with one hand at his waist, on the hilt of a sword that poked out from his jacket.

"Whatever else this has been, it has certainly been an entertaining afternoon," he added.

Shadow blustered, his face purple enough to be a grape at this point. He looked torn between fear and outrage. What was Lucien doing there? I hadn't even spotted him in the crowd before.

"Prince Lucien, you make a mockery of this council. Your father –"

"You deign to presume you understand my father's will better than his own son?" Lucien snapped.

His entire demeanor changed in a flash. His eyes were cruel and unwavering. His hand pulled on the pommel of his weapon. The hilt of it looked like pure ice. I had never seen him with the sword before but understood innately that he always had it wherever he went. I imagine there must be a magic to where that blade is stored, because I've certainly seen him with nowhere for it to hide, if you know what I mean.

Shadow's rage was rapidly melting in the face of uncertainty. Did he dare challenge the prince of his Great House openly in a courtroom filled with witnesses? He finally bowed his head in acquiescence.

"Forgive me, my lord. I was caught up in the passion of upholding our Great House's reputation."

"The Court of Shadows is built on the principles of might, invention, and discovery. Yet, I sit here and watch as you cut this woman off repeatedly. If you had heard Miss Alacore out from the beginning, you would have learned that the girl she stands beside was *not* a victim of the trafficking ring. In fact, I escorted Miss Alacore to the park earlier this morning where she found further clues to the missing girl's whereabouts. Naturally, had I known what she was walking into, I never would have left her side."

His last words were spoken to me. A softness in them conveyed something else. Was it more guilt?

"You see even in the eleventh hour, even knowing her future stake as Warden was on the line, she could not find it in herself to turn her back on the plight of another fae. Miss Alacore rescued this girl only a few hours ago. She is the victim of an entirely different nefarious scheme in our province. So, in less than twenty-four hours, Lanie Alacore has had a direct hand in stopping two wicked plots that have impacted the least fortunate of Willow's Edge."

Lucien looked at each judge in turn as he spoke his next words. "It seems to me that these are exactly the deeds of one we would seek out as a worthy successor to Rosalie Alacore's legacy."

Shadow's mouth hung open as he slowly sank back down to his chair.

"Couldn't one also say that such an act was the subconscious destructive nature of someone who does not truly want to be Warden?" Amber asked.

Prince Lucien paused. He had said something eerily similar to me just that morning. He looked at me. "Only Miss Alacore can answer that question."

"Is that true, Miss Alacore?" Dawn asked. Her dark skin glistened slickly in the light as if she had just stepped out of the ocean. "There is no shame in admitting you have only pursued this to honor the memory of your grandmother."

It was uncanny how much her words echoed Lucien's question under the bridge. Was I that transparent? Had I truly deluded myself into believing I was pursuing the Wardenship for the right reasons? I thought about it, searching my inner self for the truth.

"You're wrong. I do want this. It's not about my grandmother. Well, not entirely. And yet it is. And there's nothing wrong with that. My entire life I felt like I didn't belong. It wasn't just about growing up around humans and not knowing I was a fae. It was more than that. I guess I can relate to Charlie in that I've always felt a deeper sense of disconnection from the world around me."

"Last winter, I discovered who I really am, my legacy. It was overwhelming. All that time I had a grandmother out there who would have died to spend even ten minutes with me. It rocked me to my core. I hear how people speak about her, and I see the impact she made on our community. Rosalie helped other fae when others wouldn't or couldn't."

"I'm so proud to be her granddaughter. I was robbed of my relationship with her, but in this way I can connect to it still. All of the things I admire about who she was, they're the same things I've begun to see in myself. I don't want to be some scared florist hiding in the backroom while the world goes by. This is who I want to be. I want to help others. Being Warden wouldn't just mean keeping my grandmother's legacy alive. It would mean living a life I'm proud of. And the thing is, I'm not going to stop even if you rule against me. I can't. Not now that I've started. I'm going to keep going, using my unique talents to support our people when others would rather turn a blind eye to their needs."

I was angry that tears were rolling out of my eyes because I wasn't sad. I was facing my fears with as much courage as I could muster, and for once I was proud of myself.

Queen Titania's brow arched, and she smirked. The Arbiter's head swung back to his normal face, glowing eyes gazing at the judges in turn.

"I've heard enough," Dawn announced. "I vote in favor of Lanie Alacore as the next Warden to Willow's Edge. All those in agreement?"

Shadow looked at her in disbelief.

"The House of Amber concurs," Amber of all people announced.

"As does the Summer Court," Summer said warmly.

The Arbiter eyed Shadow. Shadow licked his lips, looking like he had just been slapped and was trying to process how it had happened. His gaze inevitably made its way to Prince Lucien. Their eyes locked. Lucien gave a slight nod.

Shadow sighed. "The Court of Shadows aligns with the members of this council," he said, as if in disbelief of his own words.

The Arbiter pressed their hands together as if praying. "This court has spoken. Lanie Alacore will be allowed to undertake the trials to become Warden to Willow's Edge."

My heart soared. For once in my life everything aligned. Charlie hugged me from the side, and a group of fae surrounded me with clapping hands and broad smiles. Suddenly, everyone was my friend. I saw Lucien's devilish grin as he disappeared past the crowd and out the open doors.

I did it.

I actually won!

Now I could undertake the trials to become Warden. I couldn't believe it. Good things like that never happened to me. The whole thing felt like a dream that was happening to someone else.

"Why did you pinch your hand like that?" Charlie asked.

I giggled. "Just making sure I'm not dreaming."

She grinned up at me.

"I can't believe I did it. I get to take the trials to become Warden. Wait…" I paused as those words sank in. "What trials?"

Epilogue

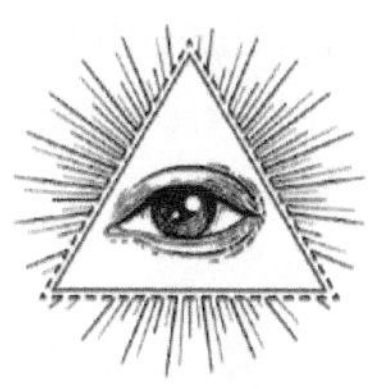

oonlight cut a dusty path across Sam's cell. Normally that light would have his blood pumping. The curse of the werebear flowing through his veins ached for release. Ached was the right word for it. Every inch of him ached.

The entire cell was enchanted with a dampening dweomer on top of the cold iron bars and walls that surrounded him. The werebear curse blunted the natural effects of cold iron on his fae blood. It was enough for him to be able to use a cold iron handle or wrap a chain of the stuff around a captive. But the amount surrounding him was too much for even the werebear curse to withstand. It hurt to stand. It hurt to lay down. It even hurt to think.

"Fucking mongrels," Sam muttered, dragging his sore fingers through his hair. He wished he could turn those fingers into a paw and tear Detective Lobo's face apart. "Stupid mutt ruined everything."

"Quiet in there, convict."

The gwyllion werewolf guarding the cellblock was a crotchety old curmudgeon. He had already opened the door once to throw Sam a beating with that whip of his, wretched bastard that he was. Sam would love to wrap his fingers around the old goat's throat and squeeze until his eyes popped.

"Yeah, sure. I'll keep it down, ya fucking billy-goat," Sam growled.

"Some people never learn," the guard said, retrieving his whip from the wall.

"Go fuck your mother." Sam spat on the floor, already on his feet and hobbling backward to the wall as the guard slid the cell door open.

The whip stung Sam on the side of his head. He cried out and covered his face with his arms, earning a few more stinging lashes to his elbows and forearm.

A loud thud broke the guard's cursing. The lashes stopped. The cell was silent.

Sam lowered his arms to find the gwyllion werewolf sprawled out on the floor, face down inside the cell. An ogre was standing just outside the open door. He had arms like tree trunks and a glower that could make a manticore's balls shrivel.

"Time to go."

"Where?" Sam asked warily.

"Get moving," the ogre said, stepping to the side.

Sam slid past him into the hallway. The ogre wore a black polo shirt and white patent leather gloves, like he was getting ready to go play a few rounds of golf. As comical as the beast looked, Sam knew better than to backtalk. They quietly stalked down the hall. Another ogre was waiting for them, holding the emergency exit open.

The night air felt cool and crisp on Sam's face. He still had dried blood caked around his right ear from where Lobo had sucker punched him. A layer of dried sweat clung to his clothes. Ugh, he would have to throw them out and buy new ones. It was a shame to waste such fine threads, but he could afford it.

Now that I'm free, I better get to the safe house, he thought. He had a sizeable stash waiting for him in the ceiling of that apartment. With that he could disappear back into the fae realm. *If I lay low for a few months, I can start the business back up in no time. Maybe I'll even hire an assassin to take out that mongrel who arrested me.*

They stalked across the overgrown field behind the constabulary. The weeds came up to his chest. The cricket chirps fell silent as they cut through their territory. There was an old highway on the other side. A black stretch limo waited for them.

Sam grinned from ear to ear. "Nice. The boss even sent a sweet ride to get me out of here. I'll tell you what, I can't wait to sink myself into a hot bath." Sam nudged the ogre on his right.

The ogre growled.

"Geez, lighten up." The door to the limo opened as they approached. Sam slid onto the backseat with an exuberant sigh. "Feels good to be out of the cage. How about we swing around to —" The words withered to ash on his tongue.

Hammered silver eyes glared back at him from across the void of seats. One of the ogres squeezed in beside him, its hulking body straining the limo's struts.

"Boss. I, uh… I didn't expect to see you out here in the middle of –"

"Of what, Sam?" the man in the shadows asked.

Sam's body grew cold as the silver eyes bored into him. Something stung his arm, like a mosquito bite. He recoiled, snatching back his arm with a yelp.

"No need to pinch a fella," he snapped at the ogre. "I would never tell them anything about your father, boss. I swear." His vision was already multiplying. The ogre's meaty fist held three needles, not one. "Wait. I didn't say anything to the wolves. Please… I –"

The limo flipped upside down as the crippling drug reached his heart.

Prince Lucien leaned forward to get a good look at the man dying across from him.

"And you never will," he promised.

Author's Note

If you enjoyed this story, it would mean the absolute world to us if you could please drop onto your favorite site and give a review of LIGHT'S LOST.

Hey there! Thank you so much for continuing this journey with Lanie and the rest of the Willow's Edge family. The awesome reviews online, and fantastic interactions with readers, both virtually and at events, have made every long day (and night) shackled to the keyboard worthwhile.

So how about that! Lanie kicked some creepy troll ass and saved the girl. Well, a lot of girls, actually. And with a little help from her friends, she's one step closer to becoming the Warden of Willow's Edge.

It's been so satisfying for us to see how much more confident and honestly just plain badass Lanie's becoming. I hope you're not too mad about the whole Lobo situation. Lanie's new FWB should help ease the sting a little.

We know there's still so many questions to answer. What's going on with our dark prince? How is he involved with Sam and his evil enterprise? Why doesn't the curse stop Lanie from being with him? What's going to happen to Deedee? How did Sacha come back from hell? And what was that about the Warden trials?

You'll find some of those answers in Book 3, which will be hitting retailers this November. In the meantime, pop into my Facebook group and join in the discussion of all things fantasy romance.

Keep reading for a sneak preview of our work in progress, Book 3 LIGHT'S WARDEN, and pre-order your copy now!

1

A manticore is essentially a mythic killing machine. They are twice the size of an average human, with the muscular body of a lion, mane and all, and the bearded face of a man. Well, not a normal man, because most guys don't sport a mouthful of twelve-inch teeth that could chew the muscles right off my bones. As if that wasn't bad enough, they also have lion tails that end in the barbed stinger of a scorpion. Those stingers inject their victim with a poison that causes such happy side-effects as convulsions, foaming at the mouth, and paralysis. Apparently, a manticore's happy pastime is to cripple their victims and force them to watch as they are slowly eaten alive. Reminds me of a few girls I went to boarding school with. Fun times.

So, to sum all that up, encountering a manticore equals rotten luck. If you ever see one, or even hear one might be within your vicinity, hoof it in the opposite direction. Or die. Those are the multitude of choices at your disposal. Only someone truly touched in the head would ever go anywhere remotely near a manticore on purpose.

I stood outside the manticore's lair, knowing this full well and wondering why I was doing something so wacked out. Was it really worth risking my life just to become a warden? The mouth of the manticore's lair was a black hole against the rocky mountainside, a stark contrast to the intertwining trunks of the magnolia trees all around me. Their pale pink flowers were so welcoming and fragrant. The cave in front of me stank of carrion and bad decisions. The rest of the forest was a wonderland, colorful birds chirping in the boughs, flying squirrels zipping overhead in the forest canopy, lush life everywhere the eye could see. I could walk in that forest for hours, drinking up its peaceful abundance.

So why enter a manticore's lair?

The beast's foul musk carried over the stench of rotten bodies. Air hit my face, then sucked away to the beat of the behemoth's snoring. It seemed the manticore fell for my trap. But if I was wrong, I was dead meat. Literally. I knew I should turn back. I was outmatched and frightened down to my bones. Nothing could be worth such a risk.

Except, it was.
I needed to become the Warden of Willow's Edge.
I took a deep breath and stepped forward.

2

A few days earlier...

It had been weeks since the fae trafficking incident. Things moved rapidly once the court ruled in my favor to take the trials to become Warden of Willow's Edge. I scarcely had time to think before I was whisked away from the province and sent to the fae realm. It seems silly now that I was so naïve as to believe the fae would just let me become warden and be done with it.

To become the Warden of Willow's Edge meant following in the footsteps of my grandmother, connecting me to her legacy, a legacy I wanted to uphold. I wanted to live a life of purpose by helping those around me. That was the entire reason for the apothecary's existence. At Alacore's Apothecary I made all sorts of helpful unguents, poultices, and elixirs. I made everything ranging from simple soothing lotions to a remedy for nightmares about spiders. Becoming Warden was just taking that one step further. It meant opening my doors to those in need, those who couldn't get the support they needed through regular channels, whether because they wanted to keep away from scandal or because the system had simply failed them.

When they had nowhere else to turn, I could use my unique talents to help them.

"And what talents might those be?" Uriel scoffed, shaking her head. "You can't even tie a proper knot, girl."

Uriel was the gladewarden. A gladewarden was apparently someone who busted your chops and delighted in making you feel ten inches tall. I suppose a more apt description would be an old crone who lived in the forest and went out of her way to make visitors feel as miserable as she was. Or maybe that was just my frustration talking. Uriel was an older woman who perpetually wore shawls and headscarves. Her faerie wings rested, folded against her back, where they protruded from holes in her shawl. Uriel oversaw my trials to become a warden. That meant she had the final say in whether I attained the mantle or not. I had been 'training' under her since the second day after the court ruled that I could take the trials. I use the word training about as loosely as my knot was coming out. She was right, my knot tying abilities suck. It didn't make her disparaging remark any easier to swallow.

"Maybe it would be better quality if you showed me how to do it first instead of just braying at me all the time like a donkey," I said.

Well, that's what I wanted to say, but it came out more like – "I'm sorry, Gladewarden." It's pretty much the same sentence. I was supposed to be weaving a net that we would use to capture gnawing gnats. There was a small cloud of them around a copse of blackberry bushes near Uriel's cottage. I didn't know why Uriel, or anyone for that matter, would want some of the nasty little critters. She never explained any of the tasks she assigned me, and I felt far more like an errand boy than a woman training and testing for the mantle of a warden.

She groaned at my apology. I think that was her favorite way of speaking, groaning and muttering beneath her breath. "Give it here then, we don't have all day." She snatched the tangle of a net I'd weaved with a scowl.

"I mean, we kind of do though, right?" I teased, trying to lighten the mood.

Uriel rolled her eyes at me. She moved her gnarled fingers deft as the legs of a spider, dancing across the twine and unraveling my shoddy work. In seconds she was tying new knots. It was too fast for me to make out the intricacies, but I leaned in close and watched, hoping I might learn something.

"You know, most fae would just use their magic to get the job done," she grumbled.

"Yes, but –"

"You want to learn to do as much as you can without relying on your magic," Uriel said. "I know, I know, you've droned on about it a thousand times."

I wasn't dumb enough to point out that she wasn't using magic to weave the net either. I'd made the mistake of getting snippety with Uriel my first week. That wonderful decision resulted in me chopping wood for *four* hours. My arms felt like cooked spaghetti for two days after that. To be honest, I didn't even know what powers Uriel possessed. She had certainly never used any magic that I could see.

Uriel lived a simple life, tucked away from the town in her stone cottage. Moss blanketed the stone edifice and thatch roof. We generally spent our sessions around the large fire pit in front of the cottage that she used for cooking and crafting. She had a weaving loom set up by her front door, with a simple rocking chair beside the fire, and a large cauldron over the crackling flames of the pit. Beside that was a long wooden table, the legs overgrown with vines, that she used to mix her ingredients. I hadn't seen the inside of the cottage, as she'd never invited me in.

"I just think it's better that I not be forced to rely on my magic to do every little thing," I lied.

The truth was, Uriel had no idea my magic was locked away deep inside me, trapped inside the foul prison of my curse. It had been tricky making up reasons not to use magic to complete my assigned tasks, but so far I'd managed. By *managed* I mean that I was doing very poorly, and I was in a perpetual state of worry that Uriel was going to kick me out of the trials. In truth, I felt that it was only a matter of time before she realized I had no magic at all. Who needed a warden that had no magic? What help could they possibly be to the other fae?

I can be helpful, I reassured myself. I had to believe there was value I could bring to the mantle, and I'd like to think there's a few others who would agree. The problem was that all of those people were back in Willow's Edge, that province overlapping the human and fae realms. Meanwhile, I was in the fae realm, far away from anyone I knew.

I worried constantly about the state of the apothecary. My good friend Tae had offered to help around the shop part time, to keep Sacha, my business partner, on his toes. Or wings. Sacha's a rather ornery imp with a penchant for complaining and predilection for lazing about. Uriel and he could have been cousins. It was good knowing Tae was there helping out.

Uriel hadn't made things easy for me and I'm certain she thought me about as useful as a cup with a hole in it.

"Voila," Uriel proclaimed, lifting the net into the firelight, and admiring her handiwork.

"You did that so fast," I complimented.

She met me with a withering look and thrust the handle of the butterfly net in my hands. "Save the ass kissing and go catch the gnawers. I need exactly four of them."

"Got it," I said. "I'll make sure we have at least four."

Uriel groaned. "Girl, I swear you're daft. Are you certain you and Rosalie were kin? I said *four*. Not three, not five, four. Exactly four. No need to go ruining a fifth critter's day just cause you're greedy."

Oh, how I'd love to punch this bitch, I thought. "As you say, Gladewarden." I bowed and headed off into the forest to collect the gnawing gnats.

"Lanie?" Uriel called.

"Yes, Gladewarden. Four." I called back, already knowing what she was going to ask.

I heard her harrumph her assent just before I disappeared into the woods. The Whispering Woods was an enchanting place that skirted the western side of The Tides. It was fascinating to see a forest untouched by the machinations of humanity. Trees grew wildly, reedy stalks of goldspire between ancient trunks of magnolias that looked like they'd been growing since the dawn of time. Magnolia flowers can grow in pinks and whites, yellows and even green. All those colors were represented in the Whispering Woods and more, with tropical canas, ferns, and orchids blanketing the forest floor. The forest was so dense that I could only see pockets of the sky overhead peeking between the tangled canopy.

I worked my way down a curving path that wound around a hill, toward the creek where Uriel had shown me the gnawing gnats a few weeks earlier. I distinctly recalled her telling me not to go near them because their *'sting is like getting kicked in the crotch.'*

The breeze shifted and the leaves overhead rustled. It sounded like a gathering of fae whispering secrets. Hence the name of the woods. I followed the bend around a massive magnolia, keeping a tight hold of my net. The left side of the path broke off into a steep descent, a red clay cliff at the bottom of which babbled the creek water. The trail I was on was lovely, a beaten red clay path skirted by mounds and mounds of purple elephant ears. A pocket of canopy let down sunlight onto the expanse of elephant ears, their massive leaves fully open, gathering every ounce of light they could soak in.

A cluster of bushes skirted the creek at the bottom of the sloping path. It was a darned place to grow, as baffling to me as were many things in the fae realm. Berry bushes tended to hate wet soil, but these were lush and overflowing with ripe fruit. I heard the gnawing gnats before I saw their black cloud. Hundreds of them buzzed about the brush, feasting on the berries.

Gnawing gnats are terrible little critters. They're like the fae equivalent of a horse fly. Each one is roughly the size of a marble, with a mouth that takes up half their face. They have rows of teeth that look like bee stingers which they use to gnaw on their food. They preferred the sugary sweetness of fruit but are more than happy to drink some blood if they're disturbed. Unlike horse flies, gnawers have little twig-like arms and claws. They're like flying reverse pin cushions and I shouldn't have been messing with them. Unfortunately, Uriel said to get them, so get them I would.

I stopped to prepare myself for this folly. I pulled my hood up and tugged the strings until it bunched up snug against my ears and cheeks. I wanted as little flesh showing as possible. Next, I tucked the hoodie into my pants and then pulled my socks up over the hem of my jeans. It was a shame I didn't have any gloves. My hands would be completely exposed. I took a deep breath and continued my march down the sloping path. I figured the trick was to fool the gnawers into thinking I was simply taking a stroll. I held my net tucked against my leg on the opposite side, out of their view.

The cloud of gnats buzzed back and forth, greedily chomping on their berries. They sounded like an army of hornets. I knew a girl in boarding girl who stepped on a hornet nest when she was home for the summer. The hornets stung her so many times she ended up in the hospital. She wasn't allergic to their stings, but after thirty-five of them anyone's body would go into shock.

Stop thinking about horrible shit, I chastised myself.

My palms felt sweaty as I forced myself to continue my nonchalant pace, staring at every shift of their nasty little swarm through my peripheral vision. Without warning I spun on my heel sideways and swiped the net across the bushes. The cloud buzzed angrily, shifting away from my paltry attack as I pulled the net back. It caught on a thorny branch.

"Fuck me," I cursed.

The swarm was already regrouping as I tugged on the handle of the net. A stream of them flew out of the net as I wrestled it back and forth trying to unsnarl from the bush. Their buzzing grew louder. They were pissed.

"Oh shit." I yanked back as hard as I could. The net ripped free. I fell backward landing on my ass on the clay path. The swarm was making a beeline for me. I could see their little mouths, row upon row of angry black teeth under beady red eyes.

Time to go, I thought, hopping to my feet.

I ran for dear life. I'm naturally a fast runner. I used to think it was because I walked everywhere, living in the city and all. Now I understand it has more to do with my unicorn bloodline. I hoofed it up the hill. The snarling gnawers buzzed just behind me. I put my head down and ran full tilt back through the woods. I leapt over a fallen log, slipped coming around a tree too quickly, and kept running until my heart felt ready to burst and my head was pounding. I didn't slow down until I smelled the smoke from Uriel's firepit.

The cottage was just up ahead, through the trees. I finally stopped, realizing the gnawers had long ago given up their pursuit and went back to their berry feasting. *Why would they give up?* I wondered with a sinking feeling in the pit of my stomach. I never actually looked at the net while I was running like a madwoman through the forest.

Did I even catch any of the devilish insects?

I broke out in a cold sweat. Uriel would kill me if I bungled up another assignment. I had already lost the stag horn and broken her rune branch. The latter was from falling out of the tree after I had cut the topmost branch from a four-hundred-year-old birch. Uriel was far more concerned with the damage to the branch than whether I'd been hurt. Most of it was broken, but the very tip was just enough wood for her to make a single rune. She'd scowled at me the whole rest of the night and well into the next week after that one. At that rate, I had to be close to flunking out of the trials.

I panted like a dog needing water as I knelt and wiped the sweat from my forehead. I hadn't even realized how tight I'd been gripping the mouth of the net. The wood Uriel used to form the hoop was elastic, bending without the slightest crack. I carefully opened it to peer inside at my imminent doom. I'd never been so relieved to see vicious little teeth before. Little black shapes writhed, pulling against the twine netting. Their teeth were gnawing futilely at the trap. The twine was spun from the reeds of a whispering willow. They could gnaw until their teeth fell out and it wasn't going to cut them free.

"Hey there fellas," I cooed. "You're stuck in there, huh? Sorry I had to ruin your lunch, but Uriel has plans for ya. Don't worry though, she's a mean old goat but I think her bark is worse than her bite." I don't know who I was lying to, the gnawers or myself. "Let's see. How many of you did I catch?"

I counted six in total. That put me two above my target.

I tsked. "Well, that won't do." Uriel was very clear about only wanting four of them. Going back with six was just as likely to land me in trouble as if I'd gotten zero. I had to free two gnats. I reached in for the gnawer closest to the mouth of the net. It felt like trying to pluck a nugget of charcoal free. The gnawer's little body twitched violently as I tugged it loose from the twine. It steadied itself with little claws, delicately laying them flat on my finger and thumb. The gnawer blinked at me with four little red eyes.

"Aw, you're kinda cute when you're not eating, huh?"

The gnawer smiled at me. Then promptly chomped down on my finger. I squealed and shook my hand in the air. It's little claws dug into my skin, and it bit me twice more. It felt like getting stung by twelve bees at once. I yelped and slapped my hand down on the ground. The gnawer released me before it hit the dirt and twirled into the air on its little insect wings. I watched in horror as two more of the gnats flew past the mouth of the net. All my flailing about had shaken them free. I dropped the net and clapped my hands together in the air.

Yes! I caught one.

I felt the buzz of its body trapped between my palms. The gnawer's compatriots fled into the trees, buzzing their victory as they made their way back to their blackberry bush. My palm stung. The gnawer was living up to its name, chomping on my hand. I shook my cupped hands vigorously back and forth until it released its hold. And then I kept shaking until I didn't feel its buzzing anymore.

I switched the gnawer to my right hand, keeping it cupped as I retrieved the net from the grass. Fortunately, the other three gnats were still trapped in the twine. I dropped the fourth inside the net and immediately pulled the mouth shut like a coin purse. My finger and palm were bleeding from tiny pinpricks of the gnawer's teeth.

I sucked on my finger as if that would help and made my way back to Uriel's cottage. She was snoring in her rocking chair when I arrived. It made my blood boil. *Of course, she's out like a light while I'm running around getting chewed up for her.*

I stood close to the rocking chair wondering how anyone could sleep with their mouth open so wide. *What if I flicked one of the gnawing gnats in there? Bet that would take the fire out of the old goat.* I loudly cleared my throat.

Uriel opened one eye, which was already trained on me.

"I'm back with the gnats," I said.

Uriel sat up and grumbled. She grabbed the cane between her legs and used it to pull herself out of the rocking chair. I felt a pang of guilt for thinking of hurting such a harmless old lady.

"As if the whole forest didn't hear ya yelping like a trapped wolf," Uriel grumbled.

Wait, so she heard me squealing in pain and she just kept sleeping? Ugh, this bitch.

"Stop staring at my bum and let me see what you've brought."

I snapped to attention and quickly followed her to the firepit. She took the net from me and frowned at my captives. "Kind of a runty little batch," she grunted disapprovingly. "You should have grabbed a couple more."

"Are you fucking serious?"

She looked at me and rolled her eyes. "Well, don't cry about it. They'll probably still get the job done. Just not as strong as I'd like it." Uriel muttered something and a soft tendril of smoke drifted from her palm into the open net.

Woah, it's her magic! I thought, getting my first glimpse at what the gladewarden was capable of.

The smoke found each gnawer in turn. I felt the air grow colder around us. A film of frostbite encircled each of the gnats and they froze in place, paralyzed except for their eyes darting back and forth.

"Fetch the kettle for me," Uriel ordered.

She kept a pole with a kettle hanging over the side of the fire pit. I used a wool pad to turn the hinged pole out of the fire, where she could reach it. Uriel motioned for me to lift the lid as she plucked the frozen gnawers out of the net. Once she had them all gathered in her palm, she swiftly clapped her hands together. It sounded like grinding seeds in a pestle. I winced at the brutality of it. Uriel rolled her eyes at me again.

"You're too soft, lass," she chided as she rubbed her hands together over the open kettle. What looked like black sand poured from her hands into the water. She rubbed them until every dry speck of the dust was gone. "Add three heads of lavender to the tea."

"You're making tea?" I gaped.

"Nothing escapes you." She turned her back to me and hobbled back to her rocking chair. "Wake me up when it's boiled enough."

I hate her, I hate her, I hate her, I seethed.

"Stop scowling and get to work," she said without looking back.

"Yes, Gladewarden."

I fell to work. I added the lavender and moved the kettle back to the heat. It would be tricky making tea over an open fire. Easy to scald the ingredients. I fell into a rhythm, letting the tea get just hot enough to boil before pulling it back. I stirred just enough to unlock their fragrance then brought it to the flames once more. The black dust was hard and crystallized. It took a few more rounds of this process, heating, stirring, cooling, and heating again, before I saw what Uriel wanted. The liquid glowed with purple swirling lights, the trails of the black dust. I smiled appreciatively at its glow.

"Put it in that bottle over there," Uriel ordered.

I jumped, almost knocking the kettle off its pole. I hadn't even heard her walk up beside me. I can get like that when I'm working at the apothecary too. I kind of fall into a trance, happily working ingredients into healing salves and the like. It's my Zen place. I recovered before Uriel could complete her scheduled grumble. She had set a glass bottle near the fire. I used a sifting cup to steadily pour the tea into the bottle.

"What made you think to hold back the lavender?" Uriel asked.

"If it stays in the tea it'll lose potency and break down that purple glow swirling inside," I said.

"How do you know that?"

I shrugged. "It feels right."

Uriel nodded curtly and pointed to a cork on her table. I brought the bottle over and stoppered it. "Why isn't the glass hot?" I asked.

"I coated the bottle in nelm oil when it was tempered," Uriel said, as if it were obvious. "Go away now. I've got lots of things to do without you tugging at my skirts."

"Yes Gladewarden." I bowed and gathered my backpack.

"Come back in two days."

There was no rhyme or reason to the span of time between my visits to Uriel's cottage. I was at her beck and call and that's all there was to it. I bowed and took my leave, eager to soak my aching feet in some hot bathwater back at the lodging house in town.

"Aren't you forgetting something?"

I paused. "Oh, um, thank you for the lesson Gladewarden." I bowed again.

Uriel scowled at me. "Daft girl. The tea. I told you to take it to Mr. Bukle's smithy."

She had said no such thing. Uriel did that quite a bit. I had learned to just play dumb and move along. "Yes, of course, my bad." I gathered the bottle and stuffed it into my backpack then took my leave. I could still feel her scowl even when I was down the hill and through the woods. I loved the view from that hike. Up on that hill you could see clear through the tree line, out to the coast where the ocean waves crashed against the rocky cliffs to the west of The Tides. I could see some of the seashell town from that vantage. My lodging was close to the edge of the woods, at the base of the hill, on the outskirts of town. I could see my front door from there.

I could also see the man waiting for me in front of it.

~~~

There's nothing like trying to solve a murder that hasn't happened yet.

The Warden mantle is within my reach. But after weeks of grueling trials in the fae realm, a meeting at the palace sounds too good to refuse. Foul play is suspected in the House of Dawn, and I've been hired to investigate.
~~~

The Patriarch of the Great House is convinced that someone is out to get him. With every high-powered fae arriving for the spring celebration this is the perfect chance to put my sleuthing skills to the test. The nobility descending on the House of Dawn all have their own secrets and agendas. I better learn who's who and how to navigate the politics of court quickly.

Dinners and dances are safer than battling monsters, right? Not in the Fae Realm…This time I may be in over my head.

Light's Warden is a gripping fantasy mystery that delves deep into the heart of the fae realm. If you enjoyed Lost Girl or the Dresden Files, you'll love the next thrilling installment in the Alacore's Apothecary series. Pre-order your copy now on our official site! www.michellemurphyauthor.com